T0036968

SISTERS OF THE SPRUCE

Copyright © 2024 Leslie Shimotakahara

01 02 03 04 05 28 27 26 25 24

All rights reserved. No part of this publication may be reproduced, stored in a retrieval system or transmitted, in any form or by any means, without prior permission of the publisher or, in the case of photocopying or other reprographic copying, a licence from Access Copyright, the Canadian Copyright Licensing Agency, www.accesscopyright.ca, 1-800-893-5777, info@accesscopyright.ca.

Caitlin Press Inc.
3375 Ponderosa Way
Qualicum Beach, BC V9K 2J8
www.caitlinpress.com

Text design by Vici Johnstone
Printed in Canada

Caitlin Press Inc. acknowledges financial support from the Government of Canada and the Canada Council for the Arts, and the Province of British Columbia through the British Columbia Arts Council and the Book Publisher's Tax Credit.

Library and Archives Canada Cataloguing in Publication
Sisters of the spruce / Leslie Shimotakahara.
Shimotakahara, Leslie, author.
Canadiana 20230522726 | ISBN 9781773861371 (softcover)
LCC PS8637.H525 S57 2024 | DDC C813/.6—dc23

SISTERS OF THE SPRUCE

a novel

LESLIE SHIMOTAKAHARA

Caitlin Press 2024

To Granny K

We said there warn't no home like a raft, after all. Other places do seem so cramped and smothery, but a raft don't. You feel mighty free and easy and comfortable on a raft.

        —Mark Twain, *Adventures of Huckleberry Finn*

the wild daisies
are celebrating...
spring's first day
—Issa

ONE

It was late by the time we got there. The sky had turned into a large shadow, which crept this way and that, and threatened to become all I could see. But animal alertness was keeping my brain bright awake, my limbs restless. It made no difference that Dad kept telling me to sit still—my legs dangled off the pier. There I sat, nestled between my two sisters, as we all waited for whoever was supposed to be coming. Our eyes fastened on the glistening black water.

Early that morning, from the deck of a steamship, I'd watched everything receding and shrinking: the cluster of clapboard houses, the store, the saloon, the white cross of the church. Fare thee well, Prince Rupert. As I looked back at the town, icy spray settled on my cheeks and it all flattened into a thin grey line and vanished completely. Then, there was nothing except choppy waves, capped with white foam. The roar of the engine filled my body.

On the ship, time juddered by. I went inside, I came out again. In, out. I'd been in this position before—salt shower making me hoarse, wobbliness in the gut from nothing solid to stand upon—but somehow, it was worse this time around. We were starting all over again, once again. This time, we didn't even know where we were going. My eyes stared out at the colourless waters, cresting and breaking with a force that came from someplace invisible, relentless. This feeling had become all too familiar in recent years.

At some point, May came to join me on the deck and grabbed at my palm. Warmth from her hand flowed welcomingly into my body.

"It'll be nice there, won't it?" Her voice faded in the wind.

"Yes, nice. Very nice, I think." I tried to sound confident, but what did I know, really?

"We'll live in a real house again? Not a basement?"

I looked down at May's petal-like face and nodded, not trusting myself to speak. In Prince Rupert, Dad had been a janitor at a down-at-heel hotel, in exchange for which we'd been granted a couple rooms in the basement. It'd been a sad existence, compared to our lives before, in a bustling mill town called Skeena.

How frightened my sister appeared, barely daring to hope. She was only seven. I adored her and she expected me to be her big sister, so I forced a smile. "We'll get a lovely house again, with a large front porch."

"What will Otousan do for work?"

Although May spoke less Japanese than me, what few words she did have—*otousan, okaasan*—she clung on to, fiercely.

"Dad will log and fish again and you'll play in the forest every day and everything will be just as it used to be. You wait and see. But no more questions for now, all right?"

She went inside, while I watched an albatross get flung across the sky like a tattered flag.

Nausea, fierce as an earthquake, came in spells that shook the walls of my stomach. Toward the end of the journey, it got worse than ever, the water suddenly all aswirl—as though a great fist were pulling us downward, toward our seabed graves. But then the fist released us, the waters calmed. And the seagulls. Always, the seagulls. You knew you were getting close to port when the flocks of gulls descended, swooping down so low that if you dared to stand outside, you had to protect your head.

And then a harbour came into focus: canoes lined the beach, boulders rising high behind. The clouds were streaked with moody violet, their upside-down images reflected upon the glassy surface.

It was the last and only stop. The few other travellers were getting off, so we did, too. We watched their backs shrink away from us, blurring into small dots in the distance. How I envied them for having purpose in their gaits, a clear destination. As we sat on the edge of the wharf, the sky darkened, engulfing us in shadows.

At last, the wood slats vibrated. A thin fellow with a weedy moustache and not much hair was approaching with a stiff wave. He was dressed in an old, crumpled overcoat and mud-spattered trousers. Without saying anything, it was clear that he was here on behalf of the Company. Mr. Brown, he said his name was. We'd have to walk to the Indian village, he said. Without asking any questions, Dad began to follow him along the beach, under the last ribbons of dim light, and so we made our way, too: me behind Dad, Mom and my sisters straggling at the line's end. All our worldly possessions were in the bags we carried.

In the distance, a smattering of bleached-out houses could be seen blurrily on the shoreline, and a single totem pole shot up, like a wave of a skinny arm.

Mr. Brown led us to the largest house, which had a long veranda, newly painted white. He told us to wait out front, while he went inside. A few minutes later he came out with a tall Indian man, who, except for his caramel skin tone, didn't much look like an Indian at all. He was dressed in a fine, dark jacket, with a matching vest beneath, the silver chain of a pocket watch secured to one of the buttonholes. His hair and moustache were more tidily groomed than Mr. Brown's. Apparently this fellow owned a boat and was going to be our skipper for the rest of the journey, down the strait into the inlet.

They haggled. It seemed the price had gone up since last month. And there were more people in our family than expected. And we were late—it wasn't going to be easy to navigate in the dark, now was it? While the Indian stood his ground, Mr. Brown got all blustery and red in the face and threatened to leave us all there. The Indian remained unperturbed and said we were welcome to camp on the beach. Bees abuzz in my gut, I looked over at Dad expectantly, but he appeared pretty powerless. Back hunched, his eyes did not stray from his feet. Mercifully, Mr. Brown relented and thrust over a fistful of cash. We followed our skipper down to the water's edge.

His boat was a small schooner with white sails that caught the wind easily and like giant moth wings carried us along the current. The feeling thrilled me, while at the same time unsettling my stomach, the black forest on both sides getting even blacker, as the sky turned to sombre flatness. The trees were higher out here than any I'd seen before, their trunks thicker, too. They formed a fortress around us, a fortress topped by daggers, or pointy teeth.

Mr. Brown's face relaxed a little. "You folks *do* speak English, I assume?"

Of course we spoke English. Why else would the Company have hired us? Of all the yellow men in this part of the world, you wouldn't find anyone who spoke finer English than my father.

"Yes, sir," Dad said. "I even taught language classes back in Japan."

"You're pullin' my leg now." Mr. Brown shook his head, his eyes brimming with curiosity. "When did ya move here?"

"Over twenty years ago, if you can believe it." My father smiled. More a smile of exhaustion than pride. His hair was thinning, the cobwebby lines beneath his eyes more apparent than ever. Too many sweaty days under the northern sun had left their mark on him.

"What about yer wife? She speak English?" His chin wagged toward my mother, seated beside me.

"Yes. Well. Some English, anyway."

"Then why ain't she answerin' for herself? Cat got her tongue?"

I watched the back of Mom's head, her glossy hair still neatly swept up in a bun, barely a strand loose, even after so many hours of travel. The white ruffles of her high-neck blouse peeked above the grey shawl. She'd wanted to wear her best clothes to make a good impression on the Company. We'd been under the belief that the Company consisted of some very important, very rich white men—not this slouchy guy who smelled of tobacco and last month's laundry.

I gave my mother a gentle nudge.

"Yes. Yes…?" This came out as barely a whisper from her lips, in Japanese.

"So she ain't mute, after all." Mr. Brown laughed, a drop of spittle flying. "Don't really matter, though. Don't need to speak, in order to cook and clean."

"My wife is indeed an excellent cook."

The boat began to rock. We were passing a drift log spit and a desolate beach, where an old canoe had been left on its side to rot.

"Your name's Sam Terada?" said Mr. Brown. "Sam's not a Japanese name, though."

"Well, it's Sannosuke, really. But people have been calling me Sam for years."

"You're one of Will Henderson's guys, correct?"

"Yes, sir," Dad said.

"You met Will back in Skeena?"

"That's right."

"Will says you can be relied on. Not that Skeena's an example for anything, make no mistake!"

Skeena had gone belly up. It still upset me to think about all my family had lost there, the consequence being we'd had to move to ugly Prince Rupert. It'd been three years since we'd left Skeena, when the American company that'd owned the mill had pulled out.

I wondered if this man had lost big money in the venture, too. But then, he smiled—a reckless, fast smile—shaking off his mood. "We're here now, my friend! That's what matters, right? And there's plenty of work to be done takin' down these beauties." He gestured at the shore, at the molasses shadows. "The government's pourin' money into it, big money. Did Will tell ya the news?"

Dad gave a small nod, while remaining quiet, attentive, like he didn't want to deprive Mr. Brown of the chance to gab on about something that clearly delighted him.

"These Sitka spruce here on the Charlottes are the only trees in the entire British Empire strong enough to build our fighter planes from. Their wood refuses to splinter, even under a shower of goddamn bullets! So everybody's countin' on us now."

He was talking about the war. The past few years, everyone had been talking about nothing but this endless war. Although it was happening far away, over in Europe, Canada was helping out, doing its part. Sending men over. Sending bulletproof trees over, too. Life would be so much easier if only the war would end, everyone said. Or in any case, we'd all have a bit more to eat, which sounded pretty good to me.

I was ready for life to take a turn for the better.

"Back in '14, I tried to enlist, sir."

"Did ya, now? And let me guess—the army told ya they're not accept in' any Japs." Mr. Brown made a face, his moustache scrunching up. "Well, that's government for you. Can't see past its own arse. You ask me? What matters most ain't a man's skin colour so much as his willingness to get blown up. And in times of war, the more the merrier! But just as well that they let ya live, 'cause you're needed here now."

May had fallen asleep on my shoulder. That girl could sleep anywhere. Izumi, on the other hand, remained tense, alert, the cords of her long, pale neck like ropes about to snap. Her eyes flashed this way and that, as though a black bear was going to emerge from the trees at any second, rise on its hind legs and lunge toward the water. Izzy, we'd started to call her, as if that'd somehow help her adjust. To my mother, though, she was always Izumi-chan. It struck me as odd that Mom had taken to addressing her eldest by this baby name. Maybe this was Mom's attempt to help Izzy feel more at home, to make up for all their years apart.

Nothing any of us did made any difference, though. My sister remained just as much a delicate, exotic flower as she'd been when she'd stepped off the boat from Japan, almost a year ago now. Everything about her baffled me, and it annoyed me that she so rarely smiled.

A sudden rise in choppiness made May come to, her eyes sweeping open. "Where… where are we?"

"We're almost there," I whispered, trying to sound certain.

Izzy put a hand to her stomach, gaze fastened on her knees.

We passed a large island, where our skipper told us there used to be farms, before the war. Before everyone with half a brain packed up and left. A couple of bald eagles swooped through the air, on the hunt for a bedtime snack, perhaps. At the bottom of the strait, where the water gathered force and the wind slammed against our cheeks, we passed a ghost town with a mill peeking out through the darkness. Little islands with sharp cliffs jumped out at us here and there. A spit jutted out, out of nowhere. Our skipper expertly steered his way around it all; nothing the landscape threw at him seemed to fluster him in the least.

Finally, we arrived at a stretch of beach. The black water was rippling with silver, with moonlight, trees rising, mountain-like, beyond.

At the edge of the beach, a crude dock had been built. We stepped off the boat and made our way toward the shore, the air abuzz with columns of insects, tickling and nipping at our skin.

On the pebbly sand, we peered into the ever-shifting shapes of darkness, trying to get our bearings. Mr. Brown led us away from the water's edge.

"Where's the mill?" Dad said.

"The mill?" Mr. Brown sucked on his cigarette, an orange ember fluttering down, like a dying firefly. "It'll be down there, a ways. Hasn't been built yet."

"But… I thought…"

"So for now, we're tyin' it all into rafts and bargin' it to Vancouver."

"Oh. I see." Dad walked in a small circle, staring at the ground.

"The men'll build the mill next, don't ya worry. Give 'em till next Sunday!" A raspy cackle. "They'll get it done if they stay off the moonshine."

At the far end of the clearing, a dozen cabins had been built. They looked flimsy and makeshift, nothing like the real houses back in Skeena; my stomach sank. Logs were piled here and there for more cabins in the process of being built, tents clustered in the background. A campfire, with a cauldron hanging above it, was still smouldering.

"Do you live here?" Dad enquired.

"Nah, I'm over in the townsite. Will lives there, too."

"Oh."

"Don't look so glum, my friend! We've got a proper house for you, at least."

Mr. Brown led us to the other side of the clearing, where the gnarl of forest resumed. An old cottage stood there, its sloped black roof covered in a carpet of bright wet moss. One window had been boarded up, where the glass had been broken.

"Who lives there?" Dad said.

"You do, now." Mr. Brown laughed again, this time with a note of pity.

ꙮ

The mildewy sofa was itchy. May's head nuzzled against my chest, her body curling into mine. I blinked, the space slowly revealing itself in the pallid morning light. Water-stained slats ran across the ceiling. Tufts of dead grass poked up between battered floorboards. The bed in the corner was covered in faded blankets, bunched around our snoring mother. Dad was nowhere to be seen.

Izzy was also up, or her eyes were open, in any case, glazed, expressionless. She sat perfectly still, straight as a rod, in the armchair where she must have slept. The chair was leaking stuffing from holes where mice might've burrowed to escape the cold. A second sofa, in not much better shape, stretched emptily across from us, abandoned by her during the night. A damp, earthy smell filled the air, like the ground was thawing.

"Izzy? You all right?"

My sister murmured something in Japanese, something I couldn't really understand. She buried her face in her hands, shoulders gently rocking. She got like this, from time to time. It was hard to believe that she was sixteen, when she acted like this snivelling baby. Although I felt flint-hearted just thinking it, the truth was that I preferred how things had been before she arrived, before I'd even known she existed. When I'd still believed that *I* was the eldest. Despite being two years younger, I still felt like I was—by a long shot, if you want the truth.

A wood stove sat in the corner, squat and sooty, an axe leaning against it. Disentangling myself from May's arms, doing my best not to wake her, I got up and inspected what remained of the fire. Using a stick, I swept the last embers into a fiery bud and sprinkled a handful of wood shavings on top to get it going again. Then I laced up my boots, grabbed the axe and headed outside.

A stone's throw away, the water spanked across my gaze. It'd thinned to a sheet of silver, reflecting the dawn sky. Sand patches and torn-off branches and islands of craggy rocks were scattered about, puncturing the surface of the low tide. Mist hung in the air: a never-ending cobweb of droplets catching the pink light.

❦

Mid-morning, Izzy was taking a nap, while my mother and I unpacked and set up the cottage.

Mom stretched her arms overhead, like her back was giving her grief again. "Get some water for us to drink, will you, please?"

"But where?" I had no intuition of the closest spring.

"I don't know. You'll have to ask, I suppose."

That would mean talking to the strangers on the other side of the clearing. All morning I'd been keeping my distance, watching them from the corner of my eye. By now the men were long gone; only a couple of womenfolk remained behind.

I went outside and spotted a youngish woman with a cloud of brown hair and a beaky nose. All *hakujin* people had rather pointy features, like their faces had been whittled with a knife. As she turned in profile, I saw the baby strapped to her back, held in place by a blanket of sorts.

There was also an older Oriental lady with a broad chin and hips to match. She was sweeping the cabins, and every so often the tip of her broom flicked out a doorway in a swirl of dust.

I approached the unlit communal campfire, carrying a pot I'd found in the cottage. The cauldron, above the charred wood, contained about a half-foot of water.

"Excuse me," I called out, feeling uncomfortable. "Is this all right to drink?"

The Oriental came outside and said something in a harsh, clacking tongue. I figured she must be Chinese.

"I'm sorry, but I only speak English." This wasn't true, really. I understood quite a bit of Japanese, which my mother always addressed me in, even if I couldn't speak it so well or read it at all. According to Mom, my Japanese was about as good as a small child's.

But what could you expect? At school in Skeena and Prince Rupert, all the lessons had been in English, of course. And the novels that Dad occasionally bought from peddlers and passed along to me, after he'd finished them, had names like *Robinson Crusoe* and *Jane Eyre*. He said there were no such tales in Japan, where literature was all about rich rulers and beautiful courtesans, rather than ordinary folks out and about in the world.

"You can drink it," the brown-haired woman said, approaching.

"Mind if I boil it?" According to Dad, it was only safe to drink water that'd been freshly boiled.

Striking a match, she lit the fire.

Her baby started to fuss. As she rocked back and forth on her heels, the whimpering subsided. Her hair blew upward, exposing watchful eyes, a tired, jumpy energy about her, and I could see that she wasn't as young as I'd first assumed. She was wearing several layers of men's shirts, with a shapeless brown sweater that was unravelling at the neck overtop, no coat. Not that I had a coat either, the damp chill seeping into my bones.

"I saw you choppin' wood this morning."

I nodded. An ache still lingered in my lower back.

"You're not bad with that axe."

"Thanks." I shrugged. The wood wasn't going to chop itself.

"How long you folks stayin' here?"

"A while, I guess. We've been hired to run the camp."

"Is that so? Hired by...?"

"Will Henderson. You know him?"

A hint of mockery twisted her lips. "Oh, *him*. The boss man."

I didn't know what to say. Why did she act like it was a joke? Uncle Will—as I'd been calling him since childhood—*was* the boss.

"So, what's yer name, kid?"

I shifted my weight from foot to foot, worrying I'd already told her too much. "What's *yours?*"

"Irene."

Irene looked perplexed when I shared my own name, hesitantly. Khya. It was an odd name, no doubt—not very Japanese sounding. Dad had concocted it, because back when I'd been born, he'd had high hopes for our life in Skeena. So he'd named me after the Khyex River, a little tributary right near the mouth of Skeena River.

As if being called Khya wasn't unusual enough, I looked on the strange side, too. I was used to people's baffled stares, as though they couldn't quite figure out where I fit into their scheme of things. My hair was cut fairly short, in the shape of a bowl. It'd been that way since I was a kid. My mother kept urging me to grow it out, but I was very much a creature of habit. And I could get away with it because I appeared younger than my age. I was short and slight, like Dad, though we both had a wiry strength.

I didn't mind looking like a boy. It was safer that way, and it had been the case for as long as I could remember. You heard too many stories about the terrible things that happened to pretty girls when they got chased through the woods. So I learned to stand with my feet planted wide apart and cross my arms, just like Dad, and if people mistook me as his son, we never corrected them.

The water was starting to steam now. "You live in one of these cabins, Irene?"

She shook her head.

"What about your husband?"

Something in her face wobbled, like a puddle hit by drops of rain. "He ain't my husband. And that man can do whatever the hell he wants!"

While she kept staring at me, as if daring me to be shocked—or not be shocked—the air seemed to tremble between us.

"Then what are you doing here?" I said, puzzled.

"My baby's father can't forget all about us. Can't forget he's got a wee mouth to feed."

"Will you be sticking around, then?"

"You think I got time to laze around? Somebody's gotta put bread on the table."

There weren't a lot of jobs women could do, in these parts. "Where do you work, if you don't mind me asking?"

Whatever I'd said must have provoked a sudden thought. Irene was looking at me with needles of interest shooting from her eyes.

"How old are ya, hun?"

"Fourteen." An oddly naked feeling washed over me, like I was a goose and she was appraising my plumpness for Christmas dinner.

"With a bit of lipstick and rouge and your hair curled all nice, I bet you could pass for sixteen." She pulled my shawl off my shoulders, scrutinizing my chest. "Don't think that you're foolin' anyone with this tomboy getup, hun."

My cheeks burned. The chirping birds faded away, like I was hearing everything through a thick, woolly layer. All I wanted was to stay as I was—halt time forever. Yet I knew it was as impossible as stopping the blood from flooding out between my legs or soothing the raw nerve endings that sent strange itches through my blistering, budding nipples.

As the woman continued to assess me, I noticed traces of fiery lipstick on her chapped mouth, cigarette-stained teeth peeking through, in the hint of an enquiring smile. At that instant, I knew who she was, what she was. In Prince Rupert, I'd seen girls like her beckoning and calling out to men on the street, from shadowy doorways, their faces painted bright as wild roses. My mother would always tighten her grip on me, as we'd rush past.

"We could use a little Oriental thing, at the house where I work. Not only for the Chinamen, let me assure you."

I backed away, startled.

"Does yer daddy treat ya nice? Or is he a mean old coot?"

A crackling shudder came over my skin. I shook my head.

"Well, that's a pity. If ya change yer mind and need an escape route"—she grabbed my wrist—"you can find me at the Rosewater Hotel in Port Clem. Just walk along the shore, headin' south. You'll have to raft over for part of the way, but you'll get there eventually."

I wrested my arm back, awash in humiliation. Who did she think she was talking to? It was bad enough that she'd pegged me as a girl, but did I look like *that* kind of girl? As I filled my pot with trembling hands, a shower of hot flecks hit my skin. I turned to leave.

"I hope yer mama knows how to take care of herself," Irene called out at my back.

"Of course, she does!"

"Good. 'Cause there ain't a lot of women, up in these parts."

Two

At some point well before dawn, I awoke to the sound of Dad's stealthy rustles. While he crept out of bed and made his way across the cottage through the gloom, I pretended to still be asleep, curled up on my sofa.

The heat from the fire had long died out. We'd taken to sleeping in our clothes, the more layers the better. After the door had creaked shut behind my father, I sat up and rotated my ankles, trying to restore some feeling in my numb toes, before pulling on my boots.

I stepped outside into the gauze of drizzle, thankful for Dad's old jacket. Hiding around the side of the cottage, I watched the men—about two dozen of them—munch wedges of bread around the unlit campfire. They'd returned very late last night, so this was my first time setting eyes on them. Most were Orientals, the others whites and Indians. They looked about the same as the guys who'd worked the mill in Skeena. The Orientals were shorter than the others and wore baggier pants with the cuffs rolled up, cords of rope tied around their waists in place of belts.

No one talked much. The meal didn't last more than a few minutes. Then Dad gave a nod and they headed for the woods.

I let them pass through the dark boundary, before darting forward to catch up. I was good at keeping my distance and crouching low, while not losing sight of the pack. Their boots made enough noise breaking branches and squishing down sodden moss to mask the sound of my own rabbit-like movements. Massive trees and lacy veils of lichen engulfed us in a world of ghostly shadows, punctured only by the occasional shaft of mauve light.

I clambered over the uneven ground, feeling my way forward by instinct. Sinkholes, cracks, coarse fragments of cobble, dead branches galore. Sudden gashes in the earth revealed the silver glimmer of water bubbling over jagged forms. Rotting stumps poked up like the mangled limbs of some half-buried giant, lying in wait to trip you and break your neck. The prickles on my scalp told me where to turn, when to halt, my nostrils drinking in the raw, oozy scents of the entire forest.

At some point one of the men shouted "Over here!" and everyone followed him out to a lagoon. I hid behind a clump of rocks, some distance from the water's edge. The air was swirling with hungry insects, challenging my ability to keep still.

It'd been a good while since I'd seen a steam donkey. This one looked bigger than the ones back in Skeena. The giant wheels had yards of steel cable wrapped around them, and there was a big boiler with a chimney on top, where plumes of steam would fly up into the sky when the thing was fired up. It looked not too different than the front car of a freight train, but this donkey wasn't going anywhere, anchored to the earth.

I watched the men getting everything set up, continuing their work from the night before. The cables disappeared down a cleared path, where they would be attached to a felled tree. This technique had been used in Skeena, and Dad was good at directing the men on how to position the cords, some even strung between treetops, like telephone wires.

The Chinese guys didn't speak much English, but that was okay, because Dad had picked up pidgin Cantonese over the years. And the Japanese guys were no doubt glad to be able to ask questions in their own tongue. Shouts got thrown back and forth, as everyone went about their work. Dad climbed a tree so he'd have a bird's-eye view, and let out a series of whistles.

As dawn was breaking, the sky streaked with pinkish wisps, Uncle Will arrived on site. He looked exactly the way I remembered him. Broad chin covered in grey-blond bristles. Tall frame, stocky as the boiler of the steam donkey itself. He wore, as usual, an old, broad-brimmed hat that shaded the merry glint of his eyes. Next to this man, my father looked like an elf. But once they'd greeted each other, once they'd started talking and planning, these differences in appearance faded away, their faces both very bright and alive, like back in Skeena.

I overheard Uncle Will say that the government had set an extraordinary target: three million feet, *per month*. That was what the Allies were counting on us to deliver for their planes, to beat back the Germans. As he and my father mulled over the setup, gesturing at parallel and criss-crossing cords and a long, smooth plank that formed a gently angled chute heading off into the water, they finished each other's sentences.

A whoosh of something like happiness passed over my goose-pimpled skin, and I didn't dare look away, in case it'd all blur into a dream. Could it actually be true? That Dad was back, back in business, back to his old self? His face glowed with renewed hope, and he looked younger than he had in years.

Maybe our luck was finally turning. I didn't want to jinx it, by getting ahead of myself, but maybe these glorious trees were going to give us our nest egg at last, so we could move to Vancouver after the war and start a business. A restaurant or noodle shop or some such, Dad said. He was confident that Mom's cooking skills would stand us in good stead. He'd been talking about this dream forever, and it'd always seemed far-fetched, but perhaps I was mistaken.

With a squeeze in my chest, I watched my father standing beside the steam donkey. The boiler had been fired up and shrill toots came out the chimney, followed by chuffing and a mushroom cloud of smoke. As the wheels spooled in the cords, a massive trunk got hauled over the earth, to the triumphant music of this din.

❦

One of the men had shot a deer. It hung for a day from a rope around its neck, off the lowest branch of a tree. Then Dad sawed off its legs, at the slender calves, and used a gently curving knife to cut into the fur around the neck. Using a smaller knife, I helped strip the creature of its butterscotch coat, revealing its deep purple flesh, as bits of white film and fur clung to my fingertips.

Once it was chopped up, my mother would put it to good use. By instinct, she was able to create recipes from whatever happened to be available. At low tide, May and I went out with baskets to the boulders covered in mounds of brownish-bronze kelp. From a distance, it looked like a woman's hair, freshly washed and combed, left to dry in the sun, but up close it was more like a mass of worms. Sprinkled with clam juice and roasted crisp, a few strands of this stuff could make salted fish surprisingly tasty.

These were the chores I enjoyed. There were other things I hated doing, like scrubbing out the *onsen*. That was the first thing the Japanese men built. They wanted the indulgence of immersing their bodies in hot water at the end of a long day. It was the only way to get truly clean, according to Dad. He and his countrymen loved their baths so much that the deep, wooden tub was fired up twice a week, a long line of naked men snaking through the forest. While waiting their turns, they'd wash their torsos and crotches with scrub cloths and pans of soapy water. Then one at a time, each man would step up into the *onsen* and immerse his entire body in the steaming bath for a few seconds, before rising clean, water gushing off his reddened back and bum and thighs.

When I was a kid, I'd caught glimpses of all this, while hiding in the trees. But now that I was older, I heeded my mother's stern warnings to keep away. She and my sisters and I bathed in the tub only rarely, because it was a lot of work to haul enough water, and it wasn't a good idea to let female flesh soak out in the open, so exposed.

Some afternoons, after my chores were done, I explored the forest. My feet padded over the velvety moss, brambles and huckleberry bushes snapping back and scratching at my ankles. Fuzzy, silk-strewn branches curved overhead, like enormous caterpillars shedding their skins. The air appeared green tinted, as though Mother Nature herself was exhaling breath after breath.

The first couple times, May came with me, until she befriended a little Indian girl, the daughter of the cook at a camp nearby. May was much better at making friends than me.

I invited Izzy to come along on my excursions, but she always declined. She said the mosquitoes devoured her skin.

I didn't mind solitude. If the mood struck, I wandered out to a beach and watched the silver rain clouds move ever so slowly, almost imperceptibly, gathering heaviness. It rained often, but never for very long.

That was how I stumbled upon the old Indian village. Strolling along the sand, I happened to notice an overgrown clearing at the wood's edge. As I approached, I could see it was clogged with bushy ferns and crippled saplings, which created a knotty layer around a big house. I didn't want to get too close because its cedar walls were covered in faded images of eyes shaped like wings, or wings shaped like eyes— opaque black circles of *something* staring out at you. Whatever they were, they were fearsome to behold.

At the centre of the house, a stump poked up from where a totem pole had been sawn off and carted away. And out front were the stumps of a few more poles, cleanly amputated. Farther down the beach were the remains of smaller houses and a cluster of simple headstones, some toppled over.

I began visiting this beach regularly. Sometimes I'd dig for clams, but mostly I just liked to let my mind drift with the great, light-infused clouds.

That was what I was doing the afternoon I first glimpsed her. A pale blotch of skin suddenly appeared at the edge of my vision, against the dark trees. Running and halting, like a spooked deer, she shot sharp glances over her shoulder and her tawny hair blew upward in puffs. Weaving in and out of the woods, she simply wouldn't stop moving. Her frilly white dress was too small and short for those lanky, awkwardly sprinting limbs.

I was about to call out to her when a big, lumbering man emerged from the trees. He had unruly black hair and a heavy beard. Panting, he leaned down to rest his hands on his knees, belly hanging down like a giant udder, face awash with fury. After catching his breath, he rushed in and out of several houses—kicking at walls, smashing what little remained. Thank God the girl had vanished by then.

"God almighty, I'll hunt you down and drag your hide back, if it's the last thing I do! So you better come out now, d'ya hear me, girl?"

A softly mocking rustle of wind was the only response.

The man noticed me standing there, watching him. He waddled forward, out of breath.

"You see a girl about yay high?" He waved a hand at the level of his nose. "She's my daughter and she's lost."

Moving slowly, I reached down into my pail, where a dozen clams soaked in water—along with a small knife, which I picked up.

"She went thataway." With the knife, I gestured at the forest, away from where she'd dashed.

The man eyed me curiously, for a good few seconds longer than was seemly. Although my heart was racketing in my head, now was not the time to show hesitation. I took a step closer—close enough to smell his foul breath, polluted with booze. His nose was ruddy and misshapen as a poisonous mushroom. "I *said* she went thataway!"

"If you're lying to me…"

"And why would I lie to you?"

A gust of wind churned up the water's surface, followed by a patter of rain. As gales whipped around our heads, the man ran off in the direction I'd indicated.

After waiting a few minutes, I made my way into the woods, exploring the area where I thought the girl might be hiding. I didn't want to scare her off. She'd come out when she was good and ready.

A colossal Sitka spruce arrested my gaze, then. It appeared slightly greener than the trees around it. Yet it was something more than its sheer scale and vibrancy that made me stop in my tracks. This tree brought to mind a corpulent matriarch, standing proud and tall, sheltering the smaller trees in her reach.

A furtive movement down at the base of the trunk caught my attention. I approached. A small face peeked up through the muscular roots, which arched in a rounded doorway. Through a curtain of glistening ferns, the girl looked at me with curiosity, fright. Pushing the fronds aside like they were strands of her own hair, she continued to eye me.

I knelt down. "Don't worry, he's gone. Is that brute really your father?"

She shook her head.

"You're safe now. So you can come out."

She made no sign of moving.

I sat down outside the tree. She'd twisted around, so I could see her better now. Her skin had an unusual hue: it was the colour of milky tea, with a handful of freckles floating atop, like tea leaves. Her nose was small and flat, like mine, her eyes narrow and slanted. Her tangled, curly mane was matted with spores and petals. I thought she might be around my age, or a bit older.

"What's your name?" I whispered.

Her eyes drifted sideways, like they were considering whether to reveal even this much. "Daisy," she replied, guardedly.

"Hi, Daisy. I'm Khya."

"Is he… really gone?"

I nodded. "Would it be okay if I came inside to join you?"

She didn't seem to object, so I crawled forward.

The air inside was very warm and damp, and there was barely enough space for us both to sit cross-legged. Our knees nudged against each other, and I could feel the heat rising from her still-panicked flesh. Through the darkness, ribbons of periwinkle light were slowly passing across her forehead. I felt like we were two fish encountering each other in an underwater cave. The whoosh of the rain and my own breathing filled my ears. And the sound of her breathing, too.

"Do you live around here?" I asked.

"No, we're just passing through." Daisy crossed her arms around her thin ribcage. Her wrists were very thin, too. Elegant, like bamboo shoots.

"You and that crazy guy?"

She made the slightest movement of her chin. "And the other girls…"

"Other girls?"

Something in her face seemed to flinch. "My sisters, I mean."

"But if he's not your father, why are you all with him?"

She shrugged, looking agitated, unwilling to speak. Her knees retracted, so they were no longer touching mine at all. She hugged her wrists around her shins.

"Where are you from, if you don't mind me asking?"

When she didn't reply, I repeated my question.

"Victoria," she said eventually, sounding cautious.

"Never been. My dad has, though. It's full of fancy hotels and rich white folks, isn't it?"

A sliver of a smirk enlivened her face. I wondered if a funny memory had surfaced.

I mimicked the expression of a haughty, rich lady, eyebrows raised high, lips pinched like an old prune. "Maid, these sheets are crumpled! Strip the bed and iron them again!" I had only an inkling that this was how such a woman would speak, based on what I'd read in novels.

But it won me a slight chuckle. Daisy's shoulders softened, as she relaxed a little. Picking up the pantomime, she pretended to have something clutched in her trembling hand. "Can't you see these silk panties aren't clean? Wash them again, wench!"

"There's a smear of blood!" I added, erupting in peals, wrinkling my nose.

She made an impish face, her freckles brightening. "You don't need to visit Victoria, 'cause you already know it. Lots of snobby white ladies, complaining there are no decent girls to shine their silverware. And then, every chance they get, they'll accuse you of nicking a spoon or bracelet."

She seemed rather knowledgeable about this sophisticated world. "Did.you work there as a maid?"

Daisy shook her head. "But I had friends in service, so they told me all the stories. If I'd stayed at the Home, I would've been hired out too, I guess."

"The Home?"

"The Chinese Rescue Home." Her eyes had an ominous glint, as though the place was famous, or infamous, and I ought to have heard of it, even out here.

"Is it an orphanage?"

"Sort of..."

I thought of the orphan asylums I'd read about in books, where the poor children were barely even fed and were flogged with branches. Only the spunkiest—like Jane Eyre—managed to survive.

I wanted to ask Daisy a great deal about her life at such a place, but I didn't want to come across as dreadfully nosy. So instead, I just said, "Why's it called the *Chinese* Rescue Home? Is it only for Chinese kids?"

She gave a nod. "Or Orientals, at least."

I felt confused. "How'd *you* get in?"

Her expression tightened, in brittle amusement, like she was used to this question, but still found it a nuisance to address. "I'm Oriental—or part Oriental—even though I don't look it much. My father's Chinese. My mother, who died, was white."

"Oh, gosh... I'm sorry about your mom!"

I didn't know what else to say, awkwardness gripping my throat. It was bad enough that her mother had died and her father hadn't been able to take care of her. But growing up neither Oriental nor white? A strange mixture of the two? Eurasians were very rare, odd, pitiful creatures.

I could remember only one prior time in my life I'd even seen a Eurasian. A little girl, with heather hair and the same curious skin tone as Daisy, had been clutching an Oriental woman's hand, out front of a restaurant in Prince Rupert. Passersby were stopping to stare and point, full of amazed giggles. And yet, the little girl had a cold, indifferent look, as if she'd grown immune to it all—chilling to see on such a young child.

Some version of the same shield of an expression had slipped over Daisy's face, and I felt like a beast, a hideous beast. I shifted around uncomfortably, knowing that she'd somehow read my thoughts, or could guess at them close enough. I wanted to apologize but didn't know what to say, because I'd never *said* anything offensive, had I? Confusion muddled my brain.

Finally, I decided, in my bumbling way, that the only thing to do was change the topic. "How'd you get away from the Home and end up here?"

"I ran away, of course."

"Good for you!" I liked her rebellious spirit and wanted to hear the full story of her getaway.

Fear splashed across her face, as though only then did she realize what she'd disclosed, in her attempt to impress me. "I shouldn't have told you that... You *mustn't* tell anybody that you know me, okay?"

"Who on earth would I tell?"

"Your parents? But *don't*—the police are looking for me!" She tightened her grip around her knees, the dirty ruffles of her oddly juvenile dress bunching up. Perhaps it was a uniform that all the girls at the Home had to wear? "The church ladies, who run the place, are after my hide!"

"Don't worry, the police don't come up to these parts."

Still, her knuckles remained white, her voice dropping to a mewl. "Are you certain?"

I shrugged, then nodded. "Till quite recently, only the Indians lived here."

Her eyes continued to dart this way and that. "I should get going now."

"But where'll you go?"

"Back to our campsite, of course."

"But that horrible man—"

"It'll be fine," she interrupted, in motion already. "His drunkenness'll wear off soon. He probably won't remember a thing."

"You still haven't told me who he is. How'd you end up with him?"

Her lips remained a lopsided knot.

It pained me to see her like this, plus I was eager to talk to her further. She seemed like she'd had such an interesting life, full of hardship and adventure. "Maybe I could get you a job at our camp? Helping out with meals and such."

She was scurrying out on hands and knees, quick as a mouse. "I'm gonna become a kitchen wench? When pigs fly!"

"Why not? You shouldn't have to stay with that brute."

"It just wouldn't work." Daisy glanced back at me, the light in her face extinguished.

"Well, I hope we'll run into each other again." My senses addled, I watched her moving with nimbleness through the roots and fronds. "Do you come to this part of the woods often?"

She was too distracted to nod or shake her head, even, as she vanished into the trees. "Remember, if anyone asks, we've never met! You've never even heard of a girl named Daisy."

THREE

The camp was growing now. Scores of new men had arrived, some barely more than boys my own age. Freckly faced kids who liked to curse and spit, freshly expelled from high schools on the mainland. Although they robbed the air of all quiet, it was good they were here, because everything got built a lot faster. Soon we had a town core of close to three hundred, and the dozen or so camps scattered around the inlet were expanding rapidly, too.

Buckley Bay was the name of the place, I learned. Apparently it'd been named after Mr. Frank Buckley, the head honcho of the Masset Timber Company, which employed us all. No one seemed to have ever laid eyes on the man, however. It was rumoured that he was long gone home to his mansion in Vancouver, leaving Mr. Brown and others in charge.

Our camp was only a ten-minute walk from the town centre, so I often wandered over to explore. The mill was a cluster of boxy adjoining buildings with sloped black roofs and giant conveyor belts penetrating its caverns. On one side, it was surrounded by piles of discarded wood and a beach of white sawdust and smoke that blew around in a great blinding haze, accompanied by a grinding racket that sent vibrations right into your jaw. The other side bordered the murky water, deep enough that ships could dock to load stacks of timber.

A boardwalk had been hastily constructed. It traced the craggy shoreline from the mill down past the stretch where there was a general store and then a few proper houses for important folks like Uncle Will, and it ended at a desolate strip of beach, clogged with driftwood, dead fish and nooses of kelp. There, at the tail end, I'd stand forever, watching the mill exhale its grey breath into the clouds. White schooners pulling rafts of logs from camps all over the inlet arrived to release their burdens at the mill.

Every two weeks, a brighter, preternaturally white dot would appear on the horizon and slowly grow larger till it took on the shape of a grand ship, called the *Prince John*. It carried in our canned goods and flour and mail, before departing with a raft of spruce. Watching this ship come and go filled my stomach with awe, like it was something godlike. And it did hold tremendous power over us, because without it, we were entirely dependant on our hunting skills to stay alive.

Occasionally, on my way back to camp, I glimpsed Irene wandering through the woods. Tarry makeup rimmed her tired eyes, her hair a messy, knotted halo. Now that there was a solid customer base in the area, she and a group of other whores came in periodically, and I'd catch sight of them doing business at dusk. Ghostly pale snatches of bare skin peeked through the trembling trees, feral grunts rising from a pair of rocking haunches.

Once when Irene noticed me walking by, she pushed the meaty body off of her and stood abruptly, skirt still bunched around her milky thighs.

"Haven't changed yer mind yet, hun?" she called out, with an obscene grin. "My offer still stands. Never too late to enter this fine profession!"

❧

Daisy was often on my mind, though our paths hadn't crossed again. The man who'd been chasing her through the woods continued to torment my imagination. Who the devil was he? Perhaps he'd kidnapped her, along with the other girls she'd mentioned. Was he a madman, with a harem in tow? The thought of anyone hurting Daisy made my blood boil.

Her sad, bright face haunted my brain, with the clarity of a photograph. There was something so rare and interesting about her face. That most people wouldn't consider her pretty in the least made me feel all the more warmly toward her, as though we shared a secret between us.

These days, whenever I went back to the beach by the old Indian village, I'd hope to find her there. I'd return to the big spruce, where our knees had touched and beads of rain had clung to her curls.

As I stared up at its sturdy trunk and followed it skyward toward explosions of feathery needles, dizziness clutched at my knees. How tiny and insignificant I felt next to this beautiful giant, whose scaly, layered bark appeared intricate and fascinating. And how had its roots grown like this, in these strange patterns of loose embrace? What was this tree's story, over the hundreds of years it'd been alive? When I dared to touch one root, it seemed to be ever so gently throbbing, with secrets and powers.

Once I crept inside the dank archway, my loneliness began to subside. The air still seemed to hold a trace of Daisy's laughter.

❧

Izzy didn't do much of anything most days. While the rest of us threw ourselves into our work, she just stayed inside the cottage, drinking tea and occasionally painting.

Her paintings, as far as I could tell, were not very good. They were bleak, deserted landscapes that lacked all colour, consisting only of black ink, watered down into shades of greyness. She painted on the floor, crouched down, rocking back and forth on her heels. Dressed in an old, dirty kimono tangled around her ankles, hair escaping her bun in wild locks, she reminded me at once of an old beggar woman and a very small child, too small to stand up and walk.

"Why do you keep watching me?" Izzy said one evening, over her shoulder.

When I didn't reply, she put down her paintbrush and turned around fully.

It was rare for my sister to speak to me. Or to anyone, for that matter. Despite my repeated attempts to be friendly, she stuck to curt answers and often didn't seem to understand what I was asking.

"Are you painting what you remember of Japan?" I said.

It was an image of a moonlit grove. At other times, it'd be dark mountains or storm clouds above a cliff.

May scampered over to look at the painting, too. "Is that where our relatives live?" Her face was lit with wonder.

Once I'd translated, Izzy gave a small shrug. "I can't speak for our whole family, but I lived in the city, not the countryside."

Although May was nodding thoughtfully, I doubted she'd understood much. So I again translated, and May's eyes widened further. Everything about Izzy fascinated her.

I was less easily impressed. "If you're not familiar with these scenes, why do you paint them over and over again?"

"They're just images I've observed in other paintings. And what else is there to paint?"

"Doesn't painting the same stuff get boring? Wouldn't you rather learn to fish and cook?" These skills would certainly be more useful to us, I was tempted to add.

Before Izzy could reply, our mother came over. She'd been standing by the stove, stirring a pot of soup, eavesdropping.

"Oh, it's different for girls in Japan—especially girls of the samurai class. You wouldn't understand, Khya, because you've never been there." A sheepish rasp escaped Mom's lips, melting into wistful silence. "Life would have been very different, for all my daughters, if we'd stayed in Japan. You certainly wouldn't be chopping wood and hauling buckets."

It was a card my mother liked to play. She enjoyed going on about how she was a samurai's daughter and had given up a great deal—a life of gentility, her days consisting of flower arranging, painting and poetry—in order to marry Dad, a farmer's son. To which he always just rolled his eyes. "If it hadn't been for the goodwill of the farmers, the samurais would have starved to death when they lost all their land. You *do* know that, don't you?" Although Mom was a few inches taller than him, Dad did not look up to her, not when she showed her snobbish streak.

"I hope that you girls aren't too unhappy here," Mom said softly, kneeling on the floor beside us.

"Unhappy? Why would we be *unhappy*?" I bristled at the pity in her voice. This was the only life I'd ever known, and it didn't strike me as half bad.

It was Izzy I felt sorry for. As a baby, she'd been taken to Japan to be raised by relatives, along with our older brother, Masao, who remained there even now. How glad I was that by the time me and May were born, our parents had let that stupid custom fall by the wayside.

I turned to May. "You're as happy as a clam here, aren't you?"

She giggled. "Why are clams happy?"

I thought about it. "Maybe because they carry around their homes with them? They're always at home, in their own shells."

But Mom's concern was directed at her eldest daughter. "What about you, Izumi-chan? I know your life is nothing like it was back in Japan."

While my sister remained silent, a sullen air about her, Mom refilled her tea. Izzy was drinking from a small bowl she'd brought from Japan, nestled in her suitcase. The white pottery had a silvery sheen, decorated with blue-grey brushstrokes that hinted at fishing boats. The delicate object appeared so out of place in our drab cottage, filling me with a confused sense of sympathy for my sister, touched by bitter resentment. It continued to puzzle me that our parents had insisted she return to us, when she clearly didn't belong here. Wouldn't she have been far happier if she'd been allowed to stay in Japan?

❧

Supper was the only meal we all took together. Everyone in the camp lined up outside our door with their bowls, into which Mom dished a hearty fish soup or meat stew, along with thick slices of her sourdough. Our cottage was as toasty as the oven she had fired up for much of the day.

Some people sat around the campfire, while others took their food into the cabins. I always wanted to go outside to join Dad, but my mother made me sit at the table with my sisters. As I chewed, I listened to the voices outside rising and falling to the crackle of flames.

Now that there were more people, groups had formed. It happened naturally, folks looking instinctively to the familiarity and protection of their own kind. Each group claimed its own cluster of cabins, just as things had been in Skeena. At the centre of each miniature community, a single man with a forceful personality emerged. For the Chinese, it was this rotund guy named Hay Kong Wong, who loved nothing more than playing mahjong late into the night. The Japanese all looked up to my father. In the case of the Indians, a flinty-eyed man by the name of Frank Turner seemed to hold authority. And amongst the whites, it was Felix Godwin.

For some reason, everyone called Felix Godwin "the Captain." There must have been a story behind the nickname, but I never heard it. Whatever the case, the name puffed him up, enabling him to act like he was in charge. Not that he had much life experience under his belt. He was a young, cocky thing—twenty, at most. A tall, broad-shouldered guy, with narrow, mint eyes and a thatch of wheat-coloured hair. That he was prematurely balding accounted for the brand new Stetson he was rarely seen without, like he'd read too many dime novels about cowboys when he was a kid. He walked with a swaggering limp, which he showed off as a badge of honour. Supposedly he'd been injured over in France, beating back the Germans.

On this particular evening, the Captain's spirits were even higher than usual. His cousin—an obnoxious, bearded guy—had just arrived to join the crew. Carl was his name. Carl enjoyed stroking the Captain's ego, erupting in gleeful laughter and grunting in assent whenever the Captain said anything, no matter how insignificant. Both their voices were boisterous with whisky, thanks to the bottles Carl had brought. I could hear every word they uttered through our walls.

"Who cooked this grub?" Carl said. "It's actually pretty tasty."

"Oriental lady," the Captain replied. "The wife of Sam."

"Sam?"

"Oriental Sam. The short little man I pointed out to you earlier."

"Oh, right." A strained pause. "Is it really true that *he's* in charge?"

A guffaw. I could picture the Captain's face reddening, under the setting sun. "For now, maybe. But don't you boys worry. I'll get this sorted out in no time."

Anger gargled in my throat. This wouldn't be the first time Dad had had to deal with arrogance from white boys. The same thing had happened at the mill in Skeena, when some workers had complained that it was demeaning to have a Jap boss. Fortunately, Dad was good at winning people over.

I sensed, however, it was going to be harder with this lot. My hunch proved correct a few days later, when I saw the Captain pull Uncle Will aside after dinner. I edged closer to eavesdrop, while gathering dirty dishes around the campfire. My father was on the other side of the clearing, smoking and chatting with some Chinese guys.

"Here's the thing, Mr. Henderson," the Captain was saying. "I understand that in the early days, you were short on men and had no choice. But now that we're all here, don't you think it'd be more appropriate to appoint somebody everyone can respect?"

"Respect?" Uncle Will almost sounded amused.

A flock of silver-haired bats emerged from the treetops and swooped erratically across the plum sky. I could feel a trickle of sweat on the small of my back.

"The more you talk, Felix Godwin, the less convinced I am that you're capable of respect. Self-respect included!"

The Captain's boys, over in the corner, were watching his every move. His face came alive, all his features contracting to a sharp point. This was how I imagined he'd look while aiming a gun at an enemy soldier.

"I know he's your friend, but there are limits to friendship, *sir*."

By now, everyone had turned to listen. A strange expression had slipped over my father. Although his eyes were wide open, they somehow had a closed appearance, as though he were staring ahead at nothing at all.

"In all my years of working with Sam Terada," Uncle Will said, with a deep scowl, "he's done nothing but prove his abilities."

The Captain appeared shaken for a split second, before increasing his bluster, if only to save face. "That so? And when push comes to shove, you reckon you can trust a yellow man?"

Uncle Will spat on the ground. "This camp has the highest yield of any on the inlet. Did ya know that, boy?"

FOUR

While chopping wood, Mom put out her back. It wasn't the first time she'd hurt herself this way. As usual she tried to carry on, only deepening the injury, and soon she was unable to endure even the lightest tasks. Bed rest was the only remedy.

This meant, of course, we all had to help out more. While I was expecting Izzy to be pretty much useless, to my surprise she was willing to roll up her sleeves. Perhaps at last she was learning how to live out here, how to use her hands as tools. In fact, she proved quite capable at making bread, her touch lighter and more intuitive than mine. This freed up my time for butchering and cooking the deer and geese that the men shot between their shifts. I was getting used to my fingernails being blackened with dried blood.

The change in routine seemed to be good for my sister. A new energy infused her complexion, adding a pinkish glow. Once she'd discarded her Japanese robes in favour of ordinary skirts, borrowed from Mom, it became clear that she had a rather comely figure, more curvaceous than women of our race usually are. It didn't take long to attract lingering stares, especially from the *hakujin* boys—randy between their monthly trips to the brothel in Port Clem. And flirting with Izzy was another way for them to undermine our father.

"What lovely creature do we have here?" the Captain said one evening, while strolling past.

My sister was crouched down—we both were—to tend the beds of beans, asparagus and potatoes at the rear of the workers' cabins. The weather was a fair bit warmer now, with summer at its dawn. Our arms were bare below our rolled-up sleeves, our skin flecked with mud and sweat droplets.

I jumped up. "What do *you* want? Our father'll be here any minute."

"Is that so? But I'm not talking to you. I'm talking to your beautiful sister."

Izzy looked up uncertainly, smiling in that docile, indiscriminate way of hers. I felt humiliated on her behalf, and a protective instinct stirred inside me. "She doesn't understand a word you're saying!"

"A woman doesn't need to talk in order to have fun." The Captain knelt down so they were at eye level.

Fortunately, I hadn't been lying about Dad. He appeared right then, carrying a bucket of compost scraps.

The Captain leapt to his feet. "You have an awfully pretty daughter,

Sam. Normally I'm not drawn to Oriental girls, but in this case, you never know, I just might have to make an exception!"

With that, the Captain turned to leave, throwing a devious wink over his shoulder.

❦

Izzy became the trophy of a strange game. At first it was just the Captain and Carl following her around, leaving bouquets of wildflowers outside our door, trying to entice her to take long strolls, deep into the forest. I kept a sharp eye and intercepted whenever I could by pulling her away from them, her body as limp as the stem of a wilted dandelion.

As other *hakujin* boys joined in, the collection of gifts grew more varied, creative. A bracelet whittled from wood. A deer-hide shawl. A primitive crown of curved branches and prickly leaves.

My sister appeared overwhelmed, but not displeased, by all the attention. Was she simply too polite to push them away or spit in their faces? Throw their homemade offerings to the ground? But then I realized—yes, there was no mistaking it—some part of her was actually enjoying it. How her complexion reddened and glowed, giggles of feigned protest bubbling up, whenever one of these boys would scurry up behind and slip an arm through the crook of her elbow, honeyed words on the tip of his tongue, meaningless to her ears. Somehow, she understood anyway. My sister knew how to flirt wordlessly, instinctively, through gestures and purrs and occasional eruptions in her pidgin English. Her foolishness and blind hunger for affection baffled me to no end.

Dad and I tried to talk some sense into her.

"Can't you see those guys aren't your friends?" I demanded. "Clearly, they're just trying to get to Dad!"

Her face swivelled away, like I'd slapped her.

"We're just telling you this for your own good." Despite his stern tone, Dad looked tired, so tired. "You keep your distance from those boys, *you hear me?*"

Izzy's chin bobbed up and down, puppet-like.

Nevertheless, the gifts continued to arrive in the middle of the night, piling up in front of our door to be discovered each morning. It was as though Izzy had died and the muddy patch in front of our cottage had turned into a memorial shrine.

Was there a part of me that was jealous? After all, this kind of fawning attention was what we girls were supposed to desire, weren't we? And I wasn't really so different looking from my sister, was I? At my mother's nagging, I'd let my hair grow out a bit, wisps curling inward beneath my chin.

Then the male attention did spread to me, and I was relieved by that throb of revulsion in my gut. Nope, it wasn't jealousy—not even close. Those oily leers and toothy grins and wandering hands that in clumsy, mock-accidental fashion brushed against my rear and reached down all too quickly to pick up the pile of wood I'd just finished chopping—as if someone strong enough to chop her own wood wasn't strong enough to carry it—no, none of those awkward gestures sent flutters and tingles through my flesh or made me feel much of anything beyond annoyance.

Although I wasn't sure what desire was supposed to feel like, I knew it couldn't be *this*. I thought that if I were ever to fall in love, it'd be a man like Rochester, who'd probably be responsible. Someone aloof, gruff, stern even, withholding of his true feelings for the longest time, until Jane Eyre breaks down his defences and then comes to his rescue, when he's crippled and blind and desperately needs her…

Not that there were any Rochesters in these backwaters. Courtship rituals here—if you could call them that—were primitive, violent.

I'd had a taste, which was more than enough. There was a certain guy with an eerie smile that melted across his thin, pasty lips whenever he'd look my way. At every opportunity, he'd sneak up and grab me and try to throw me up in the air or over his shoulder, like I was his very own kitten.

But kittens scratch and bite. One day, rather than just thrashing and squirming away, I clamped down on his ear. As a dirty, greasy taste—worse than rancid oil—spread across my tongue, he dropped me to the ground, his shriek echoing from the treetops.

After that, I became known as the crazy girl. The witch girl. The wolf girl. Don't let her anywhere near you, or she just might nip off your nose or toes or some other appendage you value more dearly.

Fine by me. It was only unfortunate that my degraded status didn't extend to my sister. The more I was shunned, the more Izzy was exalted, though it no longer seemed like she was receiving gifts from the whole crew. The weedy bouquets and crude carvings now came mainly from the Captain, who appeared to be laying claim to her, with a twinkle in the eye and a knowing laugh thrown across the blazing campfire.

❧

It was just small things, in the beginning. A missing hammer, a vanished pot. We thought we'd misplaced the stuff, or someone had borrowed it and forgotten to bring it back. But then the thief got bolder, extending his reach to handsaws and rifles. I was furious to discover that my best fishing rod had gone up in thin air. Always in the Oriental and Indian quarters. The Captain and his boys remained curiously untouched.

Yet we had no proof. Whoever was carrying out the thefts, he had a stealthy, ghost-like walk and nimble, coaxing fingers. Although we remained vigilant, things kept disappearing in the night.

One evening after supper, Dad tried to talk to Frank Turner and Hay Kong Wong about what to do about the situation. In recent days, I'd been puzzled by a certain disdain these men seemed to direct toward my father. Perhaps the fact that we now had a common enemy and thief in our midst would help them move past whatever was bothering them.

Reluctantly, Wong and Turner allowed themselves to be led into our house. Wong's fat face was already flushed from drink, though he'd long lost his jolly demeanour. By comparison, Turner was a thinner man, but nonetheless stocky. Something about him appeared at once mischievous and mellow, as though within the weathered hide of his face lived a young, impish soul. Mom, Izzy and I served tea and then stepped outside, with May in tow.

Since there wasn't anywhere for us to go, we sat on tree stumps and watched the mosquitoes buzzing around crazily, in the last of the dusky light. High above, bats were chittering and swooping in wild nosedives, like fighter planes under attack. We could hear the men's voices rising and falling inside, hushed murmurs escalating to hostile exclamations. Ignoring Mom's disapproving glance, I darted over to the window.

My eyes peered through the smudged glass into the dim interior. Dad sat at the table, with his back to me. Turner was across from him, bearing a mildly amused expression. The plate of bread and jam between them remained untouched, the tea cups unmoved from where I'd placed them. Wong had jumped to his feet.

"You think you better than us?" he hissed. He fumbled in his pocket for a letter, waving it like a dirty handkerchief in my father's face. "My wife in China, she write, you know. She tell me what you Japs do, back home!"

Dad sighed, his shoulders wilting. Clearly, the conversation had strayed far from the topic of the thief.

I'd observed that the Chinese guys were drinking more these days and their mahjong games went on well into the night, rowdy laughter penetrating the walls of our cottage. An air of recklessness surrounded Wong and his friends, who no longer acted friendly toward Dad—or any of us Japanese folks, for that matter. I gathered it had to do with the war, which continued to be all anyone talked about. There were rumours that Japan had been expanding its reach by taking over some islands in China that'd been German colonial turf, and some people seemed to believe this was the main reason Japan had entered the war in the first place. But what could any of that have to do with my father? He had no control over what a bunch of Japanese soldiers were doing on the other side of the world.

Wong kept muttering under his breath in Cantonese. Dad replied in the same language, in a placating tone, but it didn't appear to be helping.

His shiny face twisted with anguish, Wong shouted, switching back to English, "You Japs always take what not yours!"

With that, he stormed out, the door whanging shut behind him.

Dad and Turner looked at each other, in silence.

"So, that went well," Turner said, with a hint of dark merriment.

"I assume that I can count on your help, at least."

"Well, it's never a good idea to assume anything, I have to tell you."

"Oh?" My father stiffened.

"As far as I'm concerned," Turner continued, "we Haida have no reason in the world to trust you Orientals. Right from your arrival on our shores, you've been nothing but yes-men and strike breakers. If it weren't for you, our fishing unions wouldn't have been brought to their knees. Or have you conveniently forgotten about the past twenty years?"

Dad let out a strange bark, which didn't quite sound like a laugh. It faded to something more like a whimper. "Whatever your feelings are toward me, Frank, don't you think that it makes sense for us to work together? Now's not the time to let petty squabbles slow down operations."

Last month, the German army had gone on a rampage, shooting down five of our planes for every one of theirs lost. These trees couldn't be felled fast enough, according to the Allies.

"As usual, everything's about the white man's war. The white man says 'Jump!' and your scrawny ass is already in the air. Same old story." Turner gulped back his tea and grabbed a piece of bread to go. His empty cup hit the table as he headed for the door.

Dad's face glazed over with defeat. It frightened me to see him so troubled and still, his bum glued to the chair.

❦

You could notice it in the way Izzy looked at the Captain across the campfire—her eyes flitting this way and that, crinkling at the corners like origami fans, secrets folded within. In the middle of the night, I'd hear her rise and return a long time later, shadows and blankets making dark swishes around her body.

Once, when I awoke and she wasn't there on the sofa across from me, I rose groggily and staggered outside into the cold moonlight. I'd been having a bad dream, which I could only half-remember: something about a flood, everything blurring away to rushing water, or maybe it was about being aboard a capsized boat... Whatever the case, the dream had left a rocking sensation beneath my bare feet. Unsteadily, I searched around in the darkness. I checked the outhouse, finding it empty. And then I heard my sister's voice. Her laughter, her muted laughter. It sounded as though she was trying to swallow it all back.

I walked a short distance along the edge of the forest. Heading inward toward the noise, I spotted my sister—pinned against a tree, the biggest tree. Her face was as shockingly pale as the Captain's bare bum, which jiggled with vibrational energy as it thrust in and out. Whenever I'd glimpsed Irene in this position, I'd always averted my eyes, hurried past. Now, however, I found myself unable to look away, my gaze locked on my sister's expression, her strange expression. It was hard to tell if she was wincing in pain or losing herself in some kind of delirium.

My first impulse was to grab Dad's rifle and shoot this man in the bum, but I was afraid that the bullet might kill my sister, too. Pin her limp body to this guy's quivering loins forever.

So I remained perfectly still, just watching. Paralyzed. At some point, Izzy's eyes fluttered open and she might have glimpsed me, peeking out from behind my tree, for I detected a sudden urgency in her face, which shook back and forth, as though banishing me, warning me away forever. Like she was offering up her own body as a sacrifice to save mine.

But if she saw me, we never talked about the incident, and I wondered the next morning whether it'd even happened. Perhaps it was just an extension of my restless dreamlife, of my ever-growing hatred of the Captain.

FIVE

August was a wet, warm month. Mushrooms were blossoming everywhere, in patches of little white caps and fawn umbrellas. Enormous
ruffles of burnt orange lace beckoned from the thickest tree trunks, as
though the entire forest had filled with seductive ladies showing off their
underskirts. Sex was in the air. At dusk, I watched the salmon spawn-
ing in the turbulent shallows. The females swished their tails to upset
the gravelly bottom and make nests for their eggs. Never far behind,
the males swam up caressingly and squirted down their mess and kept
watch—rushing and biting at any intruder, any arrogant trout.

My sister must've wanted something similar from the Captain.
They'd been carrying on for a good while by then, having their nocturnal encounters. After what I'd witnessed, I never followed her out to the
woods again, not wanting to revisit that awful scene.

She continued on in her moony state, under the Captain's spell. Her
entire body had taken on a luminous glow, her eyes dreamy with ill-fat-
ed fantasies. It wasn't hard to see that she was desperate for the Captain
to bring their relationship out into the open. What else could have been
her aim as she walked across the clearing one evening carrying a big
bowl of stew in her outstretched arms? While everyone watched, she
strolled past the campfire, heading right to the cluster of cabins where
the white boys lived. The Captain, Carl and a few others were sitting
outside, slouched on benches, smoking, drinking, chatting.

They didn't even see her for the longest time. Eventually, the Captain looked up lazily, appearing surprised, then not so surprised. The
edges of his mouth wiggled upward, as soft snickers enveloped the group.

After handing him the bowl, Izzy just stood there for an endless
moment, as he made her wait. Uncertainty drifted over her sweetly ex-
pectant face. A shudder of disgust passed over my skin. How could my
sister be such a pathetic fool?

The timing was perfect, with Dad off to the side, witnessing everything.

"Iz, my girl," the Captain finally said, patting the seat beside him.

Her complexion abloom, she sat down, and he slung an arm around
her shoulder. When he whispered something in her ear, her whole body
came alive—even stray tendrils of hair, quivering as she laughed, seemed
to exude a brilliant energy.

While eating his stew, the Captain resumed chatting with his
friends. But more than once, he glanced at my sister. He *was* fond of

her, I was surprised to realize. He bore a slightly wounded look, some surfeit of bright feeling he didn't want to acknowledge flickering across his gaze. I didn't know if it was love, or anything close to love, but he did have affection for her, I could see, and I had a strange premonition that in the future I would remember this scene, frozen in my mind like a photograph.

The feeling passed and everything returned to ordinary life: just a bunch of coarse men joshing around in the company of a beautiful girl. But for once, they kept their voices low. They no longer felt the need to be so loud, since they'd so effortlessly humiliated my father in front of the entire camp.

❧

Poor Irene. She was desperately trying to expand beyond the townsite, which had until now provided her customer base, so I often glimpsed her wandering around our camp at dusk, unsteady from too much drink. Although the men tolerated her presence, they mostly shooed her away these days, like a stray, persistent cat. There were better pickings now. I'd overheard folks talking about how a guy named Handsome Joe had set up a big white tent, about a mile down from Buckley, open for business till the wee hours. No longer did men have to trek to Port Clem for a decent roll in the hay.

One afternoon, Uncle Will sent me on an errand. He needed me to deliver an important letter to the manager of another camp, some distance away. I didn't mind the journey. I liked walking along the beach for hours, with only my own thoughts for company.

When I caught sight of the billowy tent, curiosity pricked my innards and I couldn't resist slowing down. Set back from the shore, it peeked through the trees in bright snatches of whiteness. As I got closer, I could see that the cloth was actually far from white, rather dingy.

The campsite wasn't in the best shape either. Shards of emerald glass sprinkled the ground, catching the sun. A bottle or two had been smashed to smithereens. Next to the sloppily made fire, a wooden chair, missing a leg, perched lopsided. A black top hat—like the kind a magician would wear—lay in the mud, crushed down.

In a hammock strung between two trees, an obese guy lounged on his back, snoring heavily, head lolled away from me. His crumpled burgundy trousers pooled on the ground, one bunched-up leg still clinging to a thick ankle. His hairy thighs reminded me of sleeping pigs, his underwear as begrimed as the tent. Could this be Handsome Joe? He certainly didn't look at all handsome. As he began to twitch and gurgle, I backed away.

A rustling movement within the tent made me slip behind a tree, just before a little blond thing emerged from the flap.

She reminded me of a bedraggled fairy, in her gauzy, pink skirt that flounced outward and ended well above her bottlecap knees. The layers had turned brownish, as though she'd been rolling around in the dust for hours. Her silky top was far too large, one berry-like nipple blinking out from the gaping neckline. She appeared not much older than eleven. It startled me to find such a young soul here, and I didn't know what to make of her presence. Was it possible that she was the fat man's daughter?

She dipped her hands in a pot of rainwater and splashed her face, shaking drops from her hair in the manner of a shaggy dog.

A moment later, a taller, older girl came out of the tent and let out a wide yawn. Her lipstick was smudged, giving her homely face a swollen appearance. A brown housecoat hugged her chubby frame.

"Molly," she commanded the younger one, who was doing a half-hearted jump resembling hopscotch, "why aren't you starting the fire? One of the gents brought bacon last night, remember?"

Molly scurried off for kindling and fresh wood, while the older girl sat down on a rock and lit a cigarette, looking bored.

After the fire was going, the two of them bunched up strips of bacon to be pierced by long sticks. In silence, they roasted it over the flames, drops of fat crackling and sizzling and making my stomach rumble.

The man in the hammock began to stir, his fleshy forehead rolling forward. I could see now that he had a heavy beard, like the butt of a big black sheep. The face, still asleep, started to look kind of familiar. Uneasiness crept over my skin.

The tent flapped open again. This time—to my horror—it was Daisy who slipped out. She just stood there, blinking in the sunlight for the longest time. Then she joined the other two girls around the fire.

Daisy had slept in an old plaid shirt, so large that it came down to her knees. Strands of silver tinsel, from whatever glamorous getup she'd had on the night before, still clung to her curls. Her eyelids were smeared with shimmery charcoal that she'd rubbed into thunderclouds in her sleep.

"Pass me a piece?" she said. "Pretty please?"

"Just one," said the older girl. "After all, *I* was the one who earned it."

"I'll give you a lollipop?"

"I don't want your fucking lollipop."

A bee whirred in to settle upon my cheek. As I swatted at it, all three faces turned to stare at the mesh of branches I was crouched behind.

"Something's out there," Molly said anxiously. "A bear?"

"Too small," the tall girl said. "A wolf maybe?"

Clearly, she was as much of a city girl as Daisy. There were no wolves up in these parts.

"What're we gonna do? Daisy, grab that axe!"

"Why me?"

"You're eating *my* bacon."

"Why don't we wake up Handsome Joe?"

"You do that, sweetheart, and you'll *wish* you only had a wolf to do battle with."

Dragging the axe behind her, like a lame leg, Daisy inched forward.

It was too late to run away now. I had no choice but to wait there, lost in the sound of my stuttering pulse. When she was close enough to recognize me, I peeked out and whispered her name.

Her face swerved away, like I'd flung a pan of hot oil at her. After a moment, she managed to raise the axe unsteadily, in a pitiful attempt to look frightening. As the sleeves of her shirt fell down to her elbows, a mauve-brown sheen of bruises on her forearms alarmed my eyes.

"Scram!" she hissed.

I turned and ran, the forest spinning all around me. A whirl of greenness.

"What was it?" Molly called out, behind.

"Just some peeping Tom," I heard Daisy reply. "Nothing to worry about, I think."

ψ

It was sundown by the time I got back to our camp. I went straight to Dad. The long walk hadn't done anything to calm me down. My face was burning with fiery emotions, my thoughts in a state of mutiny.

"Something wrong, Khya?" my father said, upon taking one look at me.

"I—I passed by the white tent today."

"What white tent?"

"You know! Handsome Joe's."

Dad's forehead turned shiny. He evaded my unblinking gaze. "I don't know anything about that place. And I don't want you anywhere near it."

"The girls there are young, Dad. *Very* young. I think some of them have been kidnapped!"

He sighed, staring up at the fading sky. "Well, what do you expect *me* to do? It's better that the men have a place to blow off steam."

"What about those poor girls?"

"What about them?"

"Can't you talk to the guys? Tell them not to go there. Tell them to go to Port Clem instead. Talk to Uncle Will. Tell him to shut the tent down!"

"Oh, Khya." How old Dad appeared, the skin around his eyes like parched earth. Though he did seem moved by my plea, he seemed equally annoyed by my assumption that he had power over the situation. "Do you honestly believe it'd make any difference?"

"Think about how you'd feel if it was one of us. Me or May or Izzy!"

"It's precisely because I want to keep my daughters safe that I'm willing to put up with the tent girls."

It was startling to see him so resigned, concerned about only protecting his own turf. Shadows were gathering in the sunken parts of my father's face, and it was the same face I'd always known, yet it somehow appeared different, so different. The accusations of Frank Turner and Hay Kong Wong remained in my memory, and I was beginning to wonder whether they might contain a grain of truth. Perhaps Dad wasn't the man of high principles I'd long thought he was. And I just couldn't take it! I couldn't bear to think that he might actually be right—that Daisy was a sacrifice needed to secure my own safety, as if the price for protecting one girl was that another girl got offered up to the appetites of men. Why *her*? Why did she have to be the one thrown to the wolves?

The disappointment cut both ways. Dad was looking at me as though I'd let *him* down, by proving to be so very naive, by putting him in this awkward position.

☙

The following night, a commotion roused me from sleep. Dad could be heard bellowing outside our cottage, amidst many other raised voices and feet pounding toward the woods. Fright cleared my head like a splash of cold water, waking me up fully. I threw on a sweater and hurried out to join the crowd.

While I raced along the path, pushing my way through the swirling forms of darkness, branches sprang back and hit me in the face. I lost my footing and tripped on a gravelly rut, my knees absorbing the force. I got up and kept on running. A hot, suffocating feeling filled my head.

Men were packed around the *onsen*. Orange flames shot up, wild and blinding. Folks were screaming at each other to get buckets and they were running to the beach to fill them up and heaping water into the tub's sizzling depths. Then running back for more. I grabbed a bucket to help, but someone elbowed me aside, and I ended up soaked down one side of my body. Waves of heat and wetness hit my cheeks in alternating slaps, and billows of smoke rose from the blaze into the murky air, making my eyes sting. Dad was rushing about trying to direct people's activities. Yet it was pretty clear that the tub was ruined beyond salvation.

While we remained in a frenzy, there were a lot of others just standing around, idle. Chinese and Indian guys. Meanwhile, the white boys were nowhere to be seen. Why weren't people doing more to help us? But their grim mouths and downcast gazes seemed to conceal flickers of satisfaction.

Following a vague instinct in my gut, I ran back to camp. There, I discovered that the Captain and Carl's cabin had been emptied out, along with the neighbouring cabins that'd belonged to their crew. They were nowhere to be seen—none of the white boys were. Finally, I found a couple of stragglers packing their gear, rolling up their bedrolls. When I demanded where they were going, the taller one grunted, "'Nother camp, down south."

The Captain must have been planning this desertion for days. Despair blackened my mind. I headed back to his cabin, planning to search for clues… but clues to what? It was already clear what he'd been scheming.

That was when I found my sister. She was crouched down in the middle of the bare room, arms wrapped around her knees. She was rocking back and forth, like she always did whenever she'd paint on the floor.

I leaned down next to her. "Is something wrong?"

It was a ridiculous thing to ask, I realized, as soon as the words had left my mouth. Izzy just looked at me, her eyes all filmy and dull, like those of a dead fish, left on the shore to rot.

"He was supposed to take me with him… He *said* he would…" Her voice broke off, weeping.

I cringed at what she'd revealed. When I opened my mouth, nothing would come out. Finally, I managed to whisper, "It's better that you didn't go with him."

"*Why?* Because Father would never forgive me?" A warble of mocking laughter.

It was chilling to see her in this state. And yet, much as my heart broke for her, I also kind of hated her at that moment. I couldn't understand the deep hostility she harboured toward me and our family. What had we ever done to deserve this?

"It was *me*, you know."

"You?" I said, perplexed.

Her lips tightened, as though suppressing a grin, or savouring a secret she wasn't sure she wanted to part with yet.

"The thief! Everyone assumed it was the Captain or one of his boys stealing our stuff. But it was *me*. I wanted to do it."

Crackling shivers passed over my skin.

"I was helping him to create a stockpile," she whispered. "Things we'd need after we left."

I tried to sift through her words for shards of meaning. "Why are you telling me this?"

"If not you, who could I possibly tell?"

I searched my sister's face for any trace of guilt, but all I could see was a thick layer of self-pity, devastation. And a flicker of something curiously close to enjoyment.

"Mother likes to act like I led a charmed life in Japan. As though our relatives are still rich and they treated me like their own daughter and I never had to lift a finger, with all the servants waiting on me. But it was *nothing* like that, I have to tell you!"

"Oh?"

"No one cares about the samurais anymore. Surely, you must realize that? Samurai origins mean nothing these days. And this has been the case for over fifty years! You can buy their swords at flea markets for a few coins. The old warriors have been reduced to drunks and hunchbacks living on the streets."

My knees went unsteady, the air sucked right out of my throat. "Mom doesn't know this?" I heard myself utter.

"Of course she knows. How could she not? Why do you think she married our father—of all people—and moved to this backwater?"

I thought about Mom's wistful reminiscences, her bold claims about all she'd given up. My jaw tightened, confusion gathering in a dull ache. "Why the dickens would she lie to us?"

"Maybe life out here has made her turn funny in the head. Or maybe it helps her feel better about how she and Father abandoned me."

I stood up, indignant. "That's not true—they always sent money to the relatives to take care of you and Mas!"

"Well, I can't speak for Masao. Maybe the relatives entrusted with his care were kinder than the lot I ended up with. And boys are more valuable than girls. I guess that's why he's been allowed to stay."

"You could've stayed in Japan too, if our parents hadn't gotten it in their heads that you'd be better off here, for some strange reason!"

"No, Khya." Izzy looked at me like I was so dim-witted she almost felt sorry for me. "Money! It was all about money. Whatever amount our parents were sending to the relatives was never enough. And then it got to be even less, after Father lost everything. So, you see, our kind-hearted relatives began to treat me as nothing more than a maid. My clothes are all hand-me-downs or things I stole right before coming here. And I also stole that teacup you like." A tear trickled down her cheek. "They wrote to our parents to say that they were going to put me out on the street. Even as a maid, they didn't want me anymore. That's the real reason I find myself here!"

Shock washed over me in hot waves, my throat cinching.

"I've never had a home—not here, not anywhere," she sobbed. "But the Captain was going to change that…"

Despite her misery, I sensed that it was giving her a slight pleasure to be carrying on and burdening me with her confession. It was like she felt I deserved to be the one to bear it, since our parents had abandoned her as a child, rather than me. It was the least I could do for her, she must have thought. And still, we'd never be even.

Six

After the *hakujin* boys left, it became clear that the Indians were getting itchy feet, too. I saw Frank Turner and my father talking one evening after supper, a tense air about them. I crept closer and sat down on a tree stump, like I was minding my own business. My ears strained to catch what they were saying, over the crackling fire.

"We've made enough money for the season," Turner declared. "We've got our own fishing to do now."

"Six dollars a day isn't enough for you to stick around?" Dad replied. "You can't make close to that fishing."

"I don't care if the government pays a hundred bucks a day! We've had enough of lopping down these trees. We were fools to come out here in the first place."

It was clear from the way the Indians looked at us that they viewed us as cursed. Maybe they felt the fire had been nothing short of our own fault. Maybe they saw it as nature's way of sending us a message, settling an old score.

The Chinese workers weren't far behind. Although not all of them took off, most did, with Hay Kong Wong leading the way. I wondered if he and his crew were headed down to the other big logging post, at Thurston Harbour, where the *hakujin* guys had already gone.

To my surprise, Dad didn't try to stop anyone. He took his abandonment with slack indifference.

After the exodus, however, a sombre mood rolled over him. His quietness—the quietness of the entire camp—was the hardest to bear. With the steam donkeys idle, nothing but the warbling of birds and rustling of branches filled the air.

Mr. Brown didn't often come out to visit, preferring to let Uncle Will run the show. So it was alarming to see Mr. Brown arrive, a few days after the fire. I watched him, from a distance, as he disembarked from his boat at the dock, his face in a tight braid of fury.

It's happening again, I thought with despair. Everything's going belly up. And this time, we'll be lucky if Dad finds a job as a janitor.

I never found out what Uncle Will said to save us from that fate. Or maybe there was simply no time for sacking anybody, with the war machine at full throttle; anyone who had the ability to take over my father's job had already vamoosed.

Nevertheless, we knew that Mr. Brown had a close eye on us now, and it wouldn't take much for us to be sent packing.

❧

Izzy rarely left the cottage. In fact, she hardly got up off the sofa. Dad didn't make a fuss, since he had more pressing things to contend with, so we all kept up the charade that she'd fallen ill and just needed bed rest. After a few days, though, I was worried, very worried. How long was a broken heart supposed to last for?

I crouched down next to my sister, her eyelids red and puffy. "You'll feel much better if you get up, Iz. You can help me make lunch, okay?"

Her face remained blank, unresponsive. I nudged her shoulder.

"I had a dream last night..." As she turned, a tear came to a head and dribbled down.

"What did you dream?"

"That the Captain came back for me."

It boggled my mind. How could this man retain such a hold over her, even now? "How can you still be so stupidly in love with that scoundrel?"

Her lips twisted, trying to suppress a sob. Then she looked direct- ly at me, with sparkles of hatred in her eyes. "You see, Khya, he wasn't the first man who'd..." Then, in a lowered tone, she said something I couldn't understand with my limited Japanese.

"Come again?"

"A man in the house where I grew up. In Japan. An uncle, I suppose he is. He's married to one of Mother's sisters."

"What about him?"

"Well, when I was a little girl... he used to come into my room at night... And as I got older, he became more persistent."

Izzy was watching me very carefully, her eyes wide open, aglow. It was as though she'd been saving this card for a long while, and my stunned reaction did not disappoint her.

"With a white man, I thought it'd be different... And it *was* differ- ent. The Captain was so sweet and tender, at first." She buried her face in her hands.

"Oh, Iz..." Bleak emotions overpowered my ability to speak. How could Dad have let this happen? Had he actually believed that this was the best way for my sister to be raised—thrown upon the mercy of vile relatives? With that as her childhood, no wonder she'd fallen prey to the Captain's manipulations.

"I thought that coming here would be a fresh start."

"And it still can be! Maybe your dream was a premonition—maybe the Captain *will* come back for you."

This sprang to my lips thoughtlessly, instinctively. Not that I believed it at all. At that moment, I was willing to say anything to dull the ago-nizing ache in my chest and restore my sister to the land of the living.

Later that afternoon, she did get up, though she remained listless, incapable of even peeling potatoes. Then the strange rituals began. She must have been hiding away all the little gifts that the Captain had used to seduce her. Now, it all emerged: shrivelled fistfuls of wildflow-ers disintegrating into brown dust, pink clamshells clattering together on a string in a child's necklace, a crown of twigs and dead blossoms. She spread out all her loot in the corner. When I tried to gather it up to throw it away, she grabbed my wrist with the force of a possessed woman.

"Let go—you're hurting me!"

"Leave it, Khya. It's *mine*."

My hand recoiled.

And there, in that shadowy corner, Izzy would kneel for hours, arranging and rearranging all the stuff. Sometimes, her eyes dropped closed, her lips moving silently, as if chanting some secret, hypnotic spell. Right hand raised in the air, her index and middle fingers appeared to be drawing a series of criss-crossing lines.

"What on earth are you doing?" I demanded.

When she remained in this trancelike state, I shook her by the shoulder, more roughly than intended.

Her eyes as they slowly opened retained an unfocused, milky ap-pearance. "The last symbol will protect us," she murmured.

"What the devil are you talking about?"

The alarm in my voice seemed to draw her back to reality. Lucidity flowed back into her face, and she looked rather afraid.

❧

We needed more men. Although work resumed, without more labour-ers we'd never meet our government quotas. Dad and Uncle Will went away on a recruitment mission to the mainland. A week later, Uncle Will returned alone, with a dozen Oriental guys huddled behind him in the boat. They looked older and more docile than expected, their teeth browned with decay.

On the beach, Uncle Will was pointing toward the cabins, telling the men to get settled.

"Where's Dad?" I asked, approaching.

"He's going to be away a while longer, Khya. He's on a ship to Japan as we speak."

"What? *Why?*" I lurched forward, unable to believe my ears.

"He's scouting more workers over there. We need fresh blood. Men we can trust."

"Why didn't he tell us he was going?"

"It was a last-minute decision. We were hoping it wouldn't be necessary, but as you can see it's slim pickings on the mainland. He told me to tell you to take good care of your mother and sisters."

"But… how long will he be gone?"

"A month or two, maybe. I told him to get a move on it, but the ship takes time to travel back and forth across the Pacific." Uncle Will talked on about how the Canadian government was expediting the immigration process for those coming to assist the war effort. "Spruce soldiers" was what our loggers were now being called. I was only vaguely listening as I tried to get my head around this turn of events.

So that was it. Without a word of warning, Dad had set sail for the other side of the world. After the stunt the Captain had pulled, wasn't he worried about leaving us alone? Evidently, he had other, more important stresses to deal with.

"Don't worry, Khya." Uncle Will threw me a wink. "I'll be here for you and your family, and you've got Kenji and Shig, of course."

Kenji and Shig were my father's best workers. But they were young and reckless at times and prone to drink. They'd be just as caught off guard as the rest of us by Dad's departure.

"Don't look so glum." Uncle Will ruffled my hair, like he used to do when I was a kid. "You're in charge till your father gets back."

❦

It turned cold that night, summer swiftly over. Chilly dampness seeped into the bones of my feet. Since sleep was a hopeless prospect, I got up to tend the fire. Mom was also restless; her body rocked about, making the bed rattle and squeak, her back still giving her grief. And on the sofa opposite me, Izzy was making strange gurgling noises, as if sobbing—or being choked—in her dreams. Only May appeared calm, curled up cat-like at the edge of Mom's bed. Yet she'd reverted to sucking her thumb, which she hadn't done in years.

Mom had taken the news of Dad's departure stoically, it'd seemed at first. Then a mood of bitterness had crept over her.

"I can just imagine all the stories of adventure he'll use to lure those poor fools out here! The beauty of the trees, the abundance of fish. Your father still likes to think that he's Christopher Columbus." A rough snicker caused her to wheeze.

Although the door to our cottage was locked, it was a flimsy, useless lock. Dad's rifle leaned against the wall behind me, within easy reach. Even though the war was taking place on the other side of the world, I could feel its tremors in the windblown branches of our trees.

SEVEN

I was fishing, up to my thighs in a cold, fast river. Stripping line off my reel, making long aerial casts across the shimmering surface, then letting the line flow with the tide. Didn't take long for a big one to bite, my rod almost bent double. Quickly, quickly, I began hand-hauling in, as the silver streak jumped up and splashed up a storm, leaving me drenched. And that was when, through the spray of droplets, I caught sight of Daisy in the salal bushes. Her hair was loose and flecked with amber in the afternoon sun, and she was wearing a man's white shirt, cinched in with a thin belt, giving the impression of a very simple dress.

My line went slack—the salmon surged away. This was the first time we'd seen each other since our awful run-in outside the white tent.

"Uh, hello."

"Hello," she said shyly. "I heard about the fire. I'm so sorry."

"We're just lucky no one got hurt, I guess."

"Who set it?"

"The Captain and his boys, no doubt."

"Figures."

I nodded, not trusting myself to speak. It startled and revolted me to realize that Daisy knew those men, but of course she did—they were her prime customers. She seemed to sense my discomfort and froze up, like a small animal being hunted.

"Where's Handsome Joe?" I worried he'd be after her hide for sneaking off.

"Passed out drunk, I hope." She held up a fishing rod I hadn't noticed. "I'm supposed to be learning how to use this thing, so we don't starve to death."

"I'm surprised you guys aren't packing up, heading south." Now that our camp wasn't teeming with men anymore, business had to be suffering.

"The other camps around here are still full enough. And from what I've heard, your dad's bringing more men soon."

A hot, unsteady feeling assailed my body. Shame. As unmistakeable as an itchy blanket suffocating my face. For the first time in my life, I wanted to apologize on my father's behalf, for how he was enabling this life of slavery for girls like Daisy. But no words came to my tongue.

On the other hand, I couldn't deny that a wee bit of joy flickered in my heart, because Daisy was going to be staying.

"I can teach you how to fish, if you'd like." It was a small thing I could do to make her life a little easier.

Her face lit up, and I felt the cloud of exhaustion thinning and vanishing from my brain. Kicking off her shoes, she waded out to join me in the bracing water.

❉

To my delight, Daisy and I fell into a routine of meeting at the river every few days. Although from dusk onward she had to work, she had some freedom during the day. Handsome Joe no longer kept such a tight leash on his girls. For one thing, Daisy told me, there was nowhere for them to run. Even if they made it to Port Clem, what was a girl to do there except more of the same? And the brothels there were known to be crowded, rowdy places, where girls had to deal with thirty customers a night. The lineups were so long that men were expected to get in and out in five minutes and not take off their trousers and boots. It was startling how matter-of-fact Daisy was talking about it all.

Besides, some time ago, one of her friends had tried to run away. She didn't make it far. A couple days after her disappearance, her body was found a few miles down the beach. The guys who'd had a little fun for free, before their bloodlust took over, hadn't even bothered to bury her body. After that, Handsome Joe loosened the reins—the dead girl had set an example.

Most days, I did the fishing and gave Daisy half the catch. She never really developed a knack for it. Her willowy arms lacked the strength to reel in fast, and she'd get distracted by the silvery flies drifting around her hair. That was fine by me. I was content to let her sit cross-legged on the shore, while she puffed away on cigarette after cigarette, the light slanting across her freckled nose, a sort of dreamy, lost-in-thought look behind the smoke veil.

Gradually, she began to tell me about her life. It took patience, for she was as secretive as you'd expect of a girl on the lam. The Head Matron at the Chinese Rescue Home had surely alerted the police after Daisy and a handful of others vanished one evening, with the help of a quack healer named Evans. Evans had come to the Home offering his services for free, since he'd heard some of the girls were sick. But it'd just been a ploy to get close to them.

"He cupped his palms around my ears," Daisy said, raising her hands to show me. "He said he could read my body's energy fields and I was surrounded by a silver aura, but it was dimmer than it should be, because my energy had been depleted. It was so lovely to feel the warmth rising from his hands. He didn't even need to touch me. And then he gave me these tiny magnets to tape to my inner wrists. They were so cool and soothing against my skin."

It didn't take much for Evans to win the girls' trust and convince them they needed healing. "We did need healing," Daisy said. "Our legs and backs were covered in bruises, for Head Matron had quite the temper. And the mixed kids got it worst of all. If we were bad, we'd be locked away in the basement for days. The missionaries and church ladies, who run the place, hated us even more than the pure Chinese. It's like they blamed us for polluting their race. We had to work harder than anybody to secure even a lowly place in heaven."

"Couldn't you tell your father what was going on?" But as soon as I'd said it, I realized it was a stupid question. If her father had unloaded her at an orphanage, it wasn't likely he'd cared enough to visit.

She admitted, "He's not been in my life much."

I didn't want to make her more uncomfortable by prying.

"He's not a bad guy, though. Really, he isn't. When I was little, he used to be so nice, baking me cookies and cakes all the time. He was the cook at the boarding house where we all lived back then."

Seedy boarding houses and brothels often employed Chinese cooks; I'd seen them taking out the trash and smoking in the back alleys of Prince Rupert. I wondered about how Daisy's mother had supported herself, but that wasn't something I could ask.

"Although my parents were sweet on each other, it wasn't easy with him being Chinese," she continued. "People on the street always looked at us so funny, and kids at school made fun of me to no end. So after Ma's death, Dad gave me to the Chinese Rescue Home. I got in 'cause I was thought to be at risk of becoming a whore." She added that the Home was supposed to be a haven for Oriental prostitutes—or "slave girls," as the church ladies who'd started the place liked to call them.

"Slave girls?"

"Well, it's true that some of us were bought and sold back in China. But most were just neighbourhood girls, fallen on hard times."

"Did you ever see your dad after he left you there?"

Daisy said that he was busy working at a restaurant in Chinatown by then. About once a year around Christmas, he'd come by the Home. Then, the visits abruptly stopped. She thought he might have gone back to Guangdong, where he was originally from.

It wasn't hard to see how a girl so alone in the world would fall under the sway of a fraudster healer. "What did Evans promise you and the others?"

"He said that he owned a strawberry farm in the valley. We were all going to live there and make jam and bake bread. And he would heal us. It sounded so lovely! I'd never been to a farm before. So one night, me and three others, we climbed out our bedroom window and met Evans out back, just like he'd told us to." Her look of reverie faded. "We soon discovered the farm didn't exist. Evans didn't waste any time. He already had buyers lined up—Chinese men who wanted young wives. But since no one wanted a mixed girl, I got sold to Handsome Joe. Funny how I've become the very thing the Home was supposed to prevent me from being."

My sinuses smarted, as if I'd been swimming too long. I didn't want Daisy to see me tearing up over her story. Her wrists and forearms were, as usual, covered in blooming bruises where Handsome Joe or other men had handled her roughly. It infuriated me to see their fingerprints all over her delicate skin.

"This can't go on! We have to get you *away*."

"Away…?" Daisy said the word like it had no meaning, like it was in a foreign language.

"Away from this life, of course!"

Alarm brightened her gaze. If she'd contemplated escape before, she'd not allowed her mind to travel far down the path.

"Aw, it's not so bad here." Perched on the bank, she swung her feet down to swirl in the water, kelp ribbons catching on her pale toes. "Maybe one of my regulars will want to marry me after the war? It does happen, you know." Her eyes had a whimsical sheen, which faded to mere resignation. It was the most she could hope for, in her mind.

⚘

As the autumn days grew colder, Izzy continued to crouch in her corner, playing with the Captain's gifts, arranging them in odd configurations. New things had been added to her collection, too. A dead moth, its dun wings frozen outward. A skull of a mouse or small rat, the snouted bone worn smooth with age.

One evening my sister became entranced by a half-dead mosquito staggering about drunkenly. It took flight in a last burst of energy, crashed against the window and plunged down.

"Poor thing." She knelt beside it.

Our mother, resting in bed, shifted her weight. The springs squeaked and rocked.

I grabbed a rag to swat at the bug, but Izzy blocked my arm.

Frustration swelled in my temples. "The Captain's not coming back! You've got to accept it and stop acting like a madwoman."

The bug had stopped twitching by then, its glittery wings strangely pretty. My sister reached to pick it up, but my foot got there first.

"You don't know *anything*, Khya!" She clutched her stomach, as though some wild creature were running around inside her, making her whole body heave and sweat.

As I bent down, her skin had a musky scent, touched by sour sweetness, like an old apple rotting, fermenting. I was struck by how familiar the odour seemed. Too familiar.

It thickened, like a sauce boiling, and a whiff of bile emanated from her open lips. Crossing her arms, she doubled over, and the truth slammed against me. These were the same scents that'd wafted off Mom before her miscarriage a few years back.

"How—how far along are you, Izzy?" I stuttered, horrified.

With an imploring look, she ran outside to retch. I followed, weak at the knees.

After releasing a stream of porridge, she wiped her mouth and stood to face me. "It's going to be all right, because Mother gave me herbs and remedies. I've been taking them every day."

"*What?* Mom knows about this already?"

"She guessed the truth, a while back."

I was the one who'd been slow on the uptake, so distracted by the woes of our camp that I'd failed to see what was right under my nose.

"Since I've been throwing up, it must be working, right? Maybe the baby's out of my system already?"

An involuntary snicker died on my tongue. Izzy actually believed that it was possible to vomit up a fetus? If only it could be so easy. My poor, deluded sister. As she cleared her throat, her eyes brimmed glassily, like a part of her soul was dissolving, drowning. She was already mourning her baby's impending loss, her last tie to the Captain.

"What did Mom give you exactly?"

A small sack of a rust-coloured powder got thrust toward me. I sniffed its mildly fiery sweetness from my fingertips. It was just cinnamon, ordinary cinnamon. Then Izzy pulled from her pocket a handful of dried crimson berries. The goji berries I'd seen Mom buy from a peddler, back in the summer.

"Mother says that if I eat enough of this stuff—raw, with no water—it's likely to kill the baby." She sprinkled a generous pinch of cinnamon on her tongue. It made her cough fiercely.

And there were other odd things Mom had her doing. Shoving bouquets of wild parsley up her crotch. Drinking endless cups of tea made from tansy flowers, which grew in a big patch of riotous yellow in the forest. Tansy was poisonous and putrid smelling. I certainly hoped Mom knew what she was doing.

While I had faith in her ability to cure colds and soothe aching bones, I had a feeling something like this was going to prove more difficult. What if it didn't work? Would Izzy's life be ruined forever? Where would she and the baby even live? Certainly not with our family, as long as Dad remained at the helm! Was my sister headed for the same wretched fate as Irene?

❧

"All that parsley up the twat's gonna do is make your pee turn bright green," Daisy said.

She and I were sitting at the river's edge, our fishing rods idle on the grass beside us. A couple of days had gone by since I'd found out about Izzy's predicament.

"Maybe you have a better idea?" I figured that Daisy might know of girls who'd been in the same situation.

"Izzy needs to see a doctor."

"A doctor? But she wants to get *rid* of the baby."

"There are doctors who'll do that, if you pay 'em enough. Some of these men aren't even real doctors, though it's best if you get a real one—less chance you'll bleed to death."

A slap of shock. I'd never heard of this procedure before. "You know girls who've actually done this?"

"Oh, sure." Her gaze slipped away, down the water.

I prayed that Daisy wasn't talking about herself.

As if reading my mind, she shook her head. "Not me. But a few of the girls at the Home had gone this route."

The clouds, drifting across the sky, appeared unbearably heavy.

"You have to go to Victoria, if you want to find this kind of doctor," she added.

Well, that was out of the question. I had nowhere close to the kind of money needed for boat tickets, not to mention the doctor's fee. And the thought of some strange man—who might not even be a real doctor—cutting the baby out of my sister's womb? Would she even recover? Or bleed to death on the spot? It was too harrowing to fathom.

"What about the Chinese Rescue Home? Do you think they'd take Izzy in?"

"They would, but I wouldn't advise it, Khya." Daisy's mouth tightened like a child's small fist. "The ladies who run that place are mean. Real mean."

"If it's either that or being out on the street, though—"

"I'd take the street."

I sighed, feeling drained. "I have no idea what we're going to do then."

"What about the Captain?"

"What about him?"

"Does he know about Izzy being with child?"

I shrugged, then shook my head. How could he? He and Izzy hadn't had any recent contact.

"Do you think if he knew about the baby on the way, he might come back and marry her?"

The thought hadn't crossed my mind. I never wanted to see that weasel again, let alone invite him into our family. But then I recalled the way he'd looked at my sister, when he thought no one was watching. That unexpected shimmer of genuine warmth in his gaze. Maybe Daisy's idea wasn't so insane, though I still didn't like it one bit.

"How would I even get in touch with that man? He and his boys went south, far south." Thurston Harbour wasn't even on our island.

"I'm friendly with a peddler who comes around every so often. He goes to all the camps, including Thurston Harbour. If you write a letter, I'm sure I could get him to deliver it."

As Daisy spoke, her face came alive, like a rain puddle struck by sudden sunrays. How desperately she wanted to believe that marriage was every sad girl's last shot at a decent life. And yet, much as I hated to admit it, maybe in this instance she was right.

EIGHT

So I took Daisy's advice. I wrote a short, blunt note, conveying the fact of my sister's pregnancy, telling the Captain he had to come back and make things right. Then Daisy passed it along to her peddler, and we waited. Days went by, weeks. God only knew how long it'd take for the letter to get there and compel the Captain to respond. I still hadn't told Izzy about what I'd done, not wanting to get her hopes up.

It was a terrible time, for there was nothing I could do. Nothing except worry. Izzy continued to drink her poisonous tea and choke back cinnamon, which left her skin with the ruddy hue of a sunburn. Although her vomiting had subsided, it was painfully clear that she'd failed to expel anything: her waist was thickening by the day, her stomach cresting in a gentle hilltop. Her fingers clawed at it, while she undressed at night.

"It's the strangest feeling," she said. "It's like ants are crawling around inside me. I'm so itchy! But I can't scratch deep enough."

I tried to imagine what it'd be like to have a baby inside me, but the closest I could come was a bad case of indigestion, which Izzy seemed to be suffering from, too. Burps thundered out from her throat, at all hours.

"You have to stop drinking that tea," I told her. "You're just making yourself sick."

"It's working, though—I can feel it."

"It's *not* working!"

"What's going on?" May piped up, from the armchair. She'd been asking a lot of anxious questions lately, intuiting that some disaster was afoot. One of these days, someone would have to explain that she was soon to become an auntie. But now was not the time, not when I had more pressing things to settle.

I called out to our mother, flat on her back in bed. She wasn't very responsive. "Mom," I hissed again, "your remedies aren't effective! We have to come up with a real plan."

"Plan?" She rolled around to face us, her eyes dull as slate. "Do you think that when I was a girl, I ever imagined I'd end up here? I gave up planning a long time ago."

When on earth would Dad be getting back? He'd been gone over a month already. I couldn't see his return making my sister's plight any easier—the news of her pregnancy would surely throw him into a rage. And yet, I found myself almost welcoming it. At least then our next step might become clearer.

I could no longer think for all of us, my joints achy, my eyelids sluggish all the time. It was like I was seeing everything through a grey mist, which sleep did nothing at all to lift.

ꙮ

I awoke in the middle of the night to a deep, guttural moaning. Izzy was in agony as she twisted about on the sofa across from mine. Even in the gloomy absence of light, I could see that she was clutching at her belly. I went over and placed my hand atop hers, trying to still her scuttling fingers.

"Are you in pain?" I whispered.

Her fingers splayed wide, as though trying to shield her womb. "Oh... it's all my fault..."

"Nothing's your fault... Shhh..." Stroking her damp forehead, I attempted to soothe her.

In a burst of energy, she jumped up and hobbled to the door, with me behind. The night air woke me up fully, a slap to the senses. Glancing at the outhouse, some way in the distance, Izzy decided instead to drop to a squat, in the shadows. As *shi-shi* hissed out her bladder, her elbows rested upon her knees and she buried her face in her palms. After she'd finished relieving herself, she remained frozen in this position.

Through her muffled sobs, it was hard to understand what she was saying. Gradually, I began to piece it together. It had something to do with her fear of having unleashed an evil spirit. The patterns I'd witnessed her drawing in the air, over her pile of the Captain's worthless gifts, were tied to a form of black magic she'd learned in Japan. No one had ever taught her how to use it, but she'd often seen our great-uncle practising it in his study. Izzy had thought she could employ this magic to banish the malicious spirit who'd driven the Captain away. Yet she worried that instead, she'd managed to summon forth a bad spirit who'd now taken possession of her baby. The punishing kicks inside her belly were far more vicious than what a wee infant could be responsible for.

"Oh, Khya," Izzy wept, dolefully, "the ghost is right inside my core!" Her hands made sweeping motions down her torso, like she was trying to usher the thing out, banish it forever. "It just won't leave me!"

My sister had gone mad. The revelation hit me with a dull thud. I was coming to realize that insanity wasn't an absolute state, like it was portrayed in novels, where mad people ran about on all fours, their hair turned into matted fur, no trace of humanity left. In real life madness could creep up on you, in different intensities and forms. Mom's long periods of despondency, her body afflicted by never-ending pains. Izzy's deranged belief that a ghoul had laid siege to her unborn child! I worried that if left to fester, her madness might increase until she became no different than the madwomen of books. Would we eventually need to lock her away, like Rochester's first wife, Bertha Mason? Confine her to a shack? Tie her up? I cringed at the thought of it.

"The spirit is hungry, so hungry..." My sister shook her head in distress.

"Why is it hungry?" I asked, with forced gentleness.

"Because it has no home, poor thing! It's desperate for a home, like all *muenbotoke*."

Mom had told me about the *muenbotoke* when I was a young child. Japanese folk stories were full of lonely, mischievous ghosts, who wandered the countryside and attacked the weak and vulnerable, by laying claim to their bodies. But I'd never taken these tales as anything more than folklore, fiction. Did Izzy honestly believe that such a spirit had taken possession of her baby?

"Oh, Khya, it's gnawing at my innards!" Her face paled in revulsion.

I reached out a hand to help her to her feet. Despite my effort to stay composed, it was terrifying to see her in such a state.

NINE

And then one misty morning, Dad reappeared just as unexpectedly as he'd vanished. When I stepped outside, still groggy with sleep, the air was like a never-ending cloud. Clinking voices could be heard in the distance, and as I headed toward where they seemed to be coming from, I half-wondered if I was still in a dream.

The haze blurred away. There was my father, on the beach, in the centre of it all—a bit gaunter and greyer, no doubt. Yet while he laughed and chatted with the men around him, a feisty quality animated his face.

About a dozen guys surrounded him, a bunch more visible behind, on the dock. The two boats were already turning around to pick up more newcomers, I suspected.

They were an odd hodgepodge. Many had the rough look of peasants: blunt, shovel-like hands, raggedy hair, glassy-eyed expressions. But others stood far apart, as if fearing contagion. These men had travelled in their best kimonos, heavy grey and black robes, with thick lapels. Their hair was cut in ordinary, helmet-like shapes, which looked strange atop the traditional clothing; topknots had been outlawed in Japan since the fall of the old regime. Nevertheless, it was clear from the swagger these men carried themselves with that they descended from samurai lineage. Now that times had changed, they'd have to rely on their money-making skills, rather than swordsmanship, to win honour.

Some of the men my father appeared to know quite well. I even heard someone call him their *itoko*, or cousin. They all seemed to speak the same dialect as us, the Fukuoka tongue.

A tangle of emotions caught in my throat as I approached my father. I wasn't nearly as relieved to see him as I'd thought I'd be. Something acidic, like resentment almost, stirred in my gut. While he'd been off adventuring in Japan, we'd been left to fend for ourselves.

When I searched for the words to tell him about Izzy's pregnancy, nothing came to me, my voice like a dried-up river. What if he decided to send her back to Japan? Wash his hands of her entirely? His lack of sympathy for the tent girls continued to bother me, and I wasn't sure that I could trust him to act honourably where his own daughter was concerned. Maybe we girls were better off dealing with her situation ourselves. But how? No brilliant plan had come to me yet.

Mom had recently resumed an old ritual, as if it might help solve our problems. Every morning, she lit sticks of incense and laid out small plates of food in front of a makeshift shrine in the corner of our cottage.

When I was young, she used to do this daily, until Dad—who thought all religions were bunk—had complained that she was wasting perfectly good grub. But now, Mom had returned to her original habit, compulsion. These offerings were supposedly for her deceased family members.

Although I normally had no patience for this sort of thing, some small part of me wondered if there might actually be something to it. Had our family endured no end of bad luck due to our neglect of ancestral spirits? By letting them go hungry and unnourished, had we provoked their ire? Was this why Izzy had been driven to lose her mind?

Not that I could share any of these thoughts with Dad. He'd dismiss me as a superstitious lunatic.

"Hello, Dad." I crossed my arms. "Your trip went smoothly, I assume?"

"Oh, more than smoothly." Smiling distractedly, he was already delegating tasks to the new workers in his midst. When he turned his attention back to me, he said, "Everything's fine here, is it?"

"Um… I guess."

"I knew I could rely on you to take care of things. You always do."

Yet he didn't sound particularly grateful or impressed. It was just what he'd come to expect of me, all my life.

❧

Izzy's newfound plumpness didn't appear to catch Dad's eye. Perhaps he thought the kimonos she'd resumed wearing were simply a means of finding comfort in familiarity. I braced myself for the day when Mom would let the cat out of the bag, and then all hell would break loose. But she and Dad hadn't been on the best terms since he got back. I wondered if she, too, felt disappointed in him for leaving all the hardwork to us women.

One afternoon, while Mom and I were cleaning the kitchen, I tried to talk to her. "So when are we going to break the news to Dad?"

"What news?"

"The news of Izzy's pregnancy, of course!" Frustration bubbled up inside me.

Mom threw herself into wiping down the counter, her arm making big, energetic arcs. "Oh, your father has a lot on his mind."

"What's the new baby going to be named?" May interjected from the corner, where she was sweeping the floor. A few days prior, I'd let her in on the secret and explained that she was going to become an auntie.

"That's for Izzy to decide," I said.

"Will it be an English or a Japanese name?"

"I dunno. You'll have to ask Izzy." I turned back to our mother. "Look, Dad's going to find out soon enough. He's not blind—she's really starting to show. Isn't it better if he hears it from one of us?"

Keeping her eyes down, Mom continued to scrub. Why was she being so complacent?

"We have to get Dad used to the reality that there's going to be a baby here. And maybe you could pass it off as your own?" I'd heard about this trick being used in other families, where grandparents claimed their daughter's offspring as their own. If Mom started to dress like Izzy, in loose kimonos, she could make herself appear pregnant.

"The baby will look different, because the father's *hakujin*," Mom said flatly. It was as though she'd already dismissed this option, a long time ago.

"Yes, but… not till it's older." Babies just looked like babies, like little bundles of flesh. Would an Oriental baby really look so different than a baby that was half-white?

"And what then, Khya?" Mom's face glowed with sudden hostility. "As the child grows up and looks different, am I supposed to just… pretend that I had an affair with a *hakujin*?"

The disgust in her voice made me flinch, as despair gathered in hot pools behind my eyelids. Although the same blood flowed through our veins, there'd never be any place for this kid in our family. That was the dismal truth.

❧

The man fished with such ease, elegance. That was the first thing I noticed, while hiding in the salal bushes. He cast line through the air with the precision of an expert dart thrower, his rod moving like an extension of his limber arm. The line sliced through the water almost imperceptibly, with very little splash. It looked so effortless, seamless, the way all his motions came together—never any gaps of hesitation, panic. Even when struggling with a big fighter fish—stalking its final, tortured efforts down the shore—his face registered nothing more than mild amusement.

It wasn't the first time I'd seen this guy around camp. How could I miss him? He bore an uncanny resemblance to Dad. This guy was a smidge taller, perhaps, but just as lithe and wiry. He seemed quite at home in his new surroundings, as if it took little effort to adapt and move back and forth between Japanese and English. And he dressed in regular old clothes, like any logger, blending in.

By then, the man had noticed me spying on him, I sensed. My suspicion was confirmed when he turned to look directly at where I was crouched, half-hidden.

"The thing to remember," he said, like we'd been engaged in conversation all along, "is to kill with as little pain as possible. The fish tastes better that way. Did your father teach you the Japanese method?"

Slowly, I rose to a standing position. "He did." I knew the technique he was referring to, but I never used it. It was easier to conk the fish on the head.

A silver spike, about the size of a small screwdriver, flashed in the stranger's palm. As he inserted it into the brain, right between the eyes, the fish opened its mouth in one last O. There was a simplicity—a beauty—to the way this man killed, like it was the most natural thing in the world.

"You know my father?" I said, guardedly.

He nodded.

"How do you guys know each other, if you don't mind me asking?"

"The old days."

"You and he were childhood friends?" How little I knew about my father's youth. He never said much about that period of his life.

"Let's just say that if I'd had any friends, your father might've been the closest thing to it."

"What's your name, mister?"

"Dice."

"Dice?"

"Short for Daisuke."

Yet something about the flecks of white light in his eyes made me think of a pair of dice, dancing around in the palm of a muscular hand.

☙

Although the camp was well populated again, nothing was the same. Before, there'd been no one looking over our shoulders all the time. Oh sure, Uncle Will was supposed to have been supervising Dad. And ultimately Mr. Brown called the shots. Though in truth he rarely used to show his face, preferring to stay close to his mistress's apartment in Port Clem.

Now, things were different. All buoyancy had been sucked out of the chilly air. Mr. Brown showed up every few days to poke around, his glare like a solar eclipse. I overheard him arguing with Uncle Will about lagging quotas and lost dollars. After Uncle Will tried to placate him, Mr. Brown stormed about—barging into cabins, rifling through people's stuff, searching under cots. Triumphantly, he clacked together half-empty bottles of sake, which the newcomers had brought with them from Japan.

"I'm running a tight ship from now on!" He drained the bottles for all to see, booze pooling at his feet, creating a mud puddle. "And anyone who don't like it can *git!*"

Since most of the new loggers didn't speak much English, it fell to Dad and Dice to translate and help them cope. How odd to see that Dad had a double; the same way that folks instinctively turned to him, now they could just as easily turn to Dice. Neither man appeared too happy with this arrangement, so for the most part they continued to ignore each other, an edgy, competitive energy emanating from their flesh.

Occasionally, however, they'd be forced to overcome their wariness, as some pressing matter compelled them to consult in hushed whispers, off by themselves under the shadow of trees, heads bent close. It was unsettling how their faces seemed to blur together, as though they were actually the same face, caught from slightly different angles. At moments like those, I could see it was inconsequential that they didn't much like each other, because they were united by a bond far deeper than friendship.

❦

The noise got louder than ever, in the ensuing days. Blasts and explosions, like something inside your head was being blown apart. Those daring young men—head-riggers, they were called—would climb the tallest trees in boots with spikes coming out the soles. Although Dad was too old by then, Shig was as nimble as a squirrel. When he was high enough, he'd axe off the treetop or set slow-fuse dynamite to blow it off, before scurrying down.

The walls of my skull always trembled, as the ground shook and trees all around quivered and swayed and rained down tattered, ashy scraps. It was like the air had had its breath sucked right out of it, a sensation never to be forgotten. A clammy, gritty residue clung to everyone's skin.

Suddenly, everything seemed to be moving faster, too. Trees toppled down every hour. Astonished screams ripped open the sky when head-riggers fell—their splayed bodies momentarily caught and cradled by branches, before descending to the ground. Once, I was present to see it happen. Every twitch and contortion of the man's falling limbs appeared magnified somehow. If very lucky, these poor souls broke legs and arms. More often, the injuries were worse, fatal. The hastily built hospital up the inlet was said to be overflowing. Everyone knew somebody languishing there, fighting to hang on to his last breath.

It was a bleak, cloudy day when Shig got flung from a treetop, arms spread-eagled as if trying to fly. Although I wasn't there to witness it, the image still got burned into my memory. Apparently, by some miracle, he survived, but could feel nothing from the waist down. We never found out what happened to him, after the hospital shipped him back to his mother on the mainland.

And yet, life went on, at this accelerated pace. A man got killed, and everyone paused for a few minutes of silence, before the corpse got moved to the side. Then it was back to work as usual.

❦

Izzy continued to wander aimlessly through her days, a strangely complacent quality about her. I couldn't understand it. Whenever I tried to impress upon her the urgency of her predicament, she simply turned away, hiding within the billowy folds of her unbelted kimono. Did she believe that when Dad found out the truth, he'd welcome her baby into our family, without hesitation? Could she actually be so deluded?

One morning, I noticed that she had on a pair of thick white socks, pulled high. In Japan, it was believed that the nerves running up a pregnant woman's ankles connected to her womb, so it was important to keep the feet warm and protected. These distinctive socks marked my sister as being with child, plain as day.

I grabbed her by the elbow and said under my breath, "You don't think that Dad's going to notice your socks?"

She stepped around the mess of last night's campfire, which we were supposed to be cleaning up. "Let him think whatever he wants. Everything's going to turn out fine, you'll see. I've been in touch with the ghost."

"The ghost haunting your womb?"

She pressed her lips together, secretively.

"You're making no sense. I thought you wanted to be rid of the ghost!"

"It's protecting me now. It's going to ensure that my baby has a smooth passage into this world."

I stared into her placid expression. Whatever fanciful thoughts about ancestral ghosts I'd indulged in before, it now struck me as pure claptrap. Seizing my sister's shoulders, I gave a good shake, like I might jar her out of this terrible blindness.

Mom was making her way over. Squinting under the sunlight, she regarded Izzy with concern. Yet it was me she addressed, sternly. "What are you so upset about, Khya?"

"Golly, I wonder!" I gestured at Izzy's barely concealed belly and white socks.

"Calm down. I gave your sister those socks."

"And *why* would you do that?"

For a second our mother appeared almost sheepish, but the emotion quickly vanished, impossible to read. "It's not good for Izumi-chan to get worked up. Just rest. Lie down in the hammock or go for a stroll. Enjoy some fresh air, while you still can."

I pointed at the dishes that remained scattered around the fire. "Actually, I could use a hand with all this. She can take a break later."

"But there might not be time, later…" Something seemed to catch in Mom's throat.

I didn't understand why she was in such an odd mood. "Why on earth wouldn't there be time later?"

"Oh, I just meant… sometimes, in the final months of pregnancy, a woman has to stay in bed," she mumbled.

This, too, made little sense, especially since my sister was nowhere close to birthing time. Too tired to argue, though, I let Mom's comment pass.

❀

Later that afternoon, when Izzy usually helped in the kitchen, she was nowhere to be seen. I thought she might not be feeling well, resting in the hammock out back. But she wasn't there. When I asked Mom where Izzy could be, she was as much in the dark as me.

Worried that my sister might have fainted—pregnant women were known to be frail—I searched everywhere. The edge of the woods all around camp. The meadow where she used to gather wildflowers. When she was still nowhere to be found, I began to panic.

Did we need to convene a search party? Comb the woods?

Dad would know what to do. As I reached the stretch of shore where he and his guys had been working since yesterday, I failed to spot him amidst the loggers. Waving to Dice, I enquired about my father's whereabouts.

"He left by boat, right after lunch," Dice said, perplexed. "Didn't he tell your mother? He said he's going to be away for a few days, if not longer."

"A few days?" Sun danced across the water's surface, blindingly bright. I was sick and tired of my father's vanishing act. "Where the dickens is Dad going?"

"Victoria, he said."

"*Victoria?* Why Victoria?"

"Well, um…" Dice appeared embarrassed. "I didn't want to ask, but I assume it has to do with your sister. He took her with him."

"*What?*"

It dawned on me then that pretty much everyone knew about Izzy's shameful condition, Dad included. Mom had already let him in on the secret, or he'd figured it out himself and confronted her. Dad had been quietly making plans to deal with the situation, and Mom was in on it, too! Her guilt-ridden behaviour earlier left little doubt. My face smarted at her betrayal, though I didn't know why I felt so surprised. She hadn't hidden her ill will for the baby.

"Did Izzy seem all right to you? Was Dad *forcing* her to leave with him?"

"I didn't see them heading off, though I'm sure that wherever he's taking her, it's for the best."

"Where *has* Dad taken her?" The knives of brightness off the water kept punishing my eyes. "What's in Victoria?"

Dice shrugged, looking uncomfortable.

But in my heart, I already knew.

The Chinese Rescue Home.

Dread surged into my veins, my heels sinking down into the oozy mud. After dislodging them with a splatter, I sprinted down the shore, toward the white tent.

TEN

I ran over the pebbly sand so fast that my heart seemed to be volleying forward, threatening to burst through my ribcage. I had no inkling where Daisy would be at this time of day—I hoped I wouldn't have to pull her from the clutches of some disgusting john. But if it came to it, I felt capable. The one good thing that had come of Dad's deception was it'd awakened an anger inside me that made me feel vividly alive.

As it turned out, I didn't have to search far. She was sitting on the beach, a short distance from Handsome Joe's tent. A blue pail stood on the sand, neglected, while she stared out at the water, smoking, chin resting upon knees. Typical Daisy. Although she was supposed to be digging for clams, she preferred to escape into a daydream and nicotine haze. She didn't come out of the spell until I was pretty much right in front of her.

"What's wrong, Khya?" She jumped up upon taking one look at me.

"It's Izzy—my father's taken her to the Chinese Rescue Home!"

Daisy's hands shot up to her face. "He *didn't*..."

"He *did*." I relayed what little else Dice had told me.

"What now?"

"I have to go there, of course! I have to bring her back."

"That's not going to be easy." Her spindly arms crossed around her chest, like they were trying to hold her ribs together. "Head Matron will be keeping a close eye on everyone after me and the others escaped."

"I have to do *something*. What else can I do?"

"How would you even get the money to go all the way to Victoria? A boat ticket costs a fortune, you know."

I hadn't been prepared for her to be the voice of reason. I sank to the ground, sand getting under the cuffs of my pants. The burst of energy that had fuelled my run over left me suddenly depleted.

"Maybe I'll stow away on one of the schooners?"

"Where'll you hide? Right next to the boiler, along with all the rats, for days on end?"

"Maybe I'll make off with Handsome Joe's stash. That should be plenty to cover the trip."

"Don't even joke about that."

I rested my forehead on my knee tops, plain out of ideas.

When I looked up, she was crouched beside me. "Maybe there's no point going to the Home right now, Khya. It's better to let Izzy give birth there. Head Matron treats the pregnant girls all right—much better than the rest of us—because she wants the babies to be born healthy, pretty. It's easier to get them adopted that way."

"Adopted?" It'd never occurred to me that this would be the fate of the baby. "What if my sister doesn't *want* to give her child away?"

Daisy fussed with a stray curl unfurling over her ear. I felt, not for the first time, that a good many sad, unspeakable things were being communicated through the nervous twitches and rustles of her body.

"Oh, all the girls give their babies up," she said eventually. "It's better that way, Head Matron says. God's will."

"God's will? In a pig's eye!"

"But here's what I'm thinking, Khya." Her eyes regained their intensity and focus, compelling me to calm down and listen. "What you really need to do is get down to Thurston Harbour. Find the Captain. Tell him what's happened, so *he* can go to the Home and claim Izzy."

"That lout never even replied to my letter!"

"Well, I don't know... My peddler said he delivered it, along with a stack of mail for other folks. Maybe your letter somehow got lost in the pile, maybe the Captain never even received it."

A lot of maybes. Maybe the Captain was a lecherous bastard.

"At least you actually have a shot at making it to Thurston Harbour," Daisy continued. "It isn't that far away."

"Oh?"

"Folks go down there all the time. It's on Moresby Island, the other big island, down south."

I knew we were on the biggest of the Charlottes, Graham Island, but beyond that my sense of geography was hazy. Daisy, on the other hand, seemed to know how to get around; she was chattering on about certain paths and stopping points and where to catch a ride on a boat at some little town. She must have gathered this information from her clients, who travelled up and down the Charlottes.

"Since you clearly know the way, I appoint you our navigator."

"What, Khya? I *can't*..." She stiffened in terror, at the mere thought of what I was suggesting. "Handsome Joe would *kill* me..."

"*Staying* is what'll kill you, my dear."

A flicker of something like hope—maybe—danced in her gaze.

I threw an arm around her shoulder, daring myself to dream that through sheer force of personality, I could convince her to be my travelling companion. "It's settled. You're coming with me! Otherwise, I'm bound to get lost and fall into a bog and drown."

ᴪ

Together, we hatched the plan. Some small, scared part of Daisy must have long been fantasizing about escape, because I could tell, as we talked, it wasn't the first time she'd thought about this stuff. But her fear that Handsome Joe would come after her was merited, no doubt. What was to stop him from tracking her down and dragging her back? Or would he fly into a rage and slit her throat on the spot? Dump her body into a hole in the woods for animals to dig up and feast on? As we discussed these cheery prospects, Daisy ran her hands through her hair and glanced over her shoulder with every breath, as if expecting to find his florid, hateful face there already.

An idea glimmered at the back of my mind. I was thinking about the last book I'd been reading before I had to quit school, so we could leave Prince Rupert. How annoyed I'd been that I hadn't had time to finish it. It was about this scrappy rascal named Huck Finn. So engrossing was the story that it was hard to resist nicking it, and besides, the school library had more than one copy. Yet if Dad ever found out, I'd get in no end of heck. So I never found out what happened with Huck and Jim floating down that river on their raft.

No matter, though. The key lesson was at the beginning, when Huck manages to fake his own death, in order to get away from his violent churl of a father.

"What if Handsome Joe thinks that you're already dead?" I proposed. "He can't kill you if you're dead, right?"

"You want to... *what*?" Daisy squinted at me in confusion. "Kill me first, so he's deprived of the pleasure of doing me in himself?"

Thoughts were coursing through my brain too fast. I struggled to slow down my disjointed speech so Daisy would have a hope in hell of understanding. It didn't help that she hadn't read the novel.

"It's about a kid named Huck Finn," I explained, "and he figures the only way he'll have a decent life is to run away from home, forever. To prevent his maniacal dad from coming after him, Huck contrives the scene of his own death."

"So, let me get this straight," Daisy said, blanching. "We're going to make it look like I'm dead. But *how*? If I'm actually still alive, what do we use for my dead body?"

"Not all murder scenes require a corpse, you see." I conveyed that in Huck's case, he smashes in the door of their cottage and leaves an axe, coated in pig's blood, in the corner. He plants his bloodied shirt in the middle of the floor, along with more splattered blood. He even creates a trail of gore to make it appear that his bludgeoned body has been dragged off. All to outwit his dastardly father.

"Well, where are we gonna get all that blood?" Daisy asked.

"I'll kill a deer, I guess?" Though I wasn't thrilled by this prospect. Hunting took time, and I wasn't sure that Daisy and I would be strong enough to haul the carcass ourselves.

She, too, didn't appear confident that it'd work.

"What about...?" she pondered, her eyes falling shut.

"What? You've got another idea?"

"Suicide... Suicide's not uncommon for girls in my line of work."

I mulled it over: instead of murder, suicide. It could work, couldn't it? Suicide was bound to be less gory than murder. "How do we fake a suicide scene?"

"I'll write a note bidding farewell to the world, of course."

"Okay... But what about the problem of the corpse, once again?"

"No need for a corpse. My note will mention that I'm going to swim out into the ocean, the pockets of my dress filled with rocks."

"That's brilliant!" Daisy's nimble mind would get us to our destination, I felt sure of it.

My own note, addressed to Mom, could be much more straightforward. It would convey that I'd figured out Dad had taken Izzy to the Chinese Rescue Home in Victoria. I was going there to bring her back, because I couldn't stand for her to live in such a dreadful place. Mom shouldn't worry about me, because I was more than capable of taking care of myself, as she was well aware.

My biggest concern was that she'd go straight to Dice or Uncle Will. But they had a lot on their plates, especially with Dad away. I figured it was possible that Mom would wait a couple days, not wanting to trouble them, unless absolutely necessary. Just like when I was a mischievous child, inclined to go off exploring in the woods, my mother would let me tire myself out and come back on my own. Upon realizing how far away Victoria was, I'd have no choice but to return, tail between my legs. This was what Mom would be betting, I hoped. By the time she got truly worried, Daisy and I would already be at Thurston Harbour, if luck was on our side.

⚘

There was only one time we could depart, with any hope of evading detection. During the daylight hours, the inlet was far too busy. Nighttime was no easier, though, because those were prime business hours at the white tent, and Daisy's absence was sure to be noticed. Our only chance lay in that brief interval between night and dawn, after the tent had cleared out, and none of the loggers had gotten up yet to start the day.

That evening, I pretended to go to bed as usual, but remained very much awake. For hours, I lay there listening to Mom and May snore, my brain abuzz with so much excitement and worry. In the distance, I could hear the rise and fall of nocturnal revelry, as men trekked down the beach to Handsome Joe's, and then made their way back, an hour or two later, all energy spent. It was then—when that rare blanket of quietness descended and all you could hear was the rustle of trees and chitter of bats—that I knew it was time to rise, ever so stealthily. Before slipping outside, I left my note to Mom on the table and grabbed my satchel of provisions, which I'd discreetly packed earlier.

I was to meet Daisy on the beach, a half-mile down from the tent. While waiting for her, I hid in the bushes, which provided a slight bit of shelter from the cold wind. Crouched down, curling into myself, I braced myself for disappointment and abandonment; a big part of me feared she'd chicken out at the last minute, if she hadn't already. But then I caught sight of her running toward me across the pale sand, and a wave of giddy warmth submerged my flesh.

Quickly, we created the scene of her suicide: we placed her little red purse, with the note tucked inside, in the middle of the beach, along with a pair of her beat-up shoes, which weighted down not only the purse's strap, but also her favourite purple shawl, the fringe blowing around crazily like a woman's hair. A couple of heavy rocks, of the kind she'd supposedly put in the pockets of her dress, ensured that nothing got carried away in the wind. Arranged just so, under the moonlight, these mute possessions filled me with a swell of emotion—they spoke so woefully about a lost girl's last moments on this earth. For a horrible instant, I nearly believed that Daisy was dead, drowned.

"We have to get going." She grabbed my arm, snapping me out of my trance.

Down the beach was a flimsy dock, where a canoe and a raft were resting.

"Where are we going?" I rubbed my tired eyes.

"I told you already—we need to boat across to Port Clem, before we hike to Tlell."

I didn't particularly want to steal somebody's boat. "Can't we just get to Port Clem by foot?"

"Not really. It'd take forever."

So we took the canoe, since it'd be faster than the raft. I perched down at the stern, while Daisy stepped into the prow, the boat rocking so much it seemed we were going to topple for a bad moment. I showed her how to kneel for stability and grasp her paddle properly.

"Don't worry, I've done this before." To prove she was an expert boatwoman, she threw her entire arms into the motion, using the paddle like a shovel, covering me in a great, icy splash.

"Relax," I called out. "It'll go a lot easier if you caress the water. Let its pressure do the work for you." I demonstrated the right stroke.

After a while, she got the hang of it, and our paddles sliced through the glistening, black waves in synchrony. We were moving forward at a surprisingly decent pace. My eyes scanned the formless shores, constantly changing and receding, as if no more stable than the water itself. The smudgy trees at the water's edge were like ghosts from another realm.

That wavering eye of fiery light in the distance… Could it be Port Clem? I certainly hoped so, for that was where we were heading.

"I can't believe we're actually doing this," Daisy whispered.

The fear in her voice comforted me a little; she, too, felt way out of her depth.

Pushing my paddle away from the canoe, I corrected our direction slightly. "So what does it feel like to be a dead girl?"

She chuckled in surprise, the realization only now hitting her. "Weird, but kind of amazing, to tell you the truth. Like I've been reborn."

"You *have* been reborn. You should have a new name."

"You too, Khya."

She added that this was a wise idea, because who knew who might come looking for us? We needed to erase our old identities. I heartily agreed; Handsome Joe might not believe that Daisy had drowned herself.

"So what do you have in mind?" she said. "Jane? Mary? Mildred?"

I couldn't imagine responding to any of those names. "Are you talking about for you or for me?"

"I dunno. Both of us, I guess?"

Silence took over. It wasn't that easy to choose new names.

"You select something for me," Daisy said, shivering.

"Well… how about Ash?"

I told her that Ash had been my beautiful, black dog, back in Skeena. How I still missed him. The way he used to nuzzle his lustrous head in my palm and lick figure eights along my inner wrist. I longed to know what had become of him after we'd left and set him free in the wild.

Daisy said she liked the name rather well. I told her it was only fair that she, in turn, come up with a name for me.

"What do you think of Del? I have an aunt named Del. My mother's younger sister." Daisy said that Aunt Del lived in San Francisco, where she worked in a shop making fancy hats and occasionally got to sew wild costumes for circus performers, too. When Daisy's mother had still been alive, Aunt Del had come to visit them in Victoria once.

I could be Del.

Ash and Del.

Dim pools of light were misting down on us, accompanied by soft showers. They were actually snow flurries, I was startled to realize. Very rarely did we get snow in BC. Only a few times in my life had I glimpsed the dreamy white sprinkles. It seemed strangely fitting—magical, almost—like the sky was baptizing us, blessing our new names.

Ash and Del might well be boys' names, which was good. Because it was nothing out of the ordinary to hear about a pair of guys, like Huck and Jim, or Crusoe and Friday, off in the wild on their own having big adventures. But a couple of girls? Unheard of! Girls traipsing about were sitting ducks for rape, robbery and no end of trouble. If we wanted to lay low, passing ourselves off as the cruder sex was only sensible. And I'd been doing that for most my life, anyway. Daisy, on the other hand, looked anything but rough and masculine.

So I got up the courage to suggest something I was pretty sure she wasn't going to like.

"Daisy—I mean Ash—don't get upset, but I think you should cut your hair. It'll help you blend in better." I explained about girls being too conspicuous.

Her fingers touched her bouncy mane protectively. I prepared myself for her refusal, because what, if not her lovely hair, did she possess that was her own in this world?

But to my surprise, she nodded, releasing her tresses with a no-nonsense air. "Got any scissors?"

I did. My satchel contained not only scissors, but also a couple of good knives and forks, a folded tarp, a few other tools, a wedge of bread, a sack of nuts and a bottle of water. If Dad had a handgun, I would've filched it too, but all he had were rifles and they were too cumbersome.

We stopped paddling, letting the canoe drift under the first bruised light of dawn, while I clipped off Daisy's glorious locks. They floated away, like strands of seaweed, on the glassy surface.

I also had an extra change of clothes in my bag: a black sweater and dun trousers. Although they'd be too small for Daisy, who was considerably taller than me, they'd be less eye-catching than the skimpy dress she had on, beneath a bulky coat she must've stolen from some sleeping john. Her thin, bare legs had to be freezing to death. I turned around to give her privacy as she slithered into my garments.

The pants ended a couple inches above her ankles, but that was okay because she had on boots to cover the gap. With her curls now cropped, she resembled a scruffy young man. At least, this was the effect I was hoping for.

From a distance, it might work. Up close, her face was too gentle, her eyes too large and sensitive, her skin too smooth and fine, where there ought to be a sandpaper roughness. And vestiges of bright makeup still clung to her lips and eyelids. I rubbed at her skin with a handful of frigid water to try to wash it off, but even then her features maintained an indelible delicacy.

ELEVEN

By the time our canoe nosed its way onto the beach, the sky was lightening in uneven patches, the dawn of an overcast day. White plumes rose from my breath and my benumbed hands felt like they were made of cold metal. Standing on the crusty sand, Daisy and I peered into the shadows ahead. A smudge of treeline was visible, not much else. Somewhere in the distance a wild dog was wailing.

Without realizing it, I'd grabbed Daisy's hand. Although her palm was just as cold as mine, it restored some feeling to my tingling flesh.

As we headed away from the shore, the first signs of life appeared: a dead campfire surrounded by empty bottles, shining like big icicles on the sand. We made our way toward a rickety wharf. On its other side, a cluster of pale, crooked dwellings protruded from the landscape. Apart from a couple pinpricks of light, the place appeared asleep. We approached the main road, the only road: a line of uneven wooden slats, sinking into the mud.

"What now?" I said, dazed. Amazed that we'd actually made it here.

"We have to find the path to Tlell. We'll have to ask somebody where it is. But first I think we should rest a bit. The trek to Tlell's pretty far, I believe."

Timidly, we wandered up and down the empty street. Weather-beaten bars, a church, scuffed houses, hotels that'd definitely seen better days and maybe been turned into brothels. There were no benches or even front steps for us to sit on. I could hear that sad dog crying out again, along with a steam donkey warming up somewhere. It wouldn't be long till businesses opened and the day got going, I hoped.

The ground was a mess of litter and puddles of yellowish vomit. Off to the side of the road, a rotund old man had passed out, flat on his back, belly rising and falling. His hat had long tumbled off and gotten flattened by the feet of passersby. As I leaned down to inspect him, I saw that his clean-shaven face was remarkably serene, snowflakes melting on his parted lips and teeth.

"Should we wake him?" I said.

"Nah, just let him sleep it off." Daisy examined him closely. "You hungry?"

Food was the last thing on my mind. I shook my head.

"We have to eat to keep up our strength, Khya."

In a flash, she kneeled down and reached inside the man's jacket, extracting his wallet from the upper pocket.

"What on earth are you doing?" I hissed.

Her slender hand worked so quickly, effortlessly; he didn't even stir. After removing the bills, she placed the empty wallet on the ground beside him. "As I said, we have to eat."

"But this poor guy—what did he ever do to us?"

She shot me a quizzical expression. "Are you blind? Look at the way he's dressed. Expensive suit. Freshly polished shoes. Well fed belly. Clearly he's one of those government bigwigs, here to buy up spruce for the war. Trust me, he can afford to buy us a meal."

There was no point arguing with her. Daisy wasn't going to return the money.

We huddled together near the side of a building, while she chain-smoked. Gradually, the town came to life. The smell of coffee wafting out into the street lured us toward the doorway of what appeared to be a pub.

A girl with a pale brown ponytail was sweeping the threshold, as we approached. Her eyes bobbed upward and I feared she was going to take one look at our uncouth appearances and shoo us away. Yet her clean, unadorned face contained no such judgment and she even stepped aside, with a squiggle of a small smile, as if welcoming us in.

"We're not actually open yet," she said, "but feel free to take a seat and rest your feet, while the cook starts the grill."

"Oh, thank you!" Daisy exclaimed, slipping inside.

I, too, was grateful to come in from the cold. My bones ached mightily.

It was a dark, dank space, with low ceilings held up by crude beams. Beneath the greasy aroma of bacon sizzling somewhere, the air was still thick with lingering odours of drunken, pungent bodies from the night before, as well as an older, grosser scent that made me think of manure. It wouldn't have surprised me if, not so long ago, the place had been a stable.

I'd heard rumours that the provincial government had recently passed a prohibition law, but it didn't seem to be affecting the booze trade in these parts. The bar appeared very well stocked.

A garland of raggedy silver tinsel hung from the top of a doorway, a sprig of mistletoe in the centre. Could it be approaching Christmastime already?

Daisy and I perched upon the high stools. Tentatively, I called out toward the lit kitchen. We were the only souls about, it seemed. Then I saw that the blur of movement under a nearby table was not a cat or chubby rat, as I'd assumed. It was actually a woman with long, dark hair.

Down on her hands and knees, she was scrubbing.

When she stood up and looked me square in the face, I was shocked to recognize her as Irene. An older, dimmer version of Irene. Too much drink had taken its toll and leached the life right out of her. I'd been wondering, in a vague way, about what'd happened to her; she hadn't been seen around our camp, in the longest time. Competing with the tent girls had been too much of a challenge, I reckoned.

"Well, well, well..." Irene ran her hands through her matted hair and looked at Daisy and me through unfocused eyes, her words slurring. "If it ain't the high and mighty Khya Terada, here at last!"

I felt taken aback. I'd never been high and mighty with her, I didn't think. I'd always tried to be nice—or at least not cruel, like everybody else—because I felt sorry for her, and her baby daughter, especially.

"How are you doing, Irene?"

She gestured at the tattered housedress she had on, with the pride of an actress in a stunning evening gown. "As you can see, I'm doin' just magnificent!"

I averted my eyes, embarrassed.

"You've fallen on hard times, I assume? That why you've finally come to see me, Khya?"

"Well... not exactly."

"If you've come in hopes I'll open doors at the brothels, you've come too late, I'm afraid. None of the madams'll have anythin' to do with me. Though, occasionally, I'm allowed to wash sheets and scrub floors. Which ain't so different than lickin' a man's arse. But what have we here?"

Daisy's body stiffened, as Irene's scrutiny turned her way.

The woman took in Daisy's new hair, which had settled into a becoming cap of curls. Her eyes were still plumed with traces of black and gold powder, despite my attempt to remove it. With her hair so short, her eyes looked more entrancing than ever.

It dawned on me that perhaps it'd been a mistake to put Daisy in this disguise. Far from helping her to blend in, it might end up attracting more attention.

"Who is this lovely, rare creature, Khya?" Irene purred, stepping closer to us. "Is he your sweetheart? But somethin' makes me think that maybe he wants a sweetheart of a different kind, doesn't he now?"

Thanks to her flat chest, tall height and narrow hips, Daisy made a more convincing young man than I ever could. Yet all her gestures and expressions were jarringly girlish.

"There are men here who like your kind," Irene drawled.

Daisy tensed up again. I was about to grab her arm so we could leave, but a thin, sallow boy walked in from the kitchen carrying two plates. They were laden with bright yellow eggs, sunny side up, and crispy bacon. The smell of grease stirred an animal hunger in my gut.

"I assume you folks are here for breakfast?" He put down the plates and kept his eyes down, minding his own business. He appeared a couple years younger than me and Daisy.

"Give it to 'em on the house, Bobby," Irene said.

"But my father won't—"

"Don't ya worry about that man. I'll take care of 'im. He still has a soft spot for me, 'member?"

"Gosh. Thanks, Irene," Daisy said brightly. "If it isn't too much to ask, can we have some coffee, too?"

"Sure thing, hun. I was just gonna offer."

It struck me as strange that she was suddenly being so nice to us, but who was I to argue with a free meal?

When Irene returned from the kitchen with two steaming mugs, she took the stool beside Daisy. "You need a place to stay, hun?"

Daisy looked over at me enquiringly.

I shook my head. "We have to get going. Do you know how to get to Tlell?"

"Sure do, hun. At the end of this road, you'll see a clearing, bald as an old man's testicles. Nothing grows there, ever since all the trees got chopped down. On its other side, where the forest begins again, is a path."

According to Irene, all we needed to do was follow the path and keep on following it for miles through the woods. We'd come out to a beach eventually, where Tlell was located.

Her directions seemed too vague and stupidly simple. Uneasiness filled my belly. Yet she insisted that was all there was to it.

"Why are you folks goin' to Tlell?" she added.

"No reason," I said. "Just visiting an old friend of my father."

"Ain't a lot of folks out there. What's this old friend's name?"

I shook my head, irritated at myself for walking into the trap. "Never mind. You definitely haven't heard of him."

Devouring her breakfast, Daisy thanked Irene once again for her hospitality. She chugged back her coffee, but I found it too bitter and gritty, so I only drank half.

Daisy stretched her arms and yawned. "D'you know a place where we could rest for a few hours before we get going, Irene?"

She pointed up at the ceiling. "This is the best inn in town."

"How much is a room, though? We don't have much money."

"Nonsense." Irene waved a hand, as if she'd never dream of taking our money. "After you've finished your food, I'll take you two sweet things up for a bit of shut-eye."

TWELVE

At the top of the rickety stairs, Irene led us down a dim hall to a door at the end. The room had a small window, covered in frost. The air was flecked with dust that glittered in the cone of light from a lampshade, fringed in purple beads. Its mysterious, mauve glow was making my eyelids sluggish, as though everything was on the verge of blurring away, twirling into a strange dream.

"I expect you two'll be comfortable enough here," Irene said, fluffing up a pillow.

"Oh, more than comfortable, thanks…" Daisy dropped down to the bed, just as exhausted as me.

The bed had a wrought-iron headboard, elaborate as the wings of a butterfly, and I was struck by how they seemed to be trembling slightly, like getting ready to take flight.

With a glimmer of a beautiful smile—it gave me a weird glimpse of how she might have looked in her heyday—Irene turned to leave. As the door clicked shut, I couldn't be certain, but I thought I heard the faint turning of a lock, metal grazing against metal. Though I wanted to go over to check, I was just too weak. All I could do was follow Daisy's example of falling limp onto the blanket.

She was snoring already. Her face, so close to mine, had a magnified quality, which made me want to pore over all her details: the blue river of a vein meandering up over her temple; the mushroom-shaped freckle perched atop blurrier, smaller ones; the finely carved V of her upper lip; the silk-like translucency of skin that seemed to offer glimpses of hidden depths. But a tranquil feeling was enveloping me and carrying me down in a dark whoosh, and that was all right, for I knew that when I awoke, she'd still be there beside me.

❧

My head throbbed and sweat stung my upper lip, as wakefulness gradually returned. Fragments of a nightmare remained scattered in my mind, like a jigsaw puzzle… Through my grogginess, I tried to piece it together.

It'd had something to do with Mom's miscarriage, a few years ago. I'd had to help deliver the little stillborn, a gruelling experience. In my dream, it'd all come back to me in vivid images: Mom's crazed eyes, the mass of bloody sheets, twisted about her splayed loins. After an endless night of Mom moaning and panting, the poor thing that'd finally slithered out from between her legs had looked not much different than a new-born rabbit: a slick, greyish-pink crescent of flesh, with slits for eyes and a mouth, but no expression at all. Small enough to rest in Mom's palm. Though it was hard to tell, I'd sensed that the baby—if you could call it that—had been a girl. And in my dream, I'd been more certain than ever that yes, I'd lost a tiny sister.

Wherever her soul had flitted off to, I wished her the best. In the dream, I'd been setting adrift a Japanese lantern boat, as an act of mourning… The white, candlelit boat had glowed eerily against the night water, guiding my sister's soul back to the other side.

But in reality, it'd saddened me that we hadn't done anything to mourn her death, not even burning a stick of incense. Mom had said it was pointless because the baby's soul had no chance of making it into the afterlife or being reincarnated—it was too small and weak and lacked the karmic power.

The plight of the stillborn continued to bother me to this day. What became of those teeny, lost spirits? If they had not a hope of reincarnation, did they just float around in the ether, homeless, forever?

I had more pressing things to worry about, though. The light through the window had brightened and I was aware of feet plodding about, down below. What time was it? How long had Daisy and I been asleep?

I wanted to get up, but my limbs were still heavy, so heavy. After a moment, I could control nothing, including my drooping eyelids.

❧

When I awoke for the second time, there were voices. Hushed, murmurous voices, fluttering like frenzied moths above my head. My eyes opened a crack: Irene's back was toward me. She was whispering to a tall, pasty man with a jagged profile. He looked like he could be Bobby's father maybe, the owner of this fine establishment. Whoever he was, he was sucking on a long metal pipe, smoke swirling about his bald head, a sweet, pungent odour. Opium, I suspected. I recalled its distinctive scent from certain alleys in Prince Rupert.

A hubbub of drunken, laughing folks could be heard in the bar downstairs. That slip of sky, visible through our window, had now faded to slate. Had we slept *all day*? How the heck was that possible?

The truth settled, with a thud in my gut. What noxious substance had Irene slipped into our coffee?

She and the tall man went to the other side of the bed and bent down over Daisy's face. She was still snoring, dead to the world.

"You've found us a lovely one," the man said, under his breath. He reached out to caress Daisy's cheek, with creepy admiration. "These pretty boys aren't easy to come by."

An intimate rustling. To my horror, he was poking about her trousers, below the waist.

Irene slapped the man's fingers away. "You'll wake the boy, you dirty old coot!"

"Just wanna make sure we know what we're dealing with."

"So, how much d'ya reckon we can get?" Excited, Irene's voice rose an octave.

"Shhh… I'll ask around at the brothels."

"*I* can do that."

"Don't you dare. After all the trouble you've been causing around town, you'd be lucky if any of the madams even open the door to you. You've done your part. Now *I'll* take care of the business end."

"Oh yeah? How do I know I'll get my cut?"

"Guess you'll just have to trust me, since I'm the only friend you've got left in this town. And when have I ever let you down, darlin'?"

Bile was spreading across my tongue in a bitter residue that reminded me all too well of that foul coffee. Whatever Irene had spiked it with, the drug's mind-altering effects could still be felt, like polluted water swishing about in my skull. Thank God I hadn't drunk that much of it, but what about poor Daisy?

Irene was lightly shaking her shoulder, testing her. Daisy didn't even stir. "They're still out cold. It'll be a while before they come to."

"Should we tie 'em up? Gag 'em?"

"It'll mess up their faces. I want 'em to look pretty for the madams. Don't worry—I'll be just outside. The first sign of noise or trouble, I'll come runnin' in. You just get a move on your talks with those madams, Ewan."

"What'll you do if they wake before I get back?"

"Offer 'em some water, 'course. Tainted with more of the same."

"Careful that you don't accidentally kill 'em." Ewan stifled a grim laugh. "Don't want to be burying bodies now."

"You just get a move on."

After they'd left and locked the door—this time, the clicking was unmistakable—I sat up dizzily, terror clearing my head. What on earth had we fallen into?

"Daisy?" I sputtered, peering into her slack face. Lightly slapping her cheek, I placed my other hand over her mouth.

Her eyes opened, like shutters in a storm. I placed a finger to my lips, as I released my cupped palm.

"What... what happened?" She tried to prop herself up on her elbows, but I could see she was still very much feeling the effects of the drug.

I gripped her arm. "We have to get going, before Irene and Ewan get back. And they'll have others with them, this time."

"What others? Who... who's Ewan?"

I conveyed what I'd discovered about Irene and Ewan's plan to sell us to the brothels.

Astonishment shot across Daisy's expression as she bolted upright. "I should've known better than to trust that Irene. Bitter old whores are the worst."

I was already over at the window, trying to push up the sash. But my fingers slipped and fumbled, finding nothing to grip on to—there *was* no sash. I stared through the cold, misty glass, shot through with tiny octagons of black wire.

"It can't be opened?" Daisy said fearfully, behind me.

"I guess that's why Irene put us here."

"What... what now?"

Sweat was bathing me all over, leaving me soaked as if thrown off a boat, at gunpoint.

"Khya?"

Not even Daisy's pleading voice could pull me out of my bleak state. *I* was responsible for our wretched fate. If it hadn't been for my mad idea to come out here, Daisy would still be back at Buckley, her life no worse off. Now who could say what sort of hell we were in for?

❦

At some point, my voice returned to me, like that of a small child. "So what's it like working in a brothel?"

Daisy cast me a panicked look. "You won't do well, Khya... They don't like girls who fight back."

"Ha!" I crossed my arms, self-pity fading to disgust. I was proving myself anything but a fighter at the moment.

My eyes fell upon my satchel, which had toppled to the floor by the bed. My brain cleared a little. Why hadn't I thought of it sooner? We had knives and other tools of use in this situation. When our captors returned, we'd stab them in their necks and eyes, with the element of surprise on our side, and manage to get away!

But my heart plummeted as I rifled through the bag, nearly empty. Irene wasn't stupid: she'd taken away my scissors and knives and forks and even the bowls and sack of nuts, leaving only the stale bread and water bottle and tarp. Daisy's shoulder bag had been ransacked, too. Her cigarettes were gone, and all the money she'd stolen had in turn been stolen from us. Most of her other stuff—makeup and cheap jewelry—had been left untouched, too worthless to be of interest even to Irene.

Hopelessness gripped me once more. Meanwhile, my hands continued to search through Daisy's bag, in the way that a chicken with its head cut off continues to run around the yard for a while.

Ouch! Something at the bottom pierced my finger. It was the narrow handle of a hair comb, thinner than a chopstick. I pulled it out of the bag.

"We can use that," Daisy gasped.

"Really? How?"

She'd already seized the thing and was huddled at the door, peering through the keyhole, her brow furrowed. "I learned a thing or two at the Chinese Rescue Home. This isn't my first time being locked up."

Inserting the instrument into the tiny black hole, she fiddled around, her ear pressed close, as though listening to the inside of a seashell.

After a few minutes, her confidence faded. The lock wouldn't give. I kneeled down to see if I could help, but the comb was no more useful in my clumsy, panicked hands.

THIRTEEN

The woman Irene ushered into the room was a squat, red-faced creature, with glossy black hair in a too-perfect bun. I was pretty sure it was a wig. She had on a black velvet shawl, and many clunky rings pinched her sausage-like fingers. An oxen guy, with the same squished-together facial features, young enough to be her son, loomed behind like her shadow. Ewan stood at the edge of the room, looking tense.

For the occasion, Irene had miraculously transformed herself, by powdering and painting her face and donning a silky dress in jewel green that swished about her knees. "Mrs. Hill, these are the two love-lies that Ewan told you about," she said eagerly, twirling a hand in our direction.

Daisy and I had returned to bed. We'd decided it'd be wise to appear as drowsy and weak as possible. The last thing we needed was for Irene to drug us again.

"Aren't they just the prettiest things you've ever seen?" Irene prodded.

Mrs. Hill snapped her fingers, her beady eyes flashing with impatience. "Stand up, so I can have a gander at you all."

When Daisy and I hesitated, Irene and the beefy guy grabbed us by our arms and yanked us to our feet. Daisy let out a frightened yelp, which made my blood boil. But with Ewan standing in front of the door, now was not the time to pull anything. Sadly, the commotion of music and rowdy voices from the bar was loud enough to muffle our cries for help. The night was in full swing.

The madam strode toward Daisy, eying her with interest. "What have we here? Have I found myself a prairie nymph with something special between the legs?" She licked her lips and smiled, with big gaps between the teeth.

Daisy remained quiet and still, while Mrs. Hill moved closer, inspecting her. "Open your mouth, child. Wide as possible."

Daisy complied, as this hideous woman peered inside. God only knew what she was checking for—what on earth could mouth size have to do with a madam's business? Without warning, she slipped a hand around Daisy's bum and gave it a squeeze, the other hand going for her crotch.

"Hey!" I shouted, indignant.

I leapt forward but Mrs. Hill's henchman grabbed me from behind, restraining my arms. He cuffed my ear, which released a terrible ringing.

But what upset me most was that Daisy budged not an inch, under the assault of this woman's palms.

Mrs. Hill's back stiffened, as she failed to find what she was seeking between Daisy's legs. With pinched lips, she delivered a cracking slap across Daisy's cheek. It left a streak of blood, due to one of those sharp rings. Astonished, my sweet friend just stood there—not even raising her hands to shield herself from further abuse. With a growl, I struggled to break free, but the brute's arms easily held me in place, like I was in a straitjacket.

"She's just another stupid girl, *common as vermin*," Mrs. Hill spat.

All hope was draining from Irene's face. Nevertheless, she managed to find her tongue. "Okay, so you can have these two nymphs for a lower price, eh?"

"Nymphs?" The madam rolled her eyes. "Are you in need of glasses, woman? These two are plain as mud."

Ewan released an agitated sigh. Now that the truth had come to light, he just wanted me and Daisy off his premises, immediately. "I'm sure they're worth *something*. And the little Oriental girl's kinda cute, don't ya think? You've got Chinamen at your crib."

The lout said over my head to Mrs. Hill, "We could use a couple more girls, since Betsy and Annie both got the clap."

"Well, that doesn't mean I want these urchins." Though Mrs. Hill seemed to be mulling it over. "This one's trained already, I can see," she said eventually, wagging her chin at Daisy. "But the feisty yellow girl knows damn all about life and men."

"So, I'll have fun teachin' her the tricks of the trade." The beast's sweaty paws tightened upon me, as he leaned down to kiss the top of my ear, making me shudder. "And if she still ain't no good with customers after that, we can always use another laundress."

"*Fine.*" Mrs. Hill frowned, like we'd wasted too much of her precious time already. "Twelve bucks for the pair of 'em, not a penny more."

When Irene demanded fourteen, the madam laughed and headed for the door, but Irene quickly relented. And so we were sold, like a pair of slaves, the cheapest kind.

While bills exchanged hands, I couldn't believe that this was actually happening. My head felt light and fuzzy, like it was on the verge of floating away from my body. Was this nothing more than a horrific nightmare, from which I couldn't manage to awaken? Yet the calloused fingers of the brute manhandling me were real, too real. He stuffed my arms through my coat. Reluctantly, I shoved my feet into my boots and threw my satchel around my neck. I tried to get Daisy's attention, praying that she'd have some sense of what to do next, but her eyes remained timidly downcast.

Ewan stepped out of the room and returned with rope to bind our wrists behind our backs. As I squirmed and struggled, the fibres cut into my skin, my shoulders aching badly.

Then we were pushed out into the dark hall. The thug remained right behind me, steering me forward, his fat fingers acting like they owned my flesh. Behind us, Mrs. Hill was similarly keeping a tight leash on Daisy.

Now that Ewan and Irene had received payment, they couldn't give a fig what happened to us. With a vague gesture, Ewan told Mrs. Hill to sneak us out the rear. Meanwhile, he and Irene turned in the opposite direction, heading down the main staircase to the bar, from where wild revelry and uncaring laughter wafted up, thickly. If I screamed out for help, the only result would be I'd get my head smacked again.

With my hands tied back, my balance was off. It wasn't easy to descend the ladder-thin stairs at the back of the building. When I tripped and lurched forward, the lout pulled me up, giving me a moment to recover. That was when I realized that although he'd bound my wrists with violence, his knots were not the foolproof kind. Because I'd been fighting him as he'd tied me, there was a bit of slack. If I wriggled and made use of the sweat on my palms, the binding just might loosen enough...

"Quit dawdling, girl." He whacked the back of my head.

At the bottom of the stairs, a fug of oily odours hung in the air. The kitchen door was open wide enough to expose an aproned young woman with a round, flushed face, by the stove. She dipped a finger into a steaming pot and licked it heartily. As she glanced up at me and Daisy being herded forward—like lambs sent to slaughter—her eyes enlarged. It was the same girl who'd been sweeping the doorway when we'd arrived! Her eyes widened further, in horror, as she recognized us, too. She looked like the wholesome type, with caring in her face, hair neatly pulled back. Perhaps she felt guilty for having invited us into this bleak establishment and delivered us to this fate. I saw what might be our only chance and I wasn't going to let it go to waste.

"Help us, please!" I shrieked. "They're kidnapping us for the brothel!"

"It's true!" Daisy echoed.

The thug walloped my head again, so hard this time that I saw stars. He tried to force me forward but I let my knees go limp, and it wasn't so easy for him to drag me with my arms bound back.

The maid had frozen up. But I thought I could detect pity in her eyes. Perhaps we weren't the first captives she'd witnessed being forced through these doors.

Still down on my knees, I stretched my fingers as straight as they'd go, attempting to shrink my knuckles. While the rope scorched my raw skin, I continued wriggling and wriggling. An image of my stillborn little sister flashed in my mind. Although her face remained a formless lump of flesh, the tiny slits comprising her eyes and mouth now appeared to have come alive, and she was smiling slightly, urging me on. My wrists suddenly slipped free. My hand plunged into my pocket, where I'd stashed Daisy's comb. When the thug reached down to yank me up, I let my body rise and drove the comb's handle right into his eye.

He staggered back, screeching in pain.

Mrs. Hill was quick enough to react. "You stupid slut!" she bellowed and lunged toward me.

Just as she was about to tear my eyes out—an eye for an eye—a frying pan came down on the back of her head. Her body fell like a sack of potatoes, on top of me. I stumbled back and she collapsed to the floor.

Daisy was clutching the pan in her trembling hand, braceleted rope still clinging to her wrist. Evidently she'd also managed to writhe free. Her face was slick and luminous with sweat.

We didn't have time to catch our breath. While Mrs. Hill appeared unconscious, her henchman was only injured in one eye. Taking stock of the situation, he pounced toward Daisy with a vicious scowl, blood trickling down his cheek. My heart seized up, yet I was too far away to do anything.

Grabbing a rolling pin off the counter, the maid stepped up behind the man. She brought the utensil down on his skull with a crack. He collapsed to the ground.

"Oh my God!" My pulse was thundering in my ears.

Our eyes locked, me and the maid. She was older than me, by about five years, her gaze at once scared and steely. Her thin nose was slightly crooked, from some old injury maybe. In that instant, we might've been soldiers on the same side in the midst of a harrowing battle, so it didn't matter that we were perfect strangers. An air of authority swept over her, as though she knew she outranked me.

"*Run*," she mouthed.

When Daisy and I remained stock-still, she repeated her command louder. She pointed at the back door, rolling pin still in hand.

How grateful I was to this woman, who had no reason in the world to help us. Regaining our senses, Daisy and I were only too willing to follow her directive and scurry out, while whispering our incoherent thanks. How she'd deal with the two unconscious bodies in her kitchen was beyond me.

What chaos we'd left her with! Hesitating in the doorway, I glanced over my shoulder at the terrible scene, but Daisy grabbed my arm and yanked me forward.

FOURTEEN

The wintry air stung my cheeks, like I was a newborn slapped to life. Daisy grabbed my palm and we broke into a sprint. I let her pull me in whatever direction she chose, glad that in the midst of this heady confusion, I could rely on her navigational skills.

She soon slackened to a brisk walk, forcing me to slow down, too. The last thing we needed was to call attention to ourselves, so running madly wasn't wise. Continuing down the street, we kept our eyes lowered and moved swiftly, pulling our coats around our shivering chests. Gangs of loggers, looking for some release at the day's finish, swam past in a blur at the edge of my vision.

"Christ, did that really *happen*?" My thoughts kept slipping away from me like water running through splayed fingers. "How...? How long do you think it'll be before Mrs. Hill and that beast come to?"

"Dunno—five minutes, maybe?"

"So at any moment, they'll be up and after us?"

"They'll be dizzy and confused for a while, I hope. And that bastard may never see anything through that eye again."

"What...?" Queasiness bubbled up in my gut. "You think I might've *blinded* him?"

"Jesus, Khya, keep your voice down! I—I don't know what to think. Nothing like this has ever happened to me before. But it didn't look good what you did to his eye. At least he's still got the other one to see through. Serves him right."

In the darkness, I strained to see ahead: beyond the road's end lay nothing but sudden flatness, where only moss covered the gently sloping ground. No salal or huckleberry bushes, no understorey at all. All that broke up the stark monotony were rotting tree stumps and a handful of miniature conifers, so stunted it was like they were meant for dwarves.

"That must be the clearing Irene mentioned," Daisy said.

Who knew whether Irene had been telling the truth about this being the way to Tlell? After how dreadfully she'd deceived us, we had no reason to believe she'd been honest about anything. And another thought troubled me, too. "I wonder if Irene will remember that we asked for directions to Tlell?"

"You think the police will question her about where the criminals"—Daisy gestured frantically at the two of us—"are heading?"

"As I've said before, there aren't any police out here." It was Mrs. Hill's thug I was more worried about. As soon as he came to, would he head out to track us down? Or with his eye in bad shape, would he at least wait till morning?

Daisy grabbed my arm, like she could read my thoughts. "We don't have time to dawdle! If you're still interested in finding the Captain, this is the only route to Thurston Harbour. So we'd best get going."

She was right. What choice did we have? We had to keep moving forward.

As we crossed the wet clearing, moss squelched beneath our boots, tree stumps poking up and tripping us occasionally. Moisture leaked through to my already damp feet. While I was bemoaning their state, Daisy's hand shot out in warning.

Lo and behold, standing in our path, blocking our way, was a pair of giant, hoofed creatures! They resembled deer, yet they appeared much too muscular and menacing. I wondered if they could be some kind of caribou, but I'd heard that caribou had gone extinct from these islands—and besides, they always had antlers, didn't they? These two creatures had bare heads, except for their big, pitch-black ears.

Deer were skittish animals. At least, that'd always been my experience. They feared being hunted and pranced off to the cover of trees at first sight of humans. These two animals, however, boldly stared back at me and Daisy, with bored indifference in their ebony eyes. The fatter one leaned down its muzzle to feast at the top of one of those sad, minuscule trees. The other one remained in our way, and it didn't back off when I moved toward it with an aggressive stomp.

Without warning, it rose on its hind legs, hoofs kicking up and scratching wildly through the air.

"Run!" Daisy screamed.

She was already dashing toward the forest's edge, with me not far behind.

We didn't slow down as we threw ourselves forward, headlong—fighting our way through the dense gnarl of trees and brambles, our hands soon torn and bleeding, our feet slipping, tripping. There were no well-worn paths here, or if there were, we certainly couldn't find them.

"Khya! Where *are* you?"

It startled me how far away Daisy sounded, her voice muffled by endless leaves. How had we gotten separated, already? I thrust an arm through the punishing tangle. What a relief when she clasped on to my clammy fingertips! We didn't let go of each other, while making our way forward. Every step was won with another scrape as we pushed aside branches only to have them fly back, exacting their tolls.

After a while, we realized that we could slow down. That monstrous deer had long lost interest in us. Hands on knees, we rested, winded. A sharp cramp cut into my waist. A bloody streak under Daisy's right eye jumped out at me.

"You're hurt!" I reached out to examine the wound.

Fortunately, it turned out to be just blood from a gash on the back of her hand, which she must have rubbed across her cheekbone. Beneath the blood, I could make out the thin scratch from Mrs. Hill's ring, which incensed me all over again.

Continuing onward, we stumbled upon an area where the trees thinned out. Luck being on our side for once, it turned out to be more than that. It was a trail winding around trees through the knee-high growth.

"Sweet Jesus, d'you think this is the path to Tlell?" Daisy exclaimed.

It was the only path we'd come across. Wherever it was heading, we were heading there, too.

I led the way through the inky gloom, with Daisy a step behind, clutching at my shoulders. Tiny brown and white owls peered out at us, with riveting yellow eyes from the lower branches of trees. One emitted a skin-crawling whistle.

Huckleberry and salmonberry bushes grew shoulder high and the salal and devil's club shot up well above our heads. The moist air misted our faces and chilled our noses.

My knees ached, my feet were soggy and cold. My tongue, on the other hand, was dry as an old shoe. We paused at a spring and cupped our hands for a drink. I filled my bottle and we passed it between us, while continuing to trudge onward. We were on the lookout for berries, but the only ones we could find were an eerie white. Since I didn't know whether they were poisonous, I urged Daisy not to eat them. We shared my bread instead, our last and only food.

Eventually, we dared to talk about what had transpired back at Port Clem.

"What's going to happen when the authorities discover what occurred in that kitchen?" Daisy said nervously.

What authorities, though? And would Mrs. Hill and her thug report the incident, even if they could find anybody in a position of power? Or would they deal with the situation themselves? This seemed more likely to me, because those who live outside the law generally don't look to the law for justice. Of course, they'd be mad as rabid dogs at Irene and Ewan for their part in delivering us. And Irene was already an outcast in town. I pictured her getting the beating of her life, well deserved.

But that kind, courageous maid, who'd come to our rescue! Thinking about her upset me greatly. "I certainly hope the maid doesn't end up getting blamed…"

Daisy said, trying to sound hopeful, "After you stabbed the guy in the eye, he was deranged with shock. Maybe he won't realize that it was she who snuck up behind and struck him. She could act like she was just an innocent bystander, while we escaped."

Would Mrs. Hill and the lout believe that? I could picture them interrogating her and roughing her up, poor thing. It was too awful to contemplate, after she'd stuck her neck out for us.

"There's no point thinking about it," Daisy said, flatly. "There's nothing we can do to help that girl now."

Sadly, she was right. We fell into dreary silence.

I wanted to talk about something else, if only to distract me from my guilt-ridden conscience. "Did I mention that I had the oddest dream back there?"

"Oh?"

I told her about my tiny, stillborn sister and the queer dream she'd engendered.

"That sounds terrifying, Khya!"

I shook my head, reflecting. Possibly, it'd been a good omen that my wee ghost of a sister had come to visit me in my dream. And maybe in more than just my dream? At the instant my wrists had slipped free of the rope, I'd felt that she was somehow there watching over me, giving me strength. I was aware that this sounded crazy, of course. Was I turning as feeble-minded as Izzy, believing that ghosts could offer protection to the living?

I decided against sharing any of this with Daisy. It'd only frighten her more and convince her that I was losing my grip.

After we'd been walking for a very long time, probably many hours, we passed the foot of a lake. Just beyond, a shimmer of light caused us to halt—a yellowish orb was glowing out at us, through the fat trees. As we edged nearer, the light transformed into a small log cabin, its window illuminated by candlelight.

"I've heard about this place." Daisy said, excitedly. "On the path to Tlell, there's a resting point, where folks can spend the night. This must be it."

I was relieved by this sign that we were heading in the right direction. Yet sleep was the last thing on my mind, despite the numbness in my feet. Nor was I in the mood to befriend whoever had lit the candle. For who could say that our fellow traveller wouldn't drug us and tie us up and peddle us to a brothel?

"You're not tired, are you, Daisy?"

"After what happened the last time we closed our eyes?" She snorted grimly, her thoughts identical to mine. "I say we best keep moving."

Fifteen

We came to a river and followed it downstream, until it vanished into a limestone cave. Over the rutted mud we continued, exhausted. This had to be the longest night of my life. Left, right, left, right... Onward, we trudged. Clumps of moss appeared to be exhaling silvery clouds, though it was probably just my tired eyes playing tricks on me.

Without warning, the forest ended. Wide-awakeness flooded my skin, reviving my senses. Gales of wind were whipping hair and sand into my eyes, soaking my face with stinging moisture. We were at the edge of a stark, windswept beach.

The tide was coming in violently, a spew of white froth. The sky was still black, relentless. Against the sandstorm, my eyes struggled to stay open long enough to scan the shore for any signs of settlement, but there was nothing in either direction. Nothing except rock piles and enormous, crumbling dunes, which ran parallel to parts of the shoreline, like giant, toppled sandcastles.

How we longed to find some place to rest and keep dry. Robinson Crusoe, even at his most desperate, had his cave to retreat to while waiting out the torrential rains. But there were no caves around here—or if there were, we'd never find them.

Finally, we came across an abandoned canoe. Pulling it inland, we turned it on its side. We curled up behind it, clutching on to each other for warmth. My tarp offered the thinnest blanket.

I must have, surprisingly, been able to doze off. When I came to and stood shakily, uncurling my achy spine, the sky had lightened to a pearly colour. Daisy was up already, staring out at the rippling water, her back toward me. Sensing my presence, she looked back and smiled, wearily.

All we could do was walk. We didn't have much of a plan. Daisy had heard there were boats you could catch from Tlell southward. Yet we didn't have any names of boatmen, and who knew if we were even near Tlell? We strained our eyes, praying that a village was about to appear around the bend. All we could do was keep moving, hoping.

Although it wasn't as windy as last night, the drizzle remained steady. As we followed the shoreline, no cottages miraculously burst into view. A crane swooped through the air, on the hunt for breakfast, and groups of little birds with bright blue feathers and wild black plumes drifted through the sky, like snooty ladies in decadent hats. After a while we noticed coin-sized depressions in the sand, and we dropped to our knees to dig for clams, simply for something to do. We had no way of cooking them, since Irene had confiscated my matches and pot.

I scanned the horizon, praying to glimpse a ship—even a capsized one—drifting toward us. If it hadn't been for that blessed, wrecked ship, which offered up tools, guns and food for Crusoe to pillage, how would he have ever survived?

Yet the waters remained flat, no precious shipwreck on its way. We retreated to a cluster of rocks where we simply tried to conserve energy. Our clothes were soaked through, our flesh wet and miserable. The hunger that'd been tormenting me earlier that morning had given way to numbness. A soft chanting was filling my head, as though the ocean waves were trying to speak to me, indistinctly. I looked over at Daisy, who was curled up with her chin pressed to knees, her back shivering, convulsing.

All of a sudden, she seized my arm. Her spine straightened as she squinted and leaned forward. Then she was gesturing at a pale blur down on the beach: tawny wings, edged in black feathers, were flapping around a blood-red crown, and when those wings flared open their undersides flashed a deathly white. It was a crane, limping about lopsidedly, its bill extended like a pair of open scissors. A man was down there, immersed in the feathery confusion, trying to subdue the panicked wings.

I barely dared to trust my eyes. Was this scene real? Or a figment of my delirious imagination?

Yet Daisy saw it, too. She was grabbing my wrist and we were running toward the action.

"Help us, please!" she cried, as we approached.

"We're lost!" I added.

The man didn't seem to hear or even see us. He was entirely focused on tussling with the crane as he tried to hug it from behind. But the bird wasn't submitting, and they continued to stagger about, in this drunken dance. Chords of trumpeting sobs, from the creature's throat, echoed down the beach.

He was a short, compact fellow with a certain innocence about his childlike face, which contrasted oddly with his receding silver hairline. The crane was almost as tall as him, and as its massive wings expanded, the man got slapped many times. His cheeks were cherry bright, blood trickling down from his nostrils.

At last, the bird had tired itself out, pushed to the verge of fainting. Venturing closer, I saw the poor thing was missing a foot; one thin leg jutted out, like a cracked-off branch.

Only then did the man register my presence. He froze up and stared at my moving lips—as though I were saying something far more ominous than just my name—and he pushed me away and used his body as a shield, like he was worried I was going to harm the bird. Picking it up and staggering under its weight, he let out a heaving grunt and slowly headed inland, not uttering a single word.

Daisy and I followed, while keeping our distance. He was making his way into the woods, wading through the high grass. A short distance in, a cottage with a sloped, moss-covered roof appeared through the trees. I hoped this man didn't live alone. I prayed that he had a wife who'd be more talkative and kind.

But as we approached, it was another old man we saw. He was sitting on the porch, his big, club-like feet up on a crate.

Slowly, he got up. "What have you found us, Bertie? You should've just let the poor thing be… There's nothing we can do for it, and you're lucky it didn't beat ya to death."

Bertie just stood there, nodding dumbly. The other man lightly cuffed the side of his head, like one would do to a naughty youngling.

Daisy and I crept forward.

"And who are these two ragamuffins?" The man put his hands on his hips.

"I'm Del," I said. "And this here is Ash."

"We got lost," Daisy said. "We're very cold and tired."

"A couple of runaways from one of the camps, I assume?" he said.

Daisy and I remained silent.

"You wouldn't be the first to show up on my doorstep. The logging camps are hiring far too young. Boys like you can't take all the rowdy drinking and bullying that goes on there—am I right?"

After a moment of hesitation, we nodded.

I was relieved that this man took us for a couple of wayward boys. The farther Daisy got from her old life, the more her flickering, sweet smiles and feminine gestures were falling away.

"Well, come inside then, my friends. I'm Lester." His face cracked open in a wide smile, as he continued to size us up. He had near-set eyes and a lantern jaw covered in a scraggly beard.

"I see you've already met my brother, Bertie. Not much of a talker. Deaf since birth. But the animals like him just fine—even when he's more likely to hurt than help them."

Lester stared at the crane, which Bertie had placed on a grassy knoll beside the house. The bird's chest was rising and falling in shudders. "Don't touch it, Bertie! You'll only make it more terrified." Lester went over and pantomimed touching the heaving feathers, then made a cross with his forearms, staring at his brother sternly and shaking his head.

Lester filled a bowl with water and left it beside the crane's unconscious head.

"Is it going to be okay?" Daisy said.

"We'll see. Even when these birds have lost a foot, they can often manage to fly. It might just need some time to rest and recover from the shock of my stupid brother's attack."

The situation didn't appear optimistic to me. The bird looked like it was on the brink of death.

Holding the door open, Lester ushered us into his cramped, foul-smelling lair. Never had such a mixture of putrid, oozy odours hit me all at once—a punch in the nose. Equally powerful were the shrieking chirps and doleful cries. As my eyes adjusted to the dim light, I took in the cast of furry and feathery creatures in wire cages that lined all four walls. Having guests seemed to agitate them, so I tried not to peer in at anyone too closely. All too nearby, the heart-shaped, brown and white face of a marten pressed against the mesh, looking at me appraisingly. Although cute, martens were wily hunters known to attack even deer, by jumping down from trees and going straight for the neck.

"What... what is this place?" Daisy murmured.

"I guess you could say it's a kind of rescue home, or hospital," Lester said.

She flinched when he said "rescue home." The Chinese Rescue Home. Sometimes those who appeared to be do-gooders had other, less savoury motives.

"What's the point of it all?" A little cream-coloured owl stared out at me, with true suffering in its eyes. "Wouldn't it be better to let them die? And become food for other animals?"

Lester shrugged. "That's the law of the jungle, I suppose. But what'd happen if we humans let ourselves go that way? We'd be at each other's throats all the time, the bigger, stronger folks gangin' up on the little guys. Life would be nothing but war and bloodshed."

"The war is raging, over in Europe," Daisy said.

"Case in point." He nodded glumly, while lighting his pipe. "So I do what I can to save a few furry lives, or at least make their deaths less painful. And animals are, as you point out, a lot more worthy than us. They kill each other just for food, not for something as stupid and pointless as war."

❧

Lester promptly put us to work helping out with the animals. Without any hesitation, he gave us boys' work. Catching crickets and digging for worms to be fed to the smaller birds. Mashing up dead mice into a disgusting, grey paste to be squeezed out the corner of a bag into the mouths of young owls. For me, the work was no grosser than the skinning and butchering I'd been doing since childhood, but I worried that Daisy would be too squeamish. She surprised me by rolling up her sleeves, with only a slight grimace.

At the end of our first day, Lester cooked an odd, swampy stew that had no meat in it at all, just vegetables and lentils. We ate it up, without complaint, out of pure hunger. Lester said that he and his brother never ate meat, out of respect for the animal world. Although I wondered why the animals were allowed to have a carnivorous diet, but not us, I managed to hold my tongue—I didn't want to be seen as giving back talk.

After we'd finished eating, Lester made a pot of weak tea that tasted of pine needles. While sipping it, we continued to sit at the table out front of the cottage, as the sky darkened in moody patches. The crane was still at rest on its back. I wondered if it even had a heartbeat. Bertie kept sending it woeful glances.

"So, tell me about yer folks," Lester said, looking at me with belated curiosity. "You a Chinaman, I gather?"

Without thinking, I nodded. After all, the whole point of assuming a new identity was to get away from your real one.

"Say somethin' to me in Chinese, why don't ya?"

"Oh, I don't speak it," I muttered, blushing.

"How can you be from China, then?"

"I was born in Canada, you see."

"Didn't yer folks speak the mother tongue?"

Shooting Daisy an anxious look, I said the first thing that came to me. "Both my parents are dead. I grew up in an orphanage in Victoria."

"That's right," she backed me up. "I'm an orphan, too. Del and I got to be friends at the orphanage."

Lester scratched his beard. If he doubted our story, he didn't say anything. And then he was more concerned with a black-eared deer grazing at the edge of the yard. Although it wasn't as enormous as the pair that'd bullied us at Port Clem, it was still unnervingly plump.

"Shoo!" Lester shouted, clapping his hands.

But the animal remained unperturbed, chomping away on shrubs and grasses.

"They're a pesky nuisance, and they breed like rats."

"Why are the deer around here so unafraid?" Daisy asked. "They don't act like deer at all."

"My father and his lot are responsible for that. When they brought

their families out to these islands, we were the original homesteaders."
The old man's face softened in reminiscence. "Yessiree, we packed all
our furniture and farming equipment onto a boat and sailed out here. I
wasn't even ten at the time. On the boat, I played with the pair of fawns
we'd brought along for the ride. All the farming families were doing that.
As soon as we reached shore, we set 'em loose."

"How could they survive?" I said. "Wouldn't they get eaten by bigger creatures?"

"The problem is just that. There aren't nearly enough bears to keep
their numbers in check. And these black-tailed deer, they're *always* hungry. They'll eat bare every sapling in sight. The poor crab apple trees
can't sucker anymore, lots of trees can't. So the soil gets too dry for
auklets to make their nests. And now, with the logging companies
clearing big stretches, it'll be easier than ever for these deer to stuff
their bellies on whatever's left of the undergrowth," Lester predicted,
with an unhappy air.

I thought about those pitifully stunted trees back at Port Clem.
Maybe they'd never grow any higher, with these deer around.

In a burst of frustration, Lester grabbed his rifle from the porch and
fired a couple of warning shots. At last, the creature cantered off.

"So what was it like here, when you were a boy?" I asked. "Where
was your family's farm?" This little, rugged patch hardly seemed like
farmland.

"Oh, it was nowhere close, much farther inland." Stillness settled
over his face and I suspected that his childhood had not been an altogether happy time. "Out here, there are no farms. Nothing but a ram-
shackle cottage here and there, with miles between."

"Are we far from Tlell, then?" Daisy said.

"Tlell? This *is* Tlell."

"But where's the town?" I demanded.

"There's no town. Tlell's just the name for this stretch of shore."

Daisy's face tensed up, mirroring what I was feeling, too.

"We heard there are boats you can catch from Tlell, southward," she
said. "Where do they dock?"

"There's no official pier with a ticket booth, I can tell ya that much."
Lester's eyes drifted, thinking. He said that he had an Indian friend who
ferried folks around from time to time. Aside from him, Lester didn't
know of any boatmen. And he had no way to get in touch with the Indian, whose habit was to drop by unannounced, usually with a bleeding
animal in tow.

"You don't know where the man lives?" I pressed.

"I don't know if he lives anywhere. He's always on the move, in his boat. I seen him once at a dock, a ways down the beach, south. So you might catch him there."

It wasn't much, but it was better than nothing.

By then, we were immersed in darkness. Lester set up a tent for me and Daisy, since the cottage had only one bedroom, which he and Bertie shared. I was glad to be spared sleeping in close quarters with all those caged animals, reeking and squawking. Although the tent was flimsy and did little to block the cold, Lester gave us a stack of rough, dun blankets, which Daisy and I curled up under.

"What are we gonna do?" Daisy's voice was fragile as a cobweb. "Just wait till the Indian boatman magically appears?"

To this, I had no comforting reply. "We'll figure it out," I mumbled at last.

SIXTEEN

To my astonishment, when I awoke the next morning, the crane had vanished.

"You see!" Lester said while coming outside, a steaming mug in hand. "A bit of rest is all it takes. I seen birds that looked like their necks got broken. But if you leave it on the ground, a day later the thing just might return from the dead, good as new."

Daisy was still asleep in the tent. I wanted to wake her to share the nice news but I figured it was best to let her catch up on much needed rest.

Although Bertie never spoke a word, he had his own way of showing emotion. When he discovered that the crane had left us, he ran in circles around the spot where it'd lain and released high-pitched toots, while clutching at the empty air.

As Lester smiled his wrinkles deepened, and I noticed a long scar along the side of his cheek, disappearing into the beard. It'd faded to a pale seam in the skin—a very old injury, I guessed.

"What happened to your face?" I said.

"Oh, this?" His hand crept up to finger the scar, with curiosity, as if rediscovering it after a long time. "An older boy gave me this gift, not long after we moved to the Charlottes."

"Ouch. What happened?"

"He had a beef with me, because his father had a beef with my father. They'd both staked a claim to the same piece of land."

"Oh?"

The corners of Lester's mouth twitched upward, with bleak amusement. "We came out here for peaceful farm life, but that turned out to be just a damn illusion. When the government tried to lure homesteaders out here, their pamphlets talked of virgin land. Rich, rich soil. Trees like giants. 'The early bird catches the worm'—that's what one pamphlet said. And my poor father was just dumb enough to fall for it."

"The government lied?" I stared off into the trees, puzzled. "But it *was* untouched wilderness, wasn't it? Most of this land still is."

The old man chortled. "That's just how things look on the surface. In truth, the land's been staked for decades. Well before small-timers like us arrived, the big companies had already moved in. Companies owned by rich men in big cities, on both sides of the border. They gobbled up the best turf and just held on to it, lettin' it sit idle. Bidin' their time, till these trees became profitable enough to log. Thanks to the war, they hit the jackpot." He shook his head, bitterly.

I felt bad for Lester and his folks. "So why didn't you guys go back to the mainland, if all the land was taken?"

"I didn't say that. There was still land available. Inland. Where the ground's rocky and irrigation's a nasty challenge. That's the turf we homesteaders got stuck with. But since my father had invested his last dollar in gettin' us out here, what choice did we have? We tried to make the land bear fruit."

"And did you have any success?"

Lester made a sour face. "That soil barely grows even the puniest firs. After a couple years of breakin' our backs, we were beat."

"So what did you do then?"

His eyes glinted at some old memory. "By then, my father had decided it couldn't hurt to seize a bit of prime waterfront, up on Masset Inlet. He didn't realize that the company that'd staked it had a watchman stationed there, along with his family." He touched the scar around his beard.

"The watchman and your father came to blows?"

"Yep. My father lost a finger in the battle."

I hesitated to ask anything more. "And... your scar?"

"The watchman had a son, a couple years older than me. But I was tall for my age, so I put up a decent fight. The other boy had a knife up his sleeve, however. So, while his injuries healed quick, mine left me with this reminder of what happens when folks encroach upon company land."

✤

After spending a couple more days at Lester's, Daisy and I were very antsy. Still no sign of his Indian friend. In fact, since we'd arrived, not a new soul had come within eyeshot of the cottage or beach.

Nevertheless, Daisy remained on edge that Mrs. Hill had reported our assault to the authorities by now. I, on the other hand, continued to doubt that the madam would turn to the law, even if there were any police on these islands. In truth, I might've welcomed the sight of a police officer wandering down the beach toward us. It was starting to feel like me and Daisy and these two odd brothers were the last surviving humans on the face of the earth.

At night in our tent, we whispered about what to do next. Lester was getting all too comfortable with me and Daisy doing the most menial, unpleasant chores, like cleaning out the animals' cages, disposing of their endless piles of poop. Daisy was desperate to move on—fearing that the law was on our tail—but I was more hesitant. Where would we go? Even if we managed to find the Indian's dock, how likely was it that he'd happen to be there? Cold, hungry, with no place to sleep, what would we do? Wait at the dock, forever? It seemed to me that the safer move was to stay put and do whatever we had to in order to earn our keep, till the Indian paid Lester a visit.

When I said as much to Daisy, she didn't look pleased. "That could take *weeks*."

"You think I don't realize that?"

We were falling far behind schedule. By now, Izzy would be imprisoned at the Home, the harsh realities of what lay before her setting in. And Mom would be beside herself with worry over my prolonged disappearance. She'd be setting off alarm bells, calling upon Uncle Will and Dice to find me immediately. And I wondered if word of our attack on Mrs. Hill had made its way to Buckley by now. Gossip moved quickly out here, folks desperate for any form of scandal as entertainment. One way or another, were we going to pay for what we'd done to Mrs. Hill and her lout?

"We have to get a move on," Daisy said under her breath, chewing at her fingertips. Ever since Irene had filched Daisy's cigarettes, nibbling at her fingernails had become her substitute. "Lester's not right in the head… There's something funny about him."

"Aw, he's just an eccentric old man. Pretty harmless."

"He's *not* harmless." She said that in her line of work, a girl got a sense about these things.

"Too much time on his own, with no one but his deaf brother to talk to. Who wouldn't go a little peculiar?"

"That's just it, Khya! Don't you find it strange that these men are living out here, even now? Why didn't they go back to the mainland, like everyone else, at the start of the war?"

"They just prefer animals over humans," I insisted. "Nothing wrong with that."

❦

Lester wasn't a good cook, so we offered to take over the preparation of meals. On any given day, Daisy would be at the stove, stirring a steaming pot, while I chopped up turnips—as birds in cages all too nearby chirped their never-ending sorrows. At this time of year, there wasn't much in the way of wild herbs to add flavour. It was doubtful that our concoctions would be much tastier than Lester's.

But I had another reason for wanting to spend time in the tiny kitchen. If Daisy were to insist that we set off on our own soon, we'd have a better chance at survival with some tools. So every now and then, I'd nick something: a paring knife, a fork, a spoon, a needle and thread. I had to be discreet and not get greedy. Though I was itching to take Lester's magnifying glass, it seemed too likely that he'd notice its absence.

"Keep an eye on the door, will you?" I murmured to Daisy, one afternoon.

She looked up from the bubbling pot. "Why? What are you planning to do?"

"I just want to peek in the bedroom." Its door was always closed, and Lester had emphasized that we were not to go in there.

"But why? It's too risky, Khya!" Daisy continued to hold Lester in fear, believing him to be unhinged.

"Maybe Lester has a wad of cash hidden in the dresser. If we manage to find the Indian skipper, we'll need money to pay for our boat rides, right?"

"Well, what do I do if Lester comes in?"

I told her to stand near the window and keep a lookout. If he was coming up the path, she should cough loudly and shout "Stew's ready!" That'd be my signal to get out.

Before Daisy had a chance to object, I slipped through the door, its hinges squeaking.

The bedroom was small and cramped. My eyes gradually adjusted to the darkness. Without a single window, the only light came through crevices in the log walls. Two saggy cots, side by side, covered in grey blankets, took up most of the space. On the nightstand was a candle stub, and inside the drawer were a few more candles. I pocketed one, along with a book of matches.

A couple shelves stretched out along the opposite wall. They contained the brothers' few garments of clothing, messily folded, as well as a dusty copy of the bible. On the upper shelf, some black blankets were piled, and they looked softer than the ones Lester had given me and Daisy for our tent. I reached out and touched one, contemplating whether to risk stealing it.

That was when I noticed some objects had been hidden beneath its folds. I backed up, startled: *a line of yellowed skulls was staring out at me.* Some were oblong shaped, with big, gaping eyeholes and protruding fangs, like they might have belonged to wild cats or martens. Others had dramatic, curving beaks, which looked as dangerous as hunting knives. They'd been eagles or hawks, I suspected.

The half-dozen skulls continued to quietly watch me, with chilling amusement. Quickly, I came to agree with Daisy's assessment of Lester. How could he and Bertie sleep with this gang of skulls staring down at them?

As my trembling hands tried to reposition the blanket, I couldn't help but notice a larger, lumpier thing still concealed at the shelf's other end. Overcome by curiosity, I lifted the dark fabric and found myself face to face with a bigger skull. It was a human head—of *that*, I had no doubt. Its gleaming, crooked teeth were still intact, and they appeared to be smiling, with a grim ferocity.

A voice punctured my spell. Daisy was calling out to me, yet I remained transfixed.

Plodding footsteps. The door groaned open and I could sense Lester's looming presence behind me, Daisy rustling in the shadows.

"I told ya not to come in here." Though he sounded angry, he did not seem altogether surprised.

"I… I'm sorry…," I faltered, fear rushing over me, all too late. I didn't dare to turn around.

"You wonderin' who that head belonged to? You can save yer tears. Cry over these other fine animals who lost their lives. They deserve yer sympathy far more."

"Did your father…?" The question died on my tongue.

Daisy erupted in a coughing fit, like she desperately wanted me to stop talking.

"Did my father *what*?" Lester said tauntingly, daring me to ask.

"The company's watchman?" I whispered. "Your father killed him, in the end?"

He stroked the side of his cheek. "Remember I told you that the watchman had a son? When he grew up, he took over his father's job. And then… well… things between us got ugly again."

I'd heard enough, my stomach a roiling swamp. I wasn't going to press for details. Daisy, too, looked very unwell.

"But if anyone ever comes pokin' around here, lookin' for a human skull, I'd say it's just the head of my father. He and I were always thick as thieves, and there's no law against keepin' a dead loved one close by."

"Don't worry," I sputtered. "We won't tell anyone what we've seen!"

"Best that way. Now, it's late, so you boys are welcome to spend one more night." Though it was pretty clear from Lester's expression that we'd worn thin his hospitality. "First thing tomorrow, I'll expect you *gone*."

Seventeen

Before dawn, Daisy and I left stealthily, without saying goodbye to our hosts. Through the dreary shadows on the beach we scurried, our eyes hungry for anything resembling a jetty. A few miles passed. Nothing. As the sky began to lighten, I wondered if Daisy would finally be willing to discuss the skull. Last night she'd shaken her head and looked ill whenever I'd tried to talk to her about anything at all.

"So you were right about Lester being a crackpot," I ventured.

"A *crackpot*?" She rubbed at her nose and turned to face me at last. "That man's a goddamn *murderer*!"

"Okay, okay." I held up my hands. "I should've listened when you warned me about him."

I could only pray that Daisy wouldn't stay angry for long. We continued walking over the rough sand, the water like a never-ending mirror.

Eventually, I dared to break the silence. "It's not like Lester had no reason for doing what he did. Just like we had our reasons for attacking Mrs. Hill and her thug! If we hadn't defended ourselves—"

"It's not the same thing, Khya!" Daisy glowered at me.

"You don't know that. Lester could've been defending himself."

I thought about the kitchen maid who'd bravely come to our rescue. She hadn't premeditated her assault on that monster, any more than I'd been planning to jab a comb into his eye.

I remained tormented with worry about what'd become of the poor woman. Had she stuck around till Mrs. Hill and the brute recovered consciousness? Or had she fled the scene? Skipped town, maybe? I thought that was what I might do, in her shoes.

"We didn't kill anyone," Daisy said insistently. "Mrs. Hill probably just has a bump on her head. And the other guy... well.., you only need one eye to see, right?"

⚘

The farther we walked, the more I seemed to be slipping into a light trance. By afternoon, it was starting to feel like we had no destination at all. Daisy still wasn't talking much, her foul mood persisting. Did she think that I was as much a crackpot as Lester? How was I ever going to win back her trust?

It looked, from a distance, like a big pile of manure, smack dab in the middle of the sand. We had no inkling of what it was, at first. As we got nearer, however, my heart shuddered.

I'd never seen a dead whale before. I wasn't prepared for its sheer size or the way its sad head, mottled in white blotches, had flopped to one side. Eyes closed, in anguish. Big jaw, with fleshy, grey tongue exposed, frozen in some final unspoken word. Its neck area was covered in pink stains, from wounds that were the handiwork of a whaling mission, most likely.

A sobbing shriek escaped Daisy's throat and echoed for a very long time, as she ran down the beach, away from it all. I chased after her.

Neither of us could keep it up for long, slowing down, winded.

"Are you all right?" I said, but she didn't seem to hear me.

As we resumed walking, Daisy turned utterly silent. She ignored all my attempts to cheer her up. It frazzled me to see her like this. Giving up, I sank into muteness too, and we trudged on in this horrible state for what felt like an eternity.

🌱

A faint image teased my exhausted eyes, as dusk was edging in. Two men, who appeared very small, from this far off, were standing in the middle of a line that jutted out into the water. The plumper of the pair had unruly brown hair blowing about in the wind. The other man had a pale, narrow face; he was Oriental, I thought.

The whole scene struck me as mirage-like, not to be trusted.

Nevertheless, I said to Daisy, "Are my eyes playing tricks on me?"

Her face came to life. "Sweet Jesus!"

We exchanged wild glances and broke into a sprint. Pain shot up through my ankle, but I ignored it and kept running.

The men were no longer engaged in conversation. The Oriental fellow followed the more rotund guy—the Indian skipper?—down the wharf to where the water deepened. It looked like they were getting into an old fishing boat, a squat, white thing. Daisy and I were screaming at the tops of our lungs for them to *stop, wait for us, wait for us, please,* waving our arms like a couple of girls escaped from an asylum. But our cries, if the men heard them, must have sounded too similar to squawking gulls.

Daisy was faster than me, with my hurt ankle. By the time I reached the dock, if you could call it that—it was nothing more than an enormous tree trunk, flattened on top—she was already standing at its far end, crying out at the choppy waves, at the boat that was shrinking to the size of a child's toy.

I joined her—no longer running, for what was the point? There we stood, staring out at the grey-blue glassiness, at the receding white blotch. Our lifeboat. The sky was deepening to raw twilight. In a couple hours, night would descend, and where would we even sleep? I closed my eyes in despair.

When I peeked them open, Daisy's neck was craned forward. Something peculiar was happening: the white blotch appeared to be getting larger, not smaller. What on earth was going on? As it came into focus again, this time travelling astern, I could see it was one of those work-horse double-enders, the kind typically used for gillnetting; they cut the water more easily than boats with square rears. Scuffed white paint, dark green trim. Looking out at us, from the stern, was the Oriental guy, and as the boat drew nearer, I could see that he had a pair of binoculars held to his eyes.

Daisy clasped my clammy hand, and we both stood there in shock.

As the boat approached, the Indian skipper joined the Oriental out back. They were using paddles to control their direction. The Indian shouted instructions over his shoulder. A cloud of frustration surrounded his broad face, his hair a windblown mess. The Oriental, stiffer in his movements, appeared in an equally bad mood.

Around this point, something about their faces began to niggle at my brain. And then their features suddenly lost all blurriness, like I was viewing them through a magnifying glass. The Indian was Frank Turner and the Oriental fellow was Dice!

When they got close enough, Dice hurled me a rope. I caught it and tied the boat down. He regarded me with no small indignation.

It was Turner who spoke first. He, too, had thunder in his gaze. "You've got ten seconds to explain what the hell you're doing here, Khya! What business have you got being out here all alone?"

"But I'm not alone." I gestured at Daisy.

He and Dice glared at us, unimpressed. Neither disembarked or moved at all, as if to make clear they might very well continue on in the direction they'd set out. Leaving us to rot on the wobbly jetty.

"I thought you ran off to Victoria," Dice said at last. "Your poor mother's sick with worry. She sent Kenji there to chase you down. And now you have the nerve to turn up *here?*"

"Well…" How to explain? And poor Kenji, off on a wild goose chase in the city! What world of trouble had I stirred up for everybody?

"So, Khya, you never answered the question," Turner said. "*What in God's name are you doing here?*"

It occurred to me that I could put the same question to him. "I thought that when you and the other Indians left our camp, you were going back to the fishing life. That's what you *said.*"

He shook his head, like he didn't want to talk about it.

"Where are all your tribesmen?" I pressed.

Daisy shot me a reproachful glance, like if I knew what was good for me, I'd shut my trap.

Turner let out a raspy snort. "Tribe? What tribe? Measles, greedy white men and all those fucking logging companies have pretty much put the nail in my tribe's coffin."

Meanwhile, Dice kept watching me with scrutiny. "You're on your way to Thurston Harbour, aren't you? Trying to find the lout who dishonoured your sister?"

I stared at my feet.

"Looks like they're headed in the same direction as you, then," Turner said.

"You're going to Thurston Harbour, too? We can tag along with you then!" Daisy exclaimed.

"That's perfect," I added.

"Not on your life." Dice was shaking his head, fury unabated. "You two are heading right home."

"Do you have any idea what it's taken for us to make it this far?" I snarled. I held up my bruised, scabby hands. "And my ankle's hurting bad. It might even be broken." I rolled up the cuff of my pantleg. While I doubted it was anywhere close to broken, it *was* swelling up slightly.

"Yeah, so if you insist that we go back," Daisy continued, "it's only proper for you to come with us to make sure we get there safe and sound."

"Dad would expect nothing less of you," I said, recalling the curious bond that this man had with my father.

"Well, they've got a point," Turner piped up, while Dice sank into sullen rumination. "But I have to tell you that the fee you just paid me is non-refundable."

"What?"

Mirth danced in Turner's eyes. "On the other hand, if you wish to continue your journey, I'm willing to let these two ruffians come with us. At half price, since they're scrawny and don't take up much space."

Daisy and I traded panicked looks.

"But I'm afraid we don't have any money…," she said.

"Oh, don't you worry about that," Turner replied. "This gentleman has enough to cover your tickets, I presume?"

Dice stared out at the water, in fuming silence.

"And then, once we get to Thurston Harbour, I'm willing to ferry these mischief-makers back to Buckley—for a modest fee, of course—so you won't have to lose time on your important business. Sounds reasonable, don't you think?"

"Oh, more than reasonable!" Daisy looked delighted. The prospect of us not sleeping on the cold beach was pushing her to agree to anything.

Dice eyed her with contempt. "Who *are* you? What are you doing here, anyway?"

"He's my friend, Ash," I said.

Turner rolled his eyes. "She's a runaway harlot, clearly. Dressed like a boy for what reason I can't imagine."

"In that case, she can be left right here on the beach," said Dice.

"What? *No—I'm not going anywhere without Daisy.*" I clutched her hand.

"Ah, Daisy," Turner said. "So she does have a real name."

Dice remained surly as ever. "I'm not in the habit of paying the travel expenses of perfect strangers."

"We can't just leave her here. What if the girl gets attacked?"

"There's no one around for miles. Who's going to attack her? And if you're so concerned, *you* can waive the cost of her boat ticket."

A gloomy air came over Turner, but I sensed he was going to take mercy on Daisy.

"So, are we heading out?" he said, eventually. "If so, you owe me some more money."

An inscrutable expression had slipped over Dice's face, frighteningly calm. What calculations were humming along in his brain? I could picture him ever so casually preparing to hand over some cash, and then, at the last second, stabbing his little silver spike right between Turner's brows. His killing method no different for a man than for a fish.

But then, after some haggling, cash exchanged hands calmly enough. Daisy and I found ourselves boarding the boat, the sky rapidly darkening to night.

I offered to help steer, but Dice told me to sit down and shut my trap—I'd done enough already. When I couldn't stay still, he threatened to tie me to my seat, and I could see, in the cold steel of his eyes, that he wasn't joking. It dawned on me that the main reason he hadn't killed Turner and stolen his boat was that only Turner knew how to get to our destination.

While I was curious about what business was drawing Dice to Thurston Harbour, I had enough sense to know that now was not an opportune moment to ask questions.

Eighteen

That first night aboard passed in a blur. The sky was black as coal, mist stinging my cheeks with something like tears. I curled up, on deck. Tired aches gripped my limbs, my eyelids as sluggish as sandbags. I struggled to stay awake, having a dim sense that Daisy had already drifted off on the bench beside me. And then a solid pair of arms was lifting me up, like a small child, and carrying me down into a musty cave. It was Frank Turner, his hair scratchy against my forehead. By the time my body was being set down on some slight cushioning, I was nearly asleep again.

Some time later, I awoke with a start in a space with a very low ceiling. Apart from a trickle of grey light down a short staircase, the cabin was as dark and airless as a coffin.

As my eyes adjusted, I noticed Daisy asleep on the crude mattress beside me. She appeared trapped in some awful dream, her eyelids clenched. I wondered if I should wake her but decided it was more important to let her rest.

My bladder ached, about to burst. A large bowl was on the floor in the corner. I didn't know if it was meant for washing one's face, eating from or relieving oneself in, but for the time being it was going to serve the latter function. At times like this, how I envied men's ability to aim their yellow arcs out into the ocean. Once I was done, I pulled up my pants and decided to go up and see where we were.

My ankle felt worse this morning, so I climbed the stairs gingerly.

Dice was sitting on deck. He looked over at me like I was his prisoner and he wasn't sure what to do with me yet.

"Good morning," I said.

"Hardly." He gestured around us at the thick, white fog, unrolling in enormous layers that bandaged over everything.

Frank Turner was at the helm, in the sheltered portion. He steered with remarkable calmness, bordering on boredom. It didn't do much to reassure me.

"How can he see a thing?"

Dice shrugged, trying to act unfazed. "He says he's seen far worse, in his day. Just a bit of fog."

Every so often it would thin out in patches and I'd glimpse these slips of faraway, brilliant greenness. Then the fog would shift, blanketing everything once more. How far had we drifted? Were we being swept out to sea? Panic clutched at my innards.

I noticed a jug of rainwater on the table. "Mind if I have a drink?"

Dice nodded.

As I limped across the slippery floor and chugged back a refreshing burst, I felt his eyes gliding over my backside and legs.

"That ankle of yours is in rough shape," he said.

"Aw, it's nothing."

"Let me take a look."

When I hesitated, he leaned back, in a disarming posture. Softly, he said, switching into Japanese, "You're afraid of me, I can see, but there's no need for that. We're on the same side here."

"Oh? And what side is that?"

Dice continued to eye me with perplexity, like I was a novel type of frog or bird he'd never before encountered, and something about my spots or feathers confounded his understanding. "I have to say you're nothing like girls in Japan."

"I'm not like Izzy, you mean."

He smiled, recollecting. "She is indeed classically Japanese. An old-fashioned beauty. Timid and lovely."

I wondered if this man had started to hold a torch for my sister.

"It's a terrible shame what that lout did to her." His jaw hardened.

I nodded. "It's a mystery what she ever saw in the Captain."

"She had no choice in the matter, of course! *He violated her.*"

"I don't know about that. She claims to be in love with him, if you want the truth."

Dice's forehead creased in disgust. "Nonsense. That villain forced himself on her."

I went over to join him on the bench. Fog was moving in, immersing his face in great swirls of white dust.

"So tell me a little more about your sister…," he resumed, trying to act casual. "She didn't grow up in Canada, I understand?"

"Our parents sent her and our older brother to Japan to be raised by relatives."

"That must have been a lonely childhood for your sister."

I thought about how much she'd suffered. The terrible things that she'd endured. It made me sick to my stomach.

"That's the cost of progress," Dice remarked, not hiding his sarcasm. "*Now we should learn from and adopt the successes of the West.* That's what Emperor Meiji told us all. Suddenly, he was no longer sacred and revered, hidden from public view. He was out and about, in his swallowtail uniform on horseback, singing the praises of modernization, touring factories and schools—no different than a Western politician. And men like your father followed his command and headed out to this wretched wilderness to learn from the West."

Dad had told me about the startling changes that'd swept through Japan during his childhood. Castles had been attacked and burned to the ground, the nobles all slain or left to commit *seppuku*. Stark black ships crowded the harbours, bringing in strange-looking foreigners with ghost-white faces and bulbous noses and unnaturally big hands. The first time my father saw railways, he hadn't been able to get his head around how these vehicles could magically pull themselves—without horses, without oxen, without anything.

"Well, what's wrong with learning from the West?" I said.

"Nothing, if you put that learning to proper use. Study the English language and go off on a grand adventure, like your father! Learn how canneries and mills do things out here, the kinds of new machinery that can be used. But don't you see? The whole point of that knowledge was supposed to be that he would bring it home. *To Japan.*"

"I think that Dad originally intended for us to move back. Then he ended up liking life in Canada rather well."

"Look what good came of that!" Dice splayed his hands angrily. "*Your family's blood has been forever sullied by the barbarian.*"

While I didn't much like the Captain, I hardly considered him a barbarian.

"How did you and my father first meet?" Their relationship continued to baffle me. At times, it was like they were almost brothers, so invested was Dice in our family. Was it possible that he actually was kin?

He leaned closer, an air of secrecy about him. He looked like he was assessing me. Assessing whether I might have some hidden value to him. "It's a damn shame you're not a boy."

I made a sour face, confused by his comment.

"What do you know about our hometown, Fukuoka?"

I shrugged. I'd never been there. I'd never been anywhere in Japan.

"Fukuoka perches on a narrow strait, but that strait widens into a dark ocean that encompasses all of Asia. *Genyosha,*" Dice whispered, repeating the word for dark ocean, as though the word alone contained a multitude of meanings, secrets.

Genyosha...

Blurry memories were floating up in my brain. As a kid, I'd overheard Dad talking about the Black Ocean Society with his buddies, always in hushed tones. I hadn't known what it meant and I still wasn't entirely sure.

But over the years, I'd gotten the impression that such secret societies were dangerous, revered groups in Japan. They'd been founded by ex-samurais and their descendants, enraged about having been stripped of their land and status. Even the most powerful politicians were rumoured to have ties to these criminal organizations, which reputedly did all kinds of things from rigging elections to murdering troublesome individuals.

When Dad was a kid, his family had been very poor and needed him to help put food on the table. I wondered if he might've gotten pulled into the Black Ocean Society, as an errand boy or something. Dad and Dice both had a canniness about them, evolved from their early days of doing God only knew what.

Dice seemed to sense that he'd said too much, more than I wanted to hear. He picked up his fishing rod and wandered to the rear of the boat, while I tried to push our conversation from my mind. Eventually, I went down into the cabin to check on Daisy.

❦

When my sweet friend awoke, she was dreadfully nauseous, seasick. She vomited all over the cabin floor, poor thing. I cleaned up the mess and nursed her with cups of rainwater to prevent dehydration. In a weakened state, Daisy fell back to sleep.

Finally, for lack of anything else to do, I returned upstairs. The fog was starting to clear, like nothing more than puffs of smoke, revealing an endless expanse of sky. I was relieved to see that we'd remained close to shore, the glistening green of the forest's edge.

I approached Turner at the steering wheel. "When are we going to get there, do you think?"

"A couple more days."

"That long? Isn't there any way we can go faster?"

Irritation flickered across his brow. "What do you want me to do, Khya? I don't control the blasted weather!"

I sat down on the damp bench. Dice was also out there, taking apart a sablefish on his lap. He used a long knife to cut lengthwise along the top and opened up the glistening, pearly flesh to remove the spine. Then he sliced off a generous strip and snacked on it, hungrily. He held out a shiny hunk in my direction, but I shook my head, disgusted. My family had never been in the habit of eating raw fish. It wasn't safe, Mom insisted.

"Suit yourself. It's delicious when it's this fresh."

Turner cut the engine and came to join us, letting the boat drift with the current. Staring out at the water, he lit a cigarette.

The edges of his lips curled upward. "So, did you hear about the murder in Port Clem?"

My blood ran cold, as I stared back at him. "*Murder?*"

He seemed to be enjoying my stunned reaction. "Never a dull moment in this wilderness, eh?"

I couldn't find my voice, my face in a state of paralysis. But violent brawls broke out in these logging towns all the time and occasionally led to bad endings… This murder might've had nothing to do with me and Daisy, or so I prayed.

"What happened?" Dice enquired, with interest.

"On my way out here, I stopped at Port Clem for supper," Turner explained. "I headed to my favourite pub, but it'd been shut down because someone had been killed there a couple days prior."

A persistent roaring filled my head, like the sound of a waterfall. My thoughts kept getting swept away on it, as my mouth opened and closed with a snap, no words emerging.

"Who was the victim?" Dice said.

"An old, mean broad, named Mrs. Hill. Madam at the biggest brothel in town. Got whacked on the head with a frying pan, if you can believe it! Died on the spot."

Mrs. Hill—*dead*?

Yet I didn't doubt in my heart that it was true. For I couldn't forget how forcefully Daisy had brought that pan down upon the woman's skull.

"It really is the wild west out here. Lawless and crazy." Dice shook his head with a bemused chuckle.

"Do they know who's responsible?" I blurted. "Was anyone else hurt in the scuffle?" The ugly face of Mrs. Hill's henchman flashed in my mind, how he screeched when I stabbed him in the eye. What'd become of him? Had the maid's rolling pin done him in, too?

Dice was watching me, queerly. I was going to have to be more careful not to show an abnormal level of interest. I tried to put on the face of a busybody, eager for any scraps of gossip.

"Rumour has it that Mrs. Hill's son might be the culprit," Turner said. "Angus Hill. He's a nasty roughneck, from what I've heard."

Mrs. Hill's son—Angus—was being blamed for her death? "*How…?* How's that possible…?"

"Who knows?" Turner remained in high spirits, relishing the scandal. "He worked for his mother as muscle at her brothel, and they hadn't been getting along lately. It appears they got into a fight at the pub. Right in the kitchen, no less. Things must've got heated! Angus could've reached for a frying pan and his dear mother ended up dead on the floor."

"But… what about him?" My voice sounded distant, like it wasn't quite coming from my own throat. "Is he… also dead?"

Turner shook his head. "Angus flew the coop. Vanished into thin air. That's why everyone in town thinks he must be guilty."

Dice tut-tutted. "Even if the guy despised his mother, that's no excuse for *killing* her."

I swallowed hard. On the shore, a few totem poles were decaying, one having toppled on its side already. From the sun-bleached wood, creatures with great flaring nostrils and bared teeth and unflinching gazes stared out at me. Holding me to account.

Much about what Turner had shared didn't make sense. Why would Angus flee? Had he been so disoriented—from the blow to his head—that he hadn't been thinking straight? Where was he now? Lurking in the woods?

And what about the kitchen maid? No mention of her at all. Had she also run off and disappeared into the woods? And what about Irene and Ewan? Had they stepped forward to tell their side of things and implicate me and Daisy? Or would they keep their mouths shut, not wanting to draw suspicion to themselves and their own illegal activities?

I crossed my arms over my turbulent gut, bile rising at the back of my throat. Daisy wasn't the only one sick as a dog now.

❧

For the rest of the day, I continued to feel ghastly, my head a muddle of confusion and fright. While Daisy remained at rest down below, I couldn't bring myself to tell her about Mrs. Hill's death. The news would only make her stomach so much worse. And recounting aloud the whole harrowing mess would make it real—inescapably real. So I avoided going downstairs to check on her, because she'd be able to tell something was wrong with one look at me. Thankfully, by the time I had to go down to sleep, she was already deep in dreamland.

The following morning, Daisy appeared considerably better. In addition to water, she was able to keep down some bread and cheese, which Turner was nice enough to share with us. Still, I held off on saying anything. She would be full of frantic questions to which I had no answers—only more questions of my own.

I wanted nothing more than to pretend that we were never going to reach our destination and we two could remain lost at sea forever.

"Is something wrong, Khya?"

I shook my head. "Why do you ask?"

"You seem on edge."

"I'm just frustrated that we've been delayed so long."

"Cheer up, my dear. We're Ash and Del, right?"

A trace of childhood magic hung like stardust in the darkness around us.

⚘

Down in the cabin that night, I watched Daisy's sleeping face in the wobbling shadows for hours. The men stayed up on deck, so she and I were all by ourselves, for which I was grateful. I ventured to run a fingertip ever so lightly over the fine, golden down on her upper lip. The summer breeze of her exhalations. Confusing desires fluttered up in my gut—sweat stinging my armpits, my upper thighs. I withdrew my hand, quickly. For what if her eyes swept open and her body recoiled from my touch, in disgust?

When my lovely friend awoke close to dawn, she found me still watching over her. I preferred to remain on guard, with Mrs. Hill dead and Angus Hill on the loose. Even if we were on a boat, nowhere did I feel safe from his vengeful predations.

Daisy rubbed at her eyes. "What's wrong, Khya? You've been acting jumpy for the longest time."

I stalled, scratching my arm. Praying that if I scratched hard enough and drew blood, this whole situation might magically vanish. "I... I..."

"Now you're really scaring me! What on earth is going on?"

What choice did I have? There was never going to be a good time to spill the beans, and keeping secrets was only making me crazier than ever. With a sharp gulp, I shared with her everything I knew about Mrs. Hill's death. Daisy's jaw dropped as I let it all out in a rush of miserable whispers.

"But that means... that *means*...," she sputtered. "The police'll be on the lookout for us!"

"I don't know about that." I explained that as far as I knew, we had yet to be connected to the crime scene. And I still wasn't convinced that the police had any presence on the Charlottes.

"So what're we gonna do?" A sob choked off her voice. Her hands shot up, covering her face. "I've *killed* a woman...?"

"A despicable monster you've killed. In my defence! If you hadn't—"

"I'm still a murderer," she interrupted with a terrible moan.

It was agonizing to see Daisy in this state. And it was all my fault. If I'd never dragged her on this lunatic journey, none of this would have happened.

"What now?" she murmured, lowering her shaking hands at last.

I tried to keep up a brave front. "We lay low and continue on as planned. We go to Thurston Harbour and find the Captain, as originally intended. Thurston Harbour's far away from Port Clem—no one'll be looking for Mrs. Hill's killer there. And it's Angus Hill people are on the hunt for, not us!"

Daisy didn't appear reassured. "He ran off. So the police'll be searching for him well outside of Port Clem. In towns like Thurston Harbour. And maybe they'll be on the lookout for two girls of our description, too!"

Possibly she was right. But it was too late to turn back now. "Thurston Harbour's a big place—the biggest town on the Charlottes. We'll be safe there, blending into the crowd."

She gnawed at her thumbnail, fitfully.

"I still can't understand why Angus ran off," I pondered aloud. "Do you think getting whacked on the head affected his memory? Maybe when he came to and saw his mother's body on the floor, he thought that he'd actually killed her?"

"Perhaps. Or he figured that everyone in town would assume he did it."

Well, he'd been right about that. "So he panicked and decided to run, before folks could point fingers at him?"

Daisy nodded. Running away at the first sign of trouble made good sense to her.

"What's wrong?" I whispered.

Another grim thought had besieged her. She appeared on the cusp of tears.

"This means I can't get a job at a brothel in Thurston Harbour! It'll be too risky, 'cause Irene and Ewan might come forward and report a runaway whore of my description, so all the whorehouses'll be on the lookout…"

"Why would you get another job at a brothel?" I said stiffly. "That was never the plan. In fact, that's the *opposite* of the plan! The whole point of getting you away—"

"You live in a dream world, Khya," Daisy interrupted.

She had no confidence that she'd ever find a new line of work. It was written all over her face, plain as day. She'd come on this madcap trip simply to keep me company and now her biggest fear was that she had no way to earn a living. And the law was coming after us both.

"We'll find you a better job in Thurston Harbour. I'll help you, okay?"

Daisy sighed, her body wilting. "Okay, Del," she managed to say.

I put my arms around her and savoured the hot dampness of her tear-stained skin against my neck, my earlobe. And the next thing I knew I was nuzzling and kissing her neck—a trail of light kisses leading up to her open, salty lips. She tensed in surprise for just a second. And then her body became so yielding, offering up not an ounce of hesitation or resistance. It was blissful how our mouths seemed to be melting into each other, as our tongues flicked against one another, like the tails of playful fish. For me, all this was new, riveting. But Daisy was an expert kisser, and I had a strong suspicion that I was not the first girl she'd kissed in this way. And as her tongue continued to delicately probe and tantalize, this thought began to trouble and depress me. I didn't want her to see me as no different than all the other people who'd enjoyed and discarded her body.

She must have sensed my waning enthusiasm. Her face pulled away from mine. "What's wrong?"

"Oh, nothing…"

Her eyes tensed pleadingly. "Did I do something wrong?"

Her eagerness to please only deflated my spirits further. And then, it felt like some crucial stitching was unravelling inside me. "I shouldn't have done that—I don't know what came over me!"

"It's okay… Don't you like kissing me?"

I shrugged, seeking to act like it was unimportant. "You probably prefer kissing boys. Girls are meant to kiss boys, after all."

"Lips are just lips."

I flinched. How could she be so matter-of-fact about everything? So detached? So willing to kiss anyone?

"Oh, Daisy…"

No words of kindness or consolation came to me, though. She turned over, her back toward me, and curled up tight as a snail. I prayed that this incident wasn't going to make things forever awkward between us.

After much tossing and turning, I drifted off into a light sleep, keeping a respectful distance. But it made no difference. When I awoke the next morning, my body had snuggled up next to hers. My nose was nestled in the nape of her neck, which smelled faintly of almonds and orange rind, and how perfectly the curve of her backside fit into the valley of my upper thighs. It took a great deal of restraint to turn away, not wanting to risk waking her and doing something foolish again.

NINETEEN

We were getting close to Thurston Harbour at last. Turner said he expected we'd arrive by dusk. Later that morning, I heard him quietly talking with Dice at the stern. They seemed to be discussing what to do about me and Daisy. I edged closer and strained my ears, though I soon didn't need to, as their voices escalated.

"We'll spend the night," Turner was saying. "And then tomorrow morning, the girls and I can start the journey back and be out of your hair. Assuming, of course, that you and I can agree on a fair price for my time and trouble."

"What makes you think I'm willing to pay you a cent more?" Dice hissed. "I've paid you enough already. And it's taken an eternity to get here! I might as well have canoed myself."

Turner gestured at the shoreline. "In that case, shall I pull over right here? You're welcome to walk and swim the rest of the way."

Dice let out a harsh snort, then lit a cigarette.

It disturbed me that he no longer seemed nearly as worried about having me and Daisy in tow. Maybe he was planning to abandon us. Maybe he no longer cared if we fell into a bog or got attacked by hooligans.

Later in the afternoon, while Turner was concentrating on steering around a cluster of tiny, craggy islands, Dice sat down beside me on deck. Since Daisy was napping down below, he and I were alone.

"I have a question for you, Khya. If you're able to find the Captain, what are you planning to do to bring him around?"

"I'm going to be allowed to stay, then?"

"I didn't say that."

It was like Dice was testing me, gauging how smart I was.

"Well…" I hesitated, caught off guard. The truth was I hadn't thought this part through yet. Daisy and I had been struggling just to make it through each day. "I'm going to talk to the Captain, of course. Let him know what he's done to my sister. That she's carrying his child!"

Pity and disappointment mixed in Dice's gaze. I was proving myself to be not as sharp as he'd hoped. "You honestly think that this guy will care? That… what? He's just going to drop everything and run off to be with her?"

Doubt fluttered in my chest. "The Captain *does* adore my sister. I've seen the way he looks at her. Maybe he's going to do the right thing."

"Your sister marrying the barbarian who dishonoured her is hardly the right thing."

"He's not a barbarian," I said weakly. "I think that deep down he truly cares about her—and even loves her, maybe?"

Dice let out a guffaw. "This will be a good lesson for you."

It bugged me that he was speaking to me like a dim-witted child.

"When we get there, give it a try. Talk to the Captain. See what happens." He sucked in the last of his cigarette and tossed the butt into the water. "Meanwhile, I'm going off on my own, for a day or two."

"What? *Why?*"

"I have some things to attend to."

It occurred to me that I was still in the dark about what'd drawn him to Thurston Harbour. "Oh? Like what?"

"Since I've come all the way to this part of the world, I might as well have a glimpse of the biggest logging operation around."

From time to time, I'd noticed Dice jotting things down in a little notebook that he kept in his back pocket. Sometimes he seemed to be making sketches of logging set-ups and types of machinery. In Thurston Harbour, he'd be doing more of this, I gathered. Perhaps his superiors in the Black Ocean Society would be interested in the information.

"After all, there's nothing wrong with learning from the West." A smirk lit up Dice's face.

I had other things on my mind. "So what's going to happen after I talk to the Captain?"

"Well, I don't know, Khya. If things go your way, you just might be heading with the man to Victoria for your sister's wedding."

I didn't appreciate his mocking air one bit.

❦

It was snowing as we approached our end point in the late afternoon. I felt like the edges of my body were dissolving in the frenzy of delicate whiteness. Through it, I could just manage to discern the jagged, black trees around Thurston Harbour's narrow mouth, everything suddenly fading to greyness. We might have slipped into one of Izzy's ink paintings, where life itself appeared uncertain and smudge-like, indistinguishable from some other realm of spirits and lost souls.

But after we'd crossed into the inlet, things became more mundane. The town seemed no different than any other: a mill, surrounded by a line of pale, squarish buildings, which from a distance might have been tombstones. As we got closer, an ever-present humming filled the air. It rapidly increased in volume. The sound of machines going full throttle, like giant, buzzing wasps.

We got out of the boat, stepping onto the unsteady pier. Dazed, I just stood there for a while. It was hard to believe we'd actually made it here. I followed Daisy toward solid ground.

"What do we do now?" I murmured, turning to search for Dice.

He was gone already. Just like that, he'd vanished! Why did I feel so surprised? Dice had told me what he was up to; he'd given me fair warning.

Daisy, shivering, was still with me, thankfully. And Frank Turner was looking around, scoping out his next move.

He glanced at me and Daisy with glum unease. He wasn't thrilled to be saddled with us and wanted nothing more than to run off, I suspected.

"What are your plans?" he said.

I shrugged, feeling sheepish.

"Looks like that good-for-nothing guardian of yours has left you high and dry."

"Dice? He's not our guardian."

"Clearly."

"Look, you're free to leave us, too. We can take care of ourselves."

"Is that so? And how are you planning to go about finding the Captain, for a start?"

"We'll ask around, I guess… See if we recognize any guys from his old crew."

"Thousands and thousands of men, at scores of camps, are stationed here. Good luck finding anyone who'll even slow down to chat with you!"

Daisy let out a mewl, bursting into tears. The stress of everything—Mrs. Hill's death, the looming question of her own livelihood—it was too much for her. How useless and sad I felt. Plus, ever since our muddled kiss, things had become kind of strained between us. Although we still talked and joked, our relationship felt more uncertain and fragile somehow.

"*Now, look what you've done,*" I spat at Turner. "If you're not going to help us, just get out of our way, all right?"

The man sighed, his conscience getting the better of him perhaps. "I didn't say I wouldn't help. If you girls want a ride back with me to-morrow or the day after, I'd consider letting you ride for free. But not till I've found a few paying customers headed that way. So you won't have the cabin all to yourselves, you understand?"

I nodded coldly. What did it matter anyway? Daisy wouldn't be returning with me, that much was certain.

"In the meantime, I guess I can give you a hand tracking down the

Captain. My mother would turn over in her grave if I let you girls go poking around this cesspool on your own."

❧

The snow was getting heavier, accumulating in a white blanket, on which our feet left dark prints. I'd never encountered snow so thick before. It was clumping on my eyelashes, making it hard to see anything through the tiny icicles.

We headed away from the mill, which spewed its foul breath into the dusky sky. I was struck by the size of a new building down the street. It appeared to be a hospital, with a giant red cross at its top. And farther on was an equally impressive place, with a pitched roof and a sign that said YMCA. According to Turner, it was a rec centre, where loggers could hang out, shoot pool and try to stay out of trouble between shifts. Compared to this place, Buckley was a primitive village.

"Amazing, isn't it?" Turner said. "They're even building a wireless centre. Plus two more mills are under construction, the last I heard."

"Where's all the money coming from?"

"Magic! Haven't you heard? Money grows on trees. The trees that soon won't even be here, if this keeps up."

"It's the Americans, isn't it?"

"Who else?"

It was the same story back at Buckley, though the amount of cash that the American logging companies were investing here had to be far greater. Rumour had it that big deals were being brokered, in far-off, glittering cities. Rich businessmen were moving in, buying things up, getting their ducks in order for after the war.

A line of young guys with the buzzed hair of demobbed soldiers wandered past us toward the rec centre.

"Where are we going?" Daisy said, trailing behind me.

When Turner didn't answer, I repeated her question.

"I have to get my mail. Yup, there's a spanking new post office here, too."

Indeed there was. It took up half of a store that was a pharmacy on the other side. The pharmacy section was tidy, its shelves lined with green and brown bottles. The post office, on the other hand, looked like a storm had just hit. Potato sacks full of mail had spilled onto the floor. Battered parcels were piled in teetering towers, some having toppled over already. Behind the counter at the back stood a chubby Oriental fellow who couldn't be much older than me. Seventeen or eighteen, maybe.

"Howdy, Terry," Turner said.

"Hey, nice to see you." Terry looked up from the box he was wrapping, a stamp stuck in his uneven bangs.

"Terry Fan, these are my friends Khya and Daisy." Turner threw a gesture our way.

I glowed with unexpected delight that he'd called us his friends.

After searching through a drawer, Terry handed over a slender package and a couple of envelopes. Turner tore the tan wrapping off the parcel, which turned out to be a small blue book. He flipped through it, his face softening with pleasure.

"What're you reading there?" I said, trying to get a peek at the spine.

He ignored me and cradled the book so I couldn't see a thing.

"You must be looking forward to opening your store," Terry said.

"Sadly, I'm nowhere close to squirrellin' away enough money for that."

"You plan to open a store?" I said. "What'll it sell?"

Turner held up the volume in his hand.

"*Books?*" I'd never been in a bookstore before. It was hard to imagine a whole shop being full of nothing but books.

"After the war, I'd like to move to Vancouver. Open a little shop, live a quiet life."

His aim was fairly similar to my father's. Everyone, it seemed, just wanted to escape to the city, run a small business, and not have to kill for their supper.

Turner put the book away in his satchel and turned to face Terry. "I have a question for you, my friend."

"Okay?"

"We're looking for someone who moved here, not so long ago."

"The Captain," I blurted, excitedly. Then, I shook my head, frustrated by my own idiocy. "Felix Godwin. That's his real name."

"Felix Godwin," Terry repeated. He tilted his head back, thinking. Then, he rummaged under the counter and unearthed two mauve envelopes, bound with an elastic band. "I thought I recognized the name. Felix Godwin's been receiving letters from his mother, I think. Feminine, flowery handwriting on the envelopes, and the return address says Marie Godwin in Victoria. Or maybe she's his wife? Is he married?"

I shook my head, panic-stricken. I certainly hoped that the Captain wasn't already married.

"For some reason the guy stopped picking up his mail about six weeks ago," Terry said. "I wonder whether he might've packed it in and moved on."

My stomach plummeted. "Where would he go?"

"Back to Vancouver Island?" Terry suggested. "Maybe he wanted to be back with his family in time for Christmas."

Appalled, I rocked back and forth on my heels.

"Or maybe the reason the Captain hasn't picked up his mail is he's desperate to *avoid* his mother's plea to return for Christmas," Turner said. "He wouldn't be the first man who came out here to escape from civilization and all family obligations."

"True," Terry said.

I reached out, expecting him to hand the letters over. But Terry quickly retracted them, holding them close to his chest, indignant. "What the dickens d'you think you're doing?"

"I need to read them, of course! They might contain clues about where the Captain's gone."

A disapproving look. "I can't give these letters to you. Are you outta your mind?"

I rolled my eyes and hissed, "What the heck…? Who on earth could find out? It'd cost you nothing to just slip them to me…"

"Khya, the man could lose his job." Turner held up a hand in warning.

"More than just losing my job, I could get *sent to the clink*." Terry remained clutching the letters far beyond my reach. "And so could you. Aren't you aware that it's a federal offence to tamper with someone else's mail?"

"Oh, spare me." I couldn't believe what a couple of namby-pambies these two men were turning out to be.

After an awkward silence, Terry asked who Felix Godwin was to me and why I needed to find him so desperately. I told him that the guy was my sister's sweetheart and he'd run off, leaving her pregnant. I hoped that this would impress upon Terry the urgency of the situation.

"If the guy's abandoned your sister, how can he be her sweetheart?" he said, confused.

Fuming, I gave no reply. It didn't appear that anything I could say would make Terry relent. Discreetly, he returned the mauve envelopes to the bin under the counter.

"Since we're here," Turner said, "it can't hurt to take a stroll about town. See if anyone knows anything about where the Captain might be."

Terry nodded agreeably. "Is this Captain fellow a drinking man?"

"He sure is," I replied.

Terry recommended that we start our search at the rec centre. Apparently it was a popular nighttime venue for blowing off steam.

I thanked him for his advice, stiffly. It still irked me that he was refusing to turn over those letters.

Just as we were about to leave, I noticed that Daisy was lingering by the wall, reading a posting. At the top, it said in big letters: HELP WANTED. It was a relief to see my dear friend looking more like herself and thinking clearly again.

"Daisy, this is meant to be," I whispered in her ear. "Ask Terry if you can have the job—you'd be great working here."

She grabbed my arm, shaking her head anxiously.

"Since you're seeking another postman," I called out at Terry's back, "my friend here would be perfect."

Daisy, mortified, stared at the floor.

"She has a great sense of direction," I persisted. "I've never met a better navigator in my life. That's important for delivering mail to different camps in the area, I assume?"

Terry appeared to be sizing Daisy up.

"I've never worked in a post office before," she stammered, blushing.

"Well, I can't say we've ever had any *female* postmen before." Terry appeared a tad uncomfortable. "You *are* female, right? Your name's Daisy?"

She nodded shyly. "I just cut my hair, because, well, it's a long story..."

"You can call her Ash, if you prefer," I added.

Terry glanced at Turner. "You know this kid, Daisy or Ash, or whatever she calls herself?"

Turner nodded.

"And...? You willing to vouch for her character?"

My heart stopped as I waited for Turner to let the cat out of the bag by calling Daisy a harlot. And then she'd have no hope in hell of getting the job.

"Yup, she's a decent kid," he said, nonchalantly.

Terry resumed examining Daisy, who'd gone red to the verge of fainting. He didn't look terribly impressed. But then his eyes shifted to the chaos all around him, the heaps of undelivered mail. "I dunno... I'll have to speak with my boss. I don't know how he'd feel about hiring a girl."

"That's fine," I said, trying to keep hopeful. "How about we check in with you tomorrow?"

Terry said to come by in the afternoon. He added that he couldn't make any promises.

Although Daisy didn't appear too enthusiastic about this employment prospect, it'd be a definite step up from working in a brothel, as far
as I was concerned.

And she was right that brothels on the Charlottes might soon be on
the lookout for girls of our description, if they weren't already. We had
no guarantee that Irene and Ewan would keep silent, and it was probably
only a matter of time before Angus Hill came out of hiding, wherever
he was.

TWENTY

"Captain *who*?"Through a pair of smudgy spectacles, the old man squinted out at me.

"It's just a nickname." Maybe around here people had stopped calling the Captain that. "His name is Felix Godwin. Ring any bells?"

He puffed on his pipe, exhaling plumes around his liver-spotted forehead. When I described the Captain's appearance, the man's only reply was "Sounds like half the fellas in this room."

Unfortunately, I couldn't disagree. At this time of night, the rec centre wasn't much different than an enormous tavern. Sweaty, rowdy men crowded the place, swarming around the dart boards and pool tables, taking slugs from bottles and flasks. A handful of girls with cornsilk hair and bee-stung lips were sidling up to the high rollers.

From the corner of my eye, I could see Frank Turner chatting with strangers and making enquiries, just like I was doing. Meanwhile, Daisy hovered behind me anxiously, smoking a cigarette she must've filched off a table. I knew she was worried there might be police prowling about, on the hunt for Angus Hill or other suspects in his mother's murder. But I was trying to keep a more level head. It'd take time for news of the crime to travel to Victoria or Vancouver and then it'd take more time for the police to send an officer out here, if things even got that far. Mrs. Hill had been a vile, money-grubbing criminal. I reckoned it wouldn't be long before everyone forgot about her death and said good riddance. Or so I was praying.

Sadly, no one had any leads about the Captain. I was coming to realize that he'd been a big fish in a small pond, back at Buckley. We'd been at this for a good while and all I'd gotten were blank stares and jeering attitude and someone had thrown a hairy arm around my shoulder and breathed hotly into my ear and said he'd never slept with an Oriental gal before and he'd heard that we could do amazing things with our little yellow bodies.

Turner came over to where Daisy and I were resting against the wall. "Any luck?" he said.

I shook my head. "Isn't there a pub we should search, too?"

Turner pressed his lips together, wryly. "Haven't you heard? Around here, the new temperance law is taken very seriously!"

"What are you talking about? This place is nothing but one big barroom."

But now that he mentioned it, I *had* noticed that most fellows were drinking from bottles concealed in paper bags.

Turner shrugged. "The teetotallers turn a blind eye, I guess."

"Teetotallers?" It didn't seem there were many in this crowd.

Daisy rubbed her eyes, like she was struggling to stay awake. "Well, what now?"

"I say we call it a night, girls."

"Where'll we sleep?" she said apprehensively.

A solid night of rest would do her good, so I certainly hoped that Turner had a plan for our accommodations.

A dwarfish guy waddled into the room, wheeling a trundle buggy behind him. He was dressed in a bright yellow vest and red cap, his big, florid face beaming. He seemed to enjoy attracting attention, wherever he went.

"If it isn't Peddler Danny!" Turner looked pleased as punch, like he and this man were buddies. Turner went over to say hello and take a peek at the merchandise.

Meanwhile, Daisy and I plopped down on a bench. She was so worn out it seemed like she'd soon conk out on my shoulder.

Across the room, a face caught my attention. It was creepy how rigidly the man maintained his toothy grin, and I thought at first that was all that'd attracted my gaze. Yet the longer I looked at him, I couldn't shake a feeling of uncanny familiarity. He was conversing with a shorter, pot-bellied guy.

I clutched Daisy's arm, recognition setting in. "Good God—*that's Carl.*"

"Carl? Who's Carl?"

"The Captain's *cousin.*" Although he'd gained a bit of weight, his face was unmistakeable.

Carl chugged back the last of his bottle. Giving his friend a slap on the back, he was about to leave.

I strode across to where he was standing, as fast as my legs would carry me. "Hey—*remember me?*" I grabbed him roughly by the arm.

Carl backed up, like a spooked horse, his nostrils flaring. He attempted to shake free of my grasp, but I held on fiercely.

"Where's the Captain?" I snarled through clenched teeth. "I need to speak to him immediately."

"That's too bad, because he's not here." Again, he tried to push me off and continue toward the door.

I maintained my hold and dug in my fingernails. By now, Carl's buddy and a couple other men had turned to stare.

"If you don't talk to me about the Captain, I'll scream at the top of my lungs that he raped my sister, *you understand?*"

With a beleaguered groan, he whispered, "You've got one minute of my time, Khya, and not a second more. And lower your goddamn voice."

"Where the hell is the Captain?"

An embarrassed expression now crept over Carl's face. Something almost like shame, maybe. As he opened and shut his mouth several times, he seemed to be weighing how much to reveal. "He's… not been well" was all that came out.

"Is the Captain in the hospital? Did he hurt himself? Is that why he hasn't been picking up his mail?"

Carl shook his head, continuing to appear disheartened.

"*So?*"

"He's not been himself lately…"

"What the hell does *that* mean?" His cryptic attitude was infuriating.

"He… he's taking a break."

"A *break*? A break from what?"

"A break from life, I guess you could say." A strange, small snigger escaped Carl's throat and faded to a whimper.

"Is he even still here in Thurston Harbour?"

The man would neither affirm nor deny it.

I didn't have time for this baffling, stupid talk, only going around in circles. My head felt like a giant cowbell that wouldn't stop ringing, as if to remind me that Izzy's future was at stake.

"Are you aware that my sister is *pregnant*? That's right—your idiot cousin knocked her up! He needs to marry her, in order to give their child a decent life, *you hear me*?"

The man winced. But he didn't appear surprised by what I'd disclosed. A grim hunch took hold in my stomach: the Captain had received my letter from the peddler, weeks ago. His lack of reply had been intentional. He knew that Izzy was carrying his child and did not plan to come to her rescue. A putrid taste, far worse than disappointment, filled my mouth as I stared into Carl's ruddy face. It was like I was confronting a homelier, weaker-chinned version of the Captain. The family resemblance had never been more apparent.

"I don't know what to tell you…," Carl said, pleadingly. He squirmed away, like I was bullying him mercilessly.

It threw me off-kilter to see him like this. Was his distress just an act to get rid of me? I grabbed his arm again.

"Your sister's better off on her own, all right?" He jerked away, his eyes guilt-ridden and sad, and made for the door.

TWENTY-ONE

Daisy and I walked along the sidewalk in dismal silence, following Turner's lead. Apparently he had a friend willing to put us up for the night. But sleep was the last thing on my mind now. I'd told them both about my exasperating conversation with Carl, and they were just as perplexed as me.

"Maybe the Captain's gone funny in the head," Turner suggested. "He fought in Europe, right? We all know guys who've come back from the war not themselves. Drinking too much. Starting fights for no reason."

"But he was *fine* for all those months at Buckley," I retorted. "He was clear-headed enough to seduce my sister and turn all the white guys against my father and set the Japanese bath on fire, before skipping town."

"That's normal behaviour?"

"And that letter you sent to the Captain," Daisy said, musingly. "It must've come as a big shock to learn that Izzy's pregnant. The news could've put him in a bad way."

"Oh, yeah?" I jeered. "I doubt he's lost a wink of sleep over anything to do with my sister."

Turner stopped in front of a large dwelling, with colourful, patterned curtains in the windows. Out front was a sign that said in green letters: WAYFARER'S INN.

"You springing for a hotel?" I said, surprised.

His eyes sparkled for some reason. "Let's just say that I happen to be friendly with the owner, so my lodgings are always on the house."

Dazed at our good fortune for once, Daisy and I followed him inside.

How warm and welcoming the interior was. After spending days on that cold, damp boat, the orange glow from the fireplace was like balm to our senses. Daisy and I collapsed on armchairs in front of the blaze.

"Well, if it isn't the dapper Mr. Turner!" exclaimed a teasing voice behind me.

A big-boned brunette with fetching dimples had emerged at the reception desk. Although she was probably close to Turner's age, her smile made her look far younger, almost girlish. She was wearing a bright, flowered dress that matched the fabric of the curtains around her.

"And if it isn't the lovely Widow Stevenson," Turner replied, returning her friendly tone.

"You know what they say about widows…"

"What?"

"Good lord! There's no end of jokes about widows. A ribald lot we are."

After they'd indulged in a bit more banter, the widow led us to a room at the rear of her establishment.

I'd never been inside an inn before. The room was so inviting and attractive I was worried I was going to muss it up. On the double bed was a mauve blanket and the rug was a deeper shade of purple. And there was a fireplace here, too.

"You girls take the bed." Turner dumped his coat on a narrow sofa along the wall. With an air of unnatural casualness, he added, "The widow and I might catch up over a dram of Scotch before bed."

Daisy giggled. "We won't wait up for you."

The widow's eyes twinkled with flirtatious mischief. Yet when she saw me and Daisy staring at her, she straightened her shoulders and resumed an attitude of professional authority. Noticing how grubby we were, she added, "I'll fetch you gals a basin of hot water to wash up."

"Oh, thank you!" said Daisy.

A warm sponge bath sounded heavenly, just about now.

While the widow got us settled, Turner built a fire. Then at last they were gone, and it was just me and Daisy, perched on the end of the bed.

"A penny for your thoughts?" she said, breaking the quiet.

I watched the yellow flames lick the wood. "I can't forget what Carl said about Izzy being better off without the Captain…"

"Maybe he's right?"

I nodded. Then I shook my head, feeling desperate. "What'll my sister do with a Eurasian baby and no husband in sight?"

Even a terrible husband would be better than no husband at all. The thought disgusted me, yet there you had it.

"Get out of your damp clothes," Daisy said eventually. "You'll catch a nasty chill, if you haven't already."

I was only too willing to comply, after days of wearing the same coat, trousers, sweater, socks and boots, everything covered in layers of sea spray and melted snow. It was a relief to unburden myself of all that weight.

Huddled in front of the fire's glow, in nothing but my undershirt and knickers, I allowed Daisy to run a warm, damp cloth over my sore shoulders, neck and arms. Her gentle touch sent tingles up the nape of my neck and down through other regions of the flesh. She, too, had stripped down to almost nothing, and I was vividly aware of her pale, mottled skin shifting all around me. Her hair smelled at once salty and sweet, and I remembered the comforting weight of her head upon my chest, from the night when I'd acted foolishly. For a second, I regretted nothing about that night—nothing except my own cowardice in pulling away from her. Once again, I could feel her eyes grazing my body, as though her skin didn't even need to touch mine in order to bring forth this flickering sense of closeness, warmth. The area beneath my collarbones, where everything felt tangled in knots, seemed to be loosening slightly.

This time, it was Daisy who initiated it. Shyly, she looked into my face, like she was giving me time to jerk away. But when I remained stock-still, her eyes came alive and then her lips were covering mine and we might have been clasping on to each other, while falling very slowly down a black abyss.

At some point, the kiss reached its natural conclusion, and I could hear her soft, rhythmic breathing in my hair. We were immersed in a cloud of aromatic humidity. I wasn't sure what was supposed to happen next, or whether the kiss was going to make things awkward between us again.

But Daisy simply lay her head upon my chest, listening to my heartbeat. For once, the tightness that lived there was turning to water, to fluttering waves. I wanted to stay in this fuzzy-headed state forever.

Unfortunately, my mind soon veered back to other, far less pleasant things.

"What's it like at the Home?" I whispered.

I was curious about what Izzy was experiencing, what her daily life consisted of. Was she managing to adapt to the institution's dreary routines? Or was she terrified and unable to cope at all—plagued by worries about her baby's future?

"Not nice," Daisy said, after a lengthy pause.

"But beyond that," I said, hungry for details. "Where exactly in Victoria is it?" I wondered if, one day, I'd need to orchestrate Izzy's escape. Knowing the address would certainly be useful.

"It's on Cormorant, 100 Cormorant."

That was easy to remember. I only had to think of the bird.

"The street's a few blocks from Chinatown," Daisy added, sitting up and turning to face me. "Far enough away that the rich ladies—whose husbands fund the place—won't have to worry about getting robbed or raped on their way to board meetings."

I snorted, trying to envision what she'd described. "Is it just a bunch of snobs sitting around, sipping tea?"

"And eating scones. Don't forget that!" Daisy made an impish face.

I still couldn't quite picture this peculiar institution, which seemed to be half tea party and half prison. "What does the Home look like?"

She depicted a grey, three-storey house, the front door set behind a deep veranda, flanked by thick pillars. A brass knocker shaped like a lion's head adorned the door. The place sounded rather genteel to me.

But when I asked if she used to sit on the veranda along with the other girls, Daisy let out a scoffing grunt, like I had no understanding of their lives at all. They were not allowed to set foot outside, not even for a breath of fresh air. The front door was always locked and the backyard was surrounded by a high fence topped with barbed wire.

I swallowed hard, feeling miserable. Daisy wasn't making it easy to convince myself that if Izzy needed to stay at the Home indefinitely, she'd be okay.

"Why so quiet, Khya?"

I clenched my eyes, contemplating my sister's fate. The walls of my head were closing in on me. Was being the wife of a treacherous scoundrel better than spending her life rotting away at the Home?

TWENTY-TWO

A dim silvery light was bleeding in through the bottom of the curtains. The dawn of a colourless day. I sat up in bed, feeling panicked already, as I contemplated what the day had in store.

The sofa against the wall remained empty. Turner had found more comfortable accommodations in the widow's sturdy arms.

Daisy was still asleep beside me, and it was calming to listen to the ebb and flow of her breathing. And then she opened her eyes. Several times, she blinked at the ceiling, as though she'd forgotten where she was. I guessed that she probably found it strange waking up in bed next to me. It *was* strange. Strange and exhilarating.

But perhaps she felt otherwise and things would get awkward if we let our heads linger on these pillows, so I jumped up with a sense of purpose. I told her that we had to get a move on in our search for the Captain.

As we were heading out, we ran into Turner in the foyer. He looked more relaxed than I'd ever seen him, and the widow also appeared in good spirits as she hummed and bustled around behind the front desk, getting everything in order for the day.

"Did you sleep well?" I asked, approaching them.

Turner shot me a raised eyebrow, as though I was insinuating something lewd. "What are you girls up to now?"

"Got any ideas about where we should poke around for the Captain?"

The widow glanced up with interest. It was clear that Turner had told her all about what'd brought us to Thurston Harbour. "There's a canteen at the rec centre," she said. "That's where most loggers grab the first grub of the day."

I wondered if I might run into Carl again. I wanted to have another go at shaking him down for information. And breakfast did sound mighty good. Sadly, Daisy and I had no money.

As though she could read my mind, the widow pointed at a door off the foyer. "Right through there, I've got the best diner in town. As soon as my cook gets the grill fired up, I'll tell her that you gals eat for free."

Daisy and I thanked her heartily, as Turner hovered in the background. He said that he was going to make his rounds at camps in the area, in search of passengers for the ride back to Buckley. Sounding uncertain, he asked whether we'd be all right on our own for a while.

I didn't dignify the question with a response. Then Turner reminded us to stop by the post office in the afternoon and wished us luck. He said that Terry Fan was a good man, and Daisy would be lucky if he hired her.

✿

The men who streamed through the rec centre were far less friendly and willing to chat than they'd been last night, when their tongues had been loosened with booze. In the morning they moved briskly, just grabbing their food and paying. It came in paper bags that'd been preassembled and left out on a long table, with a cauldron of fragrant coffee at one end, making my mouth water. As they were chomping down on fried egg sandwiches, they were already in motion toward the door. Although Daisy and I tried to intercept them with our queries about Felix Godwin, all we got were curt head shakes.

After an hour of this, we were dispirited and very hungry. The canteen was closing up, all the food gone. The crowd had thinned to a handful of latecomers, who were out of luck.

We walked out to the empty street. Slowly we made our way back to the inn, under the sunless sky.

The diner was open by then. It was a narrow room containing five or six tables and a long counter, with tree stumps for stools. In front of the steaming grill stood a stout gal in a men's flannel shirt, her dark hair in a long braid down her back. A few loggers were standing about, awaiting their breakfast bags. Meanwhile, a pair of pretty, young women were chatting and drinking coffee; they were the only customers who'd bothered to sit down.

Smiling self-consciously, Daisy and I slid into the table next to theirs. They barely even glanced at us. The plumper girl appeared frazzled and busy with the baby squirming on her lap. Her friend, who wore bright pink lipstick, kept cooing at the infant, as if she was itching for one of her own.

There were more womenfolk here than in Buckley. It seemed like a good number of loggers had written to their wives and sweethearts and told them to hop on a boat out here. Perhaps after the war, Thurston Harbour was going to grow into a proper town, like Skeena had been for a time.

The gal with the braid strolled over to pour us coffee. "You must be the widow's friends," she greeted us, with a gap-toothed smile. As promised, the widow had told her to give us breakfast on the house. We said that we'd gratefully eat up anything she could bring us.

After she'd gone off, Daisy and I lapsed into quiet, still discouraged by our wasted time at the rec centre. It'd be good to get some food into our bellies. Hopefully, the nourishment would revive my brain.

At some point I came to realize that the young mother's agitated state had to do with more than just the stress of a cranky baby. She was talking loud enough for everyone in the room to hear and she didn't appear to care. Maybe she even wanted an audience.

"A madman is on the loose and no one knows damn all about what to do about it! For Chrissake, he killed his own *mother* and I don't care that she was no goody two-shoes, she was still his mother. If the government wants us to move out here and raise families, they need to *do something* to protect us."

Daisy and I exchanged stunned glances, our spines as straight as flagpoles.

"You're absolutely right," the other woman said, in a somewhat calmer voice. "According to my husband, the IMB has a wireless. They've used it to get word to the Vancouver police."

The IMB was the Imperial Munitions Board. From what I understood, it was part of the British government. They'd set up an office in Thurston Harbour, as well as another one close to Buckley, all for the purpose of buying up timber for the Allies' planes.

"*Ridiculous*," the young mom said, shaking her head in disgust. "We don't even have a mayor, let alone a police force! And those British bigwigs could care less if Jack the Ripper was on the prowl, so long as they get their hands on our top-grade spruce."

"Well, at least the police have been alerted. Maybe they'll send an officer from Prince Rupert?"

"That's a laugh. You think Prince Rupert's much better off than us? If the police send anyone, it'll have to be from Vancouver and that'll take days."

My thinking exactly. I breathed a sigh of relief.

"There's a retired policeman living not far from here. Didn't you hear? Rumour has it that he might step in."

The baby began crying, its wails going ignored. "Really? What d'you know about the man?"

"He's quite old, apparently."

"I wonder why he moved out here."

"Look in the mirror and ask yourself the same question, my dear!"

The two women burst into semi-hysterical peals. They looked at each other like they must've been crazy to venture out here.

"Apparently the detective's fond of birdwatching," mused the calmer woman. "Maybe that's what attracted him here, before the war. You get more interesting species than in Vancouver."

"He's from Vancouver? That's good! He'll be familiar with violent crime."

Vancouver was known to be our nation's most dangerous city. Murders and holdups were said to be weekly occurrences.

"He was the one who solved the case of that governess killing her charges. She was a real cold one—you could see it in her face, in her newspaper photo."

"A *female* killer?" Clutching her baby closer to her chest, the woman shuddered at this perversion of nature.

"She was sentenced to hang, not surprisingly."

"Amen to that!"

The cook was approaching us with big plates of food and a cheery smile, but Daisy and I failed to muster much enthusiasm. Our appetites had rapidly vanished.

❧

After leaving the diner we had nowhere to go, so we wandered up and down the main street, trying to keep a low profile. Daisy was more on edge than me. I kept reminding her that nothing had really changed—no one was investigating Mrs. Hill's death. Not yet, anyway. But Daisy kept swivelling her head, like she expected to find a team of coppers on her tail already. It was too risky to keep asking around about the Captain, she claimed.

Our queries about him had nothing to do with what'd unfolded in Port Clem, I pointed out. She shook her head, looking pale and ill, like she wasn't up to hearing my voice of reason. Finally, I went into a few shops on my own to speak with whoever would spare me a moment, while Daisy waited outside. Little good that it did. Thurston Harbour was a big, bustling place, where it didn't seem that shopkeepers knew the names of most of their customers.

In the early afternoon, we made our way to the post office. I was praying for some good news to lift our spirits. As soon as we walked in, however, Terry told us that his boss had been called away to deal with an emergency at another post office. Terry hadn't had a chance to chat with him about the matter of hiring Daisy.

Upon seeing our crestfallen faces, he said that he could pay us both to help out for the afternoon at least. "As you can see, the Christmas season's hit us hard." Indeed, the mountains of mail appeared to have grown even larger over the past day.

So Daisy and I set about sorting envelopes and parcels, according to Terry's instructions. Loggers who lived close to town picked up their mail, while those at outlying camps got it delivered. I was grateful to have something to keep my mind off other, more troubling matters. Many packages had been so battered in the course of their long journeys that they needed patching or rewrapping. I hoped that Terry could see how diligent Daisy was about this work, much more so than me. Hopefully, when his boss returned, he'd put in a good word for her.

In the late afternoon, when men got off work, the place became very busy. The line of loggers, their arms laden with last-minute Christmas presents and stacks of cards that should've been mailed out weeks ago, stretched through the door. It got to the point that Terry asked me to help him at the counter.

While I greeted customers, it couldn't hurt to ask if they happened to know a fellow named Felix Godwin. All I got were perplexed stares. When Terry appeared annoyed that I was slowing down the process, I let it drop. I had bigger fish to fry. For I hadn't forgotten about those mauve envelopes, addressed to the Captain, in the bin below.

Once the line had been reduced, Terry said that he was going to use the outhouse. As soon as he'd slipped out the door, I ignored the customer standing before me and dropped to my knees. I rummaged around, my pulse going like a piston. Thanks to their distinctive colour, it didn't take long to locate what I was seeking. I shoved the two envelopes down the back of my trousers.

When Terry returned, I forced myself to let several minutes go by, because I didn't want to attract suspicion. At last, I casually announced that it was my turn for an outhouse break.

The wind chilled my face as I darted around the side of the building. Both envelopes were tightly sealed, so it was futile to try to ease them open gently. Ripping one open with my sweaty fingertips, I extracted a sheet of mauve stationery.

> My Dearest Son,
> I feel I must write you dear altho I've had no reply from you in ages. I wonder how you are managing out in the wilderness and whether that poor leg of yours is still sore and troublesome? I should be so relieved to get a letter from you. But I'm sure you've written me several and they are just lost in the mail, the postal service being so new to the Charlottes. It's taking the mailmen out there some time to learn the ropes, I imagine.

Of course I know dear that I'll receive your letters soon, but the time seems so dull and grey without any word of you. It's just as wearying as when you were a soldier in France. I should be used to this not knowing feeling by now. If only your father were still alive, I would sleep much better. At least I have your little brother to keep me busy, tho he is no longer as sweet and obedient as he used to be. Yesterday, he told me he wants to go to the front, can you believe it? He's jolly quick on his bicycle and thinks that he could be of service to the Allies as a dispatch rider.

There has been a bit of embarrassing fuss over Nan Thompson this week. She continues to knock on our door, her eyes damp and swollen. She is hungry for news about you, tho I have none to give. I hesitate to tell you this because I know it must pain you that the poor girl has been in a bad way ever since you ended your engagement and stopped writing to her. I fear that she has been taking to the bottle! Altho it's not my place to lecture you and you know your own heart best of course, I can't help but wonder why you did what you did. Nan still strikes me as a devoted, kind girl, who would make a more than adequate wife. But you know your heart best, as I said. Far be it for me to force you to do right by the girl. I have said all on this matter that I plan to say.

Well dear I don't have much more to report now, so will close by saying that I know God will take care of you wherever you are. I put my trust in Him entirely. Don't worry about me because I am all right, just anxious to receive your letters.

Love from Mother

I read these words a second time. The looping writing appeared fragile and unsteady, reflective of the Captain's mother's apprehensive mood. It was spreading contagiously throughout my own chest.

So the Captain had been out of communication with his family for quite some time. His mother was right to be worried out of her skull. Why the devil had he dropped off the face of the earth? And he had a fiancée to boot! An ex-fiancée. Poor, spurned Nan Thompson. Clearly, my sister wasn't the first woman whose life this scoundrel had ruined.

Yet a small part of me couldn't help but hope that perhaps his loss of interest in Nan had coincided with his affair with Izzy. Had meeting my sister thrown his heart into disarray?

I opened the second envelope. This letter was much shorter and to the point.

> Dear Son,
> It has been months since I've had a letter from you. Your cousin Carl has not given me any response either. My worry increases by the hour! Since I know you'd not willingly inflict such torture on me, I can only fear that something terrible has happened to you.
>
> I plan to write letters to hospitals on the Charlottes and enclose your photograph. If I knew the name of the company that employs you, I would write them too. Yesterday I spoke to a kind officer at the Victoria Police Department, tho they claim there isn't much they can do, in wartime. Nevertheless, I will continue to hold their feet to the fire. Perhaps I'll have to draw from the nest egg your father left us and hire a private investigator. God only knows if I can find one willing to journey so far north. I trust that you will write as soon as you receive this letter— God willing—and put my bleak heart at ease.
>
> Love from your very worried Mother

I slipped the letters back inside their envelopes and pocketed them. Everything inside me was juddering madly. Was it possible that the Captain was *dead*? His poor mother seemed to think so. Yet based on how Carl had behaved when I'd confronted him, I didn't think that likely. I had the sense that he'd seen his cousin, not so long ago. Carl's caginess was due to some other reason, I suspected.

I had to get back inside. Terry would be wondering what'd happened to me by now. Briefly, I considered returning the mauve envelopes to where I'd found them, but decided against it, since they'd clearly been tampered with.

The line had gotten long again. While resuming my duties, I tried to act normal and ignore the stiff envelopes in my trouser pocket. I worried that Terry would somehow notice what I'd pulled and then Daisy would never get the job. But he was too busy greeting customers and licking stamps to pay much attention to me. He seemed to be well liked by many folks in town.

A whiskery old logger with a jowly chin leaned forward and rested his elbows on the counter, while Terry weighed his package. "So the ladies of this town have been kickin' up a fuss about this mother killer on the loose. I trust you've heard?"

Terry looked up from the scale. "Working here, there's very little I don't hear about."

"A bunch of us are headin' out tonight to search for the culprit—Angus Hill, I believe he's called. You're more than welcome to join us. It's all hands on deck."

A search party? *For Angus Hill?* I stopped moving, my face tightening in a hot mask.

Terry didn't seem terribly enticed by the invitation. "What makes you think that Angus Hill is hiding here, of all places?"

"Well, he's gotta be hidin' *somewhere*. And there are those caves in the woods, just north of town. You know, where the hobos set up camp. It'd be the perfect place for a fugitive to find shelter."

"That's where you're all going tonight?"

A gruff nod, followed by a mischievous grin. "You wanna tag along, Terry? It'll be fun to flush the bastard out. And he's got it comin'!"

"Thanks, but no thanks. I'd only be in the way. You fellas have our community's policing more than covered, I'm sure."

"Suit yourself." The man chuckled. "But it's gonna be a night to remember. That retired copper—Adler's his name—he'll be joinin' us."

"Good. I hope that you find the guy."

"Well, if ya change yer mind, we're gatherin' in front of the rec centre at eight. And spread the word, will ya?"

"Sure thing."

"Is everyone welcome to join the search?" I called out at the man's back as he was leaving.

Glancing back, he threw me a salute. "As I said, it's all hands on deck, kid."

❧

Once Daisy and I were back in our room at the inn, we saw that the widow had considerately left a plate of sandwiches on the dresser for our supper. Hungrily, we ate. I was relieved that Turner wasn't around, too busy enjoying the widow's company to worry about us. Because I had plans of my own, which I suspected he wouldn't approve of. I told Daisy about the search party setting out soon.

"You want to do *what*?" Her mouth full of food, she was looking at me like I was fit for the loony bin.

"It's our only hope. This retired detective—Adler—knows how to find missing people. That's what the police *do*, after all. So I want to talk to him about the Captain. Maybe, he'll have a hunch about the Captain's whereabouts—or provide some tips, at least. What's so crazy about that?"

"What's so *crazy*?" Daisy threw up her hands. "I don't know about you, Khya, but I'm trying to lay low, while I pray that Mrs. Hill's death blows over. Meanwhile, you want to walk right into—"

"It's better if we're not in the dark," I interrupted.

Her cheeks puffed out, her eyes flashing. "And what if you actually *find the guy*? Angus Hill will take one look at you—through his one good eye, thanks to you!"

"We're not going to find Angus Hill. The chances of that happening are very slim. He could be anywhere on the Charlottes. Or he could've even escaped to the mainland by now. This search party is just to give the women of this town some sense of comfort."

It pained me to see Daisy so upset, her sweet lips pressing together, quivering. And *I* was responsible for putting her in this state. What a beast I was! And yet the fact remained that this might be my only shot at finding the Captain.

"I don't expect you to come with me, of course. I'll go out with the search party and have my word with the detective and be back in no time."

"Khya," she said pleadingly, grabbing my wrist, "this is a *terrible* idea. Why won't you listen to me?"

But I wasn't in the mood to sit around all night doing nothing. I pulled free from her grasp. I grabbed my coat and charged toward the door, aware that it must be nearly eight already.

To my surprise, Daisy was also putting on her coat and shoving her feet into her boots. She wolfed down the rest of a sandwich.

"What are you doing?" I said.

"You think I'm gonna let you go on your own? If so, you really do have a loose screw."

TWENTY-THREE

A small group had gathered outside the rec centre. It'd started to snow, bright flakes thickening the air into a soupy vapour, swirling about everyone's heads. You could count them on one hand: five men, the whiskery fellow from the post office included. And now there were seven of us, as Daisy and I approached.

The men were talking about how the weather must've deterred a lot of folks. Evidently, Terry wasn't the only one who preferred to spend his evening warm and dry at home.

Daisy and I introduced ourselves, using our real names. After all, Terry already knew Daisy. If she was going to get the job at the post office, there was no point pretending that she was a boy named Ash.

I'd have felt safer if we were Ash and Del, because I didn't like the way the eyes of these men glided over our bodies. They took in our scruffy, unladylike appearances with curiosity.

"So you're adventuresses, are ya?" one of them said, with a snide grin.

"We're just a couple of citizens concerned about the community's safety, like the rest of you," I said firmly, so he wouldn't get any wild ideas.

"The more the merrier," the whiskery man said and beckoned us into the group. Though he didn't appear very merry. He was still sizing us up.

We began trudging along the sidewalk. Of the five men, three seemed rather drunk, the whiskery guy included. At least he was still able to walk in a straight line, his words slurring only occasionally. His name was Bob, he told us. The other two drunkards kept to themselves, passing a bottle back and forth amidst bellowing laughter, their feet heavy upon the snow, leaving big, predatorial prints. The fourth guy, by contrast, was quiet and slender. From something Bob said to him, I gathered that he was a shopkeeper in town.

I sidled up to the remaining man, who hung back at the rear of the group. His egg-shaped head had only a touch of silvery down, neatly combed back. "You must be Detective Adler?"

Those near-set, grey eyes appeared watchful and slightly amused, behind the glasses. Beneath his dark overcoat, the pale blue collar of a well-pressed shirt was visible. I couldn't remember the last time I'd seen ironed clothing.

"I retired a long time ago, so there's no need to call me detective. These days, I'm simply Joseph Adler, the name on my birth certificate. Which will one day—in the not so distant future—be the name on my death certificate, too." He said this like death was nothing to fear, almost something to look forward to.

Although he did appear old, he retained an air of alertness. He didn't look like he was on death's doorstep just yet.

By now we'd reached the end of the sidewalk. I could hear Daisy rustling anxiously behind me. The forest stretched out before us, like a wall of tangled knots.

"You wanna lead the way, detective?" Bob called back.

"You boys go ahead. I have a bad knee, so I have to take it slow."

I perceived no sign of a limp, however. Despite being on the portly side, Adler had a remarkably light tread.

We followed Bob and the others into the woods. The snow was coming down more heavily now. It must've snowed earlier in the day, too, because the ground was already blanketed in white and the dense conifers resembled fat ladies in billowy shawls. They glowed with a whiteness that verged on pale blueness, under the night sky.

"There's something I need to ask you, Mr. Adler," I said, scurrying along beside him. It was time to get to the point. "It's about my sister's fiancé. He left Buckley Bay and came out here some months ago. And now he appears to have *gone missing*. She's with child, you see, so the situation is of some urgency…"

As I talked on, elaborating my fears, the detective appeared more interested in the white wonderland all around us. It was hard to tell if he was even listening to me, while his gaze floated this way and that. Discouraged, I shoved my benumbed hands into my coat pockets.

"Is your concern that this man has abandoned your sister?" he asked eventually. "Or are you more worried that he can't return to her, because he's met a grim fate?"

It was a good question. Nothing was clear to me, the cold weather having worked its way into my skull. "Both things are on my mind," I blurted. "Yes, he abandoned Izzy in the beginning. But now I'm afraid that he couldn't do right by her even if he wanted to, because he's dropped off the face of the earth!" I told the detective about the letters that the Captain had neglected to collect from the post office. Naturally, I didn't mention that I'd stolen and read them, since Terry had emphasized that this was no small crime.

The wind picked up speed, boughs thrashing all around us. Snowballs plopped down upon our heads, and I heard Daisy softly cursing behind me.

"So where do you reckon we ought to be looking for Felix Godwin?" I said, feeling desperate.

Before the detective could reply, gales whipped around our heads, sending more handfuls of snow down upon us. As I was wiping cold wetness from my eyes, a big mound of feathery whiteness came down out of nowhere and swooped across into the cover of trees.

"A snowy owl," Adler said, his voice brimming with admiration. "They have the biggest brains of all birds, and their eyesight is far better than ours. It's no wonder that Athena chose the owl as her sacred pet."

Owls were frighteningly skillful hunters. I'd once witnessed an owl descend upon a smaller bird and swiftly kill it and swallow it whole.

My feet were soggy and cold, Daisy shivering beside me. Thanks to that owl, Adler appeared to have forgotten all about my query and was focused only on picking up the pace. In silence we made our way forward, following the drunken chatter ahead. At some point Bob and the others stepped off the main path. We traced their footsteps onto the snow-covered moss, overgrown with dead ferns and skunk cabbage, everything slushy and spongy, sinking beneath our feet. I suspected there was bog close by, but that wasn't my biggest concern. I had to be careful not to step into a sinkhole and hurt my weak ankle all over.

Branches rustled above my head. I wondered if that big owl was still up there somewhere, its bright yellow eyes tracing our every move. I peered out into the gloomy shadows, half-expecting a bear to be eyeing us hungrily through the trees.

"I feel like we're being followed," I whispered to Daisy. "Don't you feel it, too?"

She shrugged and clasped her arms around her cold body. Right about now, she was no doubt regretting that she'd insisted on coming with me.

Perhaps my jumpiness was simply on account of being tired at the end of a long day. What did we have to be afraid of here, anyway? Most likely, this evening was going to prove a waste of time.

The ground slanted downward, dramatically. Daisy and I backed up, astonished by what lay ahead. A small valley, lumpy with snow. On its other side, the bedrock rose sharply, punctured by many openings of differing sizes. They were caves, as abundant as the holes in cheese. Never before had I seen such a great number of them clustered together like this.

"Is that where the hobos live?" I said.

"A cave's not bad as a roof over your head," Adler replied.

Bob and the other three were already down in the valley, crossing its expanse. It startled me to see a dark thing in Bob's hand—had he pulled out a *gun*? And the other two drunkards also appeared to be armed! If they laid eyes on anyone resembling Angus Hill, would they shoot, without a second thought?

"How do they know what Angus Hill even looks like?" I demanded. "Has his picture been circulating?"

"Enough of these guys have visited Mrs. Hill's brothel, I'm guessing. And Angus Hill is known to be unusually tall."

His hulking frame flashed in my memory, his face suffused with hatred as he'd towered above me, his bloodshot eyes bulging like swollen boils. And now, he only had one eye to see through, thanks to me.

Daisy and I descended the steep slope, huddled around the detective. At one point, she lost her footing, but he effortlessly caught her by the elbow. I continued to suspect that his bad knee was but a fiction. Adler seemed rather nimble on his feet.

Up ahead, we watched Bob and his crew disappear into the mouth of the largest cave, a gaping, lopsided smile in the limestone. We followed in the same direction, with Adler leading the way. I wondered if he also had a gun on him. If so, he didn't take it out.

When we reached the cave's entrance, he turned to me and Daisy and said, with a rueful half-smile, that we'd best wait outside. It wasn't safe for us ladies. According to him, our job was to be on the lookout for feral animals and make sure that nothing menacing followed the search party in. What bunk! Daisy was all too happy to obey the detective's order, though. I released a hissing sigh through my nostrils, in no mood to argue.

After Adler had gone forward without us, I waited about a minute, maybe. Then I darted into the shadowy chamber, with Daisy scrambling behind to catch up and cursing me under her breath.

The floor was uneven and coarse with fragments of stone and strips of dead roots. The air was moist and fetid smelling, like too many homeless men had been freely relieving their bladders. Cautiously, we proceeded forward, into the narrowing space. Despite its generous entrance, which gave the illusion of a big cave, we soon found ourselves in something more like a tunnel, devoid of light. All we had to guide us forward was the faint hubbub of Bob and his men far ahead.

As Daisy's fingers clung on to mine, guilt kept gnawing at my innards. I shouldn't have let her come out here and throw herself in harm's way. She didn't want to be here—I could feel the terror in her icy fingertips. Should we turn back?

Yet the dark passage seemed to be widening slightly up ahead. The voices of Bob and the others were growing louder. A faint yellow glow, flickering unstably, lured us forward. It was Adler, I saw as we drew near.

He'd pulled out an electric torch, which was bathing the curved walls of the chamber in watery light.

Three very dirty, skinny men huddled in the corner. Their faces appeared incredibly pale and fragile, as though all flesh had melted away, exposing pure skeletal structure. Eye sockets. Cheekbones. Jaws. Purple shadows smeared out beneath their twitching, blinking eyes, which widened in trepidation as the louts on either side of Bob jumped about and made vicious screeches. They were mimicking apes or monkeys or some other creature of their drunken imaginations.

Meanwhile, the shopkeeper was cautiously approaching the hobos, trying not to scare them further. He had a sandwich in one hand and a thick book clutched in the other. After a second, I realized that it was a copy of the bible.

"So, you're a religious man, eh?" Bob said with a smirk. "That why you wanted to come here? You tryin' to save a few lost souls?"

Ignoring him, the shopkeeper edged closer to the cowering men and held out the sandwich.

"You here to take me off to the funny farm?" snarled one of the grimy faces.

"No, I'm here to offer you food and salvation, I hope."

As the shopkeeper thrust the sandwich forward, the man cringed and covered his head with both hands.

But the guy beside him tentatively reached for the food. He took a bite and grimaced in revulsion, before spitting a glob on the ground. "Can't you smell it…? Can't you *taste* it…?"

"Taste what?" said the third man, who appeared the cleanest and most lucid of the group.

"The taste of decomposing human flesh, of course!" Doubling over, he attempted to retch, but nothing beyond a cobweb of phlegm came out.

Adler, who'd been observing from the corner, cleared his throat, like he was calling a meeting to order. "Gentlemen, we're here on a matter of some importance. We need everyone's help."

"That's right." Bob stepped forward with an air of self-righteousness. "There's a murderer on the loose! His name's Angus Hill. We think he's hidin' out here, among you freaks. He's a big whale of a guy—ya seen anyone who fits this description?"

These rapid words were akin to machine-gun fire. The hobos jerked back, against the cave wall. Their heads ducked down, like they were instinctively seeking to protect themselves from more explosions.

"A murderer, I tell ya," Bob continued. "I'm not jokin'—this is serious business! For yer own sakes, you better spill the beans about where

Angus Hill is! Unless you want a murderer in your midst."

Far from encouraging the men to talk, this speech had just the opposite effect. One of the hobos clamped his hands over his ears, his head
receding into his neck. Although these men couldn't look more haggard,
they were actually quite young, I could see. They'd been soldiers not so
long ago, I suspected, and now grim memories of the war were haunting
them and driving them to madness. The never-ending blasts of treetops
being blown off didn't help, no doubt.

Two of the poor creatures started crawling across the floor on their
elbows, fighting to seek shelter within a flimsy tent. It was nothing more
than a couple of sheets tied to dead roots on the cave's ceiling. Bob's
pals—the drunken idiots—found this spectacle hilarious. The taller one
stormed over and demolished the tent in one swoop. The hobos let out
indignant sobs.

Yet they weren't all as helpless as they appeared. The cleaner guy,
who remained on his feet, was still capable of being roused to anger. He
lunged toward the vandal.

Jerking back instinctively, the man reached inside his coat—for his
gun. A shot went off and echoed deafeningly off the stone walls. It was
like a monstrous roar had surged up from the earth's belly.

It'd just been a warning shot. But the hobos released agonizing
moans, as though they'd all been hit by gunfire.

Before I could find out what was going to happen, Daisy was yank-
ing my arm with violent force. She desperately wanted to hightail it, so
what choice did I have?

Although she usually had a canny sense of direction, now she
seemed confused. In the darkness, we scrambled forward by instinct,
tripping frequently. Our hands traced the damp, jagged walls that con-
tracted and expanded without warning. This time, we had no chattering
voices or torchlight ahead to guide us, so we might as well have been
navigating blind.

"Khya, don't you have a candle with you?" Daisy called back.

How could I have forgotten? I reached inside my satchel and pulled
out the candle and matches I'd filched from Lester's bedroom. Everything around us flickered back to visibility, but what we saw was hardly
encouraging. The yellowy stone ceiling was so low that it nearly touched
my head, and poor Daisy had to bend her knees. Massive, craggy shapes
jutted out around us, allowing only the slimmest passageway up ahead.
We'd have to clamber and crawl over the rocks, keeping our heads low.
And where would that lead us?

"Good God, are we lost?" I stammered.

"None of this looks familiar," Daisy agreed, shrillness in her tone.

"We must've taken a wrong cut-off. These tunnels are all tangled together! Should we turn back and try to retrace our steps?"

Another gunshot went off. The echoing blast was a reminder that we hadn't migrated far from the mayhem. Not far enough.

Daisy tugged my arm, her eyes terrified. She pointed at a small stream trickling by our feet. "We'll follow it—it's bound to come out somewhere. Okay?"

I had no better plan so we slowly ventured forward, Daisy leading the way. It wasn't easy for me to hold the candle, while manoeuvring over the uneven rocks, on all fours at times. Soon my elbows and knees were badly bruised and bleeding. The humid, salty air, which smelled of rotting seaweed, filled my nostrils with a suffocating sensation. We were like a pair of injured otters, trapped within the bowels of the earth.

Finally, as the candle's hot wax was dripping off my hand, the passage began to open up. The ground seemed to be sloping downward, while the spring widened into a creek. We clung to the narrow bank, though our feet had long since become wet and numb.

Fresh air lay ahead. I could smell it as the ceiling rose and I could once again inhale and exhale, without fearing it might be my dying breath. The sound of the rushing water grew louder—joyous, almost. It echoed the feeling coursing through my own veins. When the rocks cleaved to reveal an opening ahead, Daisy and I squeezed each other's hands excitedly. We rushed forward, not caring if our feet got soaked all over.

The night air and rustling trees greeted my senses. The snow had stopped, and I stared up at the criss-crossing treetops and the black, borderless sky beyond. Daisy and I both dropped to our knees, overcome by pure exhaustion.

"What now?" I said at last.

"I guess we try to find our way back to town?"

Gingerly, we rose to our feet. And that was when we discovered that we were not alone.

Behind us, the limestone cliff revealed the entryways of several other caves. In front of one, a man was standing, watching us silently. Beneath the brim of his beat-up Stetson, he had a pair of ice green eyes. They settled upon my face, widening in amazement. Recognition.

I, too, was walloped by surprise. Could it really be *him*? The Captain's cheekbones stood out like two bent fishing rods, struggling not to snap under pull. Dirty shadows smudged the recesses of his emaciated face. But as he held my gaze, there could be no mistaking that familiar sneer.

My knees turned to jelly, my brain unable to grasp that I'd actually found the scoundrel. And then I was striding forward with speed, ready to give him a piece of my goddamn mind.

TWENTY-FOUR

A big part of me had been hoping to find the Captain gone batty, I realized right then. At least I'd have some explanation for why he'd never replied to my letter. But those cool eyes stared out at me with lucidity, their sense of superiority still intact.

"Khya...? Is it really you?"

Perhaps he wasn't all there in the head, after all. Did he think that I was a ghost or hallucination?

"What in God's name are you doing here, Khya?"

"I could ask you the very same question, you fool!"

"I'm taking a camping trip." He released a titter, which retained a trace of his old recklessness. "A man's still allowed to go on a long camping trip, the last I checked."

"You're talking *gibberish*," I spat, dizzy with fury. "How long have you been out here, living like a hobo? Izzy's in terrible trouble! Don't you care about her at all?"

The Captain lowered his gaze sheepishly. He removed his hat and stroked his head. I was taken aback to see that he was bald as an old man. Long red burns covered his scalp, where he'd shaved too roughly. His fingers scuttled over the damaged skin.

"I came here not long after I got your note from the peddler," he replied eventually. "Even before that, Izzy had been on my mind. I missed her awfully and regretted how I'd treated her... And then your note arrived. It threw me into a state! I needed to get away and think things through."

"So what happened?"

"Thinking about things led me to think about other things and I just couldn't stop thinking, so I never left."

"What's to think about?" I hissed. "Clearly, you need to marry my sister! If you don't, she and the child will have *no place in society*. Do you understand what that means? Who can say what'll become of them?"

On the edge of my vision, I was aware of Daisy looking like she wanted to vanish into thin air. It was an expression she often wore, and it never failed to stir my emotions.

"What makes you think that if I marry Izzy, her life'll be much better?" The Captain's thin, colourless lips twisted with affliction.

"Have you gone soft in the head? Of course, her life would be better, much better!"

"Would it, though?" The man looked up at me, at last.

How could he be so selfish, so cowardly? Clearly, he did have feelings for my sister. The prospect of deserting her with child had pushed him to this tormented, wasted state. And yet he seemed incapable of doing what needed to be done.

"I knew a half-breed once, when I was a kid," he said. "Danny was his name. He went to my school. We were friends... almost."

"So you see?" I leaned forward, trying to appear encouraging.

"I never knew that his mother was Oriental. Not till I ran into Danny on the street one Saturday. He was with this little yellow lady, clacking away to her in Chinese. He'd always told me and the other boys that he was a Spaniard and that was why his skin was tan. What did we know? He could pass as Spanish or Mexican to our eyes."

I didn't know what to say to this. A lump lodged in my throat. Meanwhile Daisy appeared sadder than ever, hemmed in by her own aloneness.

The first time I'd encountered her in the woods, how dumbfounded I myself had been to come across a Eurasian! How prejudiced and unfeeling I'd been, back then. It incensed me how she'd suffered all her life from endless scorn.

"You see, it's a lot easier if you're one thing or another," the Captain continued, still rubbing his scalp in agitation. "If I were Oriental, at least the kid would have some community to belong to. But a half-breed? My family would disown me! And your father and mother? You think they'll want anything to do with us? We'll all be outcasts—me, Izzy and the baby. We wouldn't even be able to walk around Chinatown without getting jeers!"

Daisy had clenched her eyelids. Her shoulders were shaking and her nose twitching, as she tried to hold inside shuddering sobs. I felt awful for her, but no words of consolation came to me. For what could I possibly say to make her feel better?

"Poor Danny," the Captain said, picking up where he'd left off. "After I told the other boys his secret, we teased him mercilessly. *Chinky chinky Chinaman sitting on a rail! Along came a white man and chopped off his tail!*" He chuckled callously, looking at me like he fully expected me to hate him.

I blinked hard, trying not to take the bait. Trying to keep focused on my sister's future. "So what are you going to do, you coward? Just hide out here forever? Starve to death?"

"Maybe. It'd serve me right, don't you think?"

"But what about Izzy and the baby?" Disappointment didn't begin to describe the emotions pummelling me. I reached into my pocket and thrust the mauve envelopes toward him. "By the way, your mother's mighty worried about you, too!"

The Captain didn't appear very interested, allowing the letters to fall to the ground. "She has my younger brother to tend to her now."

His uncaring attitude only infuriated me further. This man was of no use to my sister or any woman—he wasn't lying about that. I thought of the other girl he'd wronged, Nan Thompson. He just took whatever stirred his lust and left a trail of wreckage behind him. My head was throbbing dreadfully as I averted my eyes from his pathetic face.

A soft, intimate rumble rose above the sound of my own clipped breaths. It was as though a small creature was breathing, right within the cave of my skull! And then, I could feel her presence—a surge of angry heat, animating every part of my body—even though I couldn't actually see her. I couldn't see her, because she was deep inside me. My stillborn little sister, that was. She was protecting me, just as she'd done when Angus Hill had attacked me in Port Clem.

The Captain jerked back, his eyes flicking side to side, fearfully. He could see that I was not myself. Or rather, I was *more* than myself! Tripping backward, his arm shot out, his wrist breaking the fall. He let out a woeful yelp, though I failed to feel any pity for him.

"*You—you despicable fool.*" I crouched down next to his splayed body. At that moment, I felt it was within my reach to kill him with my bare hands.

He leapt up, in a frenzy. Although I hadn't laid a hand on him, he acted like he was under vicious assault. He scrambled off toward his cave, with me in pursuit.

But he had the advantage of knowing the space well, with no need of light. While I fumbled in my satchel for the candle stub and matches, he scurried into the cave's depths. I made my way in after him, lit candle now in hand.

In the dismal cavern, the Captain had cobbled together the barest of living quarters. The charred remains of a sloppily built fire greeted me. Farther inward, he'd set up his bedroom: an old red blanket had been laid overtop a cushioning of dead leaves. A fishing rod, a chipped blue bowl and a metal teapot were cast off to the side, along with a pile of rags or soiled clothing. The brittle leaves filled my nostrils with a mournful, ashy smell.

Above this sad arrangement a tarnished brass object dangled down from a string. It was swinging slightly, pendulum-like, tied to a dead root above. I discovered it was a compass. But it didn't work anymore. Regardless of which direction you turned it in, the arrow always pointed south.

I guessed that the Captain had hung on to it for sentimental reasons. Perhaps it was a reminder of another time, when things had had clear directions.

Seeing his meagre, unpleasant existence dampened my rage slightly. It was like the man was doing penance. He knew that he'd ruined Izzy's life and hurt her appallingly, but he couldn't figure out how to make things right. And now, I had no inkling of what to do either! I'd journeyed all the way out here on the assumption that the Captain had the ability to save my sister, yet it appeared that he was as much in need of salvation as anybody.

Daisy and I wandered in dreary silence toward the rear of the cave. There it narrowed into a slender burrow, occluded by rocks like enormous teeth. The Captain must've slithered in there to hide. Knowing how treacherous those crevices were, Daisy and I looked at each other wearily. Even if I could manage to corner the fool, what good would that do?

I released a growl—dangerously close to tears—and kicked at the wall.

Then Daisy took my limp hand and guided me out into the night air. Following her lead, we slowly found our way back to town.

TWENTY-FIVE

When I awoke, I actually believed for a hazy second that my encounter with the Captain had been a befuddling dream. But then the aches returned to my body—proof of last night's misadventures—and I watched sunlight seeping in through the bottom of the curtains.

My bad mood only intensified when I got out of bed and saw the note that Turner had left on the dresser. In tidy block letters, it conveyed that he'd found two passengers for the ride back to Buckley, so they'd be departing that very evening, after supper. The tides were good for sailing, Turner wrote. If I wanted a seat on the boat, I should meet him at the inn at seven o'clock sharp. In the meantime, he was going to spend the day trying to rustle up more passengers.

Daisy had woken by then. She sat on the edge of the bed, facing me groggily. "Is something wrong, Khya?"

I couldn't hold back a snort. "Gosh, I wonder? The Captain turns out to be a useless dunce, this whole journey has been a farce, and now Turner says that we're leaving this very evening. *So you and I are never going to see each other again.*" My voice cracked and I felt very close to blubbering like a small child.

"Oh, Khya…" Daisy cast me that lovely, sad smile of hers. Even though she remained across the room, I felt like our faces were so close that our noses were almost touching. She murmured, "Maybe we'll meet again one day, after the war? Didn't you say that your dad wants to open a restaurant in Vancouver?"

"Yeah, but what good does that do? You'll be here—working at the post office, hopefully—and I'll be in Vancouver."

"There are post offices in Vancouver. Maybe I'll prove myself such a good worker that I'll get promoted and sent to the big city."

A cartload of maybes. But it was sweet that the thought of never seeing me again distressed her, too.

"Well, what now?" I said weakly. "What are you going to do if I have to leave tonight? Where'll you even live? You'll not be allowed to stay here, with Turner gone."

Daisy looked at me reproachfully. "I'm not an idiot, you know. I chatted with Terry yesterday. He has enough room at his place. If his boss agrees to hire me, Terry says that we can be roommates."

I didn't like the sound of that one bit. While Terry wasn't at all handsome, he did have a pleasant, steady quality about him. I feared that it wouldn't take much for him to fall in love with Daisy, and then it might only be a matter of time before she'd warm to his shy, fumbling advances. Yet out in this lawless backwoods, maybe Daisy would only be safe having a man around for protection. Misery flooded my gut.

I continued to fret over whether our paths would ever cross again—whether she might stroll into my family's diner, one rainy afternoon in Vancouver years down the line—but I knew I was indulging in pure fantasy, too far-fetched to make me feel much better.

"How are you at letter writing?" Daisy piped up.

"Letter writing?" My frown lost a bit of its heaviness.

"I have to warn you," she said, blushing, "my spelling isn't great. But I'll try my best for you... Maybe the post office has a dictionary I can borrow."

Who could say whether I'd have a knack for pouring out my thoughts and feelings on paper? But for Daisy, I was willing to give it a try. That she and I had a means of remaining in contact lifted my spirits, a wee bit at least.

✤

After eating a late breakfast at the diner, we headed to the post office in hopes that Terry's boss would be back. I prayed that he'd offer Daisy employment. If not, I didn't know what to do. I certainly wasn't going to leave her in this town, without two pennies to rub together. She'd have no choice but to try her luck at the brothels, and the mere thought of that was too horrid to bear.

But Terry had no news for us. As soon as we walked in, I could see on his face that his boss was still away. The man would probably be back by the day's end, Terry speculated. He said that he'd been impressed with Daisy's efforts and would happily recommend that she be hired. Who knew whether that'd be enough to sway things in her favour, though. It upset me terribly that I might have to leave without knowing that she had a decent job.

Of course, I could refuse to get on Turner's boat, yet how would I ever find another way home? Mom would be in a state of franticness by now, terrified that I'd been kidnapped or raped or murdered or all three. And I wondered whether Dad had returned from Victoria and learned of my absence—in which case, all hell truly would be breaking loose.

I tried to put all this out of my mind and concentrate on just getting through the rest of the day. Terry said that we were welcome to roll up our sleeves and work, at the same pay as yesterday. I figured it might augur well for Daisy. Maybe when the boss finally got back, he'd walk in the door and the first thing he'd see would be Daisy nimbly wrapping parcels.

This time she assisted Terry at the counter, while I sorted mail off to the side. As my eyes skimmed names on the heaps of envelopes, I thought about those poor ex-soldiers living as hobos out in that cave. I imagined that some of these letters might be to them, from desperate sweethearts and wives and mothers. Like the Captain's mom, they'd be deranged with worry about why their letters had received no replies in the longest time. Perhaps they were right to fear the worst! Last night's gunfire lingered in my ears. Had Bob and his louts harmed some helpless soul? I felt like I should report the shots to someone, but the closest this town had to a police officer was Adler, and he was already well aware of what'd transpired.

I had bigger problems to worry about anyway. The Captain's anguished words hadn't faded from my brain. What'd made it all the harder to hear was that for once in his sorry life, he wasn't lying. Who could deny the grim road ahead for a Eurasian child, with parents whose races couldn't be more opposed? Where would such a family fit into the world? Would the poor child grow up having a single friend?

Still, the fact remained that Izzy's last hope lay in whatever protection this man was willing to offer. Even if the Captain refused to marry her, perhaps they could live like husband and wife in a rundown part of some big American city, where these mixed couplings weren't as rare? Though it'd be a hard existence, wasn't that what love compelled people to endure? And wasn't this the way things usually worked out in novels? I remembered how in the final pages of *Jane Eyre*, a voice mystically comes to the heroine's ears. It is Rochester calling out Jane's name, prompting her to return to him at last! That he's now uglier than ever—disfigured by the fire—makes no difference at all. He and Jane marry and begin a new life together. If it was possible for them, why not for the Captain and my sister?

Hopefulness thrashed about in my chest, my body willing my brain to believe that it could be so. With time, the Captain might come to see how much Izzy and the baby needed him. In confronting him yesterday, I'd planted the seeds. Soon, perhaps, regret would take root. Too late, he'd realize what a fool he'd been, kicking himself mightily. He'd want nothing more than to find my sister and make up for lost time.

My agitated hands continued to sort through mail while the dimming light outside the window made me all too conscious that late afternoon had already arrived. And that was when the return address on a certain envelope caught my attention. For some reason, the house number niggled at my brain, until another, similar address bobbed to the surface of my memory: 100 Cormorant Street. The location of the Chinese Rescue

Home. Blinking, I realized my oversight! The Captain would be utterly in the dark about where to look for Izzy, because I hadn't thought to tell him where she was. *The Chinese Rescue Home, at 100 Cormorant Street in Victoria.* It would've taken so little to drop this information. How could the man find my sister, if he had no inkling of where to search?

But it wasn't too late to fix this, was it? I had to try! Grabbing my coat in a fumbling rush, I mumbled some words to Terry about needing to go to the outhouse, though I had no intention of coming back in anytime soon. On second thought, I snatched a pen and paper off the counter, in case the Captain had strayed from his cave and I'd need to leave a note.

With that, I dashed out the door. I'd have to run as fast as I ever had, if I was going to make it back in time to board Turner's boat.

TWENTY-SIX

The woods stretched out, sprawling and formless. The sky had already dimmed to the first shades of twilight as I scurried along the path I'd travelled with Bob and the others, just yesterday. Now that the snow had mostly melted, the place looked starker, gloomier. Trees jutted up in mountainous tangles of branches, covered in infinite broom bristles.

It was easy enough to find my way to the caves where the hobos lived. *If* they still lived there. Perhaps they'd packed up and moved on, after Bob and his lunatic friends had put the fear of God in them. Whatever the case, I had no wish to enter that harrowing maze again. The challenge would be to stay aboveground and intuit my way to where Daisy and I had found our escape, a stone's throw from the Captain's hideaway.

Sound was my only friend. While trekking down into the valley— the sodden ground like a giant pillow beneath my feet—I opened my ears. I was listening for gushing water, trying to detect which direction it might be flowing, since the tunnel that'd expelled me and Daisy had contained a stream. But it probably wasn't the only vein of water in the area. Not by a long shot. I suspected that the bedrock was criss-crossed with underground creeks, all bleeding together. Although I could hear a muffled roar, it seemed at once nearby and faraway. Everywhere and nowhere.

The harder I strained my ears, the more disoriented I became, until all I could make out was the forest breathing heavily all around me, engulfing me in its mysterious sighs.

At the base of the valley, I beheld the slanted limestone, dauntingly steep. I began to hike around the perimeter, praying that I'd eventually stumble upon the Captain's hideout on the other side.

I rehearsed in my head what I might say to the man. "One day soon, you're gonna come to your senses and realize what a cruel halfwit you've been!" Then I wondered if a gentler approach would be better, since the Captain seemed in a fragile state. "My sister and the baby *need* you, don't you see? If you abandon your own flesh and blood, you'll regret it to your grave. Oh sure, it won't be easy, with folks being so prejudiced and all. But that's why the child's going to require your protection more than ever, can't you see?"

I tripped on a root and slammed to my knees, pain shooting up into my thigh bones. The murrelets hurtling high in the treetops didn't help the dizziness in my head. Swiftly, evening was descending, the air darkening to swirling murk. The ground was bumpy with big tentacles stretching out from the bases of multiple trees. I'd have to be careful not to fall again and crack my ankle. Although I was hungry for more light, my candle had been reduced to a tiny stub and I'd need it to find my way into the Captain's cave.

It served me right to be stumbling around all by myself. Poor Daisy! She'd be frantically worried about me by now. How would she feel that on our last evening together, I'd run off without so much as a word of warning or farewell?

Yet if I'd told her about where I was going, she'd have insisted on accompanying me. All her good work at the post office risked being erased, if all Terry remembered was that she'd walked out partway through a shift. And she needed his backing to get that job.

A strange, shivery feeling slipped over my skin, pulling me out of my ruminations. Craning my neck, I felt I could detect a creature nearby. I recalled the skin-crawling sensation I'd had yesterday, like I was being watched. This time, however, I didn't sense eyes upon me—it was just this niggling intuition that not long ago, someone else had tread along this very path. A bear? A human? Was I getting close to the Captain's lair? Was I about to walk right into him, while he was out foraging for his supper?

Into the gloom I blinked, like I was peering down an unlit corridor. But the Captain's pallid face failed to take shape before me. All I could make out were trees and more trees, and as I slowly advanced, everything suddenly solidified into a dark wall.

A bizarre configuration, it was. It appeared that many, many years ago, an enormous spruce had fallen to the ground. From its rotting carcass, countless new trees had taken seed and shot up—their roots and branches all blurring together in tight embrace.

It took me a long time to get around this barrier. Once I'd finally emerged on its other side, I'd lost all sense of direction, because the monstrous knotted thing blocked all view of anything that could help orient me.

Then a splotch of mauve light broke through the treetops. It illuminated a wan face in the distance. My heart took flight, as I thought it must be the Captain! But when I called out to him and he turned toward me, I could see that it was not him.

This man was shorter, slimmer. His hair was black as pitch. While I remained still as a rock, he started walking toward me.

I lurched back, as his face lost all vagueness—clear as a full moon. It was Dice. Good God! I'd forgotten all about him being here in Thurston Harbour.

"Something upsetting you, Khya? You look like you've seen a ghost."

"I… I just thought that you'd probably gone back to Buckley by now."

"Forgot all about me, did you?"

"Hardly."

He could tell I was lying, no doubt.

"I thought you were supposed to be off touring mills, gathering information about the latest types of machinery," I said, sticking my chin out.

"I finished early." Dice stroked the side of his face.

I noticed then that he had several thin, red scratches running down one cheek. The blood looked bright and fresh.

"Did an animal attack you? And what are you doing out here, anyway?"

My confused state seemed to amuse him. He looked at me like he'd been expecting me to be quicker on the uptake.

"Did you honestly believe that I was going to let that man's crime go unpunished?"

"Where…?" Panic pooled in my gut. Though I wasn't sure what my instincts were telling me. "The Captain. Where *is* he?"

Dice was in no hurry to answer. I tried to push past him, but he blocked my path. "You'll be happy to know that you were actually a great help in leading me to that villain's hiding place."

"Whatever do you mean?" I snarled, perilously close to tears.

"I have no photograph of Felix Godwin, and I've never even met him. So, how to find and identify the man? Asking around at places like the rec centre—as you and Turner did—was one option. But it had the disadvantage of calling attention to myself. If anyone ever comes looking for him, people might remember that a stranger of my description was trying to track him down, too."

The wind nipped at my skin, my teeth chattering. "Okay…? Well, what did you do?"

"You were desperately seeking to locate the Captain, too. At first, I was doubtful that you'd get very far. Then I realized that by following you, you just might lead me to our target."

It'd been Dice who'd been trailing me yesterday in this very forest, stalking my every move. He'd followed me and Daisy into the caves and tunnels, or he might've remained aboveground, listening carefully. Eventually he'd have heard me shouting at the Captain, and my raised voice had guided Dice to exactly where he wanted to be.

"What… what did you *do* to him?" I searched Dice's face, which bore a trace of schoolboy mischievousness.

He leaned back against a tree. "That man—the Captain, as you still call him—proved himself to be anything but in command. A snivelling, feeble-minded idiot. As every *hakujin* turns out to be, in the end. He got exactly what he deserved!"

The Captain was in such a frail state already. If Dice had beat him within an inch of his life, he wouldn't easily recover! On the other hand, the red lines on Dice's cheek suggested that the Captain had managed to put up a decent fight. Was he all right? Or was he curled up—bloody and half-dead—on the floor of his cave?

Taking advantage of Dice's relaxed stance, I darted away from him into the shadows, my heart thumping in my throat. The trees were thinning up ahead, and in the gloaming my eyes fastened upon the entrance to the Captain's hideout.

I dashed inside and fumbled to light my candle stub. "Where *are* you?" I cried out, my voice echoing. "Are you hurt? Don't be afraid—it's just me, Khya."

No response. I couldn't detect the rustling of a bruised body, not even a soft moan.

I advanced into the space, my candle sending ripples over the walls. The Captain's sleeping area looked no different than it had yesterday; the red blanket was laid neatly over the pallet of dead leaves. But there was no sign of him at all.

I was fingering the compass that hung down from the ceiling, when I became aware of a figure behind me.

Sadly, it was just Dice. Strolling in a leisurely manner, he was smoking a cigarette.

"What happened?" I cried. "What did you do to him?"

The string came loose, so I now held the tarnished brass object in my shaking hands. It felt impossibly heavy, as I watched its useless arrow point undeviatingly in one direction.

"It had to be done," Dice said flatly.

"You killed him, didn't you?" I whispered, horrified.

He smiled slightly, through the smoke cloud. "It was a matter of honour. Your father's honour had to be restored."

"Did Dad ask you to do it?"

"He didn't need to. But I'm sure he knows why I came out here."

My shoulders began to tremble, my eyes stinging. I buried my face in my hands. Guilt washed over me, an indelible stain. It was as though I'd had a hand in the killing, by leading Dice to the Captain, however unwittingly.

"This is why girls will never be admitted to the Black Ocean Society," Dice said with disdain.

The barb hardly even registered. I had other things on my panicked mind. "Is someone going to find the Captain's body?"

As my eyes flitted across the ground, it wasn't hard to see a band of deep ruts in the dirt and gravel. Not long ago, a corpse had been dragged out. My eyelids clenched, my brain seeking to cling to oblivion.

"He's found his final resting place in the bog. He's not the first man and he won't be the last to join that soupy grave."

"The Captain was going to come around," I cried, tears clogging my nostrils. "He loved Izzy—*I could see it in his eyes.* Given time, he would've come around and married her, for the baby's sake! I'm sure of it. But now... *now...*"

"Now," Dice said calmly, "now, we return to Buckley. Your parents are bound to be very worried about you."

I jerked away from him. "I'm not going back with you! Frank Turner's giving me a ride tonight."

"Yes. And from what he's told me, our boat's leaving very soon, so we'd best get going."

So Dice was one of the other passengers Turner had mentioned. Of course he was. The thought of spending days on a boat with this murderer turned my innards. I wanted nothing more than to run deep into these woods, but where would that get me? And if I refused to cooperate with Dice and keep our terrible secret, would I be next to find my final resting place in the black bog?

"Come along, Khya," he said with briskness. "You seem confused, but don't worry, I know the way back. You'll feel much better once we're away from this place."

While keeping my distance, I let Dice guide me out of the forest. At some point, I realized that I still had the broken compass clutched in my palm. I shoved it into my pocket. Perhaps years down the line, when Izzy and I were both old women on our deathbeds, I'd give it to her and tell her everything—the real story of what'd happened to the Captain and why she'd never seen him again. It wasn't because he'd abandoned her and the baby without a second thought.

When Dice and I reached the main street, I could tell by the sky's sombre colour that it was well past seven. And then Frank Turner was storming down the sidewalk toward us, telling us off for being late. Dice grabbed my arm—with more force than necessary, as if to remind me of the dark secret we shared—and I let myself be pulled forward, limp as a rag doll.

As I kept my eyes down, someone scampered up beside me. A warm hand clung on to my one free arm, refusing to let go. *It was Daisy.* I broke away from Dice's grasp and turned to face her. Her eyes were imploring and swollen, like she'd been weeping, and it filled me with despair to know that I was responsible.

"What happened to you?" she demanded, her sadness shifting to anger.

"I'm sorry," I mouthed, barely able to find my voice.

"Are you *all right?*"

Although I gave a quick nod, it must've been quite clear to her that I wasn't all right. *Nothing* would ever be all right again. Her bewildered eyes bored into mine, insisting upon answers, though I had none to give.

Dice yanked my arm forward, and I was almost grateful for the shooting pain. As I let myself be dragged away from my sweet Daisy, I whispered back the feeblest goodbye. I wondered if I'd ever see her again, the gulf between us growing wide and unbearable already. Looking over my shoulder, I watched her face grow smaller and smaller, until it was nothing more than a pale blotch of light.

Twenty-Seven

Without any fog, the journey only took a couple days. Down in the cabin, I slept for most of it, too exhausted to be on edge anymore. The worst had already happened. The Captain was at the bottom of a bog, and Daisy and I would never see each other again. It was better this way, perhaps, because how could I ever look her in the eye, while withholding such a terrible secret?

So there I remained in the boat's underbelly, hiding in the shifting shadows. In addition to Turner and Dice, there was a stout, jowly peddler aboard, and he came down to join me occasionally for gassy naps. But for the most part I was alone. I claimed to be seasick, in need of rest. Upon the bed where my sweet friend had lain, I buried my nose in the musty pillow, in hopes of detecting a faint whiff of her skin. I could smell nothing, though. Nothing except the foul stench of my own misery and filth. As the voices of the men on deck rose and fell in muffled waves, I prayed that we might capsize and be swallowed by the ocean.

It was evening when we arrived at Buckley. Frank Turner called down that we were nearing our destination, so I'd better pull myself together and get ready to face my father. He chuckled grimly, like if I were his daughter, he'd give me what for. Yet not even the prospect of Dad's wrath was enough to rouse me out of my miserable state.

The next thing I knew we'd stopped moving, were merely floating. As I ascended the stairs the air chilled my face, my breath coming alive in ghostly plumes. Everything looked rather different, somehow: the dock, the beach, the looming forest beyond. It was as if I'd been gone a lot longer than seven or ten days or however many it'd been. But it was hard to pinpoint what had changed in my absence. It wasn't a matter of snowfall—not even a dusting covered the sandy ground. It was something else, like the air itself had turned gloomy. Everything appeared tainted by a sense of hopelessness and impending doom.

And then the disaster was right before me, unfolding in front of my eyes. While hesitating on the dock, I watched the men light cigarettes on the beach. Before I knew it, Dad had appeared out of nowhere. His back to me, he was talking to Dice. Then my father's head swivelled toward me, his face pale and luminous with fury, but Dice grabbed his arm, in restraint. Whatever he whispered, it caused Dad to halt, the lividness draining from his expression.

They were conferring about the Captain's death, I suspected. Dice was telling my father that I knew what'd happened, that I might as well have witnessed the killing. So Dad should go easy on me. This seemed to be what Dice was conveying as he relaxed his grip. Because when my father looked back at me a second time, the anger and self-righteousness had been extinguished. Instead, there was something surprisingly close to pleading. *Don't ever try to talk to me about Thurston Harbour,* was what his gaze appeared to warn.

A burst of his violent temper was what I'd been expecting—hoping for, even. That would've maybe put me in my place and restored some normalcy to our family. But now, only uncertainty trembled in the air.

It was like Dad was seeing me anew, as a stranger. Like he wasn't sure that he could trust me, at all.

❦

Mom had aged ten years since I'd been gone. It was a shock to see her so haggard, as I stood in the doorway of our cottage. A hoary wisp framed her forehead, her skin drab and weathered. What'd happened to my pretty, genteel mother, the samurai's daughter? How had she vanished overnight?

When Mom caught sight of me, her eyes widened—crazed, terrified. It was like she believed me to be a ghost, here to confirm her worst suspicion that I was dead! But then her eyes turned hard and cold, reason setting in. She was striding toward me, one hand already raised in the air, as if striking me was the only way to prove that I was real.

Although she hit hard, more than once, the blows barely even registered. For I knew in every nerve of my body that I deserved so much worse.

Soon a high-pitched shrieking from the corner caused Mom to turn still. It was May, her face shiny with mucus and tears. As Mom stepped back, my little sister ran toward me and buried her sopping nose in my chest. She clung to me like our lives both depended on it, her hot tears quickly seeping through to my flesh. Guilt battered my conscience—what a dreadful sister I was! Until now, I hadn't thought about May at all and what my disappearance would do to her.

For the first time in a long while, I took a good look at her. Her face was losing its roundness and her front teeth had fully grown in. I realized with a start that she must be eight now… Or was she actually nine? Celebrating our birthdays had fallen by the wayside during the war.

Thankfully, May was still young enough not to hold a grudge. While Mom gave me the silent treatment, she seized my hand and wanted to know everything.

"You went to find Izzy, right?" she whispered excitedly, pulling me over to the sofa. "So, did you find her? Where *is* she?"

I shook my head, wondering how much I ought to disclose. "Izzy's in Victoria, at a home for pregnant girls, but that's not where I went. I was trying to locate the Captain, in order to tell him about our sister's predicament. I was hoping he might come to his senses and marry her."

"Oh." May's eyes flitted this way and that, while she processed my words. "And did you find him? Will he marry Izzy?"

"I *almost* did…" Something caught in my throat, a bitter glob of failure. It was Dice's fault. If he hadn't taken matters into his own hands, things could've turned out so very differently.

"You didn't find the Captain, in the end?" May looked at me with disappointment.

"Sadly, he got away from me."

"Maybe after the baby's born, you'll go back to look for him again?" She bit her lip, still trying to sound hopeful. "I'll go with you this time."

"That… that's a lovely thought."

"Don't cry, Khya." May used her sleeve to wipe at my eyes. I hadn't even realized that they'd started to drip.

Then she was hugging me again, attempting to console me with plans for another adventurous journey to save our sister. In May's innocent mind, it wasn't too late for Izzy to marry her sweetheart and give her baby a wholesome life.

"Look what I found," she said brightly, seeking to cheer me up. When she dropped to her knees, she slipped a hand beneath the sofa.

What May extracted was a flat, tin box, rusty and battered. Inside was an array of pebbles, seashells, twigs and long-dead flowers, decaying to sepia dust. It took me a moment to recognize the sad remains of the Captain's courtship. Izzy had hidden it all away for safe keeping, and here it remained, even after his death.

As I touched the smooth surface of a lovely black pebble, I felt a twinge of closeness to Izzy. I remembered her conviction that through a spell she'd cast over these objects, a malevolent spirit had been unleashed and taken up residence in her womb. And then she'd come to believe that the same spirit had turned into her baby's protector. I hoped that she still felt that way, because who, if not a compassionate ghost, did she have to rely on now?

I was in a similar boat, much as I didn't like to admit it. My stillborn sister's tiny, unformed face flickered, like a memory of a dream. If I stilled my body enough, I could hear her faint, tinkling laughter, fleeting as raindrops… Whoever or whatever she was, I needed her to stay nearby and give me the strength to carry on.

Twenty-Eight

Although Mom still wasn't speaking to me, she allowed me to resume my chores in the kitchen. In silence, I butchered meat and peeled potatoes. She'd already made clear that she didn't plan to answer any questions about how Izzy had gotten settled at the Home. But maybe Mom was as much in the dark as me; Dad could've told her nothing. For all I knew he'd left my sister on the Home's front steps, without so much as a word of farewell.

For the most part, Dice and I managed to avoid each other. While other folks had their supper in groups, he kept to himself, as had always been his custom. On the rare occasions I ran into him during the day, he'd briefly block my path, with a tight, complicit smile—a reminder of what we'd done. My skin never failed to pimple with goosebumps, my stomach churning in revulsion.

But Dice was too busy with a new project to waste much time tormenting me. He was building a cabin right behind our cottage. Every evening, he and Dad were fast at work out in the twilight, sawing planks into floorboards.

It chilled me to think about Dice living in such close proximity. Why did he have to be so nearby? Was it because he never wanted me to forget that he had an eye on me? And why did Dice need a whole cabin to himself, when he'd been content to bunk with other loggers until now? When I questioned Dad, he just looked at me flatly and told me to mind my own business.

And so I did. In my spare time I took long walks along the beach, Daisy never far from my brain. I wondered how she was making out with her new life in Thurston Harbour, and I prayed that she hadn't forgotten about me already. Though I desperately wanted to write her a letter, there was nothing of consequence that I could report, and I had no money for postage anyway. Until I managed to work my way back into my parents' favour, I'd have no pocket money for anything.

From time to time, I ventured along the sand in the direction of the white tent. There it still was, phantom-like and yet all too real, peeking through the trees and shadows. I couldn't bear to get too close. Even on the coldest days, a handful of young girls could be seen playing out on the sand; their hair caught the sun brassily. The older ones smoked cigarettes, chins perched upon knees, staring out at the relentless grey waves.

❧

The town now had a proper post office at the rear of the general store, which had expanded to stock a wider variety of goods. Whenever Mom ran out of sugar for her coffee or cornstarch to thicken her soup, she'd send me into town, with just enough money to cover what she wanted. So there I was browsing the shelves one afternoon, even though I'd already made my purchase. Longingly, I gazed at all the tins of cookies and jars of hard candies, wrapped like tiny presents in shiny paper.

"Khya, dear," a voice said, pulling me out of my abstracted state.

My eyes widened, taking in the figure by the door. It was Joseph Adler—the detective—looking out at me from behind his foggy glasses.

As he approached, his face shone warmly, like we were old friends. "Fancy running into you here!"

"What the dickens are you doing in Buckley?"

He didn't seem offended in the least by my bluntness. "I'm staying across the inlet at Port Clements, while looking into Mrs. Hill's murder."

"Oh...?"

Adler explained that the Vancouver Police Department had begged him to come out of retirement to investigate this case. He made a face, as though they'd really had to twist his arm. "It's wartime, so we all must pitch in and make sacrifices, I suppose."

The heat refused to drain from my cheeks as I stood there, still startled. "So... you're in charge now? Well, how's the investigation going?"

"My job would be a heck of a lot easier if the crime scene had been left intact. But that's too much to ask for, after all this time. The man who owns the pub scrubbed the kitchen and rounded up a couple buddies to bury Mrs. Hill's body the day after her demise."

"He didn't want it to stink to high heaven, I guess."

"That's exactly what he said. Poor guy. A murder in his kitchen's the last thing he wants to deal with. And now I'm lodged in a room right above, if you can believe it! The place doubles as the best inn in town, or so I'm told."

"*What?*" I froze up. An image of the room where Daisy and I had been held captive flashed in my mind. "You're staying at Ewan's inn?"

"Ah yes, I believe that Ewan is the man's name." Adler was watching me very closely, taking interest in my unsettled reaction.

It dawned on me then that his friendly prattle was perhaps a means of fishing for information. I was going to have to be more careful.

"So you're familiar with this Ewan character?" the detective said casually. "I'm not surprised."

"Oh? And why's that?" My shoulders stiffened.

"Well, when I interviewed folks who work at the pub, there was mention of two girls fitting the description of you and Daisy. Apparently, you were there the day before the murder?"

Too many questions were crowding my frantic mind. Who had Adler talked to already? *What did he know?* I continued to doubt that Ewan and Irene would say much about me and Daisy, out of fear of implicating themselves in criminal activity.

"Bobby mentioned us?" I blurted, without thinking.

"Bobby. Ewan's son. So you know him, too." The detective's voice bore no surprise, like he already knew this. "Yeah, Bobby's a good egg. He's been much more helpful than his father."

As he resumed watching my face—noting every twitch, every perspiring pore—it occurred to me that this run-in was probably not a matter of chance. "Did you come here *looking* for me?"

"Well, it's only a short boat ride across the water, and someone was kind enough to lend me a canoe. Perfect timing to find you here at the store."

"So what d'you want to talk to me about?"

Adler threw off a lazy shrug, like he was more than happy to let me lead the conversation and didn't want to intrude on my thoughts.

"Well...," I murmured uneasily, wishing to say as little as possible. "Daisy and I stopped at that pub for a bite of breakfast. Then we continued on from there. We were in a hurry to get to Thurston."

"You didn't by any chance have a nap first?"

So Bobby had seen Irene leading us upstairs. What else had he told the detective? "Um, yeah, I forgot to mention that."

"You rented a room?"

I nodded.

"That's strange. When I checked the inn's account book about the day in question, I saw no record of any guests making payment."

"We just wanted to rest a few hours. The barmaid let us have the room on the house."

"Is this barmaid, by any chance, named Irene?"

I nodded, feeling dizzy. I didn't like how Adler was always a step ahead of me. "She... she's a friend, of sorts." I felt certain, by Adler's face, that he'd already heard plenty about Irene and her erratic behaviour. "You chatted with her, too?"

"I couldn't, because she's vanished. Ever since Mrs. Hill's murder, no one's laid eyes on the woman. When you spoke to her, was she acting unusual in any way?"

"Irene's always kind of strange. Too much drink." I tapped the side of my head.

"Any ideas about why she would've skipped town?"

"You're the detective!" I jutted my chin out, while picturing the poor woman hiding like a wounded animal in the woods. Then I remembered what she'd done to me and Daisy, and my sympathy rapidly faded. "Maybe Irene attacked Mrs. Hill and ended up killing her? That's a good enough reason to hightail it, don't you think?"

Adler pursed his lips, his eyes not straying from my expression. Suddenly his face appeared as predatory as a hungry owl's. "So, after you and Daisy had rested a few hours, what happened next?"

"We left, without saying goodbye to anyone. We trekked onward to Tlell."

"You departed through the front or back door?"

"Uh… the back door."

"You must've walked past the kitchen. Did you by any chance see this girl?" Adler reached into his coat pocket and extracted a small photograph in a gilt frame.

It was an image of two young women in a sunny park or backyard. Their elbows linked, as they smiled with closed, painted lips into the camera. They looked like they could be sisters almost, their hair pulled up in identical buns, with a few stray curls. Yet the taller, less pretty one had an asymmetry to her face, an askew nose—I jerked back. *It was the kitchen maid*. Her bright, unflinching gaze stared out at me, with the same intense energy I recalled from our encounter. There could be no mistaking that this was the same girl.

Instinctively, I shook my head and averted my eyes.

"You sure you don't recognize the bigger girl?" He continued to thrust the image under my eyes.

I swallowed hard, striving for a tone of innocent bewilderment. "Should I? Who *is* she?"

"A newcomer to town. She worked in the pub's kitchen the past few months. Gretchen Smith is the name she's been going by, but it turns out that isn't her real name."

"Oh? How do you know that?"

"Because we searched her room at the inn. She was boarding there, in a space off the kitchen. When she fled, she left behind everything— her clothing, her birth certificate, this photograph. According to her birth certificate, her real name is Anna Lydia Iacono."

"She *fled*?" My bowels were tightening in knots.

The detective gave a quick nod. Before I could catch my breath he whipped out another photograph. My chin pulled back, as I was forced to behold Angus Hill's hateful face, brimming with lechery and poison.

"How about this fellow? You recall seeing him at the pub?"

I shook my head, while biting the inside of my mouth.

"You sure about that? You seem startled to see him."

I pretended to look again. "No, I've never laid eyes on the guy. He just looks so mean—like he'd be capable of murder. Is he a suspect?"

"He's Mrs. Hill's son, Angus. And yes, he is a dangerous man."

"Well, have you apprehended him?"

"Unfortunately, like the maid, he's also been quick to leave town. After Mrs. Hill expired on that kitchen floor, it seems that three people headed for the hills: Angus Hill, Irene, and Anna Iacono, alias Gretchen Smith. Any one of them could be guilty of murder. So you see, no easy task lies ahead of me."

I couldn't help but feel a twinge of relief that Adler hadn't named me and Daisy in his list of suspects. But the thought that Anna Iacono or Gretchen Smith or whoever she was might take the fall disturbed me to no end.

"There's any number of reasons why a woman might change her name," I said, as calmly as possible. "It doesn't mean the maid's guilty of anything."

Adler's lips pressed together, in a doubtful squiggle. "Whoever she is, we'll find out soon enough. According to her birth certificate, she's from Vancouver. My friends at the VPD will provide any help I ask for."

I gathered that Adler's next stop would be the IMB office, from where he was planning to telegraph the Vancouver police. If the poor woman had ever had a run-in with the law, he'd soon find out. With a satisfied smile, he reached into the nearest candy jar and helped himself to a generous handful.

Twenty-Nine

I wasn't surprised that the maid had flown the coop. I pictured her standing in that humid kitchen, in the seconds after she'd urged me and Daisy to run, the rolling pin strangely weightless in her hand. Anna Iacono would've been faced with two bodies on the floor—panic setting in. Perhaps she could already tell that Mrs. Hill was done for, the greyish-yellow hue of death transfixing her skin. With me and Daisy no longer present, Anna had no need to keep up her brave performance of being in command. Suddenly, she'd have felt just as young and frightened as us. Perhaps Angus Hill began to stir, prompting her to dash out into the cold night, without any of her belongings. I hoped she'd had the sense to steal a coat off the pegs, at least.

And now Detective Adler was on the hunt for her, poor soul! I prayed that he'd focus more on Angus Hill and Irene.

But a week later, when Mom sent me back to the general store, a sign in the window made me very uneasy: WANTED—$500 REWARD. As my eyes scanned down the page I learned that the logging company was putting up the money. No doubt it was to their benefit to have the murderer caught swiftly, before loggers and townspeople got spooked and headed back to the mainland. Inky faces of all three suspects decorated the sign: photographic images of Angus and Anna, followed by a not very accurate sketch of Irene. Beside each name and face was a physical description, including hair colour, eye colour, approximate height and weight, among other distinguishing features. Angus Hill was described as a "giant of a man, with swarthy complexion and stooped shoulders."

Yet it was the text beside Anna Iacono that made me shudder.

Evidently, the detective had followed through on his promise to contact the VPD. In addition to mentioning that Anna Iacono had been going by the false name of Gretchen Smith, the sign called her a "most dangerous criminal, suspected of having killed her husband, Tony Iacono, a respected plumber in East Vancouver." Four months prior, the man had been found dead in his backyard, thanks to a shovel to the head. Anna had vanished off the face of the earth. She was assumed to be responsible for his murder, because neighbours had heard the couple "violently quarrelling earlier in the day."

Wrapping my arms around myself, I reread these sentences over and over, with increasing speed. So Anna Iacono had fled her own dark past, long before she had the bad luck to encounter me and Daisy. I wasn't so shocked, really, for I remembered how she'd looked at us, like she'd known just how it felt to be in our shoes. Like she, too, had not so long ago been held captive by a vile brute. If Anna had clobbered her husband with a shovel, she'd had good reason, I didn't doubt. He must've been a vicious lout, no less than Angus Hill. The world had no shortage of men of this ilk.

"Howdy," said a gruff voice behind me.

Dazed, I turned around and saw that it was Frank Turner. A grocery bag cradled against his chest, he'd come out of the store. This was the first time I'd run into him since my return to Buckley.

"So how's business?" I said, by way of greeting.

"Not bad. I've been there and back to Thurston Harbour twice since we parted."

It was hard to believe that so much time had elapsed. Recently, my days had a way of blurring together.

"You've been seeing a lot of the widow, I guess?" I tried to sound cheery.

Turner scratched his chin, blushing. "Never you mind that."

"She's a nice lady. You're a lucky man, you know."

Changing the subject, he wagged his chin at the WANTED sign. "So, which one of these crooks did Mrs. Hill in? I'm bettin' on this Iacono woman."

"But *why?*"

"Dunno. Something about her face. She looks like she has it in her."

"My money's on Angus Hill."

"Could be. It often is within families that quarrels escalate to the point of murder." Turner pulled an apple out of his bag and bit into it noisily. "Whatever the case, we might actually get to the bottom of things with this detective in charge."

"Oh?" My face hardened, my lips set in an unnatural smile. "Detective Adler, you mean? Have you met him?"

"Sure have. He tracked me down yesterday."

"Whatever for?"

Turner peered up at the sky, as if only now was he considering the reason. "The detective's a chatty fellow. He made out like he just wanted to shoot the breeze, since I know a lot of folks on these islands. Of course, the conversation eventually came around to Mrs. Hill and what I'd gleaned from passing through Port Clem so soon after her murder. And he asked some stuff about my boating business, like the sorts of folks I take around."

"Oh?" Nervousness rustled inside me. "What did you tell him?"

"It came up that I'd transported you and Daisy and Dice to Thurston, for instance."

I placed a palm on the plate-glass window, trying to steady myself. "*What?* Why did you share that with him?"

"Because it's the truth, 'course." He looked at me oddly. "It's hardly a secret that I take a lot of folks around these islands. The detective was interested in knowing who went where when, that sorta thing."

It rattled me that Adler now had a clear picture of all our comings and goings. And why was he seeking out this information? In addition to the suspects whose faces adorned the sign, did he think that others might have blood on their hands, too?

"What's wrong, Khya? You're looking rather pale."

"I must've eaten something bad at lunch."

When Turner asked whether he should walk me back to camp, I shook my head, claiming to be fine. I wanted nothing more than to get away from his bright, inquisitive gaze, which made me feel like it wouldn't be long before my own face appeared on a WANTED notice.

❦

May was not herself these days. She followed me around constantly, like a forlorn puppy. In the middle of the night I'd wake to find her curled up at the end of my sofa, keeping watch through drowsy eyelids. Clearly, she was afraid I was going to run off again. I felt terrible. In the mornings, dark circles rimmed her eyes.

"I'm not going anywhere," I reassured her. "You need to get more sleep. Otherwise you'll never grow. You'll stay a shrimp, like me and Dad."

"Maybe I want to be a shrimp!"

I racked my brain for something comforting to say, but nothing came to me. I pulled my sister into a tight embrace, inhaling her gentle, woodsy odour.

"When is Izzy going to give birth?"

She'd asked me this many times before. "I don't know exactly. Izzy still has some time to go, I believe."

"And after the baby's born? The baby'll come here with Izzy to live?"

Although I nodded, what did *I* know? Mom and Dad had revealed nothing about their plans and I was the last person they'd confide in, anyway.

May continued to look fretful. "Hopefully, by the time Izzy and the baby arrive, the killer will be caught. It'll be safer for the baby, with the killer in jail."

Kids of all ages had been warned by their distraught mothers to beware of the three suspects on the loose. The monstrous faces of Angus Hill, Anna Iacono and Irene haunted everyone's nightmares.

Yet it wasn't long before one face could be eliminated from the list. Apparently it was a couple of loggers who found Irene's corpse on our side of the inlet, outside a cave in the woods. She'd been sleeping there, it appeared. Hiding out. Until a bear had attacked her and snapped her neck with a swift blow from a paw.

As gossip abounded—from the mouths of people who'd never even laid eyes on Irene—her dead body assumed a gruesome appearance in all our imaginations. It was said that her bare legs had a bloated, ruddy appearance, and they were covered with blackish-red lines and gouges. Her neck and chin showed similar signs of ravage. Her coat had fallen open, exposing a bright green dress, pooled around her thighs, knees splayed out obscenely. I remembered that dress all too well, so there was some truth to the gossip. I recalled the way it'd swished around her calves as she'd brazenly presented me and Daisy to Mrs. Hill for sale.

Despite what Irene had done to us, it still felt miserable to know that her drunken, racy smile would never flash before anyone's eyes again.

I could only pray that Anna Iacono—wherever she was—had better survival instincts.

THIRTY

With Irene dead and gone, I was hoping that folks would assume she was the murderer. And since she'd been killed by a bear—hardly a pleasant way to go—it was like Mother Nature had delivered up her own manner of justice. If only Angus Hill could meet an equally grisly end. Then people on these islands would have two murderers to choose from and forget all about Anna Iacono, I was hoping.

No such luck. With Irene out of the picture, people only became all the more convinced of Angus's and Anna's guilt. The killer was still out there, they gossiped on the street, their faces enlivened. It was like they'd gotten addicted to their lives being in never-ending peril.

So Adler wasn't going anywhere. When he wasn't across the water at Port Clem, he was bustling around our little town, chatting with locals in his friendly way. Upon catching sight of him, I always hurried along the sidewalk or ducked into an alley.

But one afternoon he came out of a shop and we almost bumped into each other.

"Khya, just the gal I've been looking for."

"Look, I'm in a rush today." I tried to beetle on, yet his broad hips blocked my way.

"I stopped by your camp yesterday afternoon, but you were nowhere to be found."

That'd been no coincidence. Through our kitchen window, I'd seen the detective wending his way around the cabins. I'd slipped outside and gone to hide in the outhouse.

There was no getting away from the man now. "What'd you want to chat with me about, anyway?"

He looked at me musingly. "So, how's your own investigation going, if I might ask?"

I cast him a blank stare.

"The case of your sister's lost sweetheart. Have you made any headway in locating him?"

My feet fidgeted about. How I regretted ever telling Adler about that. "It doesn't matter anymore. I gave up a long time ago."

"Oh? Why's that?"

"The Captain is clearly gone for good. He's left my sister high and dry." Tears sprang to my eyes and I wiped at them roughly, hoping the detective would mistake them as purely tears of anger.

"And how does Daisuke Tsunoda feel about your sister's aban-donment? You're familiar with the fellow, I assume?"

"Dice? He... he's just an old friend of my father's."

"I reckon he wasn't too pleased about how Felix Godwin had treat-ed Izzy, eh?"

"How should *I* know?" An ill feeling squirmed across my belly. Why wasn't Adler asking about Mrs. Hill's murder? Answering questions about that crime no longer seemed like such a hardship, compared to this turn.

"Why did you really stop searching for Felix Godwin?" The detec-tive looked at me meaningfully.

"I'd be thrilled if you have any news about the Captain! But why all these questions? Isn't it Mrs. Hill's death you're supposed to be inves-tigating?"

His eyes had gone inscrutable as blank chalkboards. Eventually, he said lightly, "Sometimes, you go looking into one crime, only to discover that it's connected to a slew of others."

Faint tremors, like an earthquake just beginning, passed through my core. "Have you *found* the Captain? Is that what you're telling me?" What I really meant was the Captain's body, of course.

Adler shook his head. His mouth looked hesitant, as though he was weighing how much to disclose.

"Well? What, then?"

"Are you acquainted with Carl Godwin?"

"The Captain's cousin? I tracked him down in Thurston Harbour, but he wouldn't say much about what'd become of the Captain. He did seem worried, though."

"After you spoke to him, his worry increased. So much so that Carl sought me out. It seems that Felix Godwin's been in a bad way for a while..." Adler appeared to be gauging my reaction, as though my face alone were a treasure trove of clues. "Perhaps he feels guilty about the mess he caused for your sister. Whatever the case, he's been living like a renunciate, deep in the woods."

"Is that so?" I attempted to seem shocked and distressed.

"Each week, Carl was taking him food and supplies, but on Christmas Eve, when Carl trekked out for his visit, his cousin was nowhere to be found. Carl believes that he might've met a bad end, and Felix's mother also holds this view. She's been haranguing the Vancouver police to get involved, and it seems that out on these is-lands, that means *me*."

The truth fluttered over my skin in clammy shivers. Since his arrival on our shores, the detective had been slyly investigating a second case. That was why he'd been teasing information out of Turner about his boating business.

While I'd once wanted nothing more than for someone in a position of authority to take the Captain's disappearance seriously, now just the opposite was true. Because if it came to light that Dice was a cold-blooded killer, it would also surely come out that I'd been involved! My foolish actions had *led* Dice to the Captain's hideout. And even if he'd been nowhere close to Thurston Harbour, my father was in on the Captain's killing, I had no doubt. Although no one in my family ever talked about why Dice had set out on that journey, we all knew—in our hearts, *we knew*—everyone except innocent May. Even my sweet mother knew, I believed.

"Isn't it possible that the Captain was out fishing when Carl stopped by?" I murmured.

"He came by again the following morning. Still no sign of his cousin. Carl searched the whole area. And it's unusual for Felix to stray far from that cave, Carl assured me."

"Well, I guess he might've had an accident? Hit his head or something. Fell into a bog and drowned. Or got killed by a bear, like poor Irene."

"Perhaps. But when I said as much to Carl, he insisted that things don't add up and he dragged me out to the cave for a gander."

"What doesn't add up?" A claustrophobic feeling was descending upon my head, as that craggy cave came back to me in too much detail.

"According to Carl, a compass was taken. It was an old, broken thing of no use or value. But it had special meaning, because it'd belonged to Felix's grandfather. It seems that the thing was stolen."

"A hobo must've grabbed it, I guess."

"Not likely. If a hobo's going to steal, why would he leave behind a perfectly good fishing rod? And there was also some food and money that the thief didn't touch."

I cursed myself for having seized that useless compass. It was now hidden away, buried at the base of the big spruce where Daisy and I had first crossed paths. Although I still hoped one day to give it to Izzy, that prospect seemed increasingly dim.

"Carl believes that his cousin was murdered," the detective added, in case I had any doubt about his meaning. "He suspects that the killer took the compass as a souvenir of the killing."

I let out a weak, incredulous laugh, like Carl had been reading too many mystery novels.

But Adler seemed to be considering the possibility seriously enough. "And then there's the matter of the curious track marks on the cave's floor, which I photographed as evidence. Carl's not wrong that it looks like a body could've been dragged out."

More curses erupted in my brain. Why had Dice not thought to cover his tracks—quite literally? Was he getting sloppy and soft in the head in old age?

As the detective kept examining my face with interest, I started to wonder if he viewed *me* as a suspect. Did he think that *I* had done the Captain in? Was he pondering how a girl as wee as me could get the upper hand on such a big guy—perhaps by sneaking up from behind and whacking a rock to his skull? Was he assessing whether Daisy and I might jointly possess the strength to drag a corpse into the bog?

"I don't know what to say." I put a hand to my feverish forehead. I feared that people on the street were watching us. Soon their tongues would be wagging about why I'd been talking to the detective for so long. "I better get back to my mother. She'll be worried about what happened to me."

Adler's eyes twinkled, like there was nothing quite so gratifying as contemplating an interesting murder. "In light of Izzy's predicament, your father is the obvious man who springs to mind. By compromising your sister, Felix Godwin brought shame on your father, and I understand that there was already bad blood between them."

"Dad was nowhere near Thurston Harbour in December. He was in Victoria with Izzy!"

"Indeed."

It was clear that the detective had already asked around about my father, gathering God only knew what information. "So…?"

His gaze drifted down the street. "So, what do I find out, while having a pleasant chat with that Indian fellow, Frank Turner? It seems that even if your father never headed to Thurston, his old buddy, Dice Tsunoda, set out on much the same schedule as you and Daisy. I wonder if he might've had his own plans for settling the score with Felix Godwin?"

A dark whirring filled my head. A colony of bats descending. In my muddled brain, it occurred to me that maybe this was what it'd take to get Dice out of our lives forever.

Yet there I stood under the dimming sunlight, tongue-tied and damp in the armpits. I couldn't shake the wretched feeling that whatever Dice was guilty of, my family and I had had a hand in it, too.

"If you have questions about Dice," I said tightly, "why don't you ask him yourself?"

"I've attempted to talk to the man several times, but he's very good at vanishing when he wants to. Something you share in common."

"Well, did you trek out to where the men are logging these days?"

"I did. Dice wasn't there."

"Did you speak to my father? He's in charge of everything."

Adler's lips curled up slightly. "He wasn't around either. You're not aware that they both left town yesterday morning?"

An ache spread out behind my eyes, like they'd too long been looking into a blazing fire. "That—that can't be."

But come to think of it, I hadn't seen my father at supper yesterday. Nor in our cottage later. I hadn't thought much of it, because when I usually fell asleep, he and Dice were still at work on the new cottage.

"Where did they go?" I demanded.

"Victoria, I was told."

"*Victoria?*" I choked on my own breath. Victoria could only mean one thing. "Did something happen to Izzy?"

"I don't know," the detective said gently.

"What *do* you know?"

He shrugged, with genuine pity in his eyes. "You should speak to your mother, dear. I'm sure she'll tell you what's going on."

THIRTY-ONE

But Mom would *not* tell me what the dickens had happened. It didn't matter how much I implored and hurled questions her way. Had Dad and Dice gone to Victoria to bring Izzy back? Was she going to give birth here, rather than at the Home? Why the sudden change of plans? And why the devil had Dice been needed on the journey?

"The less you know, the better" was all Mom would say. Her face remained closed, like the shell of an egg.

Clearly, Dad had given her orders to tell me nothing. Perhaps they thought that if I knew too much, I'd run off to Victoria in an attempt to rescue my sister. But rescue her from *what*?

Meanwhile, the detective's probing words continued to keep me up at night, in a perpetual state of unease. I certainly hoped that Dice had done a better job of sinking the Captain's corpse than covering his tracks in that cave. Was it possible for a body to float up to a bog's surface as the weather warmed?

When Dad returned from Victoria, I'd have to warn him of the trouble afoot. Hopefully, he'd have some sense of what to do, though in truth I didn't much trust his judgment anymore.

❧

One thing comforted me a wee bit, at least: I received a letter from Daisy. For weeks, I'd been planning to write her, but I kept putting it off, because it felt like lying to say that everything was fine. I worried now that she'd interpret my silence as cold and uncaring.

Nevertheless, her loopy handwriting and eccentric spellings buoyed my mood:

> Deer Khya,
> This is the first letter I ever writ. So please forgive me if it is not a vary good letter. But I'm writing to say how glum I feel about how we parted. You ware acting so odd when you came back from the woods, near crying. Why was that? I was so confuse & sad to see you like that. And why did you run off to the forest to begin with?
>
> I am sure you want news about my new life here. Terry Fan is a OK boss & he keeps his hands to himselv

even at nite. He is teaching me to cook Chinee food like egg drop soup.

There is another reasoun I must writ to you. That man you told me is the Captain's cousin (Carl is his name?) is stirring up rumors galore. Good God, he says the Captan is missing and maybe merdered! Can you beleave it? Carl is convince of somethin bad. Rumor has it the Detictif agrees. Do you think the Captan mite be deed? Who mite of kilt him?

Please writ back & tell me what you think & how things are for you at home.

Yers,
Daisy

I pictured her brow furrowing in concentration as she wrote out these words, her downcast eyes curtained by those long, pale lashes. How dreadfully I missed Daisy, all these small parts of her. Her sea of faint, nearly vanishing freckles. The delicate, always changing scent of her skin.

It tormented me to hear how distressed she'd been by my cryptic behaviour in our last moments together. I cursed myself for not pulling myself together and reassuring her that everything was all right and she needn't worry about me at all.

But later that afternoon, when I sat on a rock in the woods, with a pen in hand and a sheet of paper spread over a book propped upon my knees, still no words would come to me. For what could I say? That all was well? Ha, in a pig's eye! God only knew what was going on with Izzy and why Dad and Dice had rushed off to Victoria. And if Adler could so readily guess how the Captain had been killed, it'd only be a matter of time before he pieced together what'd happened to Mrs. Hill. Yet writing any of that would only burden my sweet friend more, and that was the last thing I wanted to do.

While rereading her letter, I scratched at a bug bite on my ankle until it was oozing and bleeding like a real wound. It shook me up that Carl was spreading rumours that the Captain had been "merdered," as Daisy put it. My eyes lingering on this word, I found myself wondering if perhaps she thought *I* might've had something to do with it! Had she guessed at some version of the truth? Did she suspect that when I'd left her at the post office, I'd gone to look for the Captain in his cave and ended up killing him? For it hadn't been lost on her how upset I'd appeared during our final moments together on that wretched sidewalk.

Was that why Daisy had written to me? Did she want some assurance that I was not a cold-blooded killer? Was she begging me to confide in her and justify my actions?

Yet I could do no such thing. Much as I longed to unburden my conscience and tell her everything, it wouldn't be wise to put any of it in writing. Ever.

So I wrote instead a few woefully inadequate lines. They sounded lifeless and cowardly, as I read them back to myself:

> Dear Daisy,
> I miss you terribly and think about you often. Life is not the same without you. But everything here in Buckley is going fine, all in all.
>
> It sounds like Carl has been letting his imagination get carried away. If the Captain has come to a bad end, he probably just tripped and hit his head or got killed by a bear.
>
> As ever,
> Khya

THIRTY-TWO

It was night when Dad and Dice returned. About a week had gone by since their departure. Mom and May were both asleep, but my brain remained all too alert, as I tried in vain to drift off on my sofa.

A sudden squeak of the door's hinges caused me to sit up. A silhouette swished darkly in the doorway. *Izzy.* The men stayed outside while she lingered there on the threshold, like she was unsure whether she still belonged here, or had ever belonged. Into the dark room she squinted, resembling a blind woman.

I leapt up and bounded toward her. I threw my arms around her stiff shoulders.

By then, Mom was also up. She lit a candle.

I examined my sister. Clearly, she was no longer pregnant. Indeed, she looked thinner than she ever had, shoulders stooped, spine curving slightly in the shape of a question mark. Yet her arms held no swaddled infant.

"Where's the baby?" I exclaimed.

"Is it a boy or a girl?" May called out excitedly as she rubbed sleep dust from her eyes.

But Izzy said nothing. She stared at the floor, like something about its flatness perplexed her.

"Let your sister rest," Mom said, drawing nearer. "She must be tired from the long journey."

That our mother didn't seem the least bit surprised by Izzy's childless state only worried me further. What the heck was going on? I remembered the horrid stories that Daisy had told me about Head Matron's adoption schemes.

"You didn't let them take the baby away, did you?" I blurted.

Izzy's hands flew up to her face, shielding her eyes.

In a stern voice, Mom said we'd discuss things in the morning. She ordered me and May to get back to bed. In stunned silence, we curled up at opposite ends of the longer sofa to leave the other one for Izzy. In the shadows, Mom tiptoed about to get more blankets.

While I remained very much awake, Izzy fell into a fitful sleep. Her teeth chattered and clacked, like that ghost was still trapped in her womb and desperately wanted to become free.

🌿

It was still dark when something roused me. Dawn was edging in ever so faintly, in murky lines of greyness. Into the gloom I blinked, aware that I wasn't the only one up. On the opposite sofa, Izzy sat upright. She stared ahead at nothing but glimmering swirls of dust in the air.

When I joined her, her eyes barely moved, shiny and unflinching. So many questions about what'd happened to the baby were pent up in my throat, but it'd be best to go gentle, if I was ever going to get her to open up. I placed a light palm upon her forearm, hoping to get her to look at me, at least.

"So what's it like at the Home?" I whispered. "How… how did you cope?"

Her shoulders made a small, jerky movement, difficult to read.

"Did Head Matron treat you all right?"

Her chin puckering, Izzy gave a tiny nod. "I was good at keeping quiet, staying out of trouble. The Matrons mostly left me alone, once they could see it was hopeless to try to teach me English."

"Daisy told me they're usually nice to the pregnant girls." I was seeking a delicate way to bring the conversation around to the baby.

"They were fine to me. Far nicer than some of the girls."

"The girls were mean?"

"Oh…" A hand twitched around her forehead, as if flicking away a mosquito.

"What happened?" I pressed.

A scowl crept across my sister's expression. "I made a mistake. A terrible mistake."

Dread gathering in my innards, I waited for her to go on.

"I trusted a girl I thought I could trust, because she's Japanese. I got so lonely for someone to talk to, you see, and she was the only one who spoke my language. I… I thought she was my friend."

"But she wasn't?"

In hushed fragments, Izzy conveyed how this girl—Sayako—had betrayed her. At the beginning of their friendship, my sister had confided many things about her deprived childhood in Japan and the more recent troubles she'd endured. It didn't take long for their quiet conversations to touch upon the father of Izzy's baby. He was a white man, Izzy confessed, pouring out her fears about how a Eurasian child would fare in this world. Sayako pretended to listen with compassion and promised to safeguard the secret.

But it didn't take long for her to spill the beans to the other girls. Soon they were all gossiping and giggling in scandalized tones about the "freak baby" on the way. Sayako, like the others, started shunning my sister, as though it was a small monster growing in her belly.

A vise was tightening around my heart. I wanted to grab all those girls by their greasy hair and spit in their ugly faces.

"They were right, though, I guess," Izzy whispered.

"Right? How can you say that?"

A strange keening sound escaped her lips, but she quickly swallowed it back, with an anxious glance at the bed where our parents were still asleep. After a lengthy pause, she mumbled, "They were right that a mixed child's an inferior creature, unlikely to survive..."

"What the devil do you mean?"

"According to Sayako, it's like when a donkey breeds with a horse. The offspring's a mule—a stupid, sterile creature. Sayako said a lot of mules die as soon as they're born, because they're perversions of nature."

I longed to knock Sayako to the ground. How could she be so cruel and a damn liar to boot? I didn't for a second believe what she had to say about mules.

The implications of Izzy's disclosure sank in, along with panicked emotions. "Where's your baby, Iz? The baby didn't...?"

A small moan died in her throat. "The baby arrived too early... and it was so very little... *too little...*"

Our parents had awoken by then. I was aware of their dull figures looming behind me. May, too, was starting to stir. I focused all my energy on keeping very still, knowing that if I budged a muscle, wails might loosen uncontrollably in my chest.

"I fell on the stairs and that jostled the baby from my womb," Izzy added, her voice squeaking with guilt. "That's why it came out too soon."

"Did you fall or did some wretched girl *push* you?" The words shot from my lips.

She remained silent, not denying my accusation.

"Better that the baby didn't make it," Mom said softly from behind us.

When I swivelled my head, Dad gave a curt nod. He looked bone tired and unimpressed with the world, like dealing with his troublesome daughters had knocked the life right out of him. Yes, I could see it in his flat, lustreless eyes and thick brows, which no longer appeared to curve at all; they formed a stark line, set against us. He wanted nothing more than to wash his hands of all us girls, I sensed.

❦

Later that morning I worked up the courage to approach Izzy in the kitchen. Although she was supposed to be peeling potatoes, she was mostly staring off into space. My arms were piled high with dirty pots and pans.

"Come," I murmured. "Let's get some fresh air. You can help me wash these, okay?"

Mom ignored us as we walked past. May was the only one of her daughters she could stand to look at and be friendly toward, these days.

After relieving my arms of some of the load, Izzy followed me along the gravelly trail to the water's edge. The sky was overcast, dingy as a never-ending stain. Wet slaps of wind assailed my cheeks, making me shiver. Izzy hadn't even bothered to put on a coat, but when I asked if she wanted to run back for one, she shook her head. We squatted down and deposited the dishes on the sand, while the frothy waves lapped at the toes of our boots.

I immersed a pot in the freezing water. As I scrubbed at it with an old sponge, my fingers lost all feeling. I searched for some words to break the silence, yet everything seemed awkward, unnatural. "Did the birthing go quickly, at least?"

"The baby arrived soon after my fall. Even though it wasn't alive, it still took its time to come out, many hours."

How awful! My face cringed and crumpled. I wondered if it'd been similar to Mom's miscarriage, preceded by a flood of briny, pink water.

"When did this happen?"

"About a month ago, I think."

Perhaps Izzy's baby had been large enough to look like an actual infant, with a proper nose and eyes and lips. Unlike that other baby's face, indistinct as a blob of clay. My little dead sister. If I listened very carefully, I could hear a faint echo to the ebb and flow of my own breaths, as though she was not far from me, even now.

"Did you know that our mother lost a baby, a few years back?"

Izzy shook her head.

Timidly, I said, "Did you get to see your baby?"

Her gaze careened away. It took some time to find her voice again. "I looked away, while waiting for the baby to cry out… Maybe I could already sense what'd happened. Then one of the Matrons threw a sheet over my face, and I just knew that the poor thing was dead."

My eyes welled with tears. It tormented me that my sister had had to suffer all alone, without a single family member at her bedside. I should've been there for her, at her side.

"I'm so sorry," I gasped.

But Izzy acted as though she hadn't heard me. She slipped a pan into the silty waves and kept her hands underwater for the longest time.

Her face appeared empty of emotion, not flinching against the punishing coldness.

"I went to Thurston Harbour to find the Captain." I needed for her to know that I had tried to improve her lot in life, however unsuccessfully.

Casting me a dim, unsurprised look, Izzy said, "On the boat ride from Victoria, Father told me about your adventure. He was very upset with you. He still is, I gather."

She didn't appear terribly grateful for my efforts. Yet what could I expect? What had all my wasted energies amounted to, in the end?

I doubted that I'd ever get up the courage to tell her that the Captain was dead. For would she find any comfort in knowing the truth? More likely she'd only despise me all the more for delivering this dreadful message.

"It doesn't matter anymore," she said in a flat tone, flicking water from her bluish fingertips. "The baby's gone, so why would the Captain care about me now? And Father has fixed things so I won't cause him any more trouble."

This puzzled me. How had our father managed to fix anything? Izzy remained just as sad and broken as ever. And yet I was the one with hot tears stinging my eyes, while she simply went about rinsing dishes.

❦

The new cabin got finished quickly now. For a few days Dice didn't resume working with the logging crew. Instead, he concentrated on putting a roof over the structure, with Kenji's aid. And in the evenings Dad pitched in too, pulling long hours. There seemed to be some sudden urgency to get the dwelling completed.

Through our kitchen window, while chopping turnips, I could see Dice going about his work. A curious look of youthfulness seemed to have slipped over his face, no longer quite so leached of colour. And there was a certain lightness to his step, even as he lifted heavy planks, like all this toil would have at its end some long-coveted reward.

"What's gotten into Dice?" I said.

Izzy stood at the counter, kneading a ball of sourdough. Her eyes darted toward our mother, who returned a complicit glance.

"What's going on?" I demanded, putting down my knife.

Mom took a deep breath, straightening her shoulder. "I guess it's time that someone told you the news. Your sister is now a married woman."

"What?"

"Married?" May squealed, scurrying over to us. "Why wasn't there a wedding party? Are we going to have a party?"

Izzy continued to pound the dough, in a cloud of silvery flour.

"Who the heck did you *marry?*" My brain could not absorb this information.

At last, she looked up at me, not hiding her indignation. It was like she saw me as a stupid, dreamy child—no more attuned to how the world worked than May. With a wheezing sigh, Izzy's chin tilted toward the window and the man bending down and grunting softly outside.

"*Dice?*" I recoiled. She'd married Dice?

My brain didn't want to put the pieces together. So this was how Dad had "fixed" things. This was how Dice had earned his reward for restoring my father's honour. In Victoria, after collecting Izzy from the Home, they must've found a Japanese church or some such place, where marriage rites were performed.

"Why, Izzy?"

She sighed again, her face closing over.

"Izumi-chan's lucky that a good man's been willing to have her, despite everything," Mom said lightly.

So this marriage had her blessing, too. Of course it did. When had our mother ever not sided with Dad or shown an ounce of independent thinking?

A couple days later, my sister moved out of our home and into the one behind. It sent the worst shivers over my flesh to think of her trapped at night within those walls, with that murderous beast. Every so often, through our kitchen window, I'd catch sight of them together: Dice would be leaning against a tree, enjoying his last cigarette of the day under the twilight, while Izzy meekly lingered nearby, in case he needed anything.

He treated her more like a maid than a wife. We'd hear him bellowing at her for the smallest infractions, through the walls of our cottage.

And yet, what could I do? Dice was my sister's husband now, so he had the right to lord over her, as husbands do.

THIRTY-THREE

Izzy's beauty rapidly faded. Her complexion lost its lustre, like a snow orchid in its final days. The delicate, graceful gestures that'd once animated her being gave way to hunched shoulders and plodding feet and clumsy hands. It was like she was seeking to render herself a hag, so Dice might keep his hands off her, his appetites unaroused. This was also perhaps a way of spiting him, by robbing him of the beautiful wife he'd coveted for so long. That woman had vanished and left behind a husk-like thing that I barely recognized as my sister.

Dice must've felt cheated. Blustery anger surrounded him wherever he went, and at night I could hear him storming about and shouting at Izzy, cursing her ugliness and stupidity. It incensed me to no end. How could Dad stand for it? Why wouldn't he do anything to intervene? Yet whenever I'd go to him and make my case, he'd just glance at me with cool resignation. "Your sister's made her own bed." That was all he cared to say.

One morning when Izzy walked into our cottage, I noticed that she had a white scarf wrapped tightly around her neck. It was made from a scrap of old sheet.

"What happened to your throat?" I asked. "Are you not well?"

Nodding, she gave a little cough.

I assumed the scarf was some kind of medicinal compress. They were used in Japan.

But later that morning, when Izzy was adjusting its folds, it slipped down and a scrap of purple skin flashed beneath.

"What on earth…?" I sprang toward her.

My eyes weren't deceiving me. A cluster of plum bruises patterned her flesh. Someone had gripped her by the throat. My eyes bulged, though why did I feel such shock? Dice's moods had been blacker than ever in recent days.

He was bored. After his adventure-filled youth, it couldn't be easy to subsist on such a small allowance of danger in this backwoods. Whenever I was forced to look his way, an antsy energy surrounded his face, and he scanned the land as if yearning for some immediate threat on the horizon. With no such target, Dice was turning his violent urges toward his wife instead.

"Oh, it's nothing." Izzy clutched the scarf to her neck, not allowing me to examine the damage further.

Over at the stove, Mom continued to stir a frothing pot. No doubt she'd heard what Izzy and I had been speaking about. Mom chose to shut her ears to it, because she was just as powerless as me. Or perhaps, like Dad, she believed that Izzy had earned this fate.

"This can't go on!" Was I the only one who grasped the urgency of Izzy's situation? *She wasn't safe in that house.*

My sister knew that she was in danger, yet I detected no fear in her. It crossed my mind that maybe death was what she was hoping for. Was she deliberately provoking Dice's wrath, in some perverse hope that he might kill her and end her misery?

"You've got to make an effort." Grabbing her by the arm, I hoped to awaken her from this terrible trance.

"An effort? An effort to what…?"

"To return to your old self," I whispered, anguish catching in my throat. Telling her to make herself pretty for Dice's benefit was the last thing I wanted to do, yet what was the alternative? More bruises and worse to come? "It's the only way to get your husband to treat you better. If you make him desire you, maybe he'll be a wee bit kinder, at least?"

"You're one to be giving marriage advice, Khya." A wry chuckle. Izzy watched me with disdain, as though I grasped nothing about these matters.

It was true that I felt out of my depth. Nevertheless, I kept pleading. "You need to listen to me—"

"And why should I?" she cut me off. "You've never understood a thing about my life and you never will."

❧

Although I still dreamed about us moving to Vancouver, that no longer seemed like much of a possibility. Instead, Mom had fallen into running a diner of sorts right here in the woods. Rumours about her cooking had spread throughout the region. What she had on her nightly menus was far tastier than the restaurant fare in town, at half the price. So we'd opened up our kitchen to paying customers; fifteen cents was the price of a deluxe supper, which folks praised to high heaven. They were mostly government officials and prospective investors passing through the Charlottes, contemplating how to squeeze every last dollar from these forests after the war's end.

Indeed, as winter gave way to spring, the Krauts' luck was running out fast. Rumour had it they'd gotten trounced in some important battles and by the summer, if luck were on our side, they'd be in big trouble. This would mean significant changes ahead in the timber trade.

Uncle Will had to laugh and socialize with these sophisticated men, but I could tell he actually didn't care for them. For the most influential guests, Mr. Brown made sure he was on site to shake hands and keep the booze flowing. As these portly fellows sat around the campfire, they could be heard extolling our western red cedars, which apparently had water resistant properties, ideal for shingles. And Douglas firs were highly desirable for house frames and flooring. No longer was there much interest in Sitka spruces, which were massive and unwieldy and not good for much other than fighter planes. I heard one gentleman in a fine brown suit predict that the future of the logging industry would be to clear out all the old growth, so crops of the same lightweight species could be planted. Easy to grow and chop down and ship out.

While these highfalutin conversations went on, at endless length, Dad and Dice kept to themselves at the edge of the group and stayed quiet, unless spoken to. Once the guests had left, they'd get down to real discussions with Uncle Will about all the work that lay ahead.

❦

One evening in early April, Detective Adler showed up at our camp, patiently waiting in line for grub. I was startled to see him after a good stretch of his absence. Rumour had it that he'd left the Charlottes due to a death in his family. Without him around to stir up trouble, Mrs. Hill's death was fading away in people's memories. It was what I'd been praying for.

But now, why the dickens was the detective back in town?

"Why, hello Khya," he greeted me cheerily.

"Hello," I replied woodenly, while handing him a bowl of stew and slice of sourdough. "So… you're back, I guess?"

"I had to return to check on my black oystercatchers and make sure their eggs didn't all get eaten."

Black oystercatchers were smallish, sleek birds, with flame-red beaks. They nested on cliffs and boulders on both sides of the inlet, hiding their eggs in small depressions. "I don't know what has you so worried. Those birds are smart about where they build their nests."

"Not smart enough, when the ravens and eagles get hungry. They're merciless murderers when the mood strikes."

"So what brings you back to Buckley?" I said, not hiding my agitation. "Just birdwatching? Or are you still investigating your cases?"

He gnawed on his wedge of bread, with vigour. "I've never stopped. There's been a key development, which is what pulled me back to the mainland."

"Oh? I thought you had a family funeral to attend."

"No, it was a work trip. Actually, I'd like to tell you about what I uncovered, if you can spare a moment."

"We're in the middle of the supper rush, as you can see." And yet how could I not be curious about what new information he was dangling before me?

The detective said he'd be more than happy to stick around till the crowd had cleared.

At that point, I took my time cleaning up, half hoping that he'd lose patience and leave. I didn't want to be seen chatting with him, certainly not with Dad and Dice around. But when I finally stepped outside, my arms laden with dishes that needed washing, Adler was still there by the fire among the stragglers, under the last of the setting sun. With a wave he headed toward me. I shot him a glare that communicated he should keep his distance.

I made like I was going down to the shore with my dishes, but then slipped behind a cabin that I happened to know was uninhabited. I put my load down on the ground and waited, hands on hips, for Adler to catch up.

"I don't have much time, so you'd better get right to it," I said in a low tone, as soon as his bespectacled face had appeared.

"Early last month, the VPD got in touch with me about some news. Have you ever heard of a place called Essondale?"

"Essondale?" I said, raising an eyebrow. "You're not talking about the insane asylum?"

"The one and only."

Essondale was an infamous, terrifying place, which folks reserved for their darkest jokes. It was supposedly somewhere out in the countryside, not that far from Vancouver. It was said to resemble a medieval fortress, and its inmates were never allowed outside, except when they were being used as slave labour to till the soil and grow the potatoes that comprised their measly diet.

"You'll never believe who was committed, not so long ago."

I shrugged, confused.

"A guy who bears an uncanny resemblance to Angus Hill."

"What...?" I leaned back against the cabin, stunned.

According to Adler, the inmate in question had been brought in a few months ago from Prince Rupert. He'd been sighted wandering around the outskirts of town, filthy and homeless and with a rag tied over one eye. This last detail, along with the man's hulking size, made him fearsome to behold. Moreover, he had no history in town and seemed incapable of saying anything about who he was—not even his own name or place of origin. Eventually, after people had complained enough, the mayor of Prince Rupert got in touch with the VPD, and it was decided that the proper place for the oaf was Essondale.

"Well… how does anyone know for certain that this is Angus Hill?" But I was just buying time. The patch over the eye left little doubt that this was him. Could he truly remember nothing, not even his own name? How could that be? Would he not recall that his maimed eye was *my* handiwork?

The detective was watching me intently. Did he suspect the alarmed thoughts coursing through my brain? "That's why I had to make a trip to Essondale myself. Although I never had the pleasure of meeting Angus Hill, I do have his photograph. So I can say without a doubt that it is him. The face is identical. Though he's become surprisingly meek and well-behaved, nothing like Angus was said to be. That's what asylum life will do to a man."

A film of sweat chilled my upper lip. I wiped it away with my sleeve, while my thoughts lurched about. "Was he able to cast any light on Mrs. Hill's murder?"

"When I interrogated him, he didn't confess, if that's what you're asking! A man who can't remember his own name—or so he claims—isn't going to fess up to killing his mother."

"You think he might be faking the memory loss? To dodge responsibility?"

"I'm not sure." His chin bobbed this way and that, weighing the chances. "There's this fancy new doctor at the asylum, Dr. Blackmore, who is what is called a psychiatrist. According to him, the amnesia appears quite genuine. Apparently it's not unheard of for folks to slip into these fugue states, which can last months or even years. It's usually provoked by some kind of trauma."

"The shock of having killed your own mother, after a violent scuffle that resulted in her damaging your eye? Well, that's trauma, I suppose."

"Hmm. Yes, that's certainly one possibility."

"You… you think there's another?"

"Do you know what hypnosis is?"

"You mean when somebody slips into a trance?" I'd heard about hypnotists performing their tricks before audiences at circuses.

"Dr. Blackmore's quite a believer in it." With a smirk, as though he suspected it all was quackery, Adler flicked a finger back and forth in front of my eyes. "Supposedly, under hypnosis, a patient can sometimes retrieve memories that've been blocked due to trauma. The doctor has had some luck in hypnotizing Angus Hill."

My breath quickened. "And...? What did the doctor discover?"

"He claims that when questioned under hypnosis about the night of his mother's death, Angus Hill does have memories. But as he recalls things, *he* was not the killer."

"Of course, not *him*! Who, then, does he say did the deed?" I chuckled scoffingly.

"There were two girls in the pub that night."

"Oh?"

"A couple of prostitutes, Angus Hill says. One was Oriental and slight in build. The other, taller girl looked like she could be some kind of half-breed. They were both dressed in boys' clothing for some reason. Remind you of anyone you might know?"

My face ached under the strain of my rigid expression. It occurred to me that throwing new lies on top of old ones was only going to worsen the situation. "Look, I've never denied that Daisy and I were at that pub. As I've said before, we rested upstairs for a few hours, before going on our merry way. Although I don't recall seeing Angus Hill, it's possible that he glimpsed me and Daisy there, and this is what his feeble memory's clinging on to. But to call us prostitutes?" I snorted. "I can't imagine where he got that idea! Do I *look* like a harlot?"

"Not you. But it doesn't take much asking around to find out that before she joined the postal service, your friend was in a rougher line of work."

A bristling sensation. It was one thing for him to be harassing me, but was he soon going to turn his accusations toward poor Daisy? I doubted she'd cope well with the pressure. Would she break down in tears and end up confessing to Mrs. Hill's murder?

"So what?" My chin hardening, I stared the man down. "Daisy delivers mail now. She's left her past behind."

"Whatever the case, Angus Hill seems to believe that she's responsible for his mother's death and you stabbed him in the eye."

"A girl of my size? *I'm* supposed to be capable of attacking *him*? And why? Why the devil would Daisy kill his mother?"

"That's not so clear from Dr. Blackmore's notes. We have our theories, of course..."

"It sounds to me like you and the doctor have very active imaginations!"

Adler grunted wearily. He knew full well that I was covering things up. Yet he had no way of proving it or getting to the truth of the matter.

And there was also some sympathy in his gaze. "If Daisy killed Mrs.

Hill, I'm sure that she had good reason. Mrs. Hill was not a kind woman, to say the least."

His eyes kept sweeping my face, coaxing me to reveal what'd transpired that night. For a long moment, I almost felt that he shared something of Dr. Blackmore's hypnotic power. It'd be such a relief to unburden my conscience in the detective's steady presence. And he'd likely agree that what Daisy and I had done was justified by our need to defend ourselves. And so, maybe no crime had actually been committed. When I opened my mouth, though, some animal instinct for survival kicked in. However merciful Adler might appear on the surface, he still represented the law. And this was about more than just me—I had Daisy and Anna Iacono to think about, too.

"I'm sorry I can't be of more help. But Daisy and I never met Mrs. Hill."

Adler glowered at me, with no small frustration. His face turned determined and mean, and I was relieved to have told him nothing.

An image of Anna Iacono surfaced in my mind. I wondered where she was now. On a train speeding across golden fields of wheat toward Ontario? Or was she already settled in some little town on the prairie, living a new life under yet another improvised name and identity? If Angus Hill had managed to make it as far as Prince Rupert, I felt optimistic that she'd succeed in escaping farther and reinventing herself once more. After all, she was a survivor. How I longed to run far away and start afresh myself.

"So what's going to happen now?" I said to the detective.

"Angus Hill stays at Essondale for as long as it takes for him to be deemed sane, I guess."

"And then? If he regains his memory—without the aid of hypnosis—would the police take his claims seriously?"

"They very well might."

I suspected that he was bluffing. Angus Hill remained a prime suspect in his mother's murder, so I doubted he'd be released to roam the streets after a stint at the madhouse. And when did you ever hear about *anyone* getting out of Essondale?

A giddy warmth—almost like gratitude—stirred in my chest. Were Daisy and I going to be let off the hook? Yet the detective was like a dog with a bone. I could see how much he still hungered for the truth.

"Well, I'll leave you to enjoy the rest of your evening," he finally said, discouraged only for the time being.

I followed him out along the path.

By then, the last of the stragglers had departed from the campfire.

Dusk was descending quickly, in grey and purple ribbons. The place was deserted, folks having retreated to their cabins.

Just as the detective was turning to go, a strident voice punctured the quiet night air. It was coming from inside Dice and Izzy's cottage. I watched in horror as my sister emerged from the door, sobbing. She stumbled off toward the woods, while Dice stood on the threshold, continuing to shout at her in Japanese. His voice was woolly and wild, like he'd been drinking heavily.

"I heard that your sister got married." Adler regarded the scene with fascination. "Married life isn't working out so well for her?"

A sinking feeling came over me. Dice disappeared inside, slamming the door.

"That man has a *murderous* energy about him," the detective added, when I remained silent. "I felt it from the beginning. A man like that— who's already killed—is likely to kill again, you *do* realize? I just hope it's not your sister who ends up in the bog this time."

My heart had begun to thwack so loud I was sure that Adler could hear it, too.

"I want you to know, Khya, you can always come to me. I can protect you girls from the men in your family."

It was a very bold claim to make, and I couldn't imagine how he'd ever make good on it. Without a word of reply or farewell, I dashed toward our cottage, not looking back.

THIRTY-FOUR

A raft of spruce floated outside the mill for the better part of a week. That was the first sign that something had changed. While before, those carcasses of trees couldn't depart fast enough, there no longer appeared much urgency. So there the raft remained, bobbing like a giant black coffin.

And so too in the forest, things were slowing down. The loggers were more likely to be perched on mossy rocks, chain-smoking on break, chatting, laughing. The blasts of treetops getting blown off still turned everything between my ears to jelly, but not with nearly the same frequency as before. Perhaps the men's labour was being diverted to taking down the smaller species that'd make good shingles and walls and doors.

For the first time in months, I could actually hear my own thoughts while wandering through the damp, green haze. Though I'd have preferred otherwise, because all I could think was that it was only a matter of time before Adler discovered some damning clue that'd connect me and Daisy to one or both of the murders. And Izzy's wretched marriage continued to torment me, along with my futile longing to see Daisy. Although she'd written me another sweet letter, I couldn't find the words to write back. My brain was a tangle of knots that refused to loosen, no matter how hard I pulled at them.

Frank Turner also had some unwelcome news. I ran into him one sunny afternoon, on the dock. He'd just climbed out of his boat, no passengers accompanying him.

"It's not your busiest season, I guess?" I said, approaching.

"Business is great, actually! But I'm not talkin' about this old skiff." He exuded boyish excitement.

"Oh?"

"The widow's sold her inn and we're off to Vancouver to open that bookshop, at long last."

"That's incredible."

Even as I tried to be happy for him, I couldn't ignore the sadness in my gut. All the decent people were departing from these islands. Soon, it'd just be the moneygrubbers and murderers I'd have for company.

"Why so glum, Khya?"

"Oh…" There was no simple answer to the question.

"I heard that Angus Hill's locked up in the loony bin. So that's one reason we can all sleep a bit easier, right?"

I attempted to force a smile, not very successfully. Talking about

Angus Hill was the last thing I was in the mood for. "How'd you get so interested in books anyway, if you don't mind me asking?"

Turner revealed that when he was a kid, he and his mother had lived in Victoria for a time, at the house of a famous judge. His mother had been employed as a maid. At night, Turner had stealthily explored the house, the library especially. By candlelight, he'd read for hours.

I liked that image of him as a boy, curled up with a text before him, in near darkness. "So what'll your store be called?"

Shy uncertainty flickered in Turner's eyes. "Dunno. We're thinkin' Trove Books, maybe? What d'you think?"

I nodded approvingly.

He said that he and the widow had rented a shopfront at the corner of Trounce Alley. If I were ever in Vancouver, I should come by for a visit.

It sounded so lovely and peaceful: a little shop, with book-lined walls, far away from this chaos and madness. Tears smarted my eyes, embarrassingly. I didn't want Turner to see me falling apart.

"Hey… what's wrong?" He handed me a hanky.

When it was clear that I had no answer, he let me have my privacy while I blew my nose.

At last we said our goodbyes and I wished him luck with his new venture, trying to really mean it.

❦

One evening not long after, Dice could be heard ranting through the walls of our cabin. What in heaven's name was going on over there? Something smashed, like a bowl had been hurled across the room. It was difficult to see how Mom could remain dozing in bed throughout the commotion, but she gave no sign of stirring. And Dad wasn't back from his solitary stroll, or wherever he'd gone. Not that he'd be of any help in this situation.

May scurried over and buried her face in my bosom. "Is Izzy all right?"

"No, she's *not* all right!" I jumped up from the sofa, while our mother remained like a dead mouse.

I headed out with a sense of purpose. Under the jaundiced glow of the moon, I banged on Dice's door and waited.

But when the door swung open, my courage faded. Dice appraised me with tight lips and icy amusement, like the murderer he was. I could smell booze on his breath.

"Khya, isn't it past your bedtime?" Blocking the doorway, he did not let me in.

"Izzy…," I faltered, grasping at straws. "She wasn't feeling well today. So I'm here to check on her."

"Go home, Khya," Izzy called out weakly, from the shadows inside.

"You heard her," Dice said. "She's fine."

But I met his gaze and hissed, "She's *not* fine."

I felt this man's eyes grazing the contours of my body, with more curiosity than usual. Suddenly I was very aware of the thinness of the loose, long shirt I wore as a nightgown in summertime.

Something appeared to have melted in his face, as he stepped aside.

Rarely was I allowed to set foot in this cabin. Though it was newly built and more spacious than the hovel where the rest of our family lived, there was nothing at all homey about the interior. From the flicker of a candle on the table, I could see my sister hovering against the back wall. Her hair had fallen loose from her bun and patches of pale scalp, where she appeared to be balding slightly, peeked through. Her face, taut with fear, shook back and forth, as though warning me away.

Dice pointed at a bowl on the ground. "I'd offer you some soup, but your sister's cooking isn't fit for a hog," he sneered.

I hadn't been mistaken about a bowl getting thrown across the cabin. Its splattered remains stuck to the wall around poor Izzy.

"*Leave her alone.* Why don't you just get on a boat back to Japan? Isn't it time for you to rejoin your brothers in the Black Ocean Society?"

The lines on his face twitched upward. It was tickling him to hear me plead. "Make no mistake that when I return to Japan, I'll be taking your sister with me. Though if I'd known she was going to turn into a worn-out shoe so quickly, I'd have thought twice about marrying her!"

I crossed my arms around my chest, in fear that if I didn't, my hands would shoot out and do something violent. The faint, plaintive voice of my little dead sister called out to me from some old, deep place.

"If you don't let Izzy be," I wagered, "maybe I ought to share with that detective what really happened in Thurston Harbour."

"What happened in Thurston Harbour?" Izzy whispered, confused.

"Nothing for you to concern yourself with," Dice muttered.

"But Detective Adler would be mighty interested," I said.

He looked at me with thunder in his gaze. "*You think I'm afraid of that fat fool?*"

If the detective got too close to the truth, he'd become Dice's next victim—his last breath choked off, as easily as a fish taken out of water.

Feeling shaken, I backed toward the door. Dice followed me out, his body exuding hot anger.

But once we were outside, a sudden creepy warmth flowed into his expression, overriding the mockery. He pushed me against the side of the cabin and ran his palms over my shoulders and breasts, which both received several kneads, painfully rough.

I was in such a state of shock that my brain could barely process what my flesh had just experienced. I simply stood there, sweating. The rustling trees filled my ears with their cryptic murmurs.

"At last, you're looking more like a woman, Khya," Dice said in my ear with a growl. "Who would've guessed that you'd turn out prettier than your sister?"

All too late, I broke out of my trance. Keeping my eyes on the muddy ground, I scurried back to our cottage, my bosom aching.

THIRTY-FIVE

I got up the next morning after a sleepless night. Everything in our cabin felt slightly different, somehow. Stranger, more fragile. It was as though the floor and walls were no more substantial than the shifting shadows and puddles of pale copper light.

How I wished to chalk up last night's events to a dismal dream! Yet the tender, bruised flesh at my chest was an inescapable reminder of reality. My body refused to forget the assault of that beast's greedy palms. How I despised myself for freezing up, letting him do whatever he pleased. Why hadn't I cried out? Why didn't I kick at his groin?

Later that morning, in the kitchen, I was a hopeless wreck. I was incapable of the simplest tasks and nicked my finger with a paring knife. Meanwhile, Izzy kept shooting me worried glances, like she sensed something wasn't right. Her scrutiny only made me all the more on edge.

So I ripped off my apron and announced that I needed a breath of fresh air. I wanted to be alone with the sky and trees, but it wasn't long before I caught sight of May scampering along behind me.

"What are you doing here?" I snapped. "Can't I even have a moment's peace?"

My sister recoiled, my words like a clout.

"I'm sorry…" I raked my hands through my greasy hair. "I just… I haven't been sleeping well lately."

"Me, too!" She appeared on the verge of tears.

"What's wrong?" I knelt down before her. Her watery eyes mirrored my own desperation.

"I don't like it here anymore, Khya!"

I sighed, nodding. Behind May, I could hear the waves coming in with hostile force—like they, too, wanted to be left alone, without the endless meddling of us humans.

"When are we gonna move to Vancouver to open a restaurant?" she asked.

"Dunno." How badly I also wished we could get the hell out of here and settle as far away as possible from the Captain's boggy grave.

"Dad promised we'd move to the city after the war, and they say that's going to be soon."

"I know, but…"

"He *promised*!"

I rubbed the crook of my neck.

"Dice could stay here and run the camp," she continued, like she'd given this much thought, "while Izzy comes with us to Vancouver."

"Izzy and Dice are married, unfortunately. Husbands and wives stick together."

May looked crestfallen. "Is Dice going to be with us *forever*?"

It was a very good question. I wondered what Dad would say if I told him about how Dice had attacked me last night. Would Dad finally remove the blinkers and see what a monster he'd brought into our family?

While I once would've had not a doubt in the world, nothing felt certain now. I watched a raven swoop through the sky, its wings flaring open like a tattered cape, talons outstretched.

❧

It took me another few days to get up the courage to speak to Dad. Besides, it wasn't easy to find a time when we could have a word in private. Most often when I'd catch sight of him, he was rushing off somewhere, with loggers at his side. Dice was usually not a step behind, and he'd shoot me wary looks, warning me to keep my trap shut. Although we'd been steering clear of each other, I couldn't escape the feral glint of his gaze from afar. And even when he was nowhere to be seen, I still felt within the range of his menacing presence.

So when I happened to glimpse my father coming out of the mill alone one afternoon, I decided to seize my chance. From where I stood at the end of the sidewalk, I could see him striding down the ramp and across the yard full of enormous piles of scrap wood, the wind blowing up a smother of white sawdust. My grocery bag clutched to my chest, I raced through the mess to join him and blinked against the gritty air. The mill's ceaseless grinding and clanging shot up in volume as I got nearer.

Dad looked at me with surprise. "Khya, what are you doing here?"

I could barely make out his words. I was reading the shape of his lips and guessing, more than anything. "I—I need to talk to you, Dad!"

We made our way away from the mill, the noise decreasing slightly. He eyed me with impatience, like there were a million other things on his mind.

Even swallowing seemed a struggle, all of a sudden.

"Well, what is it?" he demanded, hands on hips.

"*Dice*," I blurted, my face lighting up with heat. "He—he attacked me the other night!"

"Attacked you?"

"Yeah, Dad—he grabbed me *here*." Shame sizzling over my skin, I pointed at my bosom.

A long silence followed as I stared at the ground. Eventually, Dad emitted an uneasy chuckle. "That fool's been drinking too much, lately... In his stupor, he probably mistook you for your sister. He didn't mean any harm."

My ears couldn't believe what they were hearing. I stepped back, winded. "No, Dad—he wasn't that drunk! He knew perfectly well that it was me."

But he held up a calloused palm, like he didn't want to hear a word more. Like he'd heard too much already. Would it have been easier if he'd pretended that he didn't believe me? Told me off for slandering Dice with these filthy lies? Yet Dad didn't doubt the truth of what I'd conveyed and he didn't even seem that shocked. What it came down to was this: it was just a fact of life that some men had wandering, hungry hands.

"Dad," I stammered, "you've got to—"

Again, he held up that palm. Then a flicker of raw emotion passed over his face. He did feel bad for me, I could see. Though that didn't amount to much compared to all the other, more important worries and problems on his plate.

"Do you have any sense of what I'm up against here, Khya? I don't know what you expect me to do!"

"I'm sorry, Dad," I heard myself mutter. Even though what I really thought was that he ought to be apologizing to *me*.

By then, a bitter look had seized his expression, like he'd had enough of all my whinging. "Didn't I raise you to be able to take care of yourself? You know how to stand up for yourself, if any idiot gets in your way."

I stood there, stunned by this rebuke. Did Dad honestly see what Dice had done to me as no different than a schoolyard scuffle or argument with some shopkeeper over prices?

"This is the wilderness, Khya," he added, as if that somehow explained everything. "I thought that you liked life out here. Or have you become the same as your prissy sisters, longing for the comforts of the city?"

To this I had no response. The sky, vast and silty, seemed ready to swallow me whole. My father and I parted ways, in the swirling dust.

Thirty-Six

Vivid fantasies filled my head. But I'd had all I could take of dead bodies on the ground and it was no easy thing to dispose of a corpse. Fortunately, there were other more wily methods for bringing a person to an abrupt end. Carried out properly, they might even appear indistinguishable from natural causes: a severe case of the flu could lead to dehydration and sudden death.

I pictured myself cooking a very special soup, just for Dice, and possibly for my father, too. Into the rich, simmering stock, I'd slip some slivers of daffodil bulbs, as well as hearty rhubarb greens. A sprig of hemlock. Tiny cubes of that amber toadstool mushroom—such a beautiful, sinister shade of orange. And perhaps that tansy patch Mom had harvested for Izzy's teas last autumn might prove more effective at killing a grown man than a fetus?

What joy I'd take in carrying a bowl of this steaming concoction to Dice, in his cabin. "Izzy asked me to make this for you," I'd lie. "It'll help you sleep, and I've heard that you've been suffering from insomnia, isn't that so?"

The only problem was that Izzy would be right there and she might contradict my claim. Or worse yet, she could seize the bowl—after Dice had refused it—and I'd have no way of stopping her from spooning it down her own throat. Because she'd been struggling with restless nights lately. The sooty circles under her eyes, darker by the day, left no doubt of that.

On second thought, I refrained from acting, though I told myself that I hadn't given up. I was simply biding my time, not doing anything rash.

✤

And yet—life having a perverse sense of humour—*I* was the one who ended up falling ill. A few days after my confrontation with Dad, I got sick as a dog. My forehead was suddenly so hot, though I couldn't stop shivering. My mouth felt dry as sand, a foul taste coming and going in waves. Through the fog of my fever, I could hear my mother's and sisters' worried murmurs rising and falling indistinctly, the halo of a candle dancing over the wall. Although they kept urging me to drink water, nausea gripped my innards. It was a constant struggle not to retch.

A bad flu was going around. Rumour had it that it'd spread from the east and maybe come from Spain, originally. It wasn't clear if this was what I'd caught, but everyone was on edge. Dad purchased a bottle of vile syrup, which tasted like boiled pine needles mixed with sludge. I was ordered to take it three times daily. It was startling how genuinely concerned my father appeared about me now. Much more so than when I'd told him about Dice's predations.

Putrid as it was to get down, it was a relief to have the medicine's numbing effects wash over my body. As I lay on the sofa all day, my mind seemed to be coming untethered, drifting in and out of vague daydreams, my little dead sister's mewls and mutterings never far. While Izzy knelt down beside me and held a cup of water to my dry lips, I could sense the Captain's ghostly presence hovering above her shoulder. Or was that just a figment of my guilt-ridden imagination?

How it distressed me, as Izzy fussed about and placed a cool cloth upon my burning forehead. At such moments, I felt very close to telling her everything about the Captain's death. Did she still love the man, even though he'd turned his back on her? Did she secretly hold some small hope that one day he'd come searching for her? As the years wore on, how devastated she'd feel. Didn't I owe my sister the truth?

"Izzy, I…" But my throat was scratchy and sore.

She put a finger over my lips, urging me to save my energy. I could see in her gentle smile what a good mother she would've been. And in the not too distant future, she'd probably find herself with child again. Not the Captain's child, but Dice's, this time. To know that her husband had murdered her sweetheart seemed too much for any woman to bear.

So I let my sister stroke my forehead in silence and vowed again to take this secret to my grave. For what could revealing the truth accomplish? Izzy would only come to loathe her husband all the more, and that risked pushing him to new heights of cruelty and violence.

✤

I was sitting out front of the cottage, on a new rocking chair that Kenji had just finished. Building furniture from scrap wood had become his hobby, so our cabin was gradually gaining all new chairs and tables. But this was his first time making a rocking chair. He'd asked me to test it to make sure that it rocked properly. I'd been going at it for the better part of the morning, since I wasn't much good for anything else in my feeble state.

"There you are," a voice called out.

I looked up, astonished. It was Daisy—*could it truly be her*? Or was the medicine in my bloodstream making me hallucinate? She appeared to be standing at the end of the path, smiling broadly, her cheeks rosier than I'd ever seen them. She wore some kind of mailman uniform: navy blue trousers and a matching jacket, with a powder blue shirt underneath, everything too big, swallowing her up. Yet she looked as fetching as ever, a healthy glow to her skin.

"I can't believe I've actually found you!" Running over, she embraced me in a big hug, slipping the satchel of mail off her shoulder. It hit the ground, letters scattering everywhere.

Energy was flowing back into my limbs, the lethargy suddenly cleansed from my brain. "What on earth are you doing here? Don't you still work in Thurston Harbour?"

With a beautiful grin, Daisy said that the postal service was expanding its operations. They'd recently opened a big post office in the village of Masset, which was at the mouth of this inlet. She'd been transferred there. This meant that she was now responsible for delivering mail throughout this region. Every few weeks, she'd be making her way by boat southward toward Port Clem. Then she'd row across to Buckley, drop off mail at our postal counter, and come to see me for a visit.

I was speechless with joy.

"Say something, Khya." Daisy looked a wee bit concerned. "You *are* happy to see me, aren't you?"

"Of course I am!"

Her curls remained cut short and they peeked out beneath her cap and quivered charmingly as she talked, and her face flickered with ever-changing shades of emotion. Heady memories of being in her embrace came back to me, the way that her lips had unhesitatingly opened to mine...

"Because... well... you never replied to my last letter, unless it got lost in the mail? And the one letter I did receive from you was short and strange."

I kicked myself for being such a lout. How could I make Daisy understand? Yet there was still so much that I couldn't say to her—not without putting her in danger. Detective Adler was still prowling about. If he ever questioned her, I wanted her to be genuinely in the dark.

"What's wrong, Khya?"

"Oh, a lot of things have gone belly up since we last saw each other. It's hard to explain." Best to keep things vague, for the time being.

She looked at me with perplexity. "I hear that Angus Hill ended up in the asylum. That's good news, right? Everyone assumes that he killed his mother."

I nodded.

"So what's worrying you, then? Is it the Captain's disappearance? Before I left Thurston, everyone seemed to agree that the man's a goner. Carl included. The Captain's been out of sight for far too long. He must've had a nasty accident or a feral animal finished him off."

"Probably."

"You don't seem very relieved."

"Well…" I splayed my hands, searching for some explanation for my uneasy mood. "Without a dead body turning up, we'll never know for sure what happened to him. And my poor sister! You won't believe this—my father forced her to marry Dice."

"*Dice?*" Daisy's forehead furrowed deeply.

Although a part of me longed to share with her how the scoundrel had preyed on me too, I didn't want to burden her with that and make her see me as a pitiful victim.

Her frown faded, as she took stock of my father's motivations. "At least Izzy's baby'll have a father of sorts, I suppose?"

I shook my head, a fist tightening in my heart. I explained how Izzy's baby had died in her belly at the Home—no thanks to the cruel girls who'd tormented her there.

Daisy dropped down to a tree stump and lit a cigarette. I sank onto my rocking chair, beside her. The smoke swirled around our heads as we sat there in brooding, mournful silence. I wondered if perhaps I shouldn't have told her all this. Maybe it stirred up too painful memories of her own days in that bleak institution.

"I'm sorry that Izzy suffered so," she said eventually. "And the help-less baby…"

We sat there, without saying anything. I savoured the smell of her hair and skin and smoke and the rise and fall of her breath, and the slightest movements of her fine bones as she shifted around.

"Maybe it's better that the baby didn't make it," Daisy murmured. "It wouldn't have had much of a life…"

"Don't say that!" An ache stretched across my collarbones.

"But it's true. Dice would've never accepted that child—you know that. The kid would've grown up in the Home."

"Well, you grew up there and look at you now. Postmistress Daisy!"

She cracked a shy smile, mixed with a trace of wonder. It stirred my emotions to see that she was content in her new life.

When we finally said our goodbyes, with an unhurried kiss, I told her that I'd be counting the days till her next visit.

THIRTY-SEVEN

Something had shifted in the air, ever since Daisy's reappearance in my life. My parents' assumption that I was a pair of sturdy hands always available to do their bidding, free of any wages, grated on my nerves. Seeing Daisy, aglow with independence, had put these dark thoughts into my head and stirred awake rebellious instincts.

All I knew was that I couldn't go back to how things had been before. So I took my merry time recovering from my illness. Even when I was better, I feigned still being under the weather and told Mom that I was only capable of the lightest chores. Then I began extending my solitary walks. While I'd once gone off for a short break in the afternoon, I now didn't return for hours.

The beach by the old Indian village became once again my favourite place of refuge. Under the cumulus clouds, I dug for clams and boiled them up in salt water over a fire for my lunch. That, along with the tart huckleberries at the edge of the forest, would perhaps be enough to sustain me if I were to run away and set up camp here. Maybe I could sleep inside the cave at the base of the big spruce, where I'd first gotten up the nerve to talk to Daisy and she'd let me into her life.

In the late afternoons, I retreated there and curled up for a nap. Yet it was hard to relax so near to the Captain's compass, buried under a mound of dirt. A pebble jutted up to mark the spot, like the tiniest tombstone. I'd hidden it here because I'd worried that Detective Adler might come poking around our cabin. I wondered now if I should have hurled it into the inlet instead?

I was more at ease out on the shore, the bracing waves lapping over my bare feet. Although it was July and the weather was balmy, the water remained very cold, too cold for swimming. Instead, I contented myself with letting my toes sink into the formless sand, as white froth bubbled up around and numbed my ankles. Rust-coloured starfish slowly undulated below the surface on rocks and mounds of kelp, like they had all the time in the world.

Once, I caught sight of a black bear, down the beach a ways. It turned its cream snout toward the cub ambling along behind. They were hunting for crabs, the little one imitating its mother, learning the tricks of the trade.

While my brain knew that I ought to be terrified—especially after what'd happened to Irene—for some reason my body remained calm, motionless. My impulses told me that if I minded my own business, the bear and its baby would pay me no heed.

It was us humans who were the real predators out here. Men like Dice and Angus Hill and even my own father. They were the ones to hold in fear.

If only they could all be locked away at Essondale, the rest of us could go about our lives in peace.

❀

I was lingering at the end of the boardwalk, smoking a fag I'd filched from Dad's pack. Recently I'd taken up the habit, because it made me feel a wee bit closer to Daisy. Perhaps at this moment she too was inhaling a gritty stream, white plumes drifting like sea mist around her sweet face. I wondered if she thought about me half as often as I thought about her.

Despite her assurances that she was coming back, I still feared that for some reason, she'd not make it. For one thing, Handsome Joe remained a stone's throw down the beach. Wasn't Daisy worried that they might run into each other and he'd recognize her, even in her mailman uniform? How safe was it for her to be in these parts? In moving to Masset, to be closer to me, had she thrown herself into harm's way?

The silver waves glimmered emptily, filling me with a nervous feeling. There wasn't nearly as much activity as there used to be on this inlet. The same raft of spruce had been floating outside the mill for the longest time, in no hurry to go anywhere. It appeared to confirm what everyone had been gossiping about in recent days: the Krauts would be forced to surrender soon and the war would come to a halt.

Yet it was hard to believe that somehow, in my gut. We'd all been living in this state of endless woe and confusion for so long. How could the world simply go back to how it'd been before? What'd become of that gentler, more peaceful time? It seemed as elusive and unreal as a fairy tale from childhood days.

❀

May jostled my head. I rubbed at my bleary eyes, the morning sun too bright. Swinging my legs over the side of the sofa, I sat up. My sister was dressed already, her hair brushed smooth. She squinted like she was struggling to make out my features.

"Are you still not feeling well, Khya?"

Her face was pinched with worry. I sensed that she'd overheard our parents talking about me last night. About my terrible attitude and refusal to work. Through my light, fitful sleep, I'd had a faint awareness of them going on like that, in the darkness. The only reason Dad didn't dare to slap some sense into me was that I held dangerous knowledge.

If they asked what gave me the right to wallow in self-pity, I could retort that it wasn't an easy thing to have a cold-blooded killer for your brother-in-law, now was it? Especially when he had roaming hands, accustomed to making free with your body! I feared it was only a matter of time before he'd pull something again. Which was another reason I needed to stay away from our camp, as much as possible. If my parents gave me what for, I'd return it to them so fast their heads would spin.

My laziness had started to draw raised eyebrows from people in the community. This was the real source of my parents' disgruntlement. Folks were gossiping about how Sam's most industrious daughter had gone vamoose.

"I'm fine," I replied tightly.

"You don't seem fine. First Izzy and now you, too! Everyone's falling apart."

I ruffled May's hair and attempted to act like my old, unencumbered self. "It's your turn to hold down the fort and be the big sister for a while. I know you're up to it."

She looked at me with resentment. "No, Khya—*I need my sisters*."

Guilt took root in my stomach. Although I reassured her that I wasn't going anywhere, I knew that I hadn't been around much lately.

"Where do you go all day?" she demanded. "What do you *do*?"

"I walk around the woods, I guess."

I stood up and stretched my arms. Since I'd slept in my clothes, I had no need to get dressed. Grabbing my satchel, I headed toward the door.

"Don't you get lonely, with no one to talk to?"

Glancing back, I shook my head. "Why should I?" I had the rustling trees and murmurous waves to keep me company through the hours.

"Can I come with you today?" May pleaded.

"Then Mom'll truly be mad. She needs your help in the kitchen."

"That's not fair!" A pout came over her.

She was right. There was nothing I could say in my defence.

Much as I still adored May, I didn't have the energy to take care of her, in my current state. She was better off staying on Mom and Dad's good side, in the fold.

✤

The fog was coming in, in white wisps, which reminded me of small, floating spirits. In some places they blended together, clumping around the densest trees. I closed my eyes, listening, listening. The earth's hum—cooing birds and eddying waters and swaying, skyward trees and countless other pricks of sound—enveloped me.

I felt like I could stay here forever.

The more I thought about it, the more convinced I became that it was time to live apart from my family. I couldn't bear to spend another night under my father's roof. But I wouldn't entirely become a recluse—I still very much wanted to see Daisy. Would she think me crazy for sleeping in a cave of twisted roots? Would she make the effort to trek out here, whenever she passed through town? Might she even be willing to spend the night, if I could improvise a tent or shack big enough for two?

A smattering of blood-red salmonberries, low to the ground, caught my attention. Although they weren't as sweet as raspberries, they had a pleasant tartness. There was much I could forage among berries and mushrooms alone. And I could fish for salmon and plant some beans and potatoes to get me through the winter. I envisioned myself hoeing and pruning a small garden—something rather soothing about this image. I'd harvest just enough to keep my body going, my muscles firm and sinewy. Or maybe if I had extra vegetables or fish I'd sell them in town for a bit of spending cash.

On second thought, I decided against the idea. Dealing with money, even in small quantities, was a slippery slope. The first grubby coins in your palm were bound to awaken a hunger for more, men like Dad and Dice being sad cases in point.

The yellowish needles of a nearby pine caught my eye. Although the odd colour hadn't spread throughout, it was clear that the tree was malnourished, and diseased maybe. As I made my way around the area and the fog cleared slightly, I could see that several other trees also had this unnatural hue, their needles sapped of greenness.

Without warning, the fog thickened, putting me on high alert. I felt my way forward with my dewy fingertips. Prickly branches sprang back and hit me in the face, as I slowly advanced through the white swirl.

Where was I even heading? Probably, it'd be wiser to just keep still. Because if I kept going, I might end up wandering deeper into the woods and be lost.

It occurred to me that perhaps living out here in solitude wasn't as easy and idyllic as I'd pictured. Panic began to roil in my stomach, and I sank to a crouch and hugged my arms around my shins.

I thought of those poor, traumatized soldiers, who'd sought refuge in the caves around Thurston Harbour. Then I thought of the Captain in his final, guilt-ridden days, living no less like a witless hobo! And Lester and Bertie seemed equally bleak cases of people too far removed from human society… If I remained out here, would my own fate be just as grim?

At last I rose to my feet. The forest no longer seemed a welcoming place.

I needed to orient myself. I needed to get back to the beach. Yet my confusion only intensified, as though the murky swirl had entered my brain.

On the other side of that shifting white curtain, something seemed to be watching me. Some feral creature—*a bear?* Could it be? Yet I could make out nothing, no outstretched claws puncturing the white opaqueness. Still, the sense of being under surveillance wouldn't leave me. Was it merely the sky looking down, observing what a fool I was?

I managed to feel my way toward a tree trunk, relishing the stability it offered. Leaning against it, I tried to catch my breath and settle my nerves. Then I discovered the bark was sticky with pitch, which had now gummed up my hair. In a fit of curses, I backed away. And that was when a pair of sturdy arms wrapped around me from behind.

Caught off guard, it was hard to struggle. A necklace of pain stretched over my throat, draining me of all strength, all ability to resist. Luminous brightness filled my head, and through a tear in the fog I glimpsed the jewel greenness of the forest. It beckoned tantalizingly, with a beauty that scorched the eyeballs.

"Isn't it just like you to get lost in this weather?" a voice hissed in my ear, mockingly.

There could be no mistaking that voice. Dice must've followed me out here! Perhaps he'd been stalking my movements for days, planning this attack.

As he relaxed his grip, I managed to turn around to face him, which was what he wanted. I could see it in the enjoyment that sent a blank glitter across his gaze. He grasped my wrists again and I attempted in vain to wrest free. My face held him riveted. He relished watching me writhe in despair.

When the weight of Dice's torso lunged toward me, I feared we were both going to tumble to the ground, him on top, and then there'd be nothing I could do. His loins pressed against me, the darkness in his eyes leaving no question about his intent. And after he'd had his way, would he simply kill me, like I was nothing more than a wounded animal to be put out of its misery?

But I wasn't down yet. I kneed him in the groin, with all the force

I could muster. This won me an incensed groan, and his hands relaxed enough to give me a chance to free one wrist. With those fingers, I stabbed at his right eye, my nails sharp and unkempt.

This sent Dice staggering backward with a howl. Upon breaking away, I ran as fast as my legs would carry me across the thick understorey, criss-crossed with fat roots and wet patches of moss, slippery and treacherous.

Dice wasn't far behind. I didn't dare glance over my shoulder, because I knew he'd be right there, as near as my own shadow. My lungs ached and a dizzy sensation filled my head. It was futile—*I couldn't outrun him.* Might I be able to scurry into hiding, in some cave?

That glorious spruce, where Daisy and I had first met, careened into my field of vision—my last hope.

I tripped on a gash in the bedrock. The heft of the ground whammed up against my knees and shins. I felt Dice grab my foot, which got yanked back. He grabbed the waist of my trousers and rolled me over onto my back. When I raised my hands, in a last-ditch effort to fight him off, an explosive kick landed in my gut, followed by another one to the side of my head. Everything turned blurry and dim, the canopy of my spruce fading to green and grey blotches.

The next thing I knew, Dice was fumbling to pull down his pants, while that sea of greenness came back into focus, rebounding with startling clarity. Suddenly I could see all the interwoven branches hanging down like fistfuls of enormous feathers and all that bright verdure appeared to be gently throbbing, in time with something in my own core. Lichens, draping down like ghostly forms, swayed perceptibly. They were stepping forward as witnesses to what badness I was about to endure. Into those veils above, my mind would disappear for the duration of the ordeal. The forest's thrum and the soft voice of my little dead sister would offer some solace, too. She understood my bleak circumstances, because she, too, had been dealt a bad hand.

I refused to close my eyes, holding on to her presence. Fury sputtered in my brain, with Dice now heavy on top of me. The leaf sprays attached to an enormous branch above appeared to be quivering and bursting into green flames.

I had to be mad—didn't I? I had to be hallucinating!

That fiery branch broke off and fell on top of us, with crushing force.

I struggled to breathe. Dice was no longer moving upon me, his body as still as a sack of potatoes. Yet I could barely move either, my face buried in suffocating darkness. I pushed great quantities of prickly things away, my nostrils overwhelmed by dust and dirt and the waxy scent of needles. My hands forced their way up toward the light, clearing enough space for me to gulp air. Then I managed to wriggle out from under the mass, my panicked flesh hardly registering all the scrapes and bruises that this manoeuvre surely cost me.

Gingerly, I rose to standing, surveying the scene. It appeared that the thickest part of the branch had struck the back of Dice's skull and knocked him unconscious. If not worse.

But no, he wasn't dead, unfortunately. When I pulled back foliage to expose his head and ventured my fingers beneath his nostrils, they could feel spurts of warm air. Desperate, laboured breaths.

If I just left him here, would he die on his own? Or would he come to and slither out from under, just as I had done?

Before I could lose my nerve, I threw my entire weight on the branch atop his head. Using it as a bench, I sat down, my heart whapping. His face got pushed deeper into the earth, till there was no doubt that all life had been snuffed out.

He was dead.

He was actually dead.

I stood back in shock, witnessing this unfathomable scene.

My thoughts were like bats, chittering and plunging in wild patterns, nothing I could do to stop them. I peered through the vestiges of mist, desperate for someone to tell me what to do. But I was all alone, with only the trees for company. I stared up at the big spruce that'd been my conspirator in killing a man, like it might offer some much needed guidance. Its branches remained mute and still, not a flicker of green fire visible anywhere. I held on to the cold stillness within my core for as long as I could.

When I caught sight of Dice's pallid, unmoving fingers poking out from beneath the great mess, I broke into a run, horrified. Right until his dying breath, he'd been struggling to fight his way out from under. My vision blurred in a whoosh of greenness, tears bursting, mucus clogging my nostrils.

I had killed a man.

And now, I had nowhere to go. No inkling of what to do next!

A cramp cut into my waist. I sank to my knees and wiped at my stinging eyes and fought to get my thoughts in order.

By evening, when Dice failed to return home, Izzy would start setting off alarm bells. So a search party would gather—if not tonight, then certainly by tomorrow morning. How long would it be before Dice's body was discovered? It could be a day or two, or it could be months, couldn't it? And once the body was found, would it look like a pure accident, that blessed branch having done him in? Or would people suspect foul play?

Or just as likely, the body would never be found. Hungry animals and insects would get to it first and strip the bones of all flesh, beyond recognition. Dice wouldn't be the first man to wander off in these parts and be struck down by Mother Nature.

Whatever the case, one thing was clear: I needed to be gone from these wretched islands, immediately. I needed to depart today.

But if I ran away, would I ever see Daisy again? She'd assume that I'd abandoned her. Either that or she'd be tortured by worry that I'd come to a bad end. How could I live with causing her such misery?

Perhaps I could track her down in Masset and convince her to come with me, wherever I was headed. We were Ash and Del, after all. Wasn't it time for the next leg of our adventures together?

It seemed like a long shot that I'd be able to find her, however. Most of her time was spent in transit between camps, delivering mail. And she appeared happy in her new life. Why would she want to disrupt that for a life of uncertainty, on the lam, with me?

Blinking back tears, I scurried under the roots of our spruce tree. I wanted to be inside that cozy cave one last time, so I could feel close to Daisy and mull over what to do next. In the humid darkness, I closed my eyes and sought to say goodbye to her. Surely, this was the kindest thing I could do?

My gaze settled on that mound of dirt, beneath which the Captain's compass lay buried. For some reason, the object called out to me, with an almost magnetic power. Using my fingers as shovels, I dug it up. The tarnished brass felt uncannily light in my palm, as an idea took hold.

This compass was my last hope of giving Detective Adler what he wanted and bringing his investigation of the Captain's disappearance to a close. Otherwise, I worried that he'd hunt me down till the end of time.

I hurried back to Dice's corpse. I wiped the compass on the edge of my shirt, cleaning it the best I could. The bluish fingers on his exposed hand curved toward the earth. Looping the dirty string attached to the compass around his wrist, I nestled the thing beneath his palm, where it fit perfectly.

If Dice's body were ever found, the detective would hear about it, no doubt. And this compass would be nearly as good as a confession: it'd appear that Dice had murdered the Captain and kept the object as a souvenir, just as the detective had suspected.

As I stood back and regarded the scene, the air seemed to quiver with faint laughter, emanating from the dull brass clutched in the dead man's hand. I was relieved that he was gone for good—I felt no on-slaught of guilt or regret for my part in his demise. Maybe that would come later, because it was no small thing to have taken a man's life. But at this moment, it was only the forest's chortle that filled my ears.

A light buzzing passed over my scalp, my body suddenly alive and weightless, feeling on the verge of picking up speed. I wondered if this was what it meant to be slipping into delirium or hysteria. Even so, may-be my luck was changing at last.

THIRTY-EIGHT

Our camp looked different somehow, as I approached it for the last time. It was like I was seeing it through the eyes of a stranger, now. Although the cabins appeared tidy enough, there was nothing at all charming or homey about any one of them. They were just temporary dwellings for people who'd stick around for only as long as these forests continued to bleed money. The sadness and smallness of this way of life overwhelmed me, and I was relieved to be leaving.

There were a couple things I wanted to grab from our cabin, before setting out. A jacket would be useful, since it got chilly at night. And I'd pack a larger knife in my satchel, which already contained my water bottle and small knife and a handful of other tools. Aside from that, I'd be travelling light and living by my wits.

I wished to avoid running into Mom and my sisters, so I hid around the side of a nearby cabin, keeping an eye on the door of ours. It wouldn't be long before they'd head out, their arms laden with vats of stew and loaves of bread. The loggers ate lunch in the forest, wherever they were working. While Mom and my sisters were off delivering the food, I'd slip inside and retrieve what I needed and grab a wedge of bread for my own lunch. The heady excitement that'd gripped me earlier had vanished now and I wanted only to get moving, before losing my nerve.

After some time had passed, Mom and Izzy came out, their backs stooped under the weight of what they were carrying. They made their way toward the woods, and I watched their heads growing smaller, a pair of vanishing black dots. Sadness assailed me, as I wondered if I'd ever see them again. But I didn't have time to waste on letting my emotions get the better of me. Shaking off my mood, I rushed into our cottage.

May was seated at the table, eating. I backed up in surprise, having forgotten all about her. She usually went with Mom and Izzy to help serve lunch.

"What are you doing here?" I exclaimed.

She was startled to see me, too. She peered at me, with fright. "What happened to you, Khya?"

"What do you mean?"

"You're bleeding!"

I rushed over to the cracked mirror on the wall and saw that she was right. My cheeks were covered in scratches, flecked with bright blood. As were my neck and hands and arms. My shirt and trousers were torn in several spots, and my hair was matted with mud and twigs.

I could barely recognize this creature as me! My eyes had a desperate, feral look, like those of a mad girl.

"Oh, I… A bear attacked me… But I got away and I'm fine, all right?"

May wasn't reassured. Her eyes glassed over, on the verge of tears. I could tell that she thought I was lying: about the bear, about everything. She didn't trust me anymore, and who could blame her?

I fetched a cup of water from the kitchen and washed the blood off the worst of my cuts. I shook the debris from my hair. Still, I looked pretty ghastly, nothing like a normal person.

I looked like… a girl who'd killed a man. And barely escaped with her own life.

"Don't cry, May. I'm fine, everything's fine."

Although this was far from true, I *was* relieved about one thing: with Dice dead, I could depart without fearing that in the future, as May grew prettier and womanly, he'd come after her, too. His gluttonous hands would never attack anyone ever again. I drew closer to my sister, so much I wanted to share with her on the tip of my tongue. But she was too young to hear these hard truths, and when her frame stiffened, I stopped in my tracks.

"What's *wrong* with you, Khya?" she stuttered, a sob catching in her throat. Like everyone else, she'd come to view me as a lunatic, a menace.

There was nothing I could reply. What *was* wrong with me? Or was it the world that'd gone so terribly wrong?

After a long moment of listening to May sniffle, I pointed at my fishing rod, leaned against the wall. It was too cumbersome to take with me, and I wanted her to have something to remember me by.

"I meant to give you that for your birthday. You like to fish, right?"

She nodded, looking confused. "But it's yours."

"Nah, it's yours now."

Turning my back quickly, I grabbed my jacket and knife and satchel, before making for the door. I didn't want May to see me misting up, because that'd only upset her more and make our parting even harder.

⚜

I walked into town, toward the general store. Although I had no money to buy anything, I'd noticed that the garbage bins out back often contained bread loaves, barely even stale, and an abundance of tinned goods.

Today was no exception. I helped myself to the loot, putting enough in my satchel to get me through the next few days. Because who knew where I was heading and what nourishment would be available there? I had no plan, beyond stealing a boat and pushing away from these shores. Far, far away. Perhaps, after a point, I'd let my boat drift with the wind and leave my destination up to chance.

What would people think when they discovered that I was missing, along with Dice? Would suspicion be aroused that I had killed him? Or might they assume that it was the other way around—that *he* had killed *me*? This struck me as more probable, because I was just a puny girl, after all. And I'd told Dad about how Dice had menaced and molested me, so it was plausible that he might've tried worse and things had escalated to a whole other level of violence and I'd ended up dead. Unable to face up to what he'd done, Dice had absconded. It didn't seem that far-fetched, and I hoped that folks would reach that conclusion. Perhaps, as his mind travelled this path, my father would taste guilt over his own role in the tragedy.

As I hurried along the sidewalk, keeping my head down, I thought of Anna Iacono and all the other brave, pitiful women who'd been in our position before. It wasn't an easy thing to walk away from your life, with no certainty of where you were going and what'd await you and who you'd even become. Yet compared to the alternative, what choice was there? So you scurried along, seeking to be as invisible as a mouse.

At the edge of my vision, a group of loggers streamed past, chatting, laughing rowdily. It occurred to me that many of them had seen combat in Europe, where they'd killed their share of enemy soldiers. And now, they'd rejoined civilization, celebrated as war heroes. What I had done to Dice struck me as not that different than a soldier's work. If these men could walk down the street with their heads held high, why shouldn't I be able to do the same? Instead, I was embarking on life as a fugitive.

Weary tears clouded everything as I reached the foot of the main pier. The loneliness of the path ahead appeared bleak and daunting. Since it was lunchtime, the place was deserted, nothing but the great, drifting clouds for companionship. It was best for me to get used to it. I watched the waves glimmer dully, and I strained my ears for the inchoate voice of my dead sister, yet all I could hear was the mechanical grating and buzzing from the mill.

The waters ahead no longer seemed to symbolize freedom. They beckoned in the way that death beckons, like a roomy grave.

Nevertheless, my feet continued forward. Maybe I'd end up marooned on a deserted island and slowly starve to death. Even so, that fate would be preferable to what remained for me here.

While surveying the selection of small and large boats parked along the pier, I was aware of a slender skiff being rowed inland. I'd have to let the fellow come and go, and make like I was just minding my own business. After lighting a cigarette I sat down, facing away.

A voice punctured the silence, calling my name.

My head jerked up.

Daisy was smiling broadly, as she climbed out of the skiff. "So, you've taken up smoking, have you?"

I managed, just barely, to nod. The cigarette burned, neglected, between my fingertips. Daisy took it and sucked in the final puff, her eyes not leaving my face.

"What... what on earth are you doing here?" I whispered.

She held up a sack of mail. "Delivering this, 'course."

Although she'd promised that she would return, I still felt shocked to find her here. She was looking at me like I was a skittish animal and she didn't want to spook me further.

I pointed at the cuts and scratches on my face. "You're probably wondering what happened to me, eh?"

"A scuffle?"

"Uh, it was a bit more than that..."

"So are you gonna tell me what happened?"

"Yeah, but not now." Vigour was flowing back into my limbs, my brain no longer fearing that this was merely a dream. I gripped her arm. "We have to get going *now*."

"What's going on, Khya?" Daisy appeared a wee bit frightened, and I worried that like everyone else she was going to think me mad and recoil from my touch.

Things inside me were in a wild, colourful stir, and there was no time to think anything through, so all I could do was let words spew out my mouth. "I'm running away, because Dice attacked me and I had to kill him and God only knows what'll happen if I stay! So I'm running away and I want you to come with me. *Will you?*"

After the briefest second of hesitation, Daisy clasped my hand. "Okay."

"*Really?* Do you mean it?"

She gave a small nod and drew closer. She pressed her lips to mine, and I felt my whole body opening to hers, like a bud at the beginning of its bloom.

"Are you sure, though?" I said, after the kiss had ended. "You have a good job here... I don't want to ruin your life."

"Ruin my life? It's safer for me to be gone from this place. Handsome Joe's still in the area, and if our paths cross, he'll kill me, no question."

She hadn't been oblivious to the considerable risk she'd taken in returning to this area. And all because she couldn't bear to be apart from me?

We decided to leave behind Daisy's skiff, along with her sack of mail. Hopefully whoever found it would take it to the post office. A canoe was better for two, and there were several for us to choose from. I settled myself at the stern, she at the prow, just as things had been on our first journey. She removed her mailman's cap and jacket, so she'd be less recognizable. Already, she was starting to shed her old identity, as was I.

"Ready, Ash?" I called out, paddle in hand.

Daisy glanced back at me, and I caught a certain bewilderment in her eyes. I fretted that she was having second thoughts.

"Can I ask you something?" she said.

"Of course."

"When Dice attacked you, he didn't... succeed at...?" Her eyes shone with despair. "I don't mean to pry, but are you *okay*?"

All too well, I remembered the weight of that beast's body atop mine. The suffocating, pungent smell of his sweat and arousal. "Don't worry, he didn't get anywhere. I finished him off first."

"Good riddance!"

She picked up her paddle and we pushed off into the smooth waters. Later, I would tell her about how our spruce had fortuitously shed a branch and come to my rescue. Even if Daisy thought me fanciful and crazy, it'd be a relief for her to know the truth, because I wanted no secrets between us. So I'd tell her in detail about how everything had gone belly up these past months. I'd even reveal how Dice had killed the Captain and I'd kept silent, complicit. Hopefully one day the brass compass would be discovered and expose the truth.

But right now, there was no time for these complicated explanations. We needed to focus on getting away, and I was rather enjoying the companionable silence between us. There was something rhythmic about the waves' resistance and something lulling about their gentle, thudding sound. The scrim of trees bordering the inlet resembled blurry bruises, receding and fading at the margins of my vision.

"You all right, Ash?" I called out.

"The best I've been in days, actually. By the way, where are we heading?"

I said the first idea that popped into my head. "Vancouver? Shall we pay a visit to Frank Turner at his new bookstore?"

"He actually moved there and set up shop?" she said excitedly.

"He and the widow together. They seem to be getting on very well these days."

I knew a thing or two about books, I reckoned. Might Turner be willing to give us jobs, selling novels and sweeping the floor? The prospect of working at a shop full of books lifted my spirits.

"Or how about Victoria?" I mused, a second later. A certain part of me fantasized about burning the Chinese Rescue Home to the ground. I'd like to see Head Matron powerless and dispossessed, so she could get a taste of her own medicine. It was high time for the place to be shuttered.

Yet Daisy didn't appear keen to return to the city of her past.

As the waves shimmered around us, yet another idea flashed in my mind. Maybe we would start a *Silver* Ocean Society: a secret sisterhood for renegade girls. If Dice and his Black Ocean Society could gain so much reach, there was no telling what we could accomplish. Sadly, there'd never be any shortage of mistreated girls and women, who needed a leg up for their survival.

Wherever we were going, Daisy and I would figure it out together, on the fly. Just as we'd always done.

By then, we were so distant from Buckley that when I glanced over my shoulder, it was no more than a smear of smoke, slowly spreading out from the mill's chimney. It already had the quality of a remembered image: a ghostly stain across the pale sky, indelibly preserved in my mind.

A pair of gulls squawked and swooped overhead, pulling me out of my trance. The water stretched out in front of Daisy and me, like an unbroken mirror.

ACKNOWLEDGMENTS

This novel is dedicated to my late grandmother, Kayaco Esther Kuwabara, who shared with me many vivid memories and stories about her youth on the Queen Charlotte Islands (now Haida Gwaii), where her family lived from approximately 1920 until 1929. Equally inspirational to this novel was a diary kept by her father, Sannosuke Ennyu, from 1894 to 1896, when he first immigrated from Japan to British Columbia as a young man and worked in the fishing industry. This diary was recently translated by Shin Kawai and edited by my relatives William Kamitakahara and Michael Ashikawa, who generously gave me a copy. It provided me with an intriguing glimpse into my great-grandfather's mind and offered a springboard for the character Sannosuke Terada. At the same time, *Sisters of the Spruce* is a work of fiction, and I've taken considerable creative liberties in representing characters, imagining plot elements and adjusting historical timelines for narrative purposes. For instance, my novel is set during the final years of World War I, shortly before my grandmother and her family arrived on the Queen Charlotte Islands.

During the four years I was researching and writing this project, several books provided invaluable sources of historical information and inspiration—too many to list completely. Some books that stand out in my memory include: volume one of Kathleen E. Dalzell's *The Queen Charlotte Islands*; Richard A. Rajala's *Up-Coast: Forests and Industry on British Columbia's North Coast, 1870–2005*, which details the fascinating tale of the Allied war effort to access Sitka spruce timber for fighter planes; Ken Drushka's *Working in the Woods: A History of Logging on the West Coast*; Mitsuo Yesaki's *Sutebusuton: A Japanese Village on the British Columbia Coast*; John Vaillant's *The Golden Spruce: A True Story of Myth, Madness and Greed*; Ian Gill's *Haida Gwaii: Journeys Through the Queen Charlotte Islands*; Susan Musgrave's *A Taste of Haida Gwaii: Food Gathering and Feasting at the Edge of the World*; Suzanne Simard's *Finding the Mother Tree: Discovering the Wisdom of the Forest*; and Mary Lee Stearns's *Haida Culture in Custody: The Masset Band*. The character named Frank Turner in my novel is partly inspired by Tsimshian leader George Kelly, whose story is recounted in Geoff Meggs's *Strange New Country: The Fraser River Salmon Strikes of 1900–1901 and the Birth of Modern British Columbia*. In researching Dice's backstory and the Black Ocean Society, I relied on volume one of *Pan-Asianism: A Documentary History, 1850–1920*, edited by Sven Saaler and Christopher W.A. Szpilman; Joël Joos's essay "The Genyosha (1881) and Premodern Roots of Japanese Expansionism" and Sven Saaler's essay "The Kokuryukai, 1901–1920" were particularly helpful. With respect to the character Daisy, I'm indebted to Sui Sin Far's groundbreaking "Leaves from the Mental Portfolio of a Eurasian," an essay I encountered years ago in graduate school. Daisy's narrative was also developed through rich material drawn from Shelly D. Ikebuchi's *From Slave Girls to Salvation: Gender, Race, and Victoria's Chinese Rescue Home, 1886–1923.*

I wish to thank the Canada Council for the Arts, the Ontario Arts Council, the Toronto Arts Council and Access Copyright for the generous grant support I received while researching and writing this novel.

Warm thanks to Sam Hiyate and Diane Terrana at The Rights Factory for their insightful feedback on multiple drafts and lively conversation during our lunch meetings. Immense thanks to the team at Caitlin Press—Vici Johnstone, Sarah Corsie, Malaika Aleba and Pam Robertson—for their dedication and skill in bringing my novel to readers. Much affection toward my husband, Chris Wong, for keeping me company during the long, lonely years of the pandemic, while I was writing this novel, and the same goes for my close friends and family members. I look back on that strange period through the fog of a dream. And thank you to my parents for sharing with me their evocative photographs and stories from their recent trip to Haida Gwaii—and Buckley Bay, in particular.

PHOTO CHRIS GRIVAS

ABOUT THE AUTHOR

Leslie Shimotakahara's memoir, *The Reading List*, won the Canada–Japan Literary Award, and her fiction has been shortlisted for the K.M. Hunter Artist Award. She has written two critically acclaimed novels, *After the Bloom* and *Red Oblivion*. *After the Bloom* received a starred review from *Booklist* and is Bustle's number one choice in "50 Books To Read With Your Book Club," while *Kirkus Reviews* praised *Red Oblivion* for displaying "virtuosity in this subtle deconstruction of one family's tainted origins." Her writing has appeared in the *National Post*, *World Literature Today* and *Changing the Face of Canadian Literature*, among other anthologies and periodicals. She completed a Ph.D. in English at Brown University. She and her husband live in Toronto's West End.